In the midst of the multiverse,
Michael saw something else. No, not saw.
Felt. Sensed. A presence there,
dark and undulating, worming its way
through the layers of Creation.
And, in one terrible moment,
the presence saw him too.

RIFT JUMP

GREG MITCHELL

Published by Genre Experience

Cover Art by Thomas Mason
Special Thanks to Grace Bridges

Visit the author at
www.thecomingevil.blogspot.com

For Sarah

TABLE OF CONTENTS

INTRODUCTION

Rift Jump came to me, almost fully realized, as a dream back when I was in high school. Many, many years ago, in tenth or eleventh grade I had the most vivid dream where I was transported to an elaborate "mall world" and met a girl named Sara. She was small and timid and had long straight orange-colored hair that was parted down the middle with the bangs tucked behind her cute little ears. And she had the most endearing eyes.

In this dream, I saved this beautiful mall princess from an ugly, mean brute. I was nearly invincible in my love for this girl, and when I rescued her from her tower and held her in my arms, I'll never forget what she said to me:

I love you.

I woke with a jolt, like I'd just come back from another world. The dream stayed with me, and it so moved me that I wrote it down the next day, scene for scene from beginning to end, just as it came to me in my sleep. I described Sara exactly as I'd seen her and, in the place of myself, I created my high school alter ego, Michael Morrison. At the time, Michael was everything I wasn't: super cool (I mean, he *does* have a leather jacket, people), wealthy, and invincible. He was never afraid, never weak, and always had a witty, though usually ill-conceived, comeback.

I turned in my ten page opus for a grade in Mrs. Hamilton's Creative

Writing class; thus the first *Rift Jump* story—a *very* rough version of "Second Chances" that you'll find bound within these pages—was told.

That original story was very important to me as it was probably the first thing I ever wrote that I was passionate about. Sure, I've scribbled stories and pictures all my life, but I never *felt* any of them. *Rift Jump* was alive to me in a way none of my other characters or stories had been up to that point.

Throughout the remainder of my high school career, I wrote more *Rift Jump* stories, but after graduation, their printed adventures were confined to the bottom of a desk drawer—only to resurface in my nostalgic moods. As an adult, I started writing different tales of other characters and other worlds, eventually crafting my seminal work *The Coming Evil Trilogy*. I got married to my partner-in-crime, Meghan, we had kids, got a house—I grew up.

Back in early 2012, as *The Coming Evil Trilogy* was drawing to a close, I began to think about what I might like to tackle next. Almost as a lark, I thought back to those old stories from my high school years and wondered what Michael and Sara were up to these days. I read through the original stories, rolling my eyes at all the high school melodrama, and had a good laugh. Yet, underneath all the ridiculousness, I was surprised to discover that there was a *real* story to be told. Ideas that I thought I had created for *The Coming Evil*, I was amazed to learn, actually had their roots in *Rift Jump*. Excited, I set out to re-create those original stories for publication, reaching back through time to rediscover who I was as a teenager. The first edition of *Rift Jump* was published by Splashdown Darkwater in the summer of 2012, and I was happy with it. It was a weird, fun little project that brought me endless amusement.

But I knew the story wasn't done. I had one more *Rift Jump* tale to tell: the final Michael and Sara story. While writing the first book, I already had an idea of how it would all end. However, in late 2014 when I really started working on the sequel *Sara's Song*, the mythology and the characters twisted and turned in some very surprising directions. For the most part, *Sara's Song* follows the path I'd always intended, but there were certain elements that changed quite dramatically during the telling. As a writer, that's incredibly rewarding, but as I looked back over the first *Rift Jump* volume, I realized that I had missed the mark. There were a few false starts and some foreshadowing of plotlines that fell by the wayside. And, in the case of a couple characters, not enough build-up, given the roles they'd later play in *Sara's Song*.

I'm hesitant to revisit my work. The challenge in making a "Revised and Expanded Edition" is always to *improve* the material and not just make it different for the sake of being different. The temptation is there to change everything to better conform to the writer you are *now*, but it was important to me to preserve *Rift Jump* in the voice of who I was then—both that baby-faced kid in high school who first conceived all this madness, and the man I was three years ago when I adapted it for publication. There was a healthy dose of "walking between the raindrops" to expand without devastating the original intent. Most of the text has been preserved except where the events of *Sara's Song* necessitated a slight nudging to better align this first part of the tale with what's in store. But there are also new scenes to be explored, delving into relationships and characters that I—woefully—glossed over the first time around, not yet understanding their future relevance. Also, as an added treat—at least to me, because I love these things—*Rift Jump* now occupies a larger role in my uber-mythology that began in *The Coming Evil Trilogy*.

I believe it was da Vinci who said "Art is never finished, only abandoned." In this case, I feel that I've abandoned this book in a better place now. It's my hope that you, the Reader, will enjoy this Revised and Expanded Edition and view it and its forthcoming sequel side by side. They chronicle a single harrowing journey through the dark spaces between the worlds of the multiverse and, ultimately, display the power of Goodness. They also represent that very first story I wrote that meant so much to me.

Thank you for reading, and enjoy.

—Greg Mitchell
January 2015

PROLOGUE

Sergeant Kleg Holstead peeked through the gaps between boards and barbed wire that surrounded their flanks. Nervous soldiers—perhaps the last left alive on this world—shifted their weight behind him, armor and guns clattering in the quiet morning. Beyond them, deeper inside their fort, Kleg heard the soft weeping of the civilians under their care. He and his men had sworn to protect them from the beasts that roamed the planet of Chelkan. But though he lied to them, he could not lie to himself. They were going to die. All of them. It was inevitable. Even if they held out in their stronghold for a year or ten, the grey devils that bayed at the moons at night and feasted on the flesh of human stragglers by day would never go away.

The monsters had consumed the world like wildfire. *And humankind is facing extinction.*

It had happened almost overnight, when the strange visitor arrived from beyond the stars. The "alien" was human like them, and a young man, but with pale marbleized skin and white-blond hair. Contrasting with his albino appearance, the boy wore all black—leather, with straps and buckles on his jacket. Kleg had been part of the envoy sent to meet this visitor.

Before the stranger's arrival, wars on Chelkan had finally been all-but quenched. They were entering a time of unprecedented peace. Kleg had nearly forgotten the primal, maddening fear of combat, except in his nightmares, but seeing that boy in the leather jacket with the blackest eyes had changed all of that.

The boy came with a mission that day, claiming he was on Chelkan looking for something important, though he refused to elaborate. When Chelkan's dignitaries questioned his purposes and hesitated to give him aid, he offered them a "gift" from the darkness between worlds.

Then he lifted his hands and a rip in the very fabric of reality had split behind him, crackling with black energy. Out of it clambered *them*. The monsters. Kleg retreated with a few others, but the hordes massacred the rest of Chelkan's welcoming committee.

The Grey Death had come, and now all of Chelkan was going to fall.

Kleg's weathered eyes narrowed at the innumerable creatures beyond the fenced perimeter. They prowled about, their naked bodies ashen. Their rows of dulled, cracked teeth opened and closed in anticipation of their next meal against a face devoid of eyes and noses. The beasts walked on all fours, their toes curled under and their arms tapering into deadly blood-drenched insect-like spears.

"Sarge?" Private Telgan whispered from his left.

Kleg had witnessed his teenaged daughter impaled by one of those spears a week ago.

"What is it, Private?"

"Sir…request permission to speak freely."

"Get on with it, Telgan."

Telgan shuffled out of the corner of Kleg's eye. "Sir, people are starting to talk. They think…they think you've led us here into a death trap."

I have. "What do you think, Private?"

"Sir?"

Kleg faced the young man. "Give me your assessment."

Telgan paused, his face paling. He looked to his scuffed boots. Gripped his rifle tighter. "I think we can hold our position, but not forever. We'll starve long before the monsters get inside. I…I think we should keep moving."

"Where would we go? Would we just forage for food from town to town, losing more from our camp every night?"

Telgan kept quiet, the ground holding his interest.

Kleg leaned in, letting his rifle hang off his shoulder as he balled his gloved fists on his waist. "We're talking about a new world order, here, Private. This planet belongs to them, now. Stay here or leave…we're only delaying the eventual."

The young man's eyes cut sharply to Kleg, as if slapped. "You're saying we should quit?"

Kleg grew sullen. He didn't know what he was saying anymore. Just knew that his family was dead thanks to those creatures out there and the punk kid who brought them to his planet. If he didn't have these civvies under his care, he had half a mind to take a couple rifles, as many clips as he could carry, and walk through the grey hordes, blasting until they took him down.

He was ready for payback. One last guns-ablazin' stand.

Private Telgan trembled beside him, whether with fear that his commanding officer had lost the hope of survival or angry for the same reason, Kleg didn't know. Didn't care.

"How about this?" Kleg spat on the ground, hoisting up his rifle, the only thing he had left in this life. "Why don't you lead them, Private? Go on. Run out the back and I'll cover you."

"But—"

Kleg's earpiece squawked, "Sergeant Holstead? You'd better come take a look at this."

Kleg stepped away from the private, knowing the kid wouldn't do anything. People talked, people complained. They wouldn't be people if they didn't. Kleg didn't care about them or their worries or fears. If the civilians were merely worried about where they'd find their next meal, they didn't understand the reality that was staring them in the face.

They were up against total annihilation. And if they didn't understand *that*, he had no time for them.

Taking hold of the steel rails, Kleg ascended the steps to the watchtower. Eagle-eyed guards leaned at their posts, casually keeping eye on the milling extra-dimensional invaders beyond the gates. Kleg stopped before Private Rickmond, a dirty-faced youth who didn't bother saluting. Kleg wasn't offended. "What?"

The young man pointed across the horizon. Kleg placed both hands on the edge of the wall and peered closer. Hundreds of charcoal bodies danced around each other, huddling closer and closer in some sort of celebration. They had their claws squirming under the cloudy sky, their teeth chattering in a way that set Kleg's gut on edge.

"They're moving into one group," Rickmond said.

"For how long?"

"Just started a couple minutes ago. It looks like they're gearing up for something."

Kleg stiffened. Thought he saw…"Give me your binocs."

Rickmond had barely offered them before Kleg yanked them from the boy's hand. Pressed them to his eyes. "Skiv-*steen*," he cursed. "It's him."

Rickmond motioned for the others on the wall and everyone fell into position. Eager, the private hovered nearer. "Are you sure?"

Kleg felt the sting in his heart. Saw the boy standing there, like some sort of deity, amidst the growling, worshipping, no-faced monsters. The boy, dressed all in black leather like some common rebellious teen. His eyes void of life and compassion, his skin and hair pale to the point of being white. Kleg would never forget the sight of that kid nor the fear he felt when he first saw him.

A fear which only magnified when the boy looked up, directly into the binocs, and saw Kleg Holstead.

Kleg lowered the binocs, his heart hammering, now. "Then we're the last," he whispered. "The last ones on Chelkan."

"Sarge?"

Tears built in Kleg's eyes, and he lost all the bluster he felt only moments ago. All thoughts of fighting some heroic, though foolhardy, last stand were gone. He didn't want to die in a blaze of glory. He wanted to live. He wanted his wife back. His daughter. Wanted to hold them and kiss them and laugh and cling to all that had been stripped from him.

I don't want to die. Not like this.

A tumultuous roar came from the devastated streets below. Kleg's hands reached for the gun slung over his shoulder, felt its familiar grip, but his fingers were numb and heavy.

"Sir?" Rickmond hesitated, as the other snipers shuffled about, anxious and uncertain. "What do we…?"

A stampede of galloping grey figures surged ahead, trampling broken-down vehicles and upended sections of street alike. Running in their midst, sporting a wicked grin, was the kid—their master.

We're going to die. This is it.

Wide-eyed Rickmond brought his rifle to bear. "Sir! What do we do?"

Kleg remembered the last time he held his daughter. She'd just graduated from school. Ready to be a woman, forge her own path.

"Sir!"

Kleg looked to his rifle. Heard the thumping bass of the charging monsters at their gates, the screams of frightened women and children in the stronghold. He knew, then, that he couldn't save them. Not all. Maybe none of them.

But that didn't change anything. He was a man of war.

"FIRE!" he commanded, and the walls lit up with gunfire.

Rickmond moved his friends where they needed to be to best thin out the herds. Kleg left him to it and jogged down the stairs. He found Private Telgan among the terrified masses. "Get the families back! We'll bottleneck the creatures through the front gate. Distract them and maybe buy you some time."

Telgan nodded and rushed off.

Kleg raised a closed fist to the remaining soldiers. "On me! You got one order: Kill 'em all! Let's show them what happens when you try to take over *our* planet!"

The soldiers cheered, "Oveka!" and formed up, locked-and-loaded.

He grinned at his men. His army. "Oveka," he whispered and took the lead.

He was going to see his daughter again today.

Bring it on, you blargin' ghiffas.

Rickmond shrieked from the watchtower and Kleg looked up just in time to see a beast ripping the private's rifle arm off before plunging a long, crimson lance through his chest. Rickmond twisted, then fell off the wall, inches from Kleg's feet.

"Hold the line!" Kleg roared as a flood of ashen monstrosities spilled over the edge of their barriers.

He and his men opened fire, their bullets chewing through the first wave of creatures. The monsters were strong. A gunshot or two couldn't pierce their rubbery flesh.

But a hundred could.

The perversions fell like insects and Kleg shouted in vindication. It felt good to cut them down. To repay them for their horrors.

He looked to the walls where the men either retreated to the ground floor or were consumed by the flood of evil. Kleg kept firing, pushing back the droves, praying that Telgan and the others were able to get out. He knew there was nowhere else to go, but now he didn't care. The will to live—to survive—shoved all logic aside, replacing it with irrational and powerful instinct.

Thunderous pounding shook the front gates. They wouldn't be able to hold off a two-fold attack from above and ahead. There were simply too many of those things, not to mention their master, that damnable boy.

"Door!" He pointed at a battle group and gestured for their gates, assigning them to the area. Just as the men changed targets, the doors burst open.

Legions of extra-dimensional devils strode in, their barbed arms twirling, lashing, killing. Kleg lost several good men in the second and a half it took for the things to get inside. And, surrounded by their madness, the boy. Kleg ground his teeth in seething hatred.

"Kill him! Fire on the kid!"

His troops did, diverting attention from the alien armies, and focusing only on the pale youth in the black leather jacket. But the kid—

Bullets zipped all around him, perforating his animal minions, but the kid simply dodged out of the way with unnatural speed, and brought out two pistols of his own. He twirled, as if dancing around the soldiers' shots, and opened fire. Bullets tore into soldiers until the kid's guns ran dry. Deftly, he tossed them aside while simultaneously leaping through the air, kicking out. His boot caught the chin of a nearby soldier and Kleg heard the man's neck snap.

"Don't you quit!" Kleg said as soldiers hurried after the boy.

They fired, they punched, they leaped, but the kid seemed invincible, bobbing and weaving—that cocky grin still on his face. Without breaking a sweat he caught fists, popped wrists, broke arms, shattered shins, and dispatched every soldier who came at him. Kleg lost sight of the monsters tearing apart his men around him. He focused only on the insufferable teenager. The teenager who should not be here, in this world.

"Where did you come from?" he hollered in desperation, his voice growing hoarse.

The kid did not answer. Just kept killing, using the guns of his fallen foes on their brothers.

An army of the dead at his feet, the kid gave the sergeant his full attention and charged. Kleg fired his rifle, blinding light exploding from the barrel. The youth sprang into the air, pirouetting overhead, and came down with a fist that separated Kleg's jaw. The military man could not close his mouth. Pain blossomed and he felt like passing out, but he wouldn't give the kid the satisfaction. Dropping his gun, he brought out his blade. He thrust the tip forward, tears of agony streaming down his face. The kid whirled out of the way and deflected the Sarge's arm, coming up with a kick to the gut.

Kleg's breath left him and he doubled over, but kept a grip on his knife. He slashed up, cutting the boy in the stomach.

Time seemed to slow as the kid looked down, seeing a tiny trickle of blackish blood expanding on his shirt. Dripping onto the ground.

"So," Kleg grunted through pained breaths, his words garbled because of his useless jaw. "You *can* be hurt."

Enraged, the boy punched again, shattering Kleg's nose. But the old war horse pushed past the pain, the humiliation, the misery of seeing his wife and daughter taken from him. None of that mattered now, for he had wounded the boy. He had cut a god.

Kleg slashed again, again, again.

The boy flailed wildly, dodging the attacks, but the smile was gone now. Off-guard. Kleg understood. This kid was used to inciting fear and always having the advantage against a foe clinging to life.

But I want *to die. I've got nothing to lose.*

His smile held back an outburst of laughter as Kleg charged, hacking with the blade. The boy backed away, dancing away from the knife's edge, but not every time. Sometimes the metal drew yet more blood.

"Come on!" Kleg jeered. "Don't stop now!"

The boy dodged another attack, but lost balance in his retreat. Stumbled to the ground. Carried by his own momentum, Kleg landed on top of the kid, blade out.

The youth gasped and sputtered, those dark soulless eyes widening in shock and pain.

Kleg buried the knife deeper, barking laughter in the kid's face.

The sergeant rose off the bleeding boy, heaving giant-sized breaths, his insides on fire. The boy looked at the wound as though he'd never felt hurt before. As though he were above that kind of thing.

Welcome to the human race, ghiffa.

The punk laid his head back on the cracked concrete and a sublime euphoria washed over Kleg's soul. With the boy dead, Kleg turned to the grey monsters once more. He spotted a handful of his men still alive—

still fighting. The horde was thinner now, and weaker with their master lifeless. Kleg wanted to believe that Telgan and the others were far away from this place. That they found some hidden sanctuary, safe from this death and free to start a new world.

Yeah. Yeah, that'd be nice.

He felt white hot pain enter his back. Wheezing, he groped behind him. Felt the familiar hilt of his own knife.

Kleg slumped to his knees and faced the boy, still lying on the ground, the knife removed from his bleeding gut. And not dead. The kid did not grin. Instead, his face was set and somber. Resigned to his fate, perhaps, and Kleg felt the same. With war still raging around him, he crawled to the boy and sat beside him, sensing his own life ebbing away.

After a long moment of silence, the dying sergeant asked through excruciating huffs from his punctured lung, "What's your name?"

The boy took a moment to answer. "Michael," he said in a lazy drawl that made the word sound like *Machel*. "Michael Morrison."

Kleg nodded in return. "Kleg Holstead. I used to be a sergeant."

The kid—Michael—regarded Kleg with a furrowed brow. "You lost," he said.

Kleg grinned, hearing laughter from somewhere. Sounded like his daughter. "Guess we both did."

"No," the other shook his head. Looked to the swarming monsters. "There'll be more. I'm just one."

"Where did you come from?"

"Everywhere…nowhere. There are more worlds than these."

Kleg no longer felt angry. He saw the sadness in this kid's eyes. The boy was lost without his war, his victory. Kleg pitied him. "Why? Why did you do this?"

Michael looked to the sunlit sky as he lay down, his hand resting over his open wound where a thick black substance oozed. "It's what I was told to do…And I'll do it again. Another me will do it all again…Other worlds…other me…I don't matter," he rasped, his eyes turning glassy. "I'm just one of them…"

Then the kid died with that mystery still on his lips.

Kleg reached over with bloodstained hands and closed the boy's eyes. His daughter's laughter filled his hearing and he smiled. *There are more worlds than these.*

He looked forward to seeing them.

Kleg Holstead closed his eyes too, and saw his daughter waiting to embrace him.

PART ONE: LITTLE BROTHER

1

The skull's not right.

Michael Morrison turned his pencil around and scrubbed the eraser against the imperfect doodling. Coach Seevers' seventh grade American History class was anything but interesting and Michael had to find his kicks somewhere. Coach was at the board, droning on about the American Civil War, scribbling dates in large white cursive letters. Seated at the back of the class away from the brownnosers and popular kids, Michael kept his head down, working diligently at his task. With the side of his hand, he swiped away the eraser crumbs, preparing to try again to get the curve of the skull's left eye socket *perfect*. A coiling python currently occupied the right eye socket, and Michael mused it was his best snake yet. Too bad he didn't have anyone to show it to. A pang of regret prickled his heart, but he shoved it aside, shaking a few strands of stringy blond hair out of his eyes so he could concentrate on his drawing.

As he touched the pencil tip to the page, a wadded sheet of notebook paper passed his face, pelting his neighbor, Johnny Frawl. Michael glanced up to see Johnny's chubby cheeks burn bright red at the insult. Johnny was a fellow back row doodler, only his creations were muscled cyborgs, probably inspired by that *Terminator 2* movie that all the kids were talking about. Today, though, Johnny had been buried nosedeep in one of his weird books, this one titled *The Most Evil Secret Societies in History* with some guy giving a stiff, one-armed salute in front of a broken cross on the cover.

At the sound of snickers, Michael turned in the other direction where Dirk Epson and his junior high chums flipped Johnny the bird before going back to their business. Michael watched Johnny to see what he'd do, but the kid only bowed his head and shook his shaggy mane, frowning as he resumed his reading.

Michael didn't consider Johnny a friend, but he didn't loathe the kid, either. Which was more than he could say for the boy's tormentors. Setting down his pencil, Michael leaned across the aisle, whispering, "I hate those guys."

Johnny looked up, startled, at first. Relaxing, he grinned. "Yeah."

Michael eyed smug-faced Dirk Epson, feeling his heart flutter with anger. "Someone should teach them a lesson."

Johnny huffed. "That'd be cool."

"What would be cool, Mr. Frawl?" Coach interrupted from the head of the room, followed by the abrupt squeak of chairs as every student turned to regard Johnny. "Would it be cool if you were actually paying attention in my class for once? I think that would be cool."

Johnny reddened and he lowered his gaze, a small rodent in the path of a hawk.

Michael snapped back, "Leave him alone."

Coach Seevers studied him. "Care to repeat that, Mr. Morrison?"

Michael snarled. "Yeah, I said shove off. We weren't bothering anybody."

A round of gasps cut through the silence; and no one looked more shocked than Coach Seevers. His bushy mustache twitched as he marched to Michael's desk.

"Watch it, boy! You think I'm afraid of you? You've got everyone else in this school looking the other way, but you do *not* scare me."

Michael leaned forward, sneering. "You just don't know me yet."

"That's it!" Seevers slammed his palm hard on Michael's desk. "Detention. *Both* of you!"

"But I didn't do anything!" Johnny rebutted.

The bell rang and Coach retreated from the battle, his face a mix of rage and shame. Students gathered their things, whispering about the confrontation. Michael dumped his pencil and notebook into his bag, then pushed through the pointing and giggling, ready to get out of here. He reached into the hood of his baggy coat and pulled out a barely concealed headset, slipping it over his ears. Fumbling for the play button on his Walkman, he cranked up Guns 'N' Roses' new *Use Your Illusion* tape that his older brother bought last week, losing himself in the opening guitar licks of "Right Next Door to Hell".

Michael skulked down the hall, mindful of the stares and whispers he attracted. He hated it here. Hated these people and their perfect lives. They didn't know him or where he came from. An especially well-groomed cloister of school children snickered in Michael's direction, but he tuned them out, focusing on Axl Rose's screaming that voiced an inner rage he felt powerless to express. He had kids ogling him like he was a strange bug and teachers watching him with suspicion from their classroom doors, but they had all better keep their distance if they knew what was good for them.

They didn't know what he was capable of.

In a moment, Johnny was at his side, hefting a large bookbag. Johnny tugged on his coat, and Michael eased the headset off. Panting, the other boy said, "Hey, wait up."

"Yeah?" Michael asked, catching sight of Dirk and his loser friends laughing at him from across the hall. He thought to go over and break in their faces.

"You didn't have to stick up for me back there," Johnny said. "Now we're both in trouble."

"Coach Seevers is a blowhard, just like Dirk and all those guys. They don't scare me."

"What are we going to do in detention?"

Michael shrugged, watching Dirk slip through his fingers as the gang hooped and hollered their way down the hall. "I dunno. I was thinking of skipping it."

"Don't you know how much trouble that could get you into?"

"What are they gonna do?" Michael asked. "Call my parents?"

Johnny paled. "Oh. Yeah, I heard. So...you don't have a mom and dad?"

Michael gripped his bag tighter and resumed his march, Johnny keeping pace with him. "Nah."

"I'm sorry, man."

"It was a long time ago. I was just a little kid."

"Who takes care of you then?"

"My brother, Edward. Me and my little brother Seth, we all moved around a lot. Lived with relatives. But when Ed turned eighteen, he moved us here."

"Won't your brother get mad if you get into trouble?"

Michael smirked, but felt the expression slipping into a frown. "He's got more important stuff to worry about."

"Uh, you know…" Johnny stopped, shifting his weight from one foot to the other. Michael paused long enough to hear him out. "If you want, you could…come over to my house sometime. We could hang or you could eat with us or…whatever."

Michael blinked, unsure of how to respond. "Yeah. Maybe."

Johnny beamed. "Really?"

Michael shrugged. "We'll see."

"Okay, then!"

Leaving Johnny behind, Michael readjusted his headset and made his way for the exit, skipping detention as promised. Coach Seevers wouldn't do anything. Oh, sure, he'd raise hell come tomorrow, but so what? Michael had things going on at home that dwarfed whatever the public school system could throw at him. He'd only told Johnny half of the truth about his family. Times had been rough since Edward took custody of his brothers and he couldn't provide for them alone. But Rip had taken them in, offered them food, a roof over their heads. *And work*, Michael thought sourly. Rip made Edward his wheel-man, ushering the brothers into a world of crooks and murderers.

He wondered what he might be doing had Mom and Dad been alive. Maybe he'd be into sports or art club or band. *Maybe I'd have a chance at a real life.* But with Edward working for Rip, that wasn't an option anymore. Seth had only turned eleven this year, but was already a little hothead, causing problems. The kid didn't stand a chance of having a happy future. *None of us do…*

Maybe Michael *would* go to Johnny's house. Sit with his family and eat and pretend for a while that he was just like any other kid. Or maybe that would just make his reality harder.

Yeah…it'd be too hard. Tomorrow he'd tell Johnny he wasn't interested.

Reaching the sidewalk, Michael spotted bright red tresses attached to a thin girl who laughed with her friends.

He halted. Palms sweaty. It was *her*.

She combed her hair over one ear, gabbing with the other girls, and Michael wondered what they were talking about. Wondered if he could ever make her laugh like that. His throat dry and tight, he inched closer to the girl and spoke, his voice cracking, "Hey, S—"

A horn blare stopped him, mid-sentence.

The girl hadn't even noticed him standing there.

Deflated, he leveled a withering stare at the source of the interruption—a sedan parked across the street, its occupants watching him. The driver, a mound of muscle in a monkey suit, waved Michael over with two fingers. Michael huffed, pulled his coat tighter and crossed the road.

"What," he said.

"Seen Rip?" the driver asked.

"No."

"You lyin' to me, kid?"

Michael considered a smart remark. Maybe a "shove off" like he sent Seevers' way. But he decided the possible consequences weren't worth the risk. "I haven't seen him."

"You do, tell 'im Big Joe wants to meet."

The driver cranked the engine and the sedan crept away. Michael glowered after it, turned up the volume on his Walkman, and headed home.

2

Michael crossed the street to his apartment, mindful of the car that came to a shrieking halt inches from him, but unbothered. Hands still in his pockets, hood drawn, he shuffled ahead, even as the car's driver hung his head out the window and shouted after him, "Stupid kid! Watch where you're going!"

Once Michael was safely away, the driver floored the gas and sped off, still shouting obscenities in his wake. Michael merely readjusted his bag and glanced up, suddenly spotting a familiar cherry red 1969 Chevrolet Camaro SS parked on the curb, its shiny veneer glistening in the California sun, evidence of a fresh wax.

He sighed. Edward was home. Which meant he had the choice to either tell his brother about detention or count it as one more in a long list of lies he'd told. He settled on the latter.

Steeling himself, Michael made his way past the Chevy and jogged down the steps leading to his basement apartment. He unlocked the door and barged into the cramped two-bedroom apartment, slamming the door behind him. Edward sat in the cluttered kitchenette, cleaning his 9mm, a smoke clenched in his teeth. The elder Morrison was lantern-jawed, a slight, chestnut-colored pompadour slicked back from his pronounced brow, long sideburns extending to his jawline. Upon seeing his little brother, Edward fumbled to push his wire-rimmed glasses back onto his pointed nose, put the gun under the rag, and extinguish the flame, but Michael caught the unsuccessful clandestine act and smirked.

"It's not like you have to hide your gun from me. I know what you do."

Edward mumbled back, shame-faced, "Shut up."

Michael threw his bookbag on the couch and rummaged through the refrigerator, seeing week old leftovers and bottles of beer.

"Where's Seth?" Edward asked, sounding concerned, and adjusted his glasses.

"Beats me. I lost track of him after lunch."

"Come on, dude, how many times have I told you to watch out for him? You know what kind of trouble he can get into. They already caught him lifting that CD last month. I keep expecting to find this hoard of stolen crap under his bed one of these days."

"He can take care of himself. Get off my back."

"I'm trying to keep this family together, man. Don't you care about anyone?"

Michael grabbed a grape soda from the back and popped the top before downing the fizzy contents. "Nah. I've got hard enough time just worrying about myself."

Michael laughed darkly and walked down the hall to his room, slamming that door shut, too, relieved that he'd managed to dodge one of Edward's trademark grillings. He dropped onto his strewn bed covers amidst a couple comics and guitar magazines and selected an issue to peruse.

Michael *did* care about his brothers, despite what he'd said. He knew Seth was sneaking off to run wild on the streets, shoplifting and smoking cigarettes—or worse—with some of the neighborhood guys, and he knew how Edward worried. Michael thought to go find Seth, to bring him back home and ease some of his big brother's anxiety. But, he hadn't lied to Edward. Seth could handle himself after a short lifetime of practice. Besides, Michael had an even bigger problem now, worse than skipping detention. Sara Theresea.

He'd almost *talked* to her. She was so beautiful. He had to make his move soon. If he didn't, he thought he would surely die.

A soft tap at the door jarred him out of his blissful thoughts, and Michael shouted back, "What?"

The door creaked open and Rip entered, throwing a quick glance over his shoulder. Immediately Michael sat up straight on the bed.

"Hey, little dude, you decent?"

Rip was a leftover of the 1960s, his peppered hair hung long and unwashed, blending with his shaggy braided beard. He was rail thin but tightly muscled, and wearing a sleeveless shirt to show off the years of tattoos he had accumulated. All manner of strange symbols and patterns adorned his leathered skin. As usual, he was wearing his dark glasses, with a joint hanging from his lips.

Michael's tone softened, a quiet fear slowly taking hold. "Uh, yeah. What is it?"

"Got another job for you."

A knot formed in the pit of Michael's stomach and now he understood why Rip was being so stealthy. "I thought you said…I wouldn't have to do that again."

Michael thought of Edward and worried what would happen if his brother ever found out what he'd done…

"Come on, little hitman." Rip grinned, taking a seat beside Michael on the bed. "I need you. Your brothers need you. I'd ask Eddie to do it, but you and I both know he doesn't have it in him. He's a better wheel-man. But *you*, you've got the killer instinct. You're a soldier, little brother, like me. And we soldiers, we've gotta have a war."

Rip took a puff off his joint. When he'd first started calling him "killer" and "hitman", Rip had made Michael feel like a man. But, when the "Old Dog", as Rip referred to himself in his most jovial of moods, called on Michael to back that title up with action…

Stay away from me, Michael screamed inside, wishing he'd had the guts to say it to Rip's face. But Rip had been a father to them, given them everything.

"I'll make it worth your while," Rip said, clapping his hands together. "I'll set you up with something really nice to give to that little girl you've been eyeing."

Michael blushed, all at once excited at the thought of doing anything to get Sara to notice him, but also embarrassed that Rip knew his one weakness.

"O...okay," he relented at length. "What do you need?"

"I'll give you the details later."

Edward opened the door and looked more than a little shocked to see the Old Dog here.

"Rip...I didn't hear you come in."

Rip spread his arms out in a friendly gesture, as if he were just a close uncle dropping by for a visit.

"Ah, me and little brother, here, were just discussing females."

Edward offered a curious, surprised smile and turned to his brother. "Michael, you never told me you had a girlfriend."

Michael looked away, feeling very guilty for keeping things from his own flesh-and-blood that he'd shared with Rip.

"She's not my girlfriend," he spoke lowly, but Rip crowed loud and proud.

"She will be, little dude. You'll see. Give 'er time."

Rip stood and patted Michael on the knee, giving him a secret wink, then turned back to Edward. "Anyway, just wanted to stop by and give ya your cut from the last drop. Like I'm always telling you, Eddie, you're the best wheel-man I've ever had."

Rip clamped a fatherly hand on Edward's shoulder and led him out of the room while Michael lay back on his bed. The door closed behind them, thundering like a proclamation of doom.

So that was that. He was going to have to go through with it.

He was going to have to kill a man...

Again.

3

He's been here before. Sitting in Rip's faded gold 1976 Plymouth Road Runner, a Bart Simpson lunchbox on his lap. His coat nearly swallows him, and Michael feels so small in its clutches. Too small to be doing something as big as murder.

The memory is fresh, only six weeks old, but he's lived it a thousand times already, every time he closes his eyes.

Rip leans over the steering wheel, keen eyes scanning the road ahead. They've been sitting in the parked car for nearly twenty minutes, but Michael can't bring himself to open the door.

"Go on, little brother," Rip encourages, the hint of frustration in his voice.

"Are...you sure he'll even be there?"

"Oh, trust me. He'll be there. He's there every afternoon running his game."

Michael takes little solace in that fact. "But they'll stop me. It won't work."

Rip exhales sharply through his nose, then digs around his vest pocket for a joint. "The plan's perfect. They know all my other guys, but you're just some kid, yeah? Some kid with his little lunchbox, on his way home from school. Nobody will stop you. Nobody will think anything."

Michael's hand shakes. He grips the lunchbox tighter.

Rip turns to him, the smile gone, now. His face is hard, the shine in his eyes gone, as well. "Don't back out on me, dude."

"But...I'm scared."

"That's good. Being scared keeps you running. Keeps you alive." Rip checks the street once more, then discreetly reaches beneath his seat, bringing out a small, black object. He passes it to Michael and that's when the boy sees it's a gun.

"This is my old man's .38. It's a real special piece. He had it since forever, then he gave it to me. Now I'm giving it to you."

Michael's hand wraps around the weapon. It fits perfectly, tailor-made for him. The steel brings him resolve. "What's...his name? The guy I'm supposed to..."

Rip barks a loud laugh. "Does it matter?"

"I guess not."

"Look, Mike, don't shed any tears for this guy, all right? He ain't no saint. Who do you think Big Joe's got killing off my lieutenants? He's a bad man. Trust me, you're doing God a favor."

Michael eyes the weapon, turning it over in his hand. Edward has taken him shooting before, but always at the range. Always for fun. "If I do this…am *I* a bad man?"

Rip fastens a gnarled hand over his arm. Grips hard. "Ain't none of us innocent, little brother. None of us."

When Michael doesn't immediately move, Rip bangs the steering wheel. "You chickening out? That it? After all I've done for you? Maybe I was wrong. Maybe you ain't worth my time. That's fine, little dude. You and Edward and Seth, you cats head out. Best of luck to ya."

Rip turns the engine over and revs it, his hand on the gear shift.

"No, no!" Michael pleads, his eyes tearing up. "I'll do it! I will!"

"Then get out there."

Michael wipes at his eyes with his sleeve. Rip lets off the gas and turns the car off once more. His voice softens. "Hey, look. I'm sorry, all right? This is just real important. I only asked you 'cause I trust you. You got that spark, kid. Like me." Taking the joint from his mouth, he solemnly offers it to Michael. "Here. Take a pull off this. That's how I get through it."

But Michael shakes his head. "No. I can do this."

Rip brightens and gives him a good hearty slap on the shoulder. "You make me proud, little brother. Meet you on the other side."

"You won't tell Edward…right?"

"Ha." The Old Dog holds one hand to his chest and raises two fingers on the other one, his smoke clenched in his misshapen, discolored teeth. "Scout's honor."

Michael nods then slips on his headphones and turns up the volume on *Straight Outta Compton*. He stashes the gun in the lunchbox, raises his coat's hood over his head, and steps out the door. The hip hop bass pounds on his ear drums, drowning out the sounds of traffic. Keeping his sight ahead, his peripheral blurring to black, Michael marches forward. He crosses the street and makes it half a block when he spots the small crowd milling about the card shark on the corner. The guy never sees Michael coming, too busy laughing, smoking, and hustling his clients. Michael's eyes narrow, his damp hands keeping a death-grip around the lunchbox handle. The music keeps him strong, keeps him mad. Mad at his Mom and Dad for dying and leaving him here. Mad at Rip for asking him to do this.

Mad at himself for going along with it.

He prays his brother never finds out.

Michael inches his way through the crowd, undoing the latch on the lunchbox, slipping his hand inside. The card hustler is a scrawny black guy with large shades and a fade haircut. At Michael's approach, the guy glances up, mid-joke, and mouths something to him, but Michael's headphones muffle the words. Without hesitation, Michael pulls the .38 and aims it. The hustler holds up a hand in protest, dropping the cigarette out of his mouth as he scrambles, trying to stand. Michael pulls the trigger twice, catching the card shark once in the cheek, and once above the right eye.

The man slumps over, and the crowd flees like a flock of frightened birds. Michael shoves the gun back in his lunchbox, closes the lid, and races down the street, getting lost in the chaos, headed for his pick-up point with Rip. A mixture of excitement and disgust churns his stomach, but he doesn't have time to sort out his thoughts. He just has to get away.

Only, Rip isn't where he's supposed to be.

His body numb and tingling, Michael looks everywhere, but doesn't find his ride. But he knows this is wrong. When all of this happened before—for real—Rip had been there, waiting for him with a big, toothy grin. They'd escaped before the police showed up and Rip had sung Michael's praises all the way back to the safehouse where Michael got blind drunk for the first and only time.

But something has changed.

Michael races forward, the city closing in on him. Eyes in every shadow, in every window, watch him. His teachers are here. The kids at school. Where did they come from?

"Leave me alone!" he bats at them, but they point. Laugh. Whisper of the heinous crime he's just committed. "It wasn't my fault!"

Crying now, Michael races from their accusing glares, rounding a corner, then slides to a startled stop.

Nothing is right. He isn't in Los Angeles. It's not 1991 anymore. This isn't his world.

His shoes are suddenly gone and his bare feet touch down on charred concrete. Acrid smoke fills his nostrils. Somewhere in the back of his mind, he thinks he should be sick, but he feels unaffected. Looking from his toes to the landscape around him, Michael sees nothing but bodies of monsters. Ash-colored things, languishing under the hot sun, their limbs splayed. They have no faces, only mouths full of rotted teeth, and those mouths moan. They plead for help, but not in any language Michael has ever heard. Still, he thinks he understands them.

He stands in the center of a sea of death, a bombed-out city, but feels nothing but peace as his accusers are nowhere to be found. Besides the quiet pleas of the dying creatures, he hears only the soft breeze, rustling him.

A weight settles in his stomach. Throbs, like pinging sonar.

"Michael."

The boy turns around, the world spinning. Warping. Colors drain from everything until his eyes see only grey. But up ahead, he glimpses a fortress, devastated like the city. And there, he bears witness to a dazzling rainbow, undulating from the doorway.

He feels the pull in his stomach, like he's tied to a string that reels him closer.

"Michael."

He lumbers to the bright lights, unable to look away, forgetting the monsters and the broken city—he thinks this place is called Chelkan for some reason—and the death. He reaches for the light, a steady dull pulse quickening within as he nears the space and the rainbow-colored lights.

"Michael," the voice calling his name is closer. A dark shape steps out of the light. Michael shields his eyes against the brilliance, and barely makes out a boy, slightly older than himself. Pale. *White.* Wearing a leather jacket.

"Who—?"

The figure steps closer, his features revealed.

The stranger wears Michael's face.

The older teenager stands before him, an ever expanding splotch of black blood on his mid-section, but doesn't appear to be in any pain. His face betrays no emotion. He doesn't even open his mouth, but Michael already understands.

"No," he breathes.

The Other Michael nods, grim. "It's *your* time now. You'll be awakened soon."

"But I don't want—"

Rainbow lights swell from the doorway, swallowing young Michael whole as he screams.

24

4

Michael opened his eyes and woke in his own house, his own bed, with Edward standing over him. "Dude, get up. You're gonna be late for school."

Michael rose and rubbed his eyes, his stomach still trembling, like the lights from his dream were lulling him back. Edward left without another word, and Michael struggled to catch his breath and shake himself free of the vivid imagery of the dream. Still a bit dazed, he followed his brother through the quiet living room. Edward was in the kitchenette, hastily making a ham sandwich. He was already dressed with his shoes on, no doubt about to "go to work".

Giving the place an once-over, Michael turned to his older brother. "Where's Seth?"

Edward seemed to pick up his pace, slathering some mayo on his breakfast. "Already left."

Michael frowned. "What time did he come in last night?"

The elder Morrison didn't answer the question. "You'd better hurry, dude. Bus already went by, and I don't have time to drive you."

Michael sat at the barstool at the counter, eyeing his brother seriously. "Rip have another job for you?"

"Gotta pay the bills, Mike," Edward huffed defensively. "I don't like it any more than you do."

Michael thought of his own job for the Old Dog and scratched at the countertop with his thumbnail. "Couldn't we just...leave?"

Edward slowed as he finished constructing the sandwich and stood with his back to his little brother. "It's not that easy now. Big Joe's making a move on Rip's turf. This is about loyalty. About family."

"Rip's not family," Michael interjected, growing hot. "He's just using us—" He gulped. "I mean, you."

At last Edward turned, adjusting his glasses, appearing apologetic if not condescending. "You're just a kid, so you don't get it. The world's not always black and white. You make compromises. Do things you're not proud of."

Michael looked away, seething. Maybe his brother made compromises, but he never would. Never again. One day, he would have his own family, and he would never sell his soul for a buck and put them in danger. He'd protect his family from people like Rip, no matter what.

Edward leaned against the sink and crossed his arms, hanging his head. "We don't talk about it, but I'm doing the best I can, here, man. I'm not Dad—"

"You're right," Michael said, hopping to his feet. "You're not."

"All I care about is keeping this family together—"

"Save it," he said, storming for the hall. "I'm taking a shower."

5

Half an hour later, Michael sat on the edge of the steps at school, doing his best not think about his conversation with Edward or what Rip had asked him to do. Edward was wrong to work for Rip. Worse, he was *weak*. Weak for not standing up to the Old Dog.

Am I weak?

No, he was stronger than Edward. Stronger than all of them. He'd tell the Old Dog "no", and this time he'd mean it.

Shoving that aside for now, he thought of the one bright spot in his dark world and waited with bated breath for her to arrive. Before long, the maroon-colored Volvo pulled up to the front doors of the school and Sara Theresea, glowing in the morning light, stepped out of her dad's car. The wind caught her long orange-colored hair and whipped it about, almost in slow motion it seemed to Michael. Her otherworldly blue eyes sparkled. She offered a wave to her dad and hurried up the steps, mere feet from Michael.

His hands felt hot and clammy and his heart beat fast, and all he wanted was to reach out and say—

"Hey!"

Michael nearly jumped out of his sneakers and turned to see an excited Johnny Frawl beside him.

"You really ditched detention!" Johnny said. "I thought you were joking!"

Michael watched in longing adoration as his chance to talk to Sara slipped by. The red-headed girl was lost inside the school. She hadn't even looked his way.

Finally, Michael sighed and turned to Johnny. "So I ditched. No big deal."

"Coach came in to make sure you showed. You should've seen how mad he got when you weren't there."

Michael stood and collected his books. "Let 'im make a move. I don't care."

That went for Rip, too. It went for anyone who thought they could bully him or push him around. He was done with all of it.

But a terrible truth darkened his heart. He wasn't strong or invincible. He was just a kid, and there was no way he would ever be able to stand up to the Old Dog. That wasn't as simple as defying a teacher. Maybe if he told Edward what Rip had been doing... But if Edward ever found out what he'd done for Rip, Michael didn't think he could face his brother again. His stomach soured, hot tears threatening to build. No, he'd made this mess for himself. True, if he told his brother now, it might be enough to push Edward into a straight confrontation with the Old Dog. But then what? They'd be homeless, with no way to fend for themselves.

Or worse, Edward could be dead.

I can't do that to my family...

He'd just have to shoulder the burden. Seth and Edward never had to know. His brother's words came back to haunt him. *We all make compromises.*

Johnny and his behemoth bookbag joined Michael on his way up the steps, the chubby boy still snickering over Michael's absence in detention. "Man, you're going to get into so much trouble."

Just wait, Michael thought, fearing the path laid before him. *You haven't seen nothing yet.*

6

Lunchtime. Kids hurried about, laughing and chatting as they collected their trays and found their seats. Michael slumped his way through the line, quiet as a boneyard at midnight, sullenly accepting his offered mush. Amidst flying paper airplanes and conversations he'd never be asked to join, he took a place at a table far away from the others.

No one ever sat near him. No one picked on him, either. Not like they did Johnny Frawl. Johnny didn't fight back. Michael did. He saw the fear in his classmates' eyes whenever he passed and knew he had built for himself a reputation of being a "bad guy." He liked that. It kept people away. He didn't much care for people.

For the most part. Still, there was Sara.

He saw her seated at a table with some of the other kids in band. She was munching food and laughing and pointing and hugging and *living*. There was life over at that table, wonderful and new. Oh, how he wanted to go over there.

Michael had never talked to a girl before. He'd considered asking Edward how to do it, but he was too ashamed. He didn't want his brother thinking less of him; like a kid. He thought of Mom and Dad again. Maybe this was a thing a father taught his son, or maybe his mom would have firsthand experience on what a girl liked to hear from a boy who was interested.

But Michael had no idea how to be a man. Secretly he worried if he'd ever become one. Yeah, he'd *grow up*, but that was different. Fathers made men.

Michael slid his tray away. He wasn't hungry anymore.

"Michael."

He jumped, thinking Johnny was ambushing him again, but Michael was alone at the table.

The voice returned. *"Michael. It's your time."*

Suddenly, a door in his mind opened and he was back on Chelkan—
Wait. How did I know its name?

He stood and vertigo threatened to throw him to the floor. His mind whined, a sharp high-pitched shriek. He clutched at his eyes, his nose, the pressure in his skull building.

Michael staggered into someone. "Watch where you're going," a girl said. She hissed at the others with her. "He's such a *skeeve*."

Reality swayed and he half-walked, half-limped into the hallway. Out here, away from the noise of the cafeteria, the droning siren was louder than ever.

"Stop..." he wheezed.

Squinting against the pain, he looked up.

Rainbow-colored lights. Down the hall. Like tendrils, the light unfurled and curled once more, beckoning him. Around him, the halls dimmed to

Chelkan's final days, then back to lockers. In and out, over and over as Michael edged closer to the welcoming light down the hall. He reached out for the light, praying it would bring him salvation.

"*Come closer,*" the voice whispered. Then the light was gone.

"Wait," Michael said. The pain in his mind had faded, but in his gut, the steady boom-boom-boom from his nightmare returned.

His sneakers squeaked on the tiled floor as he approached a door marked BOILER ROOM. Michael looked down and saw the rainbow-colored lights flickering like worms from the crack under the door. They disappeared as he reached for the doorknob and turned.

Michael pushed his way inside and peered into the inky blackness of the boiler room. Shimmering reflections bathed the concrete walls in psychedelic colors and Michael wanted to join the light. To be in it, surrounded by it, infused with it.

"*Come down here,*" the rainbow said.

Michael crossed the threshold, lulled calm by the boom-boom-boom in his gut. Every thought of his brothers and Rip and his dead parents and this dumb city faded into the background. *This* was where he belonged. Where he was always meant to be. Where—

"Hey, kid!"

The colors retreated into the dark and Michael turned back the way he came. The janitor stood at the top of the stairs with an annoyed look on his aged face. "No students allowed in there. Get out."

Michael's head cleared and he wondered why he was standing in the boiler room.

"Uh…sorry."

7

After school, Michael sat outside on the steps, lost in thought. Following his strange blackout at lunch, he had trouble concentrating on anything else. The episode had brought back flashes of his dream from last night, filling him with a vague horror. With little effort, he could almost slip back into that other world—Chelkan—a whole planet nothing but dying embers. He'd seen himself there, older, darker. It seemed so much more real than a simple fantasy produced by his subconscious.

"My time," he muttered, repeating the words he'd told himself in that distant realm.

A streak of red screeched to a halt just in front of him, starling Michael out of his brooding. He looked up to see the Chevy, with Edward hanging out of the passenger window, looking upset. "Get in. *Now.*" he barked.

Michael frowned, collected his things, and hurried into the car. Edward took off with a sudden lurch, and Michael noticed Seth, his long dark bangs covering his hatchet-shaped face, sulking in the backseat.

"What's going on?" Michael said.

Edward sped down the street, wringing his hands on the steering wheel. He looked madder than Michael had seen him in a long time.

"What gives?" Michael tried again.

Edward threw an angry look to the rearview mirror. "Your principal called me in today. Seth was selling stolen video games to the kids on the playground."

"I was not!"

"Shut up! And while I was there, they told me all about your no-show at detention yesterday. Wanna tell me what that was about?"

Michael turned away, watching the street blur by them outside. "Sorry."

"I don't want to hear that," Edward snapped. "If you were sorry you wouldn't do it anymore. This ends now. Both of you. It's time this family starts watching out for each other." His voice softened near the end.

Michael thought something else was bothering Edward, something infinitely more dreadful than Seth's recent klepto problem and Michael back-talking a teacher.

Oh no…did he find out what I did?

Nauseous, he ventured, "What's wrong?"

Edward was quiet for a long moment, so long even Seth came out of his shell, braced his hands on the back of the driver seat, and leaned forward. Finally, Edward told them. "Rip's dead."

Michael's heart sank at the thought of the man dead. *We're all alone, now.*

But with the Old Dog gone, Michael was free. Though he worried it made him an even more terrible person, he couldn't suppress a small grin at the news of Rip's demise.

"What happened?" Seth asked.

"He got knifed last night. Big Joe's guys, most likely. Cops ID'd him this morning."

Michael's mind raced with uncertainty. "What does...what does that mean for *us*?"

With a grave look the eldest Morrison regarded his brother. "I don't know. All the lieutenants are dead, now the Old Dog's gone too. Everyone's scattering. We're on our own."

"I say we find Joe and get payback!" Seth shouted, eleven years old and bulletproof.

"Shut up," Edward said. "Don't you guys get it? You can walk around acting tough all you want, but this is *real*. Understand? People are dying and we're next if we don't leave town."

"Where will we go?" Michael asked. *I'll never see Sara again. I didn't even get to talk to her.*

"I don't know. We can try Uncle Jack's again."

"I hate that place," Seth muttered. "He gets mean when he drinks."

"We don't have much of a choice. We pack tonight."

8

Edward hurried about the apartment in a blur, haphazardly stuffing clothes into suitcases and plastic bags—anything he could get his hands on. Seth kept to himself, packing his toys, his games, his cassette tapes and CDs. Michael thought it looked like his younger brother was crying, but it was hard to tell with Seth's hair always obscuring his hard face.

Michael frowned, feeling bad for Seth most of all. He *had* friends here. Michael had no one to miss. No one who would miss him. He had hoped he might have Sara, but he supposed now that it wasn't meant to be.

Edward stormed out of his bedroom, arms laden with laundry. He dumped the clothes on the moth-eaten couch with the one broken leg and swooped for the shelf, taking quick stock of its contents. His fingers roved over a number of spines from his favorite books. Michael didn't read anything that he couldn't find on a comic book rack, but his older brother loved to read—mostly military history or fictional military thrillers. The elder Morrison chewed on his lip, muttering to himself as he quickly perused his collection, no doubt deciding what books to keep and what to leave behind.

At last he sighed, overwhelmed. "Gotta leave all of them," he exhaled. "I can buy them back later."

Michael resumed his own packing, feeling no sentimental attachment to any of his belongings. He grabbed a simple bag and placed into it a couple comics and a model hot rod that he and Edward had put together two summers ago. A couple odds and ends of things, just to humor his brothers. But it was all just junk. Nothing meant anything to him or represented who he was. He didn't have Seth's collection of music or games or Edward's love for Tom Clancy. No trophies, no pictures, no keepsakes, no newspaper clippings.

I'm a ghost, he thought, and the realization frightened him.

"Hey," Edward said, pausing in his tasks to smile. Michael saw that he held a small framed picture in his hand, and he instantly knew which one it was. In the picture, seven-year-old Edward Morrison sat in the hospital room with his new baby brother, Seth, cradled in his arms. A very pudgy Michael—all of one year of age—sat squished in the chair beside them. It was the only picture taken of the brothers together before their parents were killed in the car wreck.

Edward admired the picture with great sentiment, then set it down heavily. "We're gonna get through this," he said, and it sounded like a promise. "I don't want you guys to worry."

Seth didn't reply, still pouting on the floor, clinging to his belongings. Michael offered a half-hearted nod, but he was only half paying attention. He just couldn't shake his own dark musings.

I'm a ghost...

But he didn't want to be. He wanted his life to matter. And he decided there was only one way to make it matter. They'd be gone in the morning, but he had tonight to set something right.

Pleased with his new sense of conviction, he grinned and stood, backing down the short hall to the room he shared with Seth. "I...got more stuff I gotta get."

Edward, again lost in packing, waved him off as he tucked the phone under his chin and spoke into it. "Uncle Jack? Hey, it's Edward. Look, we're gonna be in town for a couple days, and—"

Michael smirked, hurried into his room, and shut the door. Feeling giddy and breathless, he climbed out the window, ready to greet his destiny.

9

As evening fell, Michael returned to school for the last time. If Edward stopped long enough to realize his brother was missing, he'd be furious, but this was too important. Michael knew that if he didn't take his chance now, it would be gone forever. They were leaving tomorrow and he'd never have another opportunity to tell her how he felt. He'd memorized her schedule, secretly watching her, and knew her every move.

And, today after school, Sara Theresea had band practice.

Michael waited on the school's second story balcony for practice to let out, sitting on the railing overlooking the campus. It was peaceful up here in the early evening with most of the students and faculty gone. He worried where he and his brothers would relocate. Would they ever be far enough away from Joe's men?

What if Joe ever found out about the "hitman" who took out his shooter that one afternoon at the street corner card game? What if he learned it was Michael? Michael had killed one man, but could he take on a whole army?

"Gotta have a war," Rip would have said.

But Rip was dead and Michael didn't want to have a war. He just wanted—

"Hey, Sara."

Sara, her trumpet case in hand, stopped in her tracks, then took one step back. "Hey…Michael." She put her head down and started walking faster.

Michael slid off the railing, blocking her path of escape. "Where are you going?"

"Home. My dad's waiting for me outside."

She tried to dodge him, and Michael nearly tripped over himself trying to make eye contact with her. "I need to, uh, ask you something."

"What?" Sara asked, coming to a full stop, a frown marring her beautiful features.

"I was wanting to know if you would want to…uh…go out?"

"Like on a date?"

"Um…" Michael felt his face flush with heat. "Yeah."

Then she laughed at him.

Something dark and wicked bloomed in Michael's heart, filling him with cold rage. A hungry void opened up inside. It was the same empty void he felt when the bullies picked on Johnny or when his teachers gave him a hard time.

It was the same numbing cold he felt after he killed that man on the corner.

"Stop it," he said, the familiar boom-boom-boom trembling in his belly.

"Stop what?" Her clear blue eyes taunted him. She tossed her ginger locks behind her. Her beauty and perfection now infuriated him. Emasculated him. His rage grew and the dark, sick feeling inside swelled to touch every raw nerve within.

"Don't laugh at me."

"You're not serious, are you? I mean, don't take this the wrong way or anything, but I don't want to go out with *you*."

Rejection. Humiliation. Cold. Unending cold. He'd only wanted to be understood, to be loved. He'd spent his life used and abused, passed from drunk uncle to criminal surrogate father, left out in the cold and abandoned since he was a baby. All he wanted was someone to reach out to him, to accept him.

But *she* laughed at him. The only girl he'd cared about. The only one, he was sure, who would ever understand him.

"Stop laughing at me." He clenched his fists, nails pressing into flesh.

"Oh, stop being so dramatic. Don't be a baby."

She moved to leave him there, to abandon him after castrating him. With a roar, he pushed her, wanting her to feel what it was like to be brought low. To become beneath another person. But, his aim had been wrong. He'd pushed her too hard. Too close to the railing.

Sara tumbled over the edge so fast she didn't even have time to scream.

Michael froze, his mind struggling to process what had just happened. "S…Sara?"

The loud whine returned, blurring his vision, locking out his thoughts. He grappled against it, gritting his teeth against the unbearable barrage until it passed. The feeling finally returned to his legs and he raced to the edge of the balcony. Down below, Sara's body was crippled in half, blood spilt from her head.

She was dead. *I killed her.*

Slumping to his knees, still holding the railing, Michael bowed his head, heaving deep ragged breaths. His chest tightened, and his throat burned. A terrible pressure built in him until at last it broke free and he wept. Louder and louder until his sobs turned to screams. Michael smashed his head on the stone railing. Again, and again, until he was for sure he'd cut himself.

But that wasn't enough. No, he needed to *die*.

"What's going on out here?" a woman's voice sliced through Michael's private torment. He glanced up long enough to see a teacher emerging, and fled before he could be spotted.

He hesitated once he was out of sight, tucked in the shadows around the corner. Watched in silent horror as the teacher peeked over the railing. Watched as she saw Sara.

The woman screamed, breaking out in breathless hysterics. "9-1-1!" she shrieked, sobbing loudly as she ran back into the school, still begging for help. Through the glass in the doors, Michael glimpsed other band kids and adults crowd around the woman, even as she fainted.

Michael hung his head and quietly padded down the stairs.

When he got to the courtyard below, he vomited.

10

The next morning the police arrived. Michael remained in his room, only watching through the crack in his doorway as Edward talked with the cops. When they left, Edward closed the door and leaned his head against it for a moment.

Michael finally emerged from his sanctuary to find Seth at home for once—apparently taking his brother's charge seriously—and eating a bowl of cereal on the couch.

"What did they want?" Michael asked, keeping his distance.

"Some girl named Sara Theresea died at your school last night. Did you know her?"

Michael quickly shook his head. "No. Never heard of her."

"They think she might have been murdered. There were some witnesses. They were asking around—"

"They think *I* did it?" Michael shouted.

"Calm down," Edward said, then eyed his brother, hesitantly. "They were just checking around. But I told them you were here all night."

Michael grew dark.

"You *were* here, right?"

"Of course I was." Michael muttered, turning his back on his brother, headed for his room.

"Is your stuff packed?" Edward called after him. "We're gone by noon. Whatever's not packed is staying here."

"I got it, I got it."

Someone knocked at the door, and Michael whirled toward the entrance, his breath catching in his throat. Had the cops returned?

Edward spoke through gnashed teeth, "What now?" He jerked the door open and Michael saw two greasers in tight pinstripe suits standing in the entryway.

He instantly recognized them as Joe's men...the same men from the sedan the other day at school.

They're here to finish what they started with Rip. Three bullets for three brothers and Michael's miserable life would meet its miserable end.

"The Boss sends his regards," the shorter of the duo said in a gravelly voice. "You drove cars for Rip; Joe wants you to drive for him, now."

Seth abandoned his cereal and joined Edward's side. Michael inched closer, his heart beating in his fingertips.

"Why would I do that?" Edward asked. He sounded defiant, though Michael detected concern.

The greasers looked to Seth and at Michael. "You've got a family to take care of. Joe understands that. Rip was bad blood, but there's no hard feelings with you. He'd like to extend his generosity by welcoming you into the fold."

"Tell him to go to hell!" Seth cut in.

"Quiet," snapped Edward, then turned back to the suits. "We'll have to talk it over. We'll let you know..."

"By tonight. Joe's *generosity* is limited."

Edward nodded without another word and closed the door. He turned to his brothers, his face slack, eyes vacant.

"What are we going to do?" Michael asked.

Edward only shook his head and walked off.

Seth turned to Michael, trembling. In a small voice, he asked, "What's going to happen to us?"

Michael looked at him for a moment, uncertain of what to say. *What am I supposed to do? I'm just twelve years old.* Finally, he put his arm around his little brother and held him close.

"We stick together. No matter what."

11

The black sedan pulled up to the cemetery. Michael and Edward sat in the back, Seth squeezed between them. The two burly grunts in suits occupied the front. When the sedan stopped, the guards exited, stood on either side of the car, and opened the doors for the brothers.

Michael climbed out of the vehicle, instantly met by the imposing image of a stone Grim Reaper poised over a grave. He felt a chill. *Two people,* he realized. *I've killed two people now…*

"Why here?" Edward asked, not quite able to hide the quaver in his voice.

His question was answered by the smooth baritone voice of Big Joe. "I find it peaceful. Don't you?"

"No," Seth muttered into his chest, eyeing the tombstones around them.

A dark-skinned giant of a man with long dreadlocks, dressed in a clean white suit, guffawed and dropped a sweaty arm around Edward's shoulders. "Boys, boys. We're family now. Nothing to worry about."

"We're not family yet," Edward said. "We haven't heard your terms."

Big Joe smiled. "Oh, I'm sure you'll find them to your satisfaction. After all, it's not really about what we want, is it? It's about what's best for your brothers. You've got a heavy weight on you, Eddie."

"It's *Edward*," Michael corrected under his breath, watching as the guards circled around to face them.

Big Joe didn't acknowledge him. "I'd like to ease the burden, that's all."

"For how much?" Edward asked.

"Like I said before. You were Rip's wheel-man. Now I'd like you to be mine."

Edward looked at the two gorillas. "But…you've already got all the help you could possibly need. Why bother with us?"

Joe laughed heartily, looking to his boys. "Ya hear that? We've got a smart one, here!"

Edward's jaw clenched and he shot a glance at Michael, who drew nearer to Seth to shadow him.

"Well, I guess you got me there," Joe said.

The guards pulled 9mms and Michael's stomach dropped.

Edward held up his hands. "Wait, wait—"

"I just wanted to see the look on your faces," Joe said. "Killin' should be personal, you know? You really need to appreciate the fact that you're takin' another life."

Joe fixed his beady gaze on Michael. "Did *you* appreciate it…little man?"

Edward turned to Michael. "What?"

Michael bit his lip and lowered his gaze. Big Joe sauntered over to him. "Didn't think we'd catch up with you, did ya? See, we know people. They saw you on that corner. Saw what you did."

"Michael, what's he talking about?"

Joe spun on Edward. "Rip was grooming your boy here to be the next big hitman. You were pretty smooth too, kid. Almost got away with it." Joe's dark face shriveled up in rage as he faced Michael once more. "But you don't get away with nuthin' in my city, ya hear! *I'm* the Boss Man!" He cooled and eyed Michael with a vindictive glare. "I just wanted you to know that before I kill you and your brothers."

Joe twitched his chin towards his guards, who looked terribly uncomfortable with the order. "Do it. I've said my piece."

Edward stood in front of his brothers. "No! Please! They're just kids!"

After a moment's hesitation, the gorillas raised their guns, but Michael no longer feared death in his heart. Staring down the barrel of the guns, facing these men who would see him dead…It felt natural. Right. He was born for this. Born to make war.

Michael pushed Seth to the ground and slid under Edward's outstretched arms to dive headfirst and arms wide at the knees of the nearest gunman. Michael managed to knock his would-be killer off balance, shoving him to the ground. He braced himself as the other goon pivoted, gun raised, giving Edward an opportunity to rush in and grab the weapon. The gun fired in the struggle, and Michael flinched, but it didn't look like Edward had been hit. Bending back the gunman's thumb,

Edward wrenched the gun away, and without wasting a second, turned the 9mm and fired on his attacker. The gorilla clutched his wounded stomach, still alive, but permanently out of the fight.

Edward recovered, his face flushed with exertion, and his eyes widened in horror as he saw what Michael was just now beginning to understand.

"Michael!"

Michael's legs wobbled and he fell back on the ground, his fingers numb and cold. He looked down. His palms were pooled with blood. A bright red flower had opened on his chest. The hole oozed blood, soaking his clothes and the cemetery grass. Seth knelt beside him, panicking. The gunman Michael had fought scurried to his feet, searching for the gun he dropped when Michael tackled him. Enraged, Edward turned on the brute and fired three times, killing him instantly.

Big Joe helped his wounded guard to his feet, glowering at the three brothers. Edward whipped his gun into firing position, only to be met by Joe's own gun. The two faced each other down, hatred burning in their eyes.

"I hurt your family," Joe said, straining under the weight of his bodyguard. "You hurt mine. I say that makes us squared. For now."

Edward's finger curled around the trigger, but Michael feared that Joe would be a faster shot and that Edward would be dead and Seth alone in the world.

"Edward," Michael whispered.

"Go," Edward told Joe.

Joe backed up and lowered his gun. Then he helped his wounded man into the sedan and drove off. Edward waited until they were gone before hurrying to Michael's side.

His face was calm, but his eyes were brimming with tears. "Michael…Michael, hang on…"

"Edward…" Michael said. He looked again at the blood leaking from his chest. "I'm sorry…I'm sorry for everything…"

"It's okay, little brother. It's all going to be okay, now."

But in his heart, Michael knew better. His vision dimmed, but in the black, he saw a rainbow, unfolding towards him, and his own voice spoke, *"It's time to wake up."*

White light. Michael awoke in a desert. The sun set behind large red mesas, painting the desert sky in shimmering hot pink and orange. Twilight arrived and the stars twinkled to life in the dark blue beyond the layers of warm light.

Michael looked down to his clothes, seeing that he was wearing a hospital gown.

What happened? The last thing he clearly recalled was Big Joe making his retreat. Edward was crying over him and then…nothing.

Now a desert.

Michael scratched his head, searching the empty landscape.

"Edward?" he asked, hesitantly at first. "*Edward?* Seth! Where…?"

Silence answered him and he knew he was alone. A chill crept into his bones. He crouched on the ground, rubbing at his arms, trying to keep warm, calm, and sane.

"I'm dreaming," he said, his back beginning to sweat. Despite the wide-open spaces, he felt strangely confined. "I'm dreaming. Right? Edward? Where did you all go?"

A new, scarier thought, seized him and Michael stood.

"Or am I dead? Oh no, am I dead? If I'm dead…where am I?"

"Sure ain't the Hilton," a familiar, lazy voice spoke from behind.

Michael spun around, his heart hammering.

Rip grinned back at him. "How ya doin', little brother?"

"Rip?" Michael took a step back. "I thought you were—?"

"Dead?" Rip cracked a grin, revealing a pair of pronounced fangs. "I *was*, little dude."

"Does that mean…?" Michael wasn't able to finish the thought. Tears formed in the corners of his eyes. If Michael were dead, he knew that he was surely in hell. There was no way he could get into heaven. Not with that street corner card shark's blood on his hands.

Not with Sara's blood on his hands.

He felt like vomiting again.

He swooned, and Rip held out his hands to steady him. "Hey, hey, relax, little man. You ain't dead."

"I'm…not?"

"Nah. Th'other way around, I reckon."

"I don't understand."

Rip reached into a backpack Michael noticed for the first time, and pulled out a pair of jeans and sneakers, a clean shirt, and a can of beans.

"Been expecting you. How about you change out of that skirt and I fill you in over dinner?"

13

It was Rip all right. He looked a little older—his hair was completely grey now and he had a few more years' worth of creases in his leathered face, but Michael still recognized the Old Dog. He dressed differently too, sporting torn jeans, a pair of cowboy boots, and a worn dusty leather jacket to cover up those weird tattoos on his wiry arms. With the backpack to complete the image, he looked every bit a highway drifter.

Michael wondered where he was headed. And, most importantly—

"Why aren't you dead?" he asked. He scooped another helping of beans out of the can using the knife Rip had lent him, pausing to admire the blade. It was crude, like maybe it was handmade. The metal was tarnished and misshapen, and the simple handle was adorned with a single carving of an image that might have been a lion's head.

Rip watched him take the bite and then laughed. "You lookin' to get rid of me, dude?"

Michael shook his head. The thought had actually not occurred to him. Seeing Rip alive again was the highlight of this very strange day.

"No, I just…Edward said you'd been killed."

"Well," Rip exhaled, leaning back and propping his head on his backpack, "I s'pose you could say I was dead, for a while. It didn't take. It was just an initiation. Big Joe thought he was taking me out, but he just helped me further down the road."

"What happened? What is this place?"

Rip sprang forward, eyeing the boy seriously. "I've got a heavy story to tell. You think you're ready to hear it?"

Michael shrugged. "Sure."

"No, not *sure*, little brother. This burden I carry ain't easy and it won't be for you, either. We're soldiers, dude, like I used to tell you, and I've found our war. Our *true* war."

A wave of disquiet fell over him, and Michael felt stiff. He nodded once. "Okay. I'm ready."

Rip stood and stretched, then removed his leather jacket, revealing a naked torso covered in tattoos and scars—both familiar and new. He twisted his arms about, showing off bizarre tattoos that seemed to move with a life of their own. "See these? You think I just get them for their looks?"

"I don't guess I ever really thought about it."

"Every tat has a story to tell, partner. These are mine. My Gramma Moore used to talk to spirits—those that had passed Beyond the Veil, but could come back from time to time. They told her the future, taught her medicine, kept her sharp. You see, that school you went to, it's got some dark voodoo about it. You ever feel it?"

Michael gulped, realizing he *had*. He'd felt its weird pull at lunch yesterday and that night too. That night when Sara humiliated him. When he killed her...

"That's Rage, man. It's powerful," Rip said. "It called to my gramma, just like it called to me."

"Yeah," Michael said softly. "Called to me too, I think."

Rip clapped his hands together once. "See! I knew it, little brother. You're special. You always had it in you, just like I told your brother."

Michael thought of Edward and missed him terribly.

"It's got plans for us, Mike."

"What plans?"

"We gotta be its outlaws, little dude! These old worlds...there's so much restraint, holdin' it all together. So many laws, so many rules. There used to be a time when things were pure. No law, only freedom. Freedom to do whatever we please."

Michael watched Rip as he nearly danced with energy, the fire's light flickering across the Old Dog's face, casting ghastly shadows.

"What are you talking about?" Michael asked.

"I'm talking Chaos! Pure, beautiful, liberating Chaos. Isn't that what we fought for on the streets? We wanted to make our own way, not following anybody else's rules. The Rage can give us the strength to do that, on a *cosmic* scale." Rip knelt down, bouncing on his haunches, his eyes lit with madness. "God's our worst enemy. Everything's all about order with him. Order and rules and right and wrong—bah! You gotta free your mind, dude. Break out of all that and experience the darkness between the worlds, like I have. It's so beautiful there, man. Beautifully wild."

Michael put down his can of beans, not quite knowing what he feared more—that Rip had gone insane, or that he was making perfect sense. "What worlds?"

"There's more worlds than these, Mike. I've been to a number of 'em, before the Rage brought me here."

"Why here?"

"To set other minds free. This is where all the Rage's children go when they're called—the Desert of Choosing. This is like the way station for the rest of your life, little dude. I'm here to train you and all the others, give you the heads-up, help you catch a taste of the possibilities." Rip laughed, scratching his head. "It's funny, you're not even the first *you* I've taught. It's a trip."

Michael stood, his mind unable to process any of Rip's words. "When can I go home?"

"No more 'home', little man. You're a wanderer of the worlds, like me, now."

Michael's chest tightened and he felt on the verge of tears. "B-But, Edward...Seth..."

"I know you miss them, little brother, but they ain't your family. That ain't your world no more. Don't you see you've been called to something greater?"

"But I don't want that! I want to go back home!"

Rip stood slowly, towering over the boy. His wild-eyed exuberance had left him, leaving only cold, dead eyes. "I told you, boy. You're special. This is who you are now. Who you were always meant to be. All your life, you never fit in, never belonged. Didn't you ever wonder why? 'Cause that ain't your world, little brother. You were just passing through, on your way here. To me. Deep down you've always known that. Ain't no running away from it."

Rip placed his hand on Michael's shoulder, but Michael jerked away. "Watch me."

He turned and raced out into the night. He looked back once and saw the Old Dog watching him with a fanged smile. Rip's dim eyes glinted in the moonlight like an animal's as he crowed, "You won't get far!"

Michael ignored the taunt and pushed on. He came to a hill face and climbed, kicking up dust and pebbles in his ascent. There was nowhere to run in the middle of a desert. But he knew he had to get away. Rip had always been a predator, but something inside of Rip had changed. Michael just couldn't tell what it was. He only knew he needed to run far, far from it.

He clenched the knife he'd used for supper in his teeth as he climbed the craggy rocks. His blond hair was matted with sweat; his face, hands, and clothes covered in dirt. His heart beat faster than it ever had before, but Michael was not scared. As crazy as it sounded, even to himself, he felt calm and alert.

He felt alive. Maybe for the first time.

When he heard a bestial howl echo in the night air, the tremble that shook his body was not out of terror, but anticipation.

Come on, Rip. He gritted his teeth, grinding against the metal of the blade. *I'm ready.*

From somewhere, Rip taunted him, "Trained a lot of soldiers out in this desert. Like I said, I even trained a lot of *you*. We got important work to do. Something's lost out there in the worlds, and we mean to find it. But you've got to earn your keep, dude. If you ain't got what it takes, the Rage can't use you anyhow. You've gotta prove yourself first."

Michael shut out the voice, concentrating on getting up the cliff; claiming the high ground. By the time his small fingers reached the peak of the rock, he felt the harsh pinch of boot on his hand. He growled, clenching the knife tighter. He jerked his head up to see Rip standing over him, backed by the moonlight. But Rip was no longer a man.

He stood upright as a man, but now long silver fur covered his torso and elongated arms. The creature's massive hands flexed, where blackened eagle-like talons clicked together. The face was totally canine, a wet snout pulling back to reveal jagged, mismatched fangs. Pointed ears protruded from a magnificent grey mane. But those eyes were unmistakable—it was Rip.

Fear washed through Michael's blood. What stood before him was something so wholly unnatural he struggled to understand what he saw. For one ludicrous half-second, he thought that maybe Rip was wearing some elaborate tribal wolf headdress, but the reality was so much worse.

Rip leaned over, propping his shaggy arm on his bent knee, his boot still crunching into Michael's fingers. Impossibly, he talked through his wolf snout. "Come on, little brother. Don't quit on me. The pain hasn't even started yet."

Rip ground his boot heel into the tips of Michael's fingers, working hard to dislodge him from the cliff's edge...

That's when the realization hit Michael. He felt no pain.

Michael pushed through the confusion and pulled himself higher. Rip stood now, the other boot on Michael's other hand, his eyes widening in momentary surprise.

"Now there's the spirit," Rip growled. "Shove it aside. Fight through the pain."

There isn't any pain, you freak. Michael pulled up until his chin cleared the cliff's edge.

Rip removed one foot. "Nice try, dude. But you're gonna have to do better if you wanna be worthy." Rearing his lifted foot backwards, Rip kicked out for Michael's face.

But Michael dodged to the side before he was even aware he was moving. As if on automatic pilot, he reached out with his newly freed hand, grabbed the boot at the ankle, and twisted. Rip fell back, rolling to the ground.

Michael used the moment to scurry up the ledge, bringing himself to a hunkered stance—braced for an attack. He took the crude knife out of his mouth and wiped the saliva on his pant leg. Then he held it ready with the blade pointed down.

The Old Dog slowly righted, keeping a low, crouched position. Michael bared his teeth, his breath coming out in furious gasps.

Rip chuckled, low and guttural. "You've seen what the Rage has done for me. Now you're starting to feel what it can do for you. You can't even begin to understand the power you've got in your blood, Mike. Your potential. You've just got to let it go. Stop holding back. Attack me—"

Before the wolf had finished, Michael roared and surged forward, his knife hand upraised. Rip lashed out with a ferocious claw, muscles rippling under grey fur. The claws sank deep, slicing Michael's stomach open, but he felt no sting. Not even the mildest discomfort.

The pain was just...disconnected.

Flinching in old reflex, Michael crumpled over, clutching his shredded clothes and abdomen, the knife clattering harmlessly to the dirt floor.

Rip stood to his full monstrous stature, sadness in his voice. "I'm sorry, little brother. I really am. I expected more from you. But...I guess it just wasn't meant to be. Maybe your brother was right after all. Maybe you don't have the killer instinct at all."

Michael slowly rose, his back to Rip.

"Whoa...how did you...that should have killed you," said Rip.

Michael turned to face him, and looked down to his stomach. The clothes were ruined, but there wasn't a spot of blood on him. Not a wound in sight. Marveling at the revelation, Michael faced the Old Dog and grinned.

"That's not possible," Rip said, backing away. "I cut right through you. I felt it."

Michael reached down and picked up the dropped blade.

"Unless..." Rip's face changed back to human form, a morose resignation settling in. "Unless you're *him*. You're *that* Michael. The one *she* talked about...the one who can't be killed." He sighed, his face sagging, a sad smile revealing a pronounced canine. "Been waiting a while to meet you. Funny. Thought I had more time."

Michael didn't know what the old man was saying. Didn't care. He just wanted to kill. He took a step forward.

Rip jerked in fright, then yelled, pointing towards the edge of the cliff as if it were a proper exit. "Get out! The Hand is on you! The Rage don't want no part of you! Leave! Go away!"

"Sorry, Rip," Michael said, feeling aged somehow, far beyond his twelve years. "You wanted a fight. You've got one now."

Michael charged again. He tackled Rip, stabbing him full force in the bare chest. Rip roared as Michael pushed deeper, taking them both over the cliff's edge. Michael pushed harder as they fell, wind tugging at his clothes, his hair, caressing his face. Exhilaration swelled inside, weightlessness offering freedom. In their freefall, he drove the knife into Rip's chest, the ground rising to meet them at a blurring pace. For one frozen moment in time, Rip stared back at Michael, a mix of pride and terror in his dimming eyes.

With a sickening crack, they landed on the ground below, snapping Rip's back in two.

Blood oozed from the Old Dog's nose and ears, but he managed a weak smile. "You done good…You could be the strongest Michael of all…the Rage might be able to use you yet, little brother…"

Michael dismounted Rip's body, uninjured, his own bloodlust subsiding. He grimaced, spat, "I'm not your brother," then leaned over and gave the embedded blade a sharp twist. With a final gurgle, Rip convulsed twice, and lay still.

Michael stepped back, staring down at the old man. In one horrifying moment, the weight of what he'd done sought to bury him. He'd killed again.

Only this time…he'd enjoyed it.

Overwhelmed by the guilt, the thrill, the disgust, the freedom, Michael looked to the starry heavens, tears breaking free, and let out a primal scream.

14

Three weeks later, Michael still had not found any sign of civilization. With Rip's leather jacket draped over his shoulders, he trudged the desert wasteland, starving and thirsty. The heat shimmered on the horizon that offered no hope of salvation, but Michael only wanted to fall over dead.

He wondered if he'd even be able to die. He didn't feel any pain and even his hunger and thirst were not so unbearable that he couldn't continue. Everything in his mind told him he should be dead by now, but on he walked.

Maybe I'm already dead, he thought. *Maybe that's why Rip couldn't kill me. Maybe I'm some sort of zombie…*

Even that thought did little to incite fear at this point. He'd grown numb to this desert. Nothing mattered anymore. Just walking. Maybe this was hell and he was in it, damned for being nothing but Rip's little soldier, even to the end. That sudden realization jabbed spears of despair deep in his heart. He didn't want to be a killer anymore. He just wanted to be out of this nightmare. To go home. See his brothers again.

God, I'm so sorry…

He wept and fell to his knees, sticking his face in the sand. He cried until the dirt turned to mud around him. The sobs rocked his body until no sound came out. He was absolutely and utterly emptied.

But why won't I die?

"Hi, Michael."

The voice startled him and Michael gazed into the ripples of heat, where stood a figure backed by the blinding sun. Michael fell back on the seat of his jeans, reaching for the crude knife he now kept stashed inside Rip's old leather jacket.

"Who are you? What do you want?"

The man stepped closer out of the light. He wore a long brown duster, a red scarf wrapped around his neck in spite of the heat. A flimsy Stetson hat rested atop his soft, wrinkled face. The old man smiled, his eyes baby blue behind bifocals. Michael felt instantly at ease despite the shock of no longer being alone.

"I am," the Man said with a wink, his words sinking deep into Michael's heart like life-giving water. The voice was clear and strong.

Michael frowned. "Am what?"

The Man laughed, soft but powerful, too. "You have a lot to learn. I'd like to teach you. If you're ready."

"Am I dead?" Michael asked.

"No."

"What is this place? What's wrong with me?"

The Man tilted his head to regard the sky for a thoughtful second, then faced Michael. "Let's walk for a while, you and I." Without waiting for Michael to follow, he turned and started across the desert.

Michael hurried to his feet and jogged to catch up. The heat seemed to cool and his sweat soon dried. The sun lowered, softening the harsh glare. The Man began, his voice dramatic as though he were about to tell a marvelous bedtime story, "The Rage has existed since the dawn of Creation."

Michael recalled the Rage in his own heart. The terror in his dreams, the rainbow-lights drawing him. He thought of the night he murdered Sara, and that sickening cold twisting inside him like a hungry serpent. Rip said the Rage had him in its grip, but Michael didn't want that to be true.

"As darkness, it has lurked in the hearts of angels and men, secretly feeding on the lusts and desires of the flesh until it is engorged. When fully ripened, it bursts open, spreading its infectious malice through the pores and veins of its host, corrupting them into something wholly inhuman, a vessel for the purest evil." The Man glanced down at Michael.

"For as long as the Rage has existed, though, the Light has combated it, illuminating vessels to wage holy war against the dark impulses in the thoughts of evildoers. In the past, the vessels of Light have been righteous men and women of valor, dedicated to God, and valiant in their stand against the dark force in Man. But sometimes, just sometimes, the Light chooses one of the Rage's own instruments to implement its justice."

"I don't understand—"

The Man stopped and regarded him. "It's you, Michael. The Light has chosen you. There is great darkness out there, in between the worlds, looking to enter in."

At once Michael wanted to smile. To think *he'd* been chosen for anything good…

Then he saw Sara's broken body on the ground. He'd done that to her. He was incapable of good. He shook his head and looked to the sand. "But…but why me?"

The Man laughed, but Michael felt no shame like he did when Rip laughed at him. Carefully, the Man used a knuckle to raise Michael's chin. Staring into the Man's eyes, Michael saw acceptance. Forgiveness. "The better question to ask is 'Why *not*?' The choice has been laid before you. You can serve the Light or the Dark—it's all up to you. But a choice must be made."

Michael chewed at his lip, his heart quickening inside, prompting him to choose. "I'm scared."

The Man knelt down and placed two weathered hands on Michael's shoulders and faced him as a father might, or at least, as Michael hoped a father would. He'd never known his dad. This man, this stranger here in the desert, however…Michael trusted him, though he did not know why.

"As long as my hand remains on you, you shall not die. I will protect you from harm, boy. But there is much for you to see. There are more worlds than these. They need your help."

"I can't help." Michael fought but failed to stop his brow from shrinking up, ready to shed more tears if he had any left. He looked to the knife in his hand, Rip's blood further staining its tarnished surface. "I'm a killer…"

"But you can become a hero, if you choose. The evil that sought to claim you has spread to countless worlds. Its agents are everywhere, seeking to loose Chaos. It has intended to use you for evil, but you can fight against them. With my strength, you can surely overcome them, for I have overcome the worlds. You will know evil when you are in its presence. You will use that pain to locate it and to combat it."

Michael lifted his face, warm inside for the first time since Joe's man put a bullet in his gut. He still didn't understand what was happening to him, but he wanted to listen to the Light. He wanted to trust this figure that seemed to know everything about him.

"You're…you're God, aren't you?"

The Man smiled and stood, patting Michael on the back. He picked up the pace and Michael once again hurried to keep up. "The road ahead is filled with much trouble, but I'll be with you, though you won't always see me. But know that I'm there, and I'm protecting you. Even unto the end of all things."

The solemn promise filled Michael with a burst of courage and determination, but his walk slowed as the reality settled. "I won't get to see my brothers again, will I?"

The Man hesitated and faced Michael. "Would knowing the answer change what you have to do?"

Michael hung his head, realizing he was not his own anymore. He owed the Man in the Stetson—whether he be God or the Light or whatever—everything. The boy thought of his brothers and a deep hurt bruised his heart. He wasn't for sure how he'd be able to breathe, traveling the worlds without Edward looking out for him.

I can't do this, his fear told him. But when he looked to the Man in the Stetson at his side, Michael felt certain he could do just about anything.

"I…I killed Sara."

The Man nodded, his twinkling eyes softening. "I know."

Though it didn't surprise him to hear that the Man in the Stetson already knew such things, Michael worried who else knew. Would his brothers find out? Would they hate him? Suddenly, running away sounded even better. He couldn't show his face to his family again. He would keep running; he would fix things.

I'll be a hero, and I'll make them proud of me.

Maybe, just maybe, he'd discover what it took to be a man.

"We can't change the past," the Man said in soothing, rumbling tones. "All we can do is make the most of the time we have left."

Michael nodded. "I want to," he said, his voice betraying his sorrow.

A wonderfully refreshing breeze whipped about him, sifting the sands, and revealed a single sheet of notebook paper on the ground.

"Then let's begin," the Man said.

"What's that?" Michael asked, stepping closer to the page.

"The messenger. You are my message to the servants of the Dark. It is your gateway to the multiverse—a rift into space and time."

"But it's a sheet of paper."

"Things aren't always what they seem, Michael."

He nodded, taking that in. "What...do I do?"

"Step inside and begin your new life."

There was so much he didn't understand, but Michael did not hesitate.

Nothing made sense anymore, but he was getting used to that. He considered Rip's knife one last time, then dropped it to the sand. Then, on nothing but faith, he stepped onto the sheet of paper. Instantly, a brilliant fountain of rainbow lights swirled around him, and he was sucked inside.

PART TWO: SECOND CHANCES

1

FIVE YEARS LATER

Tony Carlson had it coming.

Cold rain pelted him from above as he pulled his collar tighter, shielding himself from the raw chill of the city. But the icy grip that seized his body had nothing to do with the temperature, nor the rain outside. Death walked the streets this night, and Tony Carlson feared he was next in line to feel the sickle.

A seemingly endless line of sculpted bodies in tight-fitting designer clothes stretched in front of the club—The Electric Kitty. Even in this horrible storm, hundreds of swingers and would-be partygoers waited outside, praying for the bouncer's blessing to enter and have the time of their lives.

Tony had no time for the patrons as he crossed the street and forced his way through the line. He wasn't like them. He wasn't particularly handsome or well-kept, instead sporting shoulder-length slicked back hair, and an ensemble straight out of the 2130s. He was a hipster from another time, out of place with the trends of Now.

But at least he wasn't a sheep.

Ignoring the usual snickers and stares, Tony marched right up to the door and nodded to the bouncer.

"Go on in, Mr. Carlson." The bouncer returned the nod in grim affirmation before stepping aside to let Tony in, only to immediately reclaim his post with folded beefy arms.

Tony moved through the club, trying his best to dodge the dancing clusters of people. The club pitched back and forth like a ship at sea, as he was bombarded by multi-colored lights and a sound system that crashed against him like tumultuous waves. He recognized a few of the girls as he continued to push forward, but shunned frivolous thoughts of romance, never taking his mind off his destination.

"Hey, Tony. Wanna party?" A bouncy little pink-haired number named Cammy be-bopped her way over and clung to his arm. Her skin sparkled with Glitterslam—the new drug that was all the rage these days. Spritz some on your body, get wasted and look hot in the process. *Kids today.*

"Later." He pushed her aside.

She gaped at him. "Hey, you don't look so good."

He kept moving, leaving Cammy's bewildered stare behind. He worried his fear was all too evident in his eyes. The shadow of fate loomed large over him and, even inside, he felt that dulling cold that permeated the city's streets. Some animal part in his mind screamed "*Not safe!*" over and over, filling him with the uncontrollable urge to find somewhere to hide.

He needed help, and the only help he could think of was Salvatore "Sal" Frazetta, the owner of the West Side district. Tony ascended the metal steps, clanking his way to the top floor. Two dead-eyed guards stopped his approach.

"I gotta talk to Sal," he blurted nervously, glancing behind to make sure he wasn't followed.

The guards looked at each other as though communicating telepathically, then stood aside. Tony scurried to the large oak door at the end of the hallway. He knocked and waited for a response.

"Come in," someone said from inside, the voice muffled through the door.

Tony hurried into the private office, closing off the rest of the club. The room was dimly lit and patched in shadow. The blinds were drawn on the windows and the neon advertisements from the nudie joint across the street periodically painted the room in bright reds. A small lamp on the coffee table in front of the couch revealed a young twenty-something blonde girl, clumsily shooting up her arm with blue glow. She was one of the new girls. Some country bumpkin who had come to the big city to be a star. Sal was the kind of guy who had connections and actually could make a wide-eyed pretty girl's dreams come true, but his prospects usually ended up here in his club, instead, doped up. The city, with all its promises of pleasure, was exciting and overwhelming, and all too often these kids fell prey to the allure of the party culture. Whatever this girl might've been, now she was just another junkie hitting the blue glow. Tony flinched in revulsion at the sight; he'd never been one for the hard stuff.

"Sal?" he asked to the quiet blackness. He peered harder, until he found Sal, sitting in the shadows at his desk. Tony recognized the familiar stench of Sal's favorite brand of cigars and followed the trail of smoke to the furniture.

"Sal." Tony approached the desk and gave himself permission to sit down. "We got a problem, man."

Only the outline of Sal's face was evident in the shadows. "Why's that?"

"There's a new player in town." Tony waited to see Sal's response, but there seemed to be none in the near future. "I don't know who he is. Pete said he heard about a takedown in the South End, right? There was supposed to be some big shipment come in and Pete was sneaking over there to see what the Southers had coming. But he said when he got there, all he heard were screams coming from inside and gunfire. Pete said he got so scared he left. He said he had never heard a man scream like that."

Tony paused again, expecting Sal at any time to lose his cool. But, Salvatore Frazetta was known for his cool. "And, what's this got to do with me?"

Tony ventured, "Word around town has it that this guy took out East and North too. Now he's coming here. We already lost Sidney. I found him myself. All gutted. Like a fish." Tony shuddered at the memory. "Pete said Donovan was supposed to come by to go over the plans for the Watson operation, but Donovan never showed. Now, Pete's missing too."

Sal sat there in silence for a moment. The smoke from his cigar trailed in the air, causing Tony to choke it back, just a little.

"What are we going to do, Sal?"

"What does this guy look like?"

"Nobody knows. They say he's like a whirlwind, man. He just comes out of nowhere and once he's done, he just disappears. A real pro."

Sal was quiet. Thinking about their options, Tony assumed.

"Maybe we should leave town, Sal. Just the two of us until this whole thing blows over. Maybe this guy will leave."

His knees started shaking, and Tony chewed his nails as sweat pooled under his armpits. The smoke continued to curl through his nostrils, nearly gagging him. He looked down to Sal's cigar, wishing he would put the thing out. That's when he noticed that the cigar was burnt all the way down to Sal's fingers. But Sal remained unflinching, as if he didn't notice the heat brushing against his knuckles.

Then, the shape replied, "Can't leave until it's finished."

Tony's knees stopped shaking.

"S-Sal?"

In the quiet that followed, Tony looked deeper into the darkness, seeing the outline of Sal's body, and he went rigid as he stared, waiting— hoping to God that Sal would move.

Sal Frazetta fell face first on the desk, his throat cut and bleeding out.

Tony yelped and jumped back, knocking his chair over, just as the blinking neon advertisements bathed the room in harsh red light and revealed the awful truth. Standing behind Sal Frazetta was a man—no, a *kid*. Some punk teenager dressed in jeans, T-shirt, sneakers, and a worn leather jacket. He wore a blank expression and had pale blond hair, sallow skin, and the darkest eyes.

The eyes were the worst.

Without a cry, Tony Carlson rushed for the door. The shadowed figure moved faster and a cold, uncaring hand burst forth from the darkness and grabbed Tony by the scruff of the neck. The hand, more powerful than anything Tony had ever encountered, flung him across the room, sending him crashing over the chair in which he had just been sitting.

The shadows pulled back and revealed their dark occupant. He moved with determination in each step. A scary confidence that revealed no hint of fear or mercy. Tony shrank back against the wall, pulling himself into a near fetal position, desperately trying to keep his distance from this specter of death.

"Tony Carlson," the kid said, as if pronouncing sentence. "Time's up."

Tony screamed his throat raw.

The door burst open and the two guards from before came in, their guns drawn and killer intent painting their faces. After a quick look to their boss stone-cold dead on the table, they opened fire. Bullets exploded from their guns and dug deep into the kid's back with dull *thuds*.

However, the teenager was not fazed.

He paused in his pursuit of Tony Carlson and turned around. His eyes, those hollow dead eyes that he'd fixed Tony with, now set their sights on the guards. He started toward them. Their bullets only seemed to tear through the boy's jacket, and *that* only seemed to make him angrier.

The kid came right up on them and grabbed the gun hand of the guard on his right. Instantly, the gun crashed to the floor, while the guard's hand crackled under the pressure. The guard cried out. Still holding onto the hand, the kid with the dark eyes slapped the other guard's chest with the flat of his other hand, crushing his ribcage with a crisp crack and propelling the man backwards into the hall.

The boy took hold of the first guard and lifted him off the ground, raising him high before throwing him on top of his fallen partner. Then the kid slowly closed the door again.

And locked it.

Turning back, he focused his baleful glare on Tony and marched toward him, stalking him. Ready to strike.

Tony whimpered as he crawled up the wall, trying to avoid the boy. The boy walked right up to him, grabbed his face in his icy hands, and hoisted him up by the head.

"Please!" Tony blubbered. "Don't kill me! I'll give you whatever you want…*whatever it is!* Please! I'll change! I'm sorry! I'll change!"

The teenager, with an unforgiving blackness behind his eyes, spoke. "Sorry. Nothing personal."

2

With a flick of the wrist, Tony Carlson's neck snapped. Michael Morrison hurled the thug's lifeless body across the room and through the window. Glass shattered as Tony's body pushed through. Michael moved to the broken window and stared down at Tony Carlson lying motionless on a crumpled hot dog cart two stories below. Panicked passersby and clubbers alike scrambled and screamed. The sight gave Michael pause at what he'd done. Something pulled at him. Sympathy? Regret? No, Tony was a bad man. He deserved what he had coming to him.

Just like all the others on a thousand worlds in the multiverse that

Michael had visited.

Suddenly, he sensed a sharp *whoosh* as a switchblade knife cut the air just past his ear and plunged hilt-deep into his shoulder. Snarling, he looked to see the knife still stuck in him, then turned further to see the blonde girl from the couch, backing away as her pouty lips parted in mounting terror. The rubber string was still tied to her arm, and pink rings circled her wide grey eyes.

Michael wrapped his hand around the knife and gave a jerk, wrenching it free, before tossing it aside. Growling, he surveyed the fresh tear in his ratty jacket. "Don't. Touch. The Jacket."

The girl whimpered and staggered behind the table where she'd concocted her blue narcotic. Enraged, Michael took an angry arm and smashed aside the equipment she had used, splashing fluorescent blue liquid all over the floor. He reached down and undid the strap on her arm, throwing it to the side, then grabbed her with both hands as he had done to the late Tony Carlson. He slammed the girl against the wall, suspending her bare feet off the floor so that she faced him at eye level.

In that moment, he felt the fear in her as her body shook uncontrollably, but she was too numb from the drugs to fight back any more. She was helpless. He could kill her. Snap her in two without any effort and all of her pain would go away. He'd be doing her a favor, ending her miserable life.

It would be easy.

He studied her, curious. The girl before him was weak, and he pitied her for it. There was something in her grey eyes, such surrender there. She'd given up. Somewhere inside, he knew how that felt.

"What's your name?" he grumbled.

"C-Candice," she wept.

"Where are you from?"

She scanned his eyes, as though unsure of the reason behind his question. "Wy-Wyoming."

Michael cooled and released a heavy sigh, then glanced to the table. He reached over and picked up one of the needles to hold it before her, making sure she got a good look at its glowing contents. "Go back there. And never do this again."

The girl nodded to the best of her ability. Then he let her go.

She fumbled with the lock of the large door and stumbled into the club. Michael watched after her, his bloodlust subsiding. He wasn't sure exactly why he'd spared the girl, but he was glad he did. It felt good to give someone a second chance. He just hoped she didn't blow it.

"Hold it! Don't move!" a gruff voice barked from the doorway as a swarm of men in heavy armor filed in, automatic rifles raised. "Police!" the leader cried.

Michael snickered and held up his hands half-heartedly. "Relax, guys. I just killed Sal Frazetta for you, as well as all the other turf lords in your city." He offered a slight arrogant bow. "You're welcome."

The men in armor surveyed the mess he'd made of the room, finally spotting the kingpin's body. Through their clear faceplates, they traded dumbfounded expressions. At last, their leader glanced to Michael.

"*You* did this?"

Michael shrugged. "Just doing my job."

The man leveled his aim, struggling to maintain authority. "We're detaining you until we sort all this out."

A dark chuckle escaped Michael's smirk. "You can try."

"Tase him!"

A shorter cop at the leader's side unclipped a squarish pistol and fired off a round of electricity. Michael shrugged off the voltage and bolted for the window.

"Fire, fire!" the squad leader barked.

The police unloaded bullets on him as he ran, the slugs finding their mark, but doing no damage, save for shredding his poor leather jacket—the one he'd taken from Rip.

Michael darted for the window and leaped through the air, exiting the same way Tony Carlson had. He fell two stories and landed on the hood of a parked hovercar below. The impact blew out the front windshield and sent the car's alarm system into a tizzy. The retreating patrons yelped in shock.

Michael stood and hopped down from the car, onto the solid ground. The police lined up at the window, stunned into inaction as Michael offered a wave and crossed the street. High beams from a hovercar nearly blinded him. Repulsor engines groaned as they were thrown into full reverse, but the hovercar barreled forward along the slick pavement. Before it struck him, Michael stepped to the sheet of paper waiting for him and vanished in a flash of brilliant rainbow, ready to dish out more judgment on the enemies of the Light.

3

This isn't the life I wanted.

Seventeen-year-old Sara Bost braced herself on the wall, watching her husband shuffling through the house, gathering his wallet and his smokes.

"I'm going out," Charlie grunted, lumbering for the door.

"When will you be back?" she asked, nervously brushing back her long ginger hair over her ears.

Charlie didn't face her. "Mind your business. I'll be back when I get back. Have supper ready."

"Okay," she said, and Charlie was off, slamming the door behind him.

Sara slumped on the staircase that led to their bedroom, the empty quiet of their apartment consuming her. The place was more prison than home, and Sara remembered all the dreams she had in school—all the things she'd wanted to do with her life. How she had longed to leave this dumb bubble and travel to the other settlements, like Centric where they had the biggest libraries full of old paperbacks published a generation ago before everything went digital. Books had meant so much to her, reading of faraway adventures.

But that was before…

Charlie didn't allow her to have books. Charlie didn't allow a lot of things.

Sara shed no tears for her dreary existence today. Instead, she picked herself up and climbed the stairs to their bedroom, opening the double glass doors and stepping out onto her stone balcony. As she did every day, Sara leaned against the railing and looked down on the happy people below. Life thrived down there, while up here in her tower, Sara felt only darkness.

Looking to the skies beyond the glass dome of her enclosed village, she wondered what wonders existed out there in the heavens. But Fate had closed the heavens off to her, it seemed.

Something caught her eye, just above the rooftops, fluttering in the breeze. Sara saw a simple sheet of paper, curling along the output from the atmospheric generators. Odd. After the wars obliterated Earth's environment, trees had become a thing for the history digi-pads. Paper was a relic; certainly not something that everyone had.

She squinted against the sun's glare, watching as the sheet carried on across the horizon, and did not resist a smile. Maybe life still had a few surprises, after all. The paper danced, just for her, and she wondered where it'd come from, what it was doing here. With great interest she followed its path with her eyes until it finally disappeared over a building, landing a few blocks away. She had half a mind to leave the apartment and find where it went, but Charlie…

Her arm still hurt from the last time she thought to leave.

Frowning, Sara ignored dreams of chasing paper treasures, and gazed over her village, wishing she had something to fill the time. She thought back to those long ago afternoons spent discovering such wonderful paperback novels. With each turn of every yellowed page, she felt transported to a simpler time before the wars and Earth's ruination. There was power in those pages—a gateway to the past—that couldn't be duplicated by touch screens. She remembered running to her Mom or Dad and telling them all about her latest finds, regardless if they were interested or not.

A grin played at her lips. She hadn't thought of Mom and Dad in a while. They'd hated Charlie; told her he was no good for her. Why hadn't she listened to them?

They would be so disappointed to see her now.

Sara laid her head on the railing, her chest heaving, and sobbed after all.

This isn't the life I wanted.

4

Michael stepped out of the space-time rift in a brilliant blaze of light that somehow managed to go unnoticed by all. He glanced back to the piece of paper that served as his taxi across the multiverse as its glow dimmed. Now it appeared as common trash, stuck to the floor. Looking around, he realized he was standing in an alley. He approached the opening and beheld this new world. Like so many others, it resembled *his* world. Another alternate reality. Not home.

Never home.

Michael shook off his feeling of déjà vu, feeling only slightly disoriented from the rift. There was no time to worry about where he was. He had a job to do. He just had to find the problem, solve it very violently, and move on to the next assignment. That was the gig he'd signed up for five years ago in that blasted desert. Riding the rift, traveling to parallel and alien worlds, combating injustice, and waging war on evil men. That's what the Man in the Stetson—God, he believed—had called him to do.

The wounds he had sustained from Frazetta's bodyguards had already healed without a mark. The Man in the Stetson had been true to his promise to keep Michael from harm. In the last five years, he had been stabbed, burned, hung, shot about a trillion times, tortured, drowned, blown up, and once he even got a papercut. But nothing had managed to kill him.

He was indestructible, though that came with its own unforeseen complications. Pain was part of the human condition, and the drive to protect oneself from injury or death was an instinct shared by every being in the multiverse. With the ability to feel pain switched off, Michael wondered if he were even really human anymore, or just some machine.

Once more, his thoughts drifted to the sight of Tony Carlson, dead without a fight. Killing was so easy. Was it supposed to be this easy? But he hadn't killed the girl who'd stabbed him—Candice. That gave him some small measure of comfort. Maybe he wasn't entirely inhuman.

Not yet.

Michael picked a direction at random and marched, deciding to get the lay of the land. At first glance, he seemed to be in a mall, but he couldn't find the exits anywhere and there appeared no end in sight. A main thoroughfare split the gigantic center in two, disappearing over a distant horizon. Off that main walkway, more halls branched off like streets. Marvelous fountains decorated every fork in the hallway, and Michael scoped housing establishments at every turn. The mall itself was encased in a glass dome and the beautiful sunshine shone in on all of the apartments' balconies.

But still, no exits.

He took stock of the stores as he passed. Restaurants, grocery stores, toy stores, arcades, malt shops, every kind of store imaginable was accounted for. Although, he noted, he saw no auto repair shops, or *any* kind of store relating to vehicles, for that matter. Strangely, however, there did seem to be an overabundance of real estate agencies.

Was this it? Was the whole town a mall?

He'd been a lot of places, but never to a "mall world" before.

Some of the passing villagers gave him a wide berth, checking him over. A gaggle of attractive and well-dressed girls snickered at his outfit, and he remembered he still wore his wet clothes from the previous jump to the late twenty-second century, and his poor, ratty jacket. Maybe it was dumb to keep hanging onto it after all these years. Rip's jacket was threadbare, having taken the brunt of all his stabbings, shootings, and burnings. Unlike him, though, it was on its last leg and he'd have to throw it away soon.

A shame. He really loved that jacket.

He could certainly afford to buy a new one. Apart from his invulnerability, Michael's other "power" was an unlimited supply of money. And it didn't matter which world he found himself on—he'd always have the amount he needed, in the currency of the realm. All thanks to the mysterious Man in the Stetson, Michael's patron on this little quest.

But still, he couldn't bring himself to part with the jacket.

Michael merged with the crowds, following the traffic down the thoroughfare. He needed to find a hotel or something in this place. He was exhausted from the last job and was ready to sleep. After that, he'd try and find a store to buy a needle and thread so he could sew up the fresh gashes his jacket had sustained.

Then it hit him.

A sharp shriek halved his skull. His fingers went straight to his temples to massage the pain. Wincing, he scanned the area for a threat. Realizing it was only a migraine, he knew the danger was minimal.

Through slits, he scouted out the mall, trying to find the cause of his pain. It could have been anything. Purse-snatcher. Little boy who lost his mommy. Three-armed Trigarian assassin. Anything trivial, or maybe just a warning sign of danger. Yet, as he searched, he found nothing. No sign of trouble. No sign of *anything*.

Come on, God, lay off the headache. I'm looking, I'm looking.

Suddenly, a blast of pain pummeled his mind. At that exact moment, a bulk of a man bumped into him and walked on. The man had short, dark hair and an unruly mustache. His beady black eyes were set in deep shadows, and his yellowed teeth clenched a wilting cigarette.

A soft hum dulled his migraine, easing Michael's burden. He narrowed his eyes and trailed behind the burly man at a good distance, following him to one of the apartments. He hung back as the man knocked. The door opened and a voluptuous woman bobbled outside to kiss the large man passionately. Michael turned away, feeling a bit repulsed.

"I'll be back tonight, baby," the large man said. "Don't cool off just yet."

"Anything you say, sugar lumpins," the woman squeaked.

Michael groaned at the affectionate display. Was this a man he was meant to protect or execute? It was so hard to tell sometimes. He wished his orders were clearer, but the Man in the Stetson had not revealed himself since that fateful day in the desert five years ago. Try as he might to pray and breach heaven to get a word through, Michael seemed unable to contact his boss. Were it not for the headaches to warn him of danger and the stomach cramps to zero him in on his primary target, he would be directionless out here in the multiverse. Nevertheless, he felt under-qualified for the touchy-feely jobs. He was much better at the violence, as Tony Carlson and countless other evildoers could attest.

The large man left his lover behind and picked up the pace. Michael cursed under his breath, knowing that sleep would just have to wait, quickening his steps to cross the distance. The large ogre came to another apartment about a block away by one of the fountain centerpieces. He went for the door.

Michael didn't think he could go through another romantic rendezvous like that last one. He wasn't sure what these girls saw in this guy, anyway.

After a few beats, the door opened. Michael, from his perch behind the fountain, couldn't see this new girl; he only heard her voice.

"Why didn't you just come in?" she asked.

Michael strained to see the girl, but the hefty man made a better door than a window.

The man grumbled, "Forgot my key." Without giving it another moment of his precious time, the troll pushed past the new woman and entered, obviously not as thrilled with this lover as his last.

It was only after the large man disappeared inside that Michael saw the girl. The moment he laid eyes on her, the dull ache in his head stopped.

Everything became clear. Her long orange-colored hair. Her otherworldly blue eyes. At the sight of her, he began to shudder. His stomach twisted in knots.

This girl was his mission.

"Sara…?" he muttered in disbelief.

She closed the door behind her. He could only watch in a mix of horror and elation.

Sara?

5

Michael stayed on the fountain rim outside of the apartment until well after dark. Waiting.

Sara.

He couldn't believe this was happening.

Sara.

Her name kept rushing back to his mind, along with the painful truth that he had tried so hard to bury.

But it was an accident. I was just a kid. I didn't mean to…

The memories washed over him like a toxic flood. What terrible thing was going to happen to her that he had to stop? In all the alien worlds and alternate Earths Michael had been to, he'd never expected to see her again.

A door opened nearby.

Michael hunkered in the shadows and watched the apartment. The burly man stepped out, closed the door behind him, and began down the mall's walkway. Michael held back until the brute was out of sight. Once the man was past him and well on his way, Michael ran to the apartment door. He had to see Sara again.

He knocked. No answer. He looked up to the balcony. There she was, braced against the railing, resting her head on the palm of her hand, like a princess in a dream.

Sara. His heart jumped.

The moonlight glistened on her creamy white skin. That soft delicate skin that he had longed to touch. A tear ran down her cheek as she looked on while the troll left to be greeted by his fling for the night. Michael followed her gaze, understanding settling in.

Was that man her lover? A husband?

Michael tried the door handle. It was unlocked and he slipped inside. The house was a slum as though a tornado had passed through. He stepped up the staircase to the bedroom. To Sara. His heart still pounded from seeing her. Breaking and entering was a pretty bold move, he considered. It was likely she would freak and call the mall cops on him. But he had to see her. Had to talk to her.

As he entered the bedroom, he saw that the sheets on the bed were in disarray. A shotgun lay atop the covers. Michael walked so silently that Boloxian canine ears on the planet Shesh had not been able to detect him when he'd assassinated their dictator a couple years ago, and that was saying something.

He stood behind Sara, just out of sight, and got a better look at her wonderful face. A fresh cut was etched into her delicate skin with a blotchy red bruise surrounding it. He glanced back at the shotgun.

Michael clenched his teeth and cursed to himself.

"I'm sorry," he offered, not realizing he'd said it out loud until it was too late.

Sara yelped and turned to face the stranger. She wiped her tears away, wincing when her fingers brushed against her wound.

"Who are you?" Her eyes searched him. They were a sparkling blue, reminiscent of the life-giving waters of Dronaj in the Ufghar Galaxy. Michael had to pull himself out of their depths.

"You mean…you don't know me?" But of course she didn't. This wasn't his Sara. He had to remember that.

"Why are you here? What do you want?"

"I…I've come to help. I know what that man did to you. You have my sincerest apologies on his behalf."

Sincerest apologies on his behalf? Did he really just say that? It was true; Michael's conversations rarely ventured beyond "Repent or die", but that little poetic gem was a new low, even for him.

Sara immediately turned away and Michael cringed. He never wanted her to turn away from him. "He's my husband. Charlie…does it out of discipline. He—"

"That's crap," Michael spat. Sara faced him once more, shocked. Or was she insulted? "He's an idiot. You don't have any reason to apologize. He'll stop." Michael glowered, feeling that familiar cold power in his stomach. "I'll *make* him stop."

Her eyes widened with sudden fear.

Michael forced himself to calm. "Sorry. Look, I just want to help. I—"

Sara continued to gape at him, her posture relaxing, as if inexplicably drawn closer to him. Her eyes studied him. "You know…You look familiar to me. Do I know you?"

Michael's heart came to a dead halt. Did she know? Did she somehow remember what he did to her?

No. Not her. The other her.

"Did we go to school together?"

"Yeah, we…uh…go to school together. I'm Michael Morrison."

"I'm Sara Theres…Bost. Sara Bost." She smiled too.

"Listen, do you want to talk?" He didn't know what they would talk about. He just wanted to *talk* to her. Get to know her. Be a part of her life. They could've talked about anything. It didn't matter, just as long as they were together. Since he was twelve years old all he'd wanted was to talk to this girl.

"Talk?" She sighed and sat down on her bed. Chuckling sadly she said, "I haven't talked to anyone in months. Only Charlie…I would *love* to talk to you." She smiled, yet it quickly faded. "But if Charlie found out…" She threw a fearful look to the shotgun on the bed. A pained expression came across her face.

Michael stepped in between her and the weapon. "Don't worry. Your secret's safe with me."

6

Michael gave Sara his complete attention as she talked. From her words, he pieced together a bit of history of this world. War had ravaged the planet a generation ago, turning the air poisonous, and civilization had moved indoors to these enclosed towns. Each village was isolated, developing their own culture.

"But don't you ever think about leaving the village?" Michael asked. "Seeing what else is out there?"

Sara blew out a long breath and looked over the balcony railing. "Oh, all the time. Ever since I was little, when I first heard about the other settlements. For the longest time, I thought we were the only ones on the planet. To see what the other people are like...it'd be amazing."

Michael said, "I can get you there. I can get you out of the village."

She laughed, shaking her head. "Charlie would just love that."

"Leave him."

Her smile dimmed. "Don't say that."

Michael leaned in closer, about to reach for her hand, but pulled back at the last second. "You deserve better than him."

Sara moved away from the balcony, rubbing at her arms. "That's what everyone said when we first started dating. I told them that they weren't giving him a chance. Charlie just needed...a little extra understanding." She faced him. "He wasn't always like this, you know? He's just...I think he's hurting a lot."

Michael recalled a certain buxom beauty a couple blocks down the street and thought Charlie was definitely not hurting.

"He's all I have," Sara said with a frown.

"What about your mom and dad?" He vaguely remembered what her dad looked like.

"No." She blushed. "There was a robbery last year. Some guys broke in. I was sneaking off to go see Charlie and they..."

Michael moved for her. He wanted to wrap her in his embrace, but settled for brushing her arm. "Sorry. My parents are dead, too."

She eased away from his touch, but returned his gesture with a soft grin. "After they died, Charlie took me in. We got married. He took care of me. We've never had to worry about money and he's made sure that I had everything I needed."

Michael pursed his lips. "Money's not everything you need."

"Things changed after a while. He started pulling away from me. He puts food on the table and I clean the house and stay out of his way so he can have his *flings*. We're hardly ever intimate—" She immediately blushed and looked sharply to Michael. "And I cannot believe I just said that to a complete stranger."

He chuckled and waved off her apology. "It's okay. Really."

She exhaled. "I'm just his maid. His *slave*."

Michael hung on every word. Her pain was evident as she spoke, letting a flood of hidden hurt out.

I'm here to help her, he realized with joy. *I get to* help *her*.

He listened and cherished every word she breathed. He found himself drowning in the crystal sea that she used for her eyes. She caught him staring, but she smiled in her embarrassed way. He loved that.

"So, that's my incredibly long sob story. What about you?"

Caught off guard by the question, he moved to the balcony, looking back out over the mall. "You wouldn't believe me."

"Try me. I've been stuck in this apartment for a year." Michael glanced back at her playful eyes and curious smile. "I'll probably believe anything you say."

Everything inside of him screamed to tell her. To let her in. But there was another voice in his mind commanding him to restrain himself. This was just a job, like all the others. Once she was safe, he'd jump out of this world and never see her again.

"I grew up with my brothers," he finally admitted. "My parents died when I was just a baby. Growing up, I...got into a lot of trouble. Eventually I had to leave. I'm trying to make things better."

"So you just make a habit out of breaking into young girls' bedrooms and rescuing them from their problems?"

The two shared a small laugh and Michael grinned at his Converse sneakers.

"Yeah. Something like that."

When Michael turned back to her, he expected her to laugh in his face, but instead, he caught *her* staring into *his* eyes. Her glare was deep, exploring his soul. After a moment, Sara reddened and looked to the floor herself.

"I'm sorry," she said and laughed. "I'm staring again."

Michael leaned in. "I don't mind."

"It's just...I've never met anyone like you before. I don't know who you are in the slightest, but I...I feel like I know you."

She was so close to him that he could smell her perfume. Her lips were full and parted, and he wanted to kiss them.

"Sara, I..." He wanted to tell her everything he'd done and weep and beg for her forgiveness. He'd protect her now. He'd rescue her from whatever dragon loomed in her life. He'd be there for her, to love her.

"Sara—"

She watched him. Fell into his eyes as he moved in closer, ready to kiss her.

"SARA!" A door shut downstairs.

"*It's Charlie!*" Sara shouted in a whisper. She pushed herself from Michael. Ran to the mirror, checking her rosy cheeks. She frowned at their redness and fanned herself. "You have to go. He can't find you."

Michael approached her, chuckling. "I'm not scared of him."

"Please," she implored, taking the sleeve of his jacket. "We can talk again tomorrow. I mean…if you want."

Gently, he cupped her face, his eyes solemn. "I'll get you out of here. I promise."

Sara trembled, her eyes still searching him. He thought she might cry. "Are you real?" she whispered. "Or am I dreaming all of this?"

"I'll be here tomorrow," he told her.

Hearing Charlie's footsteps coming up the stairs, Michael released his hold on Sara and raced to the edge of the balcony.

"Wait—" she gasped.

Michael dove off, landing in a crouch safely below. He regarded her balcony once more, where Sara leaned over the railing, beaming, and then he darted behind the fountain.

He heard voices from her room and Sara disappeared inside. Soon came shouting. A slap, and then a cry.

Sara!

His hand formed a solid fist. Ice coursed through his veins and the deep boom-boom-boom shook his gut. His stiff arms quivered with barely contained anger.

"Ah, screw it," he muttered, marching for the front door, ready to kill Charlie with his bare hands. He'd killed a lot more men for a lot less.

But a palm seized his shoulder from behind. Michael twirled, bracing himself for a fight, but stopped short when he saw a wizened man in red scarf, brown duster, and worn Stetson.

"*You,*" Michael said, his heart shuddering with excitement and anger.

"Wait," the Man said, intently watching the balcony. After a moment's pause, he let out a tired breath. "It's over."

Michael turned back to Sara's room. He heard a door slam, then watched as Sara slowly walked to the doors of her balcony, her head bowed, and closed them.

Michael jerked away from the Man's hand and kept watching those closed doors, his heart going out to the girl behind them. "What are you doing? Why did you stop me? And where have you *been* all this time? I've tried talking to——"

But when he turned back around, the Man in the Stetson was gone. Michael stood in the empty space, snarling in defeat.

7

Michael paced on the roof across from Sara's apartment, fuming. He kept a close eye on Sara's room until she finally drew the curtains for the night. It was killing him not knowing what was going on in there, if she were all right. He'd turned his rage down to a simmer, but it was still there, waiting to break loose.

Why had God stopped him? More importantly, why hadn't he hung around long enough to explain himself? For five long years, Michael had been traveling the multiverse and killing the agents of Chaos in his Name. And not once—*not once, God!*—had the Almighty ever showed up in that dumb coat, scarf, and hat to offer a "hello" or a "well done". Nothing. Not one sight or sound from the Man in the Stetson. Until today.

Michael swore under his breath and sat down on the roof.

What did it mean? Why did the Man show himself *now*?

Concentrating, Michael fixated on the closed doors of the balcony, imagining Sara and Charlie sleeping inside. Were this any other job, Charlie would be dead by now, but Michael forced himself to stay clear-headed. His baser instincts told him to just kill the oaf. With that goliath out of the way, Sara would be free to lead a normal life. It was simple enough. But a murder—however justified it might seem to Michael—would only complicate matters. Once Michael was gone in the rift, Sara would be left behind, answering questions for the police, possibly being suspected as the murderer herself. With no friends to speak up for her and no alibi since she never left the apartment, not to mention she had probable cause in that her husband was an abusive lout, it would be no time at all before she was arrested, tried, and convicted. Leaving her behind to rot in a prison cell was not what Michael considered "saving" Sara.

Even if he managed to be discreet about killing Charlie, without any friends or parents, who would take care of Sara?

Did the Man in the Stetson already figure that out? Was that why he stopped Michael?

His former anger against the Man in the Stetson subsided. For whatever reason, it seemed God was looking out for Sara. Why she warranted a direct intervention, Michael didn't know—but he appreciated God's concern. Shared it. Maybe they were after the same thing, after all.

Calming now, Michael decided he'd have to figure out another way to save Sara. Something more low-key that didn't involve his usual brand of rough justice. He needed to keep this quiet, to smuggle her away from her husband and give her the strength to take her life back. The only way to do that would be to get her out of this bubble, maybe get her to one of the other settlements.

She could always come with me. As soon as the thought arose, Michael snuffed it out. She could come with him, and they'd be together. But this life wasn't meant for two. He spent most of his time in the middle of a war in some backwater dimension. He couldn't bring her along for that.

Could I?

But, maybe if she couldn't come with *him*...maybe he could stay here. There were plenty of apartments up for rent. Maybe they could run away together, get married, settle down. He thought of Sara. Her eyes, her lips, her body...

Could he leave his mission behind to stay with her?

More importantly, would the Man in the Stetson let him out of their agreement?

I was just a kid when I agreed to do this job. It's been five years. What if I want something different? What if I'm tired, God?

Besides, he was missing the bigger picture. This wasn't his Sara. She looked just like her. Smelled like her. But she was a totally different girl with her own life to lead, and he couldn't subject her to his whims because she reminded him of someone he had a crush on when he was twelve. That wasn't fair to her.

He groaned, not knowing what to do. He slept restlessly that night.

8

The next day, Michael walked the mall, checking a couple of

apartments for rent. One even had a balcony.

Yeah. She'd like that.

His plan was still to get Sara away from the village, but that required transportation and in a mall where there were no cars, Michael wasn't sure how one traveled in this dimension. He needed to learn more, but more importantly he needed to make sure Sara was out of that house.

He'd sneak her to an apartment across town and they'd keep a low profile, figuring out their next move. Then, once she was settled and Charlie was long gone, Michael planned on giving her enough money from his unlimited funds to ensure she'd never have to work, unless she wanted to. If she wanted, he'd shower her with riches and allow her to live like a princess for the rest of her life.

It's what she deserved.

Michael stopped outside of a clothing store advertising a new line of dresses. Sara would look beautiful in any one of these, and he wondered when the last time she'd been treated to a shopping spree. He grinned. He'd do that for her. He'd do anything she asked of him.

Still smiling, he managed to catch a glimpse of his own reflection in the mirror set up next to the mannequins in the display case, and what he saw startled him. When was the last time he'd really looked at himself? He was so pale and thin. And those eyes. Coal black and mean-looking. He looked… With great regret he realized he looked just like that specter from his boyhood nightmares, the gaunt skeletal figure with his face. A far cry from the child who had first stepped into that rift.

What happened to me?

He was seventeen, now. A young man. At least, he thought that's how old he was. Who was to say how much time had passed? He had counted it as five years, but was that an accurate number? Couldn't it just as easily been five *hundred* years? Time was meaningless to him now. There had only been the job.

Except now there's Sara, he told himself, firm.

"Find out what your future holds!" a voice announced from behind.

Michael noticed the commotion. Across the street, in front of a peculiar-looking store called SUPERNATURAL SURPLUS, an old mystic woman danced from behind her table. Shaking a tambourine, she cried out to passing customers.

Amused, Michael wandered across the street, dodging pedestrian traffic. The woman saw him and smiled.

"I see you take a great interest in your future."

Her accent was thick and gothic—like a gypsy from an old black-and-white monster movie Michael had seen back home—but probably fake.

"What question do you seek?" She raised a mysterious eyebrow and rhythmically encircled her hands over her crystal ball.

A grin twitched at the corner of his mouth. "Will I find true love?"

"Oh?" The woman cooed, dropping her voice to a hush. "You seek true love, do you?"

"Doesn't everybody?"

"Not everyone. Some prefer power or money."

"Not me."

The woman grinned. "Well, I prefer money. How about five creds and I read your fortune?"

Michael chuckled.

"Stop harassing the customers, Nana," an older boy's voice called from the store.

The old mystic looked through the window and called back to her grandson, minus the gothic accent, "I'm trying to find you customers!" With a huff that her charade was destroyed, she got up from her table of mystery and grumbled on her way to the store. "You don't get any paying customers around here. I try and be a good Nana and bring you some and what do you do? Ungrateful little…"

Michael smirked at the old woman as she went back inside like a scolded child, called in from the cold. A shaggy giant replaced her at the doorway. At once, Michael recognized him and warmed.

Johnny Frawl, his fellow back-row doodler from Coach Seevers' class.

Johnny approached Michael with an apologetic smile on his face. "Sorry about that. Nana gets a little carried away with the atmosphere sometimes. Can I help you find something?"

"You work here?" Michael asked, excitement tingeing his voice.

Johnny nodded with a puzzled look, as though that were obvious.

Yeah, I guess it is. Man, you really gotta work on your people skills.

"Yeah, my dad owns it," said Johnny.

"That's…that's really great. I'm really happy for you, man." Michael laughed. If the Johnny Frawl of his world had only known he'd wound up working in one of these spooky hocus pocus bookstores, on a parallel

76

world no less…

There's one for Johnny's weird books.

"Thaaaanks," Johnny said, looking uncertain. A customer approached the counter and he ducked back into the store to work. "Let me know if you need something."

Michael watched him through the window as Johnny shooed away his grandmother, who was ranting about his lack of business vision, then left the store behind.

Snickering to himself in amusement, Michael turned and headed back to Sara's apartment. A plan was slowly forming in his brain. As he approached her front door, he was still struggling with the specifics. First, he would have to confront Charlie. Threaten him to make him let the girl leave. Images of pounding the monster until he croaked were never far from Michael's mind, but he had already decided he had to play this a lot cooler. More diplomatic. Michael was not much for diplomacy, but for Sara, he would try.

He raised a fist, prepared to knock.

"Michael?" a voice from above. It was only a whisper. Michael looked to see Sara bending over the balcony, watching him with curious awe.

"Sara," he said, feeling like he could breathe again.

"Michael? What are you doing here?"

Michael climbed the side of the apartment, pulling himself to the balcony, and crawled into her bedroom. Sara stepped back, stunned.

"What are you doing here?" she whispered again, a wide smile fixed to her wonderful face.

"I've come to get you."

"Charlie's in the other room. It's too dangerous. You shouldn't have come."

But that smile said otherwise.

"I found an apartment. You can move out. Away from him. Start over."

Sara backed away, her grin faltering. "I can't."

"You have to. If you stay here, he'll only keep hurting you. And, one day, you won't be able to heal."

Sara's eyes widened then she shook her head. "No. It's too hard."

Once again, temptation tugged at him. Killing Charlie seemed the best solution…but no. That would lead to only more hardship for her.

Michael's hands were tied. How could he save her if she wasn't ready to save herself?

He placed a gentle hand on her arm. Her skin lit him on fire, but he withstood the heat. "You have to stand up to him. I believe in you."

She looked up at him, as though she'd never heard those words before. Frozen tears glistened in her bright blue eyes.

"SARA!" Charlie bellowed from the other room. "What's all that racket?"

Michael heard the brute marching closer.

"You have to hide!" Sara said, running to block the door. "He can't find you here!"

"I'll set everything up and I'll be back tonight. I *will* get you out of here."

"Why are you doing this? Why are you helping me?"

Michael hesitated, dark images of his past sin filling his vision. "I owe you one."

He stepped back to the balcony and tumbled backwards over the railing.

9

This time, Sara didn't have a chance to reach the edge to watch her mysterious friend retreat into the shadows. She inched away from the door, just as Charlie pushed through it.

"I heard you talking," he growled.

"No you didn't," Sara said, not very convincingly even to her own ears.

Charlie approached her. She could smell liquor on his breath, but she had to be strong. Michael believed in her. She had to, as well. Pulling together all her strength and the confidence that Michael had given her, Sara said, "I'm leaving you."

Charlie laughed. "What?"

"I want a divorce."

He cocked his meaty fists on his wide hip. "Oh really?"

Sara jutted out her chin, taking a deep breath. Charlie wasn't going to intimidate her.

"Where are you going to go?"

She remained silent.

Charlie chuckled and turned to walk away. "You're not going anywhere."

"Yes I am, Charlie. You can't stop me. Not this time." She was shaking, terrified and excited.

He looked back, eyes narrowing. "Where's all this coming from?"

Sara did not reply. Charlie approached again, searching her eyes, no doubt able to see the fear in her face despite her performance.

"You *were* talking to someone up here. Who's been filling your head with all this garbage?"

He leaned in, studying her. Her lips began to quiver and she muttered, "A friend."

"A friend?" Charlie guffawed in her face, and she flinched. "A friend," he said again, as if trying to get over how ridiculous it sounded. Suddenly, a wash of clarity came over his face. "You sleeping around on me?"

Sara blushed. "No. I would never do that."

"You're cheating on me!" He raised a hand and brought it down across the left side of her face. With a yelp, she spun and collapsed.

"What would you care?" she screamed back at him from the floor. "You don't love me! I'm just a servant to you!"

Charlie raised a hand again. Sara covered herself, bracing for the worst, but nothing happened.

"Ha. Go ahead then. Run off to your little lover. Your *friend*. You really think he'll want you? Look at yourself. You're a pathetic little mouse. Can't cook worth a crap, either." He bent down, getting right in her face.

She turned away, the fog of liquor that surrounded him nearly choking her.

"Nobody's going to want you. You're worthless. You think he thinks you're beautiful?" Charlie laughed so loud her ears rang.

Tears welled up in her eyes.

"Nobody's going to want you. Nobody but me. I took you in. Made you somebody. Go ahead. Leave if you want. But, without me, you're nothing. Nothing. I own you."

Charlie kissed her on the head and left, still chuckling. "Now get downstairs and make me a sandwich."

Sara picked herself off the floor and sat on the bed. Maybe Charlie was right. Nobody would want her, not if they knew how useless she was. She didn't know the first thing about loving someone or being a good wife. And, she *wasn't* beautiful. She was convinced of that. Michael wouldn't want her. Not if he knew her. *Really* knew her. No. Charlie was right.

Sara lay back on the bed, buried her head in her pillow, and cried.

10

"How much for the top room?" Michael asked the apartment manager. "The one with the balcony."

"Hundred a week," she croaked, dangling a cigarette from her liver-spotted hand.

"I'll take it." Michael reached into his jeans pocket and pulled out a wad of creds, not bothering to count out the fee she'd requested. It was enough. It was *more* than enough.

"I'm bringing a friend of mine," Michael said. "She's not to be bothered. No one needs to know she's even here."

"Yeah, I get it." The woman took the money, counting it with her eyes slightly wider. Her greedy smile faded and she eyed him. "You steal this?"

He smirked. "I've got a generous boss."

She nodded and puffed on her smoke. As she went back to gazing at her new fortune, Michael left, ready to return for Sara. Had she talked to Charlie? Would she have the strength to stand up for herself? Michael had told her he believed in her, and he wanted to, but she was so shy—living in fear. Michael felt powerless to fix that. For years he'd been busting into alien worlds, both barrels blazing, killing every bad thing that stood in his way of saving the day. It'd been all derring-do and adventure and war. But it seemed God was doing something different this go around. Saving Sara from Charlie wouldn't be enough; he had to train her to keep fighting after he was gone.

Gone...

Even if Sara didn't need him anymore—and if he'd done his job, she wouldn't—he still wanted to be with her. To spend the rest of his life making up for what he'd done to her. *Not her. The other her.*

But would she even love him? She didn't know him. They had talked so much yesterday, but it had been Sara who did most of the sharing. He had kept to himself, fearful of what she'd say if she knew the truth of who he'd been before.

It was better that he leave. But it didn't feel better.

One way or another, she would be safe tonight.

And he would be on his way. Without her.

11

Sara's hands were shaking as she made the sandwich, and the tears ran freely. The sounds of Charlie's wheezing hysterics over his favorite comedy show carried from the dark living room to the kitchen. Her body trembled with anger and sadness.

Michael would be here any moment to pick her up, and the thought of facing him and telling him she wasn't strong enough to leave with him...Fresh tears spilt and she clapped her hand over her mouth to muffle her cries. What would he think of her? Would he see her as weak like Charlie did?

Instead, she prayed that Michael would *never* come. She prayed that the whole thing had been a cruel lie, that he had never really intended to take her away, that he would just leave town and go on to greater things, never giving her a second thought.

That way he would never know she'd failed.

But Michael seemed too determined to leave her behind. No, he would come looking for her, just as he'd promised, because he was falling for her too. And, when he arrived, he would encourage her to try again, to make her case or leave regardless of her husband's feelings. Maybe, just maybe, he would rescue her himself. Maybe he would burst in here with his leather jacket and those dark, foreboding eyes and Charlie would be the one to cower in terror for once and Michael would fight for her honor. He would rough Charlie up and demand that Sara leave with him and be treated special, as she deserved.

Looking out the small window above the sink, Sara watched the corner down the thoroughfare, expecting Michael to come into view at any second. Her heart quickened as she realized time was slipping away. Michael was coming, she was sure of it, and she would have to make her decision. Leave or stay forever.

She *couldn't* stay forever. She couldn't stay for one more minute.

Emboldened by this cold realization, she looked down to the half-completed sandwich before her. In her hand was the knife she used to spread the mayonnaise and for one dark moment she thought...

Charlie's laugh echoed from the other room.

Get a grip, Sara. She shut her eyes and calmed.

Dropping the knife in the sink she forced herself to think. She could do this. If Charlie wouldn't listen to her, wouldn't give her a divorce, then she would just have to leave without it. Calmly, she finished his sandwich and pressed it flat, just like he liked it. Then she rummaged through the drain board and found his favorite glass, newly cleaned. She filled it with his favorite juice, all the while glancing out the kitchen window, waiting for her savior to arrive and signal the beginning of her new life. She prepared a TV tray, arranging Charlie's evening snack in proper order.

Before serving it she moved to the medicine cabinet. Charlie's blood pressure medicine and other stronger drugs were kept in the bathroom but, in the kitchen, Sara kept aspirin, cough syrup, and lesser pain relievers.

And a bottle of sleeping pills. Tonight they would be her passport to freedom, and she'd be on her own and finally away from him.

On her own. It sounded nice. But not near as nice as *On her own with Michael* sounded.

Carefully she popped the cap off the pills and spilled out a couple more than the average dosage required.

"Hurry up," Charlie bellowed from the living room.

"Coming," Sara said as casually as she could manage. She mashed the pills into powder with a spoon, then scooped up the small white pile and dumped it into the juice. She stirred and then dropped the spoon in the sink. Taking a deep breath to steel herself, she carried the tray into the living room and brought it before Charlie.

"What took you?" he grumbled, his focus never leaving his show. Sara didn't respond, only handed him his food. In between knee-slapping hilarity, he shoved the sandwich into his large mouth and chugged at his juice. Sara quivered with anticipation and sat on the couch next to him. She watched him closely. Waiting.

After the longest ten minutes of her life, Sara grew afraid that her plan would not work. She slouched on the couch and distracted herself with the last bit of Charlie's TV show.

Charlie mumbled something.

"What's that?" she asked.

"Drink tasted funny," he muttered, then fell silent.

Sara stiffened and scooted forward. "Charlie?"

A snore rippled through his mustache and Sara jumped to her feet. Sidestepping the unconscious ogre, Sara raced up the stairs, a thousand dreams of new and amazing experiences to come fluttering through her mind. She had to pack. She'd wasted enough time waiting for the drugs to work.

Sara flung open her closet and zeroed in on the clothes she would need for the trip. She picked out the practical outfits that wouldn't need much upkeep and even a few that would keep her warm in the winter.

I won't be back for Winter Festival, she suddenly realized, a tinge of sadness pricking her heart. Her first Winter Festival away from home.

But this isn't my home anymore, she reminded herself. She didn't know where home was yet. She would find it along the way. Until then, she needed to be prepared for anything.

She packed a few pairs of blue jeans and enough shirts to last her until she got a job and could afford to buy more. A job. She'd never had a real job before. It thrilled her.

Downstairs, she heard a knock on the door, and her heart nearly burst with excitement.

He's here!

Sara hurried to her balcony and peered over. Michael waited below.

"Hey!" she called out to him in a rough whisper.

He lifted his head to the window, his eyes alert. Sara waved and his hard face gave way to a small, fleeting smile.

"Catch, will you?" She heaved her bags over the railing.

Michael hustled to intercept the plummeting bags and gave an "oof" as they collapsed like dead weight in his arms. Smiling, Sara kicked her leg over the balcony and began the climb down. *I'm doing it. I'm really leaving.*

Once she was four feet from the ground, she gave a little leap and landed. Michael seemed a bit bewildered. "What about Charlie? What did you say?"

She shrugged, laughing. "Does it matter? I'm going. That's enough."

Michael nodded without pushing the subject, a bright smile breaking through. She was falling in love with that smile.

Sara wrapped her arms around him, unable to contain herself any longer. In such a short time together, he changed her world, saved her in every way possible. She'd been so lost, no longer the girl she'd once been, but he had given it all back to her.

"I love you," she said, burying her face into his chest.

Michael stiffened in her arms. She pulled away, ready to kiss him. Ready to be his forever if he'd only ask. But he seemed to be struggling against some internal dilemma.

"I…" he began, but closed his mouth. He didn't seem nearly as happy as Sara had hoped he'd be at her declaration of love. Was he having second thoughts? "We'd better go," he mumbled. He grabbed her bags and turned to leave. Sara joined him, but stopped to give one final look to her house.

Her home.

Not all the memories were bad. She'd miss the nights that Charlie brought home flowers or take-out when she'd been fretting over what to fix for their dinner. He'd cradled her when she wept for her parents, and promised that everything would be okay. She wondered whatever became of that man and why he'd changed.

"Good-bye, Charlie," she whispered.

She turned her back on the old place, her bittersweet nostalgia paling in comparison to the exhilaration at leaving her past behind and starting afresh. Taking a deep breath and failing to suppress a smile, she hurried to Michael's side.

Adventure, here I come.

12

Michael opened the door to Sara's new apartment and presented it to her with a flourish, relishing her reaction.

"Welcome home," he said.

Sara stepped inside, stunned silent. She moved about the apartment, surveying every room with wide-eyed wonder.

"This place is enormous," she said.

"And look…" He gestured to the back patio door. "A balcony."

She shook her head, tears building in her eyes. "It's…it's beautiful.

How could you ever afford this?"

He grinned. "I have sources."

"I'll pay you back." She rushed to him, looking very serious.

"No, you won't. It's a gift. I just want you to be taken care of. To be happy."

Sara covered her mouth and raced to the balcony. She threw open the door, took a deep breath of fresh air, and looked down. "Everything looks so new here."

Michael followed her. She turned to face him, glowing with unchained happiness. Her eyes glistened with life. She smiled, and he smiled because she did.

"Michael..." She stepped in to him, her eyes loving. "I..."

Michael bent closer to her, his lips hovering inches from her. His conscience raved at him, *You're leaving, man. This isn't your home. This isn't right.* But if this was going to be his last night to spend with her, he wanted—no, he *had*—to kiss her.

So he did. He didn't care what was right anymore.

The kiss started slow and tentative. Her lips were soft, though she held back. He pressed against her, his hand moving to the small of her back. She remained timid at first, her hands hesitantly sliding up his strong arms, to his shoulders.

Then, as if the floodgates opened, she kissed him back. Hard and powerful, nearly swallowing him whole. Michael did not resist her passions. He kissed her, their mouths opening, their tongues meeting. He felt flushed and alive, the shape of her body against him arousing him. His hand slipped under her shirt, feeling her skin burn. He wanted to feel her body, every inch of it. To experience her and love her and know her.

Like a wild animal finally loosed, Sara pulled at his tattered jacket, and he shook it off his arms. Her hands moved down too, feeling beneath his clothes, running against the taut muscles in his stomach. He had her. After all this time—all that he had been through—he finally had his Sara.

Only, as quickly as it began, it was over.

Sara pulled away from him, face crimson. "Wait," she said, panting.

As impossible as it was, Michael feared that somehow she had finally realized who he was and what he'd done to her.

Instead, she simply pulled off her wedding ring and tossed it over the railing to the fountain below. Then, she climbed back into Michael's arms and held him tight. "It…doesn't feel right yet. I'm still married, and I…" She blew out a big sigh.

"No, it's okay. I understand."

"I feel like an idiot."

He chuckled. "Don't."

"Can we just…can we just hold each other for a while?"

His hands were shaking with pent-up excitement, but he forced down his teenage lust. Kissed the top of her head. "Sure."

13

"This is incredible," Sara said, mid-chew. She closed her eyes, groaning in delight over her steak. Michael had left to buy them dinner, plates, and some silverware to go with it. He'd brought it back, along with a couple candles, and laid out a nice candlelit picnic on the floor of the empty apartment. "Dad bought us steak once years ago," she said. "Cost him a month's salary. I loved it, but it's so rare, you know? I heard that a place near Bevenshire has a ranch and they're trying to breed some more cattle."

He grinned at her rambling. "Well, you can eat steak every night for the rest of your life, if you want."

She swallowed her bite and took a sip of the wine he'd also purchased. Apparently legal drinking age was seventeen on Sara's world. "So, how is this going to work?" she asked, dabbing at the corners of her lips with a napkin. "Getting permission to travel to the other settlements is long and drawn out—and expensive."

Michael cut at his steak. "Money's not a problem. I'll stay with you, here, until the paperwork for your passport is complete."

"What if Charlie finds us?"

Michael huffed, amused. "What if he does? I won't let anything happen to you."

Sara set down the napkin, frowning. "But you don't know him. He can be mean—"

"I can be mean," Michael smirked and plopped a steak morsel in his mouth.

Sara's frown turned up. "He's also got about a hundred and fifty pounds on you."

Michael chewed, eyeing her. "Okay." He swallowed his mouthful and reached for the knife, beginning to clean it with his napkin. He couldn't believe he was about to do this, but it was time she knew. "I want to show you something. But don't freak out, okay?"

Sara snickered, her brow furrowed. "Okaaay."

He winked and stood, holding the steak knife. With one hand, he raised his shirt.

"What are you—" Her smile dropped.

Then he plunged the knife hilt-deep into his stomach.

Sara screamed at the top of her lungs and jumped to her feet.

Michael laughed, the knife still in his gut. "Hey, hey, no, no, no. It's okay, it's okay."

"*What did you do!*"

Still laughing, he pulled out the knife, but her petrified glare was transfixed to his abdomen. "Look," he told her, trying to break through her hysterics. "Look, look." He reached for her hand and pulled her closer.

"No," she snapped, jerking a clenched fist away.

"Ha, ha, Sara, look. No blood. I'm fine."

Her shoulders were high and tense, but she hesitantly reached for his stomach. "T-There's not even a cut."

She felt along his stomach, then removed her hand. Michael let his shirt fall back in place. "I told you. He *can't* hurt me. Nothing can."

She stared at him for the longest time, mouth slightly agape. "But, I…You…No." Shaking her head, she moved for the door. "I have to go. This isn't—"

Michael intercepted her, blocking her path of escape, and she tried to go around him, her eyes shut tight. "Let me go."

"Sara," he said, taking her by the arms, real easy. "Hey, look at me."

She slowly opened one eye, then the other. Faced him.

He grinned. "It's still me."

"But how is that possible? Are you a ghost?"

"No."

"An angel?"

"Hardly." Michael hesitated. He'd done so much lying over the last few years; a lie was as near the truth most of the time. Most people—no matter what dimension they hailed from—were not mentally equipped to understand the concept of the multiverse.

But he needed her to know the truth. "I'm from a different world, Sara."

Sara paused. Blinked. Chewed her lip. "I don't follow."

"I'm an alien." He shrugged, reconsidering. "Sorta."

Her brow creased, forming a little knot just above her left eye. She left the door and moved back to their picnic, but did not sit. Instead she paced, nibbling at her knuckle in concentration. "No…we went to school together."

"No we didn't. Maybe you went to school with the Michael Morrison of this dimension. I'm from another one. Back where I come from…I did some really bad things. I *died*, Sara. But then God or Fate or whatever you want to call it gave me a second chance to make things right."

She eyed him, sharp. "You talk to God?"

"Yeah." He frowned, anger flaring. "Well, mostly I talk *at* him."

"W-What's he like?"

"He has a cowboy hat."

She tittered. "This…isn't happening. You are a crazy person. Yes, a crazy person who sticks knives in his stomach."

Michael moved to her, but she circled him, keeping a fair distance. He said, "For the last five years, I've been jumping between the different dimensions, helping people like you. But I only stay as long as it takes to get the mission done, then I leave and go to the next world." He'd never been this honest with anyone. Ever. It made him feel weightless.

But Sara wouldn't face him. He felt naked and vulnerable, back to being twelve years old all over again, incapable of becoming a man, standing trembling in the shadow of the most beautiful girl in the world.

Sara backed away, still frowning. "Okay. You're, like, really serious right now."

He nodded and took a step forward, wanting to hold her. A flash of fear tempted him to take it all back, to come up with a lie to cover up the truth. Sara held out a hand to hold him at bay, not scornfully, but he could tell she needed space.

"So…I'm just…How many dimensions are there?"

He chuckled, unexpectedly, not anticipating the question. "I have no idea."

"And me? I'm just another mission?"

"No. You're…something more."

"I need some air." Sara moved to the balcony, failing to hide a flattered grin in the process. After a moment, the grin faltered and she turned serious. "When I leave the village…You're not coming with me. Are you?"

He joined her, looking only at her, savoring every last second he had with her. "No."

She hung her head, gripping the railing.

"I told you, God's got me running all over the multiverse—"

"But why?" she asked, facing him. "Why *you*? When will it be over?"

"I don't know. When God thinks I've redeemed myself, I guess." Sadder, he added, "I don't really know."

"It's not fair. I want you here." She considered him again and inched closer, gently taking his arms and wrapping them around her like a blanket.

He thought to tell her how bad he wanted to stay. How he loved her. But to do that and leave wouldn't have been fair to her.

"You're going to be fine," he said, lifting her chin so their eyes met. "It's going to be okay."

Her stare pulled him in again, and he didn't know how he'd ever be able to leave her.

I can't, God. Please don't make me. I want to stay. He prayed, waiting for some word from on high. *Come on, God,* he begged. *Where are you? Answer me for once. Tell me I can stay.*

Silence.

For years, he had done the job without asking anything for himself. But it was time that changed. He'd worked too hard, fought too long, not to get the answers he wanted. Sara was right. Why did it have to be Michael battling evil across the multiverse? When would it end? What was the end goal? Was he just supposed to be God's soldier forever? What kind of life was that?

If the Man in the Stetson wouldn't come to him, then Michael was prepared to go to *him.*

"I gotta go out for a while," he said. "Why don't we go shopping? I've got pockets full of money and I think it's time we splurged."

Sara laughed, but only barely. Sadness lingered on her face. "All right."

While she shopped, Michael had someone to meet.

Michael gave Sara a handful of creds to go buy some new clothes, directing her to the store with the dresses he had noticed earlier, then he made his way across the street to SUPERNATURAL SURPLUS to see Johnny Frawl. If this Johnny was anything like the Johnny from his world, the kid was a fount of information on the weird. Michael had never bought into all that supernatural mumbo jumbo before dying, but given the fact that he was an invincible warrior on a mission across parallel dimensions for God, maybe hocus pocus was right up his alley.

Johnny was finishing up the sale of a shrunken head for a little boy when Michael walked in.

"Hey, again. What can I do for ya?" Johnny asked, friendly and laid back.

"Question. Has anyone ever come to you wanting to induce a near-death experience?"

Johnny paused, then called to the back of the store. "Nana, you'd better take over the register for me."

Nana sauntered in as Johnny led Michael towards the back of the store and through a curtain into a cluttered study. Michael paused, surrounded by shelves of strange books on every facet of the occult. He didn't understand half of what he was seeing except to know that he'd killed a great many of the monsters represented in these tomes—vampires, werewolves, and ghouls.

"So why an NDE?" Johnny asked, taking a worn book off a shelf before shuffling through its yellowed pages.

Michael took a seat at a table in the center of the room. "I need to see God for a second. We need to talk."

Johnny laughed. "Try religion."

"No," Michael said, offering a brief smile. "I'm serious." If Johnny were going to help him, they needed to be on the same page. He took a deep breath. "Here's the deal. I'm from a parallel dimension. I work for God and he sends me all over the multiverse killing bad guys, okay? But I've got a really important question for him and he doesn't answer my calls. I need you to get me to him."

Johnny slowly closed the book, kicking up a small puff of dust.

"Okaaaay. Well, thank you for shopping at SUPERNATURAL SURPLUS. Please come again when you need something a little less crazy."

Michael sighed and stood from the table, reached into his jacket and retrieved the steak knife. As he began to pull his shirt up to expose his stomach, he said, "All right. I'm about to show you something. But, whatever you do, don't freak out."

15

Johnny hurried back to the table with much excitement and dropped a book, nearly in Michael's lap. Johnny thumbed through the pages before stopping and pointing. "Right there," he said. "Walk-ins."

Michael frowned, taking a closer look at the text. "What?"

"There've been stories of them as long as there has been civilization. No one knows what they are for sure, but many suspect that they're actually visitors from other planes of reality, sort of phasing into our own. They're there for a while, then they just vanish. From what you just described about yourself, it sounds like you're a walk-in."

Michael skimmed the book. Were "walk-ins" just rift jumpers like him? *How many more of us are there?* Rip wanted him to believe that there was a larger plan at work here. *But how do I fit into it?*

Not that it mattered anymore. Michael was here to get out of this life. No more walking in and out; he was ready to stay.

"I'm done with it," he said. "I've got to get God to let me out of this deal, which is why I gotta catch a bus to heaven."

"But you're invulnerable," Johnny said, eyeing the steak knife lying on the table. He'd handled Michael's self-mutilation a lot better than Sara had.

"So?"

"So, how are you planning on inducing a near-death experience if you can't even be hurt?"

Michael slumped. "Oh."

Johnny tapped his chin. "There could be another way, though."

"What's that?"

"Many believe in God on this world too. According to the God-followers' holy book—the Book of Revealing Mysteries—God exists *outside* of time and space. In the In-Between."

Michael stared at the occult nerd. "Yeah, that's making no sense to me."

Johnny sighed and shook his uncombed mane with a know-it-all smirk. "You do this for a living, and you don't even understand time and space?"

"Can you help me or are you just going to laugh at me?"

"Okay, okay." Johnny quieted, still chuckling a bit. He searched the room, spotted a brick wall, then moved for it. "Okay, look at this wall. Brick, right?"

"Look, I'm more a man of action, but I'm not stupid, all right?"

"No, listen. Look at the brick. Imagine this is the multiverse, with each brick representing another world or a plane of existence, yeah?"

"Yeah. Still following."

Johnny traced his finger along the grey mortar between the bricks. "Well, then, *this* is the In-Between. It's the Void between the different realities. It's the glue that's keeping everything together."

"You're saying God is there? Not in heaven?"

"No, this *is* heaven. And hell. Those things exist outside of time, like I said. God was here in the beginning and he made Creation out of the Void. But, I guess not just one world—but all of them. The entire multiverse is all one single creation, just many, many layers of it. Heaven and hell, angels and demons, they're all out *here*, though, outside of Creation on a different frequency or wavelength. Which is why I guess we can't see them unless they choose to reveal themselves. And God is over them all."

"Then how do I get to the In-Between?"

"Do you realize what kind of magick we're talking about that can crack a dimensional wall and into the In-Between?"

"I'm guessing a lot?"

Johnny raised his eyebrows. "Oh yeah."

"But can you do it?"

Johnny hesitated. "I could try, but are you sure you really want to? God and heaven are there somewhere, yeah, but so is a hell full of demons. They might cross over into our frequency from time to time, but we're talking about opening up a doorway for them—for all of them—to spill out into our world. Hell on earth, man. I don't know if I'm willing to risk it."

Michael thought of Sara, in his arms. Looking at him, pleading for him to save her. "I am."

Johnny scratched his dirty blond mop-top. "I'm not even sure you could get back even if you did cross over. We're talking about the Land of the Dead, here. Kind of a one-way trip."

"No. I can make it. I know I can. I've survived everything the multiverse has thrown my way. I can do this."

Johnny stuck his hands in his pockets, his smooth features darkening. "I don't know. I…I don't like this."

"Please. There's…there's this girl."

Groaning, Johnny smacked his head. "Aw, man."

"I love her," Michael said as Johnny paced. "I wouldn't ask you to do this for nothing. Being with her means everything to me."

Johnny cut eyes to him. "Even the annihilation of my world?"

"It won't come to that."

Still pacing, Johnny sighed. "I can't believe I'm doing this."

Michael grinned.

"If we get out of this alive—" Johnny jabbed a finger in Michael's direction.

Michael pulled out a pile of creds and dropped it on the table. "You'll be a very rich man and your Nana will be very proud."

16

Johnny spent the next half-hour cross-referencing a number of books, and then used a piece of chalk to draw an uneven circle on the brick wall. Michael stood up to the crude outline.

"Look," Johnny said, shakily. "I'm no expert, okay? I mean, I've read all the books since I was a kid, but I never tried this stuff."

"I trust you," Michael said, not sure if he really meant that.

At Michael's feet, Johnny etched more chalk on the hardwood floor; strange words in a language Michael had never seen before. "What are those?"

Johnny regarded them, then returned his nose to the book. "The secret names of God—at least, what we call God on my world. It's to keep the demons from coming through."

"That in your books too?"

"No. Just a hope, really."

Michael nodded. "Sounds good enough to me."

Johnny stepped back from the brick to admire his handiwork. He was sweating, his teeth set on edge. "Okay. This is it— Wait."

"What?"

Johnny reached into his back pocket and pulled out a utility knife, like a Swiss Army knife from Michael's world. "We need blood."

"Blood?"

"Crossing over into Death, remember? Life has to be shed. There's always got to be blood. Don't worry, it won't take much."

Michael held up a hand. "Impervious to harm, remember?"

Johnny slouched. "Oh. Crap."

"Sorry."

Johnny sighed and held the blade in his own hand, dragging it against the meat of his palm. He shrieked in pain and looked ready to throw up.

"You okay?"

Johnny nodded, still wincing, then moved to the brick wall and smeared his bloodied wound in the circle drawing. He turned back to his book and read something that Michael assumed was the mystical spell. The reading was over almost as soon as it begun.

Still, the wall stood strong.

Michael looked around, uncertain. "Was that it?"

"Yeah. Why didn't it work?" Johnny took a step away from the wall. "I thought I—"

Then the wall cracked. Brick and mortar shook loose, crumbling to the floor. Piece by piece fell away until Michael was staring through an opening in reality itself—straight into the Abyss. Starless black night gaped back at him, maddening and frigid. The yawning chasm tugged at him like a hungry vacuum. "Hold on to something!" he shouted as the brick wall gave way and fell into the vortex of black energy.

Johnny staggered back, out of reach of the black hole's pull, but Michael allowed himself to be yanked through. He looked back to the crack of reality to see Johnny standing safe beyond the vortex's borders.

Michael soared through the obsidian ether, losing all sense of direction, of time, of self. Everything he was, everything he had been or could be, was stripped from him. He knew nothing anymore, yet everything all at once. The multiverse unfolded before his mind's eye and he saw everything. Every possibility, every face, every life. He heard the thoughts of the people he'd saved, those he would save, those he'd failed to save. Sara was there—all of them. Every Sara from every plane of existence. Michael was there, too, but he didn't know which one was him. They blurred by him and he screamed, his mind cracking under the strain of so much knowledge.

In the midst of the multiverse, Michael saw something else. No, not saw. Felt. Sensed. A presence there, dark and undulating, worming its way through the layers of Creation.

And, in one terrible moment, the presence saw him too.

*Michael…*the Black called out to him, beckoning him. *Michael…*

"No," he whispered, twisting in the nothingness, trying to swim or fly away. But there was nowhere to go. There was nothing. Yet, in the nothingness, the presence slithered for him, caressing his soul, whispering to every cell in his body.

Welcome back…

"Please, God, no!"

Without warning, the Black dropped like a curtain, and Michael tumbled down—no, *up*—a winding tunnel filled with unearthly lights. He catapulted faster, his sense of identity returning. His awareness sharpened until, at last, he crashed hard into a ceiling that, a moment later, he realized was a floor. A terrible chill seized his muscles, and he shivered on the ground, rising to all fours. Black oily grass spread beneath his fingers, growing into large fungus-like vegetation, also the color of midnight. A sickening witch-light oozed from the base of the thick ebon trees, and the sky above was a deep shade of purple. There was no light source he could make out, save for the pulsating alien glow from the twisted mutated trunks. He wanted to hide, but Michael forced himself to stand.

"H-Hello?"

Snickers and whispers rippled through the folds of darkness around him, and many eyes blinked back at him. His breath left him in frosty puffs, and he shivered down to his very soul, his stomach mutated into a mass of knots. He gripped his abdomen, gasping, and slumped to his knees. His mind cried out in desperation in reaction to a threat, to danger. To evil.

He knew then that he had stumbled upon some plane of the purest

Evil. He had dared to rip open the veil and travel through, dared to see what no living man was meant to see or know. Now every blasphemous secret of the inner workings of the cosmos was laid bare, pressing on his mind, crushing the life within him.

Things prowled in the black, circling him, taunting him, watching him. Vague monstrosities carefully studied him, their shapes iridescent with that same greasy light that bled from the fungal growths. These creatures—their blackened outlines flickering like tips of flame whipping in the wind—slithered and crawled and gyrated closer to him.

Michael backed away, balling his fists. He thought he might cry, or laugh, or both, but he steadied himself and snarled. "Come on. Let's see what you got."

An inky black talon extended from the murky mass and backhanded him away. He careened backwards, end over end, landing hard in the slimy grass. Scrambling to a crawling position, he turned about and watched in horror as the stooped figures lurched for him, reaching, baying, screaming, giggling.

"Stop!" he barked. "Get back!"

At once, the quivering mass of monsters paused, looked to the horizon behind them, then scattered like crows, taking all of Michael's fear and panic with them. There, marching stern-faced across the diseased landscape, was a man of light, his countenance shining in the darkness beneath the brim of his Stetson hat.

Michael glanced up, bolstered by an overwhelming sense of safety.

"It's you!" He stood in a hurry, tearing up, thankful to be rid of those foul demonic entities.

But the Man did not reply. His expression was hard and displeased. He clamped one hand on Michael's shoulder, and together they vanished in a *pop* of white light.

17

Michael pitched ahead, tumbling onto soft green grass. He was instantly bombarded by daylight, by birdsong and crickets' chirps. There was *life* here in this place, refreshing and new, and he swallowed great breaths of air, touching his forehead to the earth, thankful to be free from that terrible domain.

"Thank you," he panted, then lifted his head. He was in a patch of overgrown weeds, near the crest of a mighty cliff overlooking a small town some distance below. Michael picked himself up and glanced about to find the Man in the Stetson standing before an old, crumbling church nearly reclaimed by the forest. With quiet contemplation, the Man regarded the dingy cross fixed above the door. Michael spotted a faded sign in front of the building that read "Good Church of the Faithful".

Michael quietly walked to the Man's side, wondering what meaning this derelict place held for him. They stood in silence, beholding the old church together. "Where are we?" Michael finally asked.

The Man closed his mouth to a line and exhaled sharply out of his nostrils. "There are better ways to get my attention. You never should have ventured to the In-Between."

The Man turned towards the cliff and began to walk down a gravel path. Michael scratched the back of his head, a bit embarrassed. "I was aiming for heaven."

The Man did not face him, but kept moving. "You missed."

"Yeah." Michael hurried to catch up. "What was that place?"

"Only one of a thousand such places that exist in the dark spaces between the stars."

A comfortable quiet between them, they carried on in their peaceful country walk until at last they reached the cliff. The Man settled to a stop, and kept a thoughtful watch on the burg below.

Michael surveyed the small town at their feet. "Where are we?"

Hands tucked in his deep coat pockets, the Man said, "A good place to talk." Hardening, he looked to Michael. "You shouldn't have gone into the In-Between."

"You said that already—"

"You've put everything at risk."

Michael frowned under the scolding, and said, "It's Sara. I *love* her. I want to stay with her."

The Man withdrew his large callused hands and gently placed them on Michael's shoulders, a soft smile warming his creased face. "I know, son. But your work is not done."

Michael thought of the Thing in the Abyss, the one that had spoken to him. It was burrowing its way through the worlds, but what was it?

It doesn't matter.

"Doesn't it?" the Man asked, and Michael flinched in surprise at having his most private thoughts answered. "You've acted selfishly," the Man went on, calm and without condemnation. "You're still letting your anger and fear control you."

Michael ground his teeth and jerked away. He paced for a moment before halting and jabbing a finger in the Man's face. "Don't. I don't know why you chose me, but don't hand me those holy platitudes. You stopped me from killing Charlie. Why? That man is evil. You hired me to kill evil people, in case you forgot."

The Man rose taller and, despite the peaceful morning, the heavens trembled with thunder as a great cloud passed them by. "Watch your tone, boy."

Michael faltered, holy terror gripping him. The Man relaxed and the darkness passed, but his intimidating glare did not fade. "Michael, you are at a crossroads. Dark times are ahead. Everything planned by those who seek to control you will soon be laid before you. The girl is important—more than you know."

"I don't get it."

"In many ways, your journey is about to begin."

He huffed. "*About* to...? What do you think I've been doing for five years?" Scowling now, he demanded, "And where were you? Five years! I've been doing this since I was twelve years old and where were you? What kind of God just drops a kid into the middle of something like this without any kind of help?" Michael felt his eyes sting and wiped at them, and seethed. "All those nights, I cried because I was lonely and scared. I thought you'd dumped me! But I didn't stop! I kept fighting, just like I told you I would, and I never expected anything but for you to maybe be around. But you were too busy or whatever, is that it?"

The Man in the Stetson did not retaliate, but carried the weight of Michael's accusations. Patiently, he replied, "I never left your side."

Michael threw his hands in the air, raving now. "I prayed to you! Every night, I prayed and begged for you to talk to me...*Now* you show up? Now? Telling me to keep my crap together and not lose it over some gutter trash like Charlie? That's really all you have to say to me after all this time? What kind of father *are* you?"

The Man studied him hard, and Michael could not avoid his eyes. Eyes that were a painting of pain and understanding. "I spoke to you," he said. "On every world you went, every step of the way, I cared for you through the kindness of the strangers you met. I thanked you through the tears of those you saved. I held you at night, and when you cried I breathed peace into your heart." Caught somewhere between a smile and a frown, he finished, "You were afraid, and I gave you strength to stand again."

Michael grimaced, feeling hot tears travel his cheeks. The Man gently touched the side of his face, smiling down on him through tears of his own. "I never left you."

Michael rubbed at his nose with the back of his hand and turned towards the town to compose himself.

From behind him, the Man continued, "I've kept you from this day until I knew you were ready to face it. I know what Sara means to you. But you must put her first. Not your own desires." The Man came to stand at Michael's side, but kept his gaze ahead. "You walk a fine line between the Light and the Dark, Michael. You can still fall into the abyss and become the person Rip wanted you to be."

"I don't want that," Michael said, firm.

"I know. That's why Sara is so important. You have a choice to make."

"I thought I already made my choice. That's why I'm here."

"You chose a path, but you must choose every day to stay on the path. Choose wisely. Decide who you will be."

Michael took a breath and faced the Man. "But you want me to decide what's best for Sara. *I'm* best for her. She needs me. I need her." His heart broke. "Please let me stay with her. Haven't I repented enough? Can't I have this one thing for a reward?"

The Man saddened. "You still think this is about penance. You grieve me, Michael. You still don't understand."

Michael blushed, ashamed.

"I'd let you stay on that world for her," the Man said. "This journey has always been up to you—the choice remains yours to continue with me or to stay behind. But if you stay, you will have no more need of the gifts I've given you. Do you understand what you're asking?"

"Yes, please," Michael blurted. "Just let me stay with her. I'm sorry…I just can't do this anymore."

The Man grew quiet, staring over the cliff, and Michael felt suddenly sad. As though something precious and rare had died. "Then you've made your choice."

White light immediately enveloped him, and Michael was violently ripped from the cliff and hurled once more through a portal of dizzying, unreal lights, finally landing on his hands and knees in the back study of SUPERNATURAL SURPLUS. He looked to his hands in shock, seeing steam rise off of them in waves, and when he turned back to the doorway to the In-Between, he saw the bricks rearranging themselves—reality repairing itself—sealing shut. Barring him from God, once again.

Michael coughed once, air returning to his lungs.

"Cool!" Johnny rushed to his side. "You *did* it, dude!"

"Thanks," Michael said.

"How do you feel?"

Michael thought of Sara. The life he could have with her now…but also of all that he'd given up. Despite his trepidation, he grinned. "Free."

18

Michael left Johnny's behind and entered the thoroughfare outside. A storm of emotions surged within. Relief was there, but mixed with it was a sense of apprehension. Rip had tried to pull him towards chaos, and God had pulled him towards order. Things were happening in the darkness between worlds—things that threatened everything.

But that wasn't his responsibility anymore. He didn't want to know what was happening, didn't want to be involved. He'd only been twelve years old when he'd been drafted. His childhood was gone, stripped from him by a God who should have had his best interests at heart. *I've earned this. This is* my *time.*

Still, he felt like he'd just set something terrible into motion.

What was that thing in the Dark? What is it the Rage Rip had talked about? What did it want? Who would fight it?

Not him. He was convinced of that. There were billions of other Michael Morrisons out there in the multiverse. Let one of them handle it. He had Sara and that was all that mattered.

He crossed the street to the clothing store, searching the aisles, guilt nipping at his soul. At last, Michael spotted her standing by a mirror outside the dressing rooms. She held a maroon crushed velvet dress up to her slender body, admiring the way it looked on her. She was so beautiful. So perfect. Michael had to believe she was worth abandoning the cause—letting the Thing in the Dark roam free.

"Hey," he said as he approached.

She smiled up at him, then paused with concern. "You okay?"

He hesitated. "I don't know. I—"

"SARA!"

Sara's face went white. Michael caught his breath. *No.*

Both of them looked to the front of the store as Charlie barged in, shoving shoppers aside, looking everywhere. In his hand was a duffel bag.

"No," Sara whimpered, her eyes widening. "NO!"

Charlie spotted them and glowered. Reached into the bag and took out his shotgun.

Michael grasped Sara by the arms and pulled her away.

BOOM!

A swarm of shotgun pellets punched the wall beside Sara. She screamed as Michael pushed her into one of the dressing rooms. "*Stay down!*"

Michael left her behind and ran towards the heavy man.

"You're gonna die, you little punk!" Charlie yelled from across the store, pumping his shotgun as he marched through the screaming shoppers.

Michael had dealt with enemies twice as big with twice as many arms holding twice as many weapons in each. But he hadn't hated any of them half as much as he hated Charlie Bost. Gritting his teeth, he climbed the counter and leapt for the brutish man.

Charlie fired another blast. *BOOM!*

Angry lead pellets caught Michael's arm, puncturing his leather jacket. He flew backward from the explosion, blood spraying in a fine red mist, and landed hard on a glass display, pulverizing the panes in a loud crash. Dazed, on the floor, covered in broken pieces of glass, he writhed in pain.

Real, physical pain.

"Oh, God," Michael muttered, holding his injured arm. *What did I do?*

Charlie stampeded towards Michael and slammed the butt of the shotgun against his face. Michael spat out a mouthful of blood and pushed up on wobbly arms. Charlie kicked him in the gut, turning him over on his back and sending him skidding a few paces down the aisle.

In the impact, the steak knife fell out of Michael's coat and clattered to the floor. He eyed it as Charlie's heavy footfalls grew closer. He might die on this world, but not without a fight.

He gripped the knife even as, with deft speed, he swept Charlie's thick legs out from under him. The ogre collapsed in a heap, his shotgun landing safely out of the way. Enraged, Michael mounted the large man and raised his knife high, his memory flashing back to killing Rip the same way. Roaring, he brought the knife down, but Charlie wrapped two meaty fists around Michael's arms, stopping them in mid-strike. Michael struggled uselessly against the larger man's strength, but Charlie jerked his arms out of the way and came up with a thunderstrike of a headbutt across Michael's nose. Michael heard something snap, his vision blurry with incredible misery. With a giant boot, Charlie heaved Michael off of him, somehow getting a hold of the steak knife in the process.

Michael staggered to his feet, slipping in his own smeared blood on the tile, and dropped to one knee. Charlie approached, taking slow steps, sneering.

"Dropped something," he chortled, then stuck Michael in the stomach.

Michael wheezed, wobbling backwards, and looked to his abdomen, where his steak knife protruded. A river of blood cascaded from his wound and he fell on all fours.

"*No!*" Sara shouted from somewhere around him, but he couldn't see her. Charlie turned his back and stalked away, and Michael bowed his head to the ground, trying to catch his breath, but unable to.

Determined not to die like this, Michael banged his fist on the floor and commanded his legs to move. He rose and ripped the knife out of his stomach. "Hey!"

Charlie regarded him, eyeing him in slight surprise.

"I'm not done yet," Michael said, gripping the knife by the blade and hurling it forward. It twirled twice in the air and embedded in Charlie's left thigh. The man gripped the handle, crying out in shock.

Michael grinned, tasting his own blood, and charged. Charlie turned, as if to retreat, but Michael leapt through the air and landed on his back. Growling, he struck Charlie's head and face with fists of unbridled vengeance. His knuckles broke on contact, but Michael embraced the pain. He thought of Sara as he beat at the man. Thought of every degradation she'd suffered at Charlie's hands.

"You'll never hurt her again!" Michael screamed.

Charlie blocked a punch and grabbed Michael's arm, throwing him off and splaying him out on the floor. Then the brute yanked the knife from his leg and scrambled for the shotgun. Michael wiped the blood from his lip and looked up in time to see the shotgun butt raining down, smashing his right eye. Blood spurted on the floor and Charlie pounded him again.

Michael saw stars with his one good eye and felt himself slipping back in that horrible void In-Between, where the dark pulsating Thing waited for him. *Welcome back*, it had said.

"No," he mumbled through loose teeth. "No…"

Michael quit struggling as Charlie put the shotgun barrel to his forehead.

"Say your prayers." Charlie spat out blood and chuckled.

Time stretched out before Michael, the store's overhead lights burning brighter. Sound became dulled and his vision blurred. Somewhere distant, he heard Sara still screaming. Saw her stepping over him, pleading for Charlie to stop. But Charlie placed a powerful hand on her face and shoved her to the floor. She reached out for Michael, weeping, and all he wanted was to touch her again. To hold her and tell her it'd be okay. *All right, God*…his heart surrendered. *You win. Please, just help me…*

Charlie froze, the gun mere inches from Michael's face. Sara's mouth remained open, but her screams had grown silent. Michael glanced around the room. Saw the panicked shoppers suspended in mid-run. The cops had finally arrived, and their guns were trained on Charlie, but they did not fire.

Time had halted, reality on pause. And in that moment, he saw the Man in the Stetson over him, frowning, sympathetic.

"It's never going to stop, is it?" Michael asked, sorrowful.

"It will. But not yet."

Michael nodded, accepting his fate, shouldering the old burden once more. The Man in the Stetson vanished in a blink, as a hundred different torments that Michael had felt a mere second ago now became as a distant memory. The lights of the store sharpened, and he could see with both eyes once more. Glancing down, his stomach was closed up, the blood vanished. His muscles were as iron again, and his blood pumped molten anger. Michael's mind focused to a deadly point as reality rebooted around him, throwing him back into a world of sound and chaos. Cops hollered for Charlie to put the weapon down. Panicked shoppers escaped, shrieking in terror.

Michael glared at Charlie, snarling.

Charlie hesitated, but Michael gripped the shotgun barrel with blinding speed and held it steady on his chest. "Do it," he snapped, defiant.

Charlie's eyes grew round in surprise, then narrowed to enraged slits as he pulled the trigger. Sara shrieked, but the pellets deflected off and struck Charlie instead. The brute stood there, swaying to the side, letting the gun drop. He opened his mouth, but only gurgled, blood oozing from his wounds. Michael stood now as Charlie fell flat on his back, dead.

Sara cried in hysterics, as the cops moved in, ushering her away from the grisly scene. Michael stood, his legs strong. He looked to his hand and clenched a fist and opened it again.

"You okay, kid?" an officer asked as more huddled around Charlie's body, checking him for a pulse.

"Never felt better," Michael said through a grimace. "Is he dead?"

Ashen-faced, a cop turned to him with a nod. "Yeah."

"Good."

Michael saw Sara off to the side, police wrapping her in a blanket and checking her over for wounds. Her sobs were dying down, now, as a female officer tried to get her story.

It was over. Sara was truly free.

19

After an hour of talking with the authorities, Charlie Bost's death was ruled an accidental death. The few witnesses to the fight testified that the gun had backfired. It was the only way they could explain what they had seen. Most people weren't wired to see miracles, even when one was staring them in the face.

Sara was free to live her life without fear of Charlie ever finding her again. Given the hell she'd been through, Michael assumed it would be cause for celebration. But she clung to Michael, her hand in his, leaning against his arm and softly crying the entire time it took them to return to the rift. Michael's weeping could wait. He'd cry on the next world, then move on, fighting evil in God's name. There was a war and it needed soldiers. Michael had accepted that now, and felt right inside.

But being right, however, was not always easy.

The two of them edged to the piece of paper that served as Michael's passageway through the In-Between to alien worlds.

"Is that it?" Sara said.

Michael nodded, staring at the paper fixed to the floor, waiting for him.

"It's not fair." She wiped her eyes.

He touched her face, drank from her eyes, wanting to remember this moment. It'd have to carry him for a lifetime. "I want to stay, but I can't. Maybe I'll be brought back and we'll see each other again. I'm sorry but…" He cracked a half-hearted grin, "You know how it is being the big hero."

Sara entered his embrace, whimpering into his jacket.

He looked around the mall, this tiny enclosed world. Everything was cloistered here, mundane and narrow. Sara deserved so much more than to be locked under a glass dome all her life.

"Listen," he said, his fingers tingling with nerves. He couldn't believe he was actually doing this. "You could…you could always come with me."

She lifted her face to him. She seemed frightened, but her bright blue eyes lit up.

"Do you want to come? I mean, chances are you'll never see your home again."

But Sara beamed. "I don't care where I have to go. I just want to be with you."

"You're sure?"

"Yes," she said with an enthusiastic smile and sparkling eyes. "Let's just leave this place."

He paused, unsure of what he was doing. His life was war. By bringing her along, he was just putting her in danger. *But I'll protect her. Nothing will happen to her. I can do this.*

They held each other tight as they stepped onto the piece of paper. Michael breathed in her scent, felt her body against his, and knew that she was his now. Whatever the multiverse had in store for him, he was ready.

He had Sara, and that was all that mattered.

The rift swallowed them in a blast of light.

20

"So that's him." The man in the hooded sweatshirt and dingy overcoat stepped out of the shadows. He watched as the sheet of paper—familiar to him, for he had one of his own—left this world, fading out of sight.

"Yes," a voice said from the shadows. It was low and even, and devoid of anything remotely human. "He has escaped our attention longer than expected. It was unwise of him to reach into the Void between the worlds. He will soon regret that mistake."

The man in the hood stiffened. "I didn't know she would be with him."

Icy and uncaring, the voice said, "Will that make this harder for you?"

"No," the Hooded Man lied. Of course it would be harder now, but he had left that part of himself behind long ago. He was his master's servant, and would do what the Rage commanded.

"Good," the thing in the shadows said.

"Where will he go now?"

"That is beyond our knowledge, but we've located him once. We will do so again. And when we do, the concerto will begin."

PART THREE: TIES THAT BIND

1

A flash of light and Sara felt herself lurch forward, landing hard on the ground. Instantly, high-pitched whines and explosions assaulted her ears. Red and green lights lit up the blackened night sky as the world detonated around her. Shapes moved in the staccato light, firing weapons at each other, deafening her. Terrified, she curled on the ground, her hands over her ears, and screamed.

Strong hands gripped her by the shoulders and yanked her to her feet. In an instant, Sara realized it was Michael. He was beside her, his hardened face surveying the landscape without so much as a hint of fear.

"Come on!" he said, the sound nearly lost to the warzone.

Michael dragged her forward. She trembled and flinched with each new blast.

"What's happening?" she shrieked, though her own words were mute to her.

Michael either didn't hear her or ignored her. A shimmering ball of red light collided into the dirt next to them, showering them in grass and rocks. Sara yelped, staggered by the shockwave. But Michael caught her fall. Nearly carrying her now, he hurried them away from the carnage and the killing shapes.

Michael raced for a small hovel away from the battlefield. He shoved his foot against the wooden door, splintering the frame. He hurled Sara inside and closed the door, sliding a small table to barricade the entrance.

"What—" Sara began.

Michael held out his hand. "Shh..." He watched the windows. Then he raced past her, scanning the rest of the room in the wooden shack.

Her senses slowly restored, Sara looked at their primitive surroundings. The rustic cabin was small and cramped, and the furniture looked crudely homemade.

Michael pushed by, once more, taking one last appraising look out the window, the night skies beyond flickering with alien-colored fire. At last Michael slid to sit on the floor, catching his breath.

Sara wondered if it were safe to talk now. Her heart was still protesting, but she felt safer. "Where are we?"

"My guess? The American Civil War."

"Which one?" Sara asked.

He grinned. "Right. I guess you had more than one on your world, huh? Well, in my world we just had the one…I think. History was never my thing."

A silver, forked shape zipped over the battlefield, raining green hell on the scrambling soldiers below. Sara heard them dying, even from here.

"Only," Michael said, "mine didn't have aliens."

"So, you're saying this is like your world, only—"

"Aliens are in there, too, I guess. Yeah. Judging by the color of the uniforms, I'd say they were Confederate soldiers fighting off the aliens."

Sara shook her head, her mind overloading.

Michael chuckled. "Rift jumping. It's a trip, huh?"

"So…" Sara stood to collect her thoughts, but Michael reached out and yanked her arm, pulling her back to the ground as another chunk of earth was obliterated in red and green lights outside.

"You gotta stay down," Michael said, his eyes full of fear. "I'm invincible, all right? You're not."

Sara nodded. "Right. Sorry."

"It's okay." He touched her hair. "You're new."

"Wait, so this is what it's like for you? You just jump in, right in the middle of a war?"

"Not always. But, usually if I show up, there's a war that's got to be fought with someone. That's kind of the job description."

Sara's body trembled, suddenly exhausted. Her future life stretched out before her, an endless parade of explosions, guns, and death. *Did I make the right choice by leaving with Michael?*

He must have sensed her doubt. He scooted closer to her, taking her in his arms. "Hey, listen, I know it's scary, okay? You kind of got a raw deal for your first jump. Usually God eases me into things. Don't let this upset you. It's not always like this all the time. There's good times too."

"I'm really tired," Sara said, beginning to weep. She felt homesick and alone, lost out here in space and time with a boy she hardly knew. "Can I...can I just go to sleep?"

Michael's face slackened, then tensed. "Yeah. I think the fighting's moving away. You try and sleep and I'll keep watch, okay?"

She huddled up in the corner of the shack. Michael draped his leather jacket on her. Sara clutched the coat, finding a small amount of security in it, and the sounds of fading gunfire lulled her to a fitful sleep.

2

Warm sunlight woke her in the morning. Sara sat up, her muscles sore from last night's anxiety and slumber on the hardwood floor. Michael's jacket lay across her and she put her arms through the sleeves. The ratty coat hung loose on her slight frame, the worn cuffs dangling past her hands. Wrapping her arms across her waist, she stood to her bare feet, wondering when she'd lost her shoes in the night. Michael must have taken them off, an attempt to make her more comfortable.

Speaking of which— "Michael?" she whispered. She still feared an attack, even though she could hear birds singing peacefully outside. He didn't answer so she wandered into the only other room of the shack. "Michael?" she called again. That room was empty too.

He's gone. He left me.

Instant fear swallowed her up and she panted, her chest heaving, tears building. "Michael!"

The door banged open and Michael appeared, his black eyes alarmed. "Are you okay?"

Sara ran to him, throwing her arms around his neck and pulling him in tight. She sobbed against his shoulder as he combed her hair with his fingers. "What? What happened?"

"I thought you were gone."

"No, no. I would never leave you. I was just outside, making breakfast. Okay?"

She pulled away from him, nodding, forcing herself to calm. He grinned now, easing her worry. "Better? Come on. Come outside with me."

Gently, he took her hand and led the way. Outside the sky was a rich, bright blue, with thick clouds blowing over. Lush green-leafed trees stood quiet watch over the Earth, perhaps mourning their brothers obliterated in last night's battle. Everywhere she looked there was sun and colors and Sara held her breath, taking it all in. Long gone were the screams, the explosions. Now, only the distant singing of birds and insects and the soothing rustling in the leaves broke up the serene calm.

Letting go of Michael, Sara walked to a nearby tree, feeling its rough bark, looking high into the sky to see its bushy top. "I don't believe it," she breathed, reverent of the ancient thing before her.

From behind, Michael laughed. "What? A tree? You've never seen a tree before?"

She shook her head, still transfixed by the towering giant. "Only in books…Trees were almost gone by the time I was born. We lived under the domes my whole life. I've…I've never been outside before."

Michael moved behind, joining her. "Beautiful, isn't it?"

Sara thought to the night before. The death, the terror. That seemed like worlds away, now, overtaken by the tranquility of this place. Were it not for the scattered pieces of junk, the solitary remains of the skirmish strewn about the grassy plain, she would never have known a battle had taken place here at all. In fact, there weren't even any bodies…

She paused. Finally turning away from the tree, Sara surveyed the landscape, but saw no Confederate uniforms. No soldiers. "Where are the bodies?" she asked.

Michael flinched and stuck his hands in his pockets. "I…uh…I moved them." He gestured far behind him, towards the left. "They're over the ridge. I…I thought they would just upset you."

"That must have taken hours," Sara said, feeling guilty that her freak-out had caused him to work so hard. He'd moved no telling how many corpses. What did that do to a person? But he'd done it all for her.

"It's okay." He smiled. "I couldn't sleep much anyway. Besides, I had to get up early to find breakfast."

Sara spotted a small fire, made with sticks bearing small mounds of meat leaning over the flames. "You went hunting?"

"Don't sound so surprised." He laughed. "McDonalds is a pretty popular franchise, but you're not going to find one in *every* dimension. We've got rabbit on the menu this morning."

It was at that moment that Sara realized how alien Michael really was. He'd been doing this for five years. Five years of dodging gunfire, of sleeping alone in abandoned buildings, of being around death, of hunting and cooking his own food. She understood now how mundane these things had become for him. He'd been a homeless vagabond, wandering alien worlds and realities, fighting their wars. How scary and terribly lonely it must have been for him all this time.

Sara reached out and touched his face, feeling his hard-set chin. "Thank you for making me comfortable. But don't..."

His smile sagged. "What?"

"I'm not your guest. You don't have to take care of me." She grinned. "I signed on for this job too. We're in this together now. You...you don't have to be alone anymore."

Michael looked like he might cry, as though no one had ever said that to him. He stepped closer, and Sara welcomed him into an embrace. "I'll take care of you now," she whispered, as he finally began to weep.

3

After breakfast, they spent the day doing absolutely nothing. Michael knew he had a mission to accomplish, but he felt no pang in his gut—no warning that danger was imminent. Thankful for the reprieve, he sat by the fire for a while, watching Sara dance around barefoot in the grass. Never before had she felt grass between her toes, and Michael wanted her to have this gift. She moved about like a butterfly, darting from one tree to another, plucking leaves, admiring their shapes, comparing them to each other.

Later they walked hand in hand by the stream that ran not far from the battleground. Michael taught her how to skip stones and they splashed in the water, laughing and wrestling. They raced each other in yellow wild-flowered fields, and Michael let her win a couple times. It was perhaps the best day of Michael's life.

More than once, he felt like a normal teenage boy, spending time with the girl of his dreams. He hoped the Man in the Stetson would approve.

As the day wore on, they returned to their humble cabin and Michael stoked the fire outside. He would have to go hunting for supper soon before all light left, but he couldn't pull himself away from Sara just yet.

They sat before the crackling flames, Michael stirring the embers with a stick. He and Sara spoke little, but the quiet was pleasant and reassuring. He glanced up to see her studying him, the corners of her lip upturned. He rewarded her attention with a smile.

"What was *your* first jump like?" she said.

He chuckled. "That was a long time ago."

"Surely you didn't forget."

"Nah, just haven't thought about it in a long, long time."

She edged closer to him, snuggling him by the warmth of the flames. "Tell me about it."

Michael set his makeshift fire poker to the side and dusted off his hands. "Let's see. I think it was a planet called Myriad Prime."

Sara laughed. "Seriously?"

"Yeah. Something like that. That was before I really paid attention to names. I was terrified. It was all I could do to focus on the mission. The planet was ruled by a race of horsehead guys who kept humans as slaves." Michael snickered and Sara joined him.

"I freaked right out," he laughed. "To this day, I still get a little jumpy around horses. Those guys were so creepy."

"What was the mission?" Sara asked, still chuckling.

Michael's laughter slowly died. "One of the horsehead guys was abducting human women, just to hunt them for sport. He'd…been at it for decades."

Sara met his eyes. "That's terrible. What did you do?"

"What I always do." He shrugged, a bit morose. "Killed him."

She nodded. After a thoughtful pause, she said, "Was it hard?"

"It's always hard. But you get used to it. After a while it's just like breathing." Michael watched the flame, his jaw tense. "Does that scare you?"

She squeezed his arm. "No."

He kissed the top of her head, breathing in her scent, his eyes misty.

Comfortable silence fell again. Michael reached for the stick and jabbed at the fire, watching the flames intently. Sara sighed, wistfully. "I don't know if I'll ever get used to this," she said after a small giggle to ease the tension.

Michael was grateful to change the subject. Brightening, he turned to her. "I think you're doing just fine. You'll be an old pro before you know it."

She tugged at his sleeve. "Do I get a cool leather jacket, too?"

He stared into her eyes, moving his mouth closer to hers. "If you play your cards right."

Their lips met. Michael cupped her chin, then eased his hands down to her arms, her waist, her back, holding her close. When at last they parted, Michael and Sara breathed hard through smiles, their foreheads still touching.

"Marry me," he whispered.

Sara pulled away, her eyes wide open and alert. "W-What?"

"I love you, Sara. I've never been more sure of anything in my whole life. I don't want you for one night; I want you for a lifetime. I want to know that it's just going to be you and me. For as long as we both shall live."

Sara blanched. Stood and brushed the grass off her jeans. "I don't know," she stammered, flushed. "After Charlie, I…"

Michael felt his spirits drop to the Earth. "Right. You're right, it's way too soon. I never should've—"

"It's not you," she blurted. "You…"

"Sara, it's okay. I get it." He stabbed at the fire pit.

Her voice wavered. "You…Do you even know how wonderful you are?"

Michael watched her as she wiped at fresh tears on her cheek, her lip trembling.

"If you only knew how long I dreamed to meet someone like you. You're everything I ever wanted in a man—strong, capable, decisive. All the things I never saw in my dad. The same things I thought I saw in Charlie before…Charlie was the fantasy, but *you*…" She wept. "Everything was so dark where I was but you…You came into my life and brought light for the first time."

Michael's heart stirred at her poetic declaration. He stood now, reaching for her, but she would not enter his arms. "Then why won't you marry me?"

She hung her head, squinting against more tears. When she looked up again, her face was hard and set. "Marriage…it's like ownership."

"Yeah. We *should* own each other."

"No," she winced, then chuckled uncomfortably, turning her back to him. "We don't own each other. We're here for as long as we want to be. I…I don't know if I could ever be married again." Sara faced him, biting her lip. "I'm sorry."

Michael felt sick inside and slowly took his seat by the fire. "Oh."

The silence returned, but this time it proved cold and lonely. Michael took the stick in both hands, bending it over his knees, gazing into the heart of the fire. Sara approached him, huddling over him in a hug, draping her long ginger hair in his face. It smelled so good. Her skin was soft and supple. He loved her, but was unsure of his heart now. Had he judged wrong? Was Sara not "the One"?

Rejection and hurt sat on his shoulders, snickering at him.

"I guess you're not in the mood, now, huh?" She smirked, though it looked more like a frown.

He got to his feet and tossed the stick into the fire. "I should go look for food before it gets too dark. Are you hungry?"

She shrugged. "Sure." She watched his eyes. "Are you mad?"

"No," he lied. "It's been a good day, hasn't it?"

Her smile widened, thrilling him. "The best."

Michael gave her a quick kiss on the lips, to show he still cared, then left to find dinner.

4

Sara gathered more sticks for the fire, the darkening gloom closing in. Michael was still off catching their meal and it was taking him longer than she'd hoped. Maybe he just needed some time to cool down. She felt terrible for hurting him. He'd proposed to her and she'd blown him off. But marriage? It was insane. After all, she hardly knew him…

But she loved him. In such a short time he had completely redefined her life—her destiny. He'd invited her to join him in the greatest adventure of all by coming on this rift jump. For how long, though? Surely it'd be over one day, wouldn't it? After that, then what? Would Michael return her home? Was that even possible?

He was her home now. For better or worse. Why wouldn't she marry him? She loved him with whatever remained of her heart. But to marry him…Sara had made those vows before. She had always honored those vows, and look what that got her. Could she make those vows again? She needed her freedom—it's why she left Charlie in the first place.

But, in her heart, Sara knew she had already made vows of her own. To stand by Michael, to be there for him when he needed her. He was so lonely. She must protect him just as he'd protected so many others. Yes, she'd made her own vows and she'd hold to them.

"Hey."

Michael's voice startled her. She saw him enter the clearing, only one rabbit in hand.

He held it up, an embarrassed half-grin on his handsome face. "We'll have to share. Got too dark."

"It's okay." She dumped her small pile of sticks onto the fire.

"Everything good here?" he asked, taking his game towards the shack.

Sara wiped the dirt on her pant leg, and combed her hair over her ears before reaching for a shard of torn metal. "I found this while you were gone." She hoped the gesture would take away all the awkwardness, put them on the same team again. "It's a piece of one of the ships."

Michael's brow knit together and he came in for a closer look, leaving his rabbit behind. She handed the shard to him and he turned it over, his frown deepening.

"It's got a plate on it. It says it's made in the United States of America. Is that…an alien planet?"

"No," Michael said, his eyes concentrating hard on the plate. "We're standing in it. It's Earth. It also says this ship was forged in 1996…"

"Is that strange?"

He nodded, looking up at her, his hardened face grimacing. "On my world, the American Civil War happened in the *1800s*, I think."

"So what does that mean?"

Michael opened his mouth, as if to answer, then froze. His fingers went limp and the metal shard slipped from his grip, landing in the soft grass. Just as Sara was about to ask what was wrong, Michael doubled over, clutching at his temples. "Aaagghhh!"

"*What?*" Sara panicked, bending over him, touching his shoulders, his back. "What's wrong? Let me help!"

"Git yer hands up!" a strange voice said.

Sara whirled and saw dark shapes moving in the firelight, aiming rifles at her. The shadows were men, and they wore Confederate uniforms. Michael rose, breathing heavy, but his pain seemed to have subsided. He stepped ahead of Sara, putting her behind him with a protective sweep of his arm.

"What do you want?" asked Michael. "We haven't done anything."

"Michael?" one of the soldiers said, desperation in the voice.

A soldier pushed his way to the front. He looked young, maybe in his twenties, square-jawed with long sideburns, though he was otherwise smooth-faced. His round spectacles reflected the flickering fire. The soldier lowered his rifle, taking tentative steps toward Sara and Michael. He seemed either ready to cry or laugh. Maybe both.

"Michael?" he repeated.

Sara felt Michael's body tense under her fearful grip.

"Edward?" Michael asked.

"Who is it?" Sara whispered.

Michael turned to her. "My brother."

5

It wasn't really his brother. Michael had to keep reminding himself of that. Edward—that is, the *parallel* Edward—brought Michael and Sara back to the Confederate camp, unharmed. The soldiers remained alert, their steely gaze fixed to the brush surrounding them, waiting for enemy attack.

"What are you *doing* out here?" Edward asked, his excitement a contrast to the caution of the rest of the camp.

Michael shared a nervous glance with Sara, who clutched at his arm, eyes darting at the shadows and skies overhead. "Well, we sort of...dropped in."

Edward shook his head, his face slack with shock. "We was sure you was dead, brother. Killed by them blamed Yanks last summer. We..."

The man stopped and sobbed. "You was dead, man. We buried an empty coffin, 'cause we couldn't find your body. If I'da known..."

Michael grieved in his heart. He'd left his own brothers behind to follow the Man in the Stetson, and had never been allowed to look back to see what became of them. No doubt they had been as upset as this Edward, mourning over an empty grave.

Everything inside him warned Michael to keep his distance. This wasn't Edward. He looked like him. He sounded like him—well, apart from a heavy Southern dialect—he even *felt* like him.

But it's not him. This isn't your brother.

But then again, Sara wasn't the Sara from his world, either, and yet he'd brought her into his life.

Watching this Edward shed tears stirred something and Michael put an arm around the man's shoulders. Edward returned the gesture, hugging Michael tight.

"I missed you, little brother," he whispered.

Michael felt his own tears building, thinking this was probably the closest to a family reunion he'd ever see. "I missed you, too."

Over his brother's shoulder, he glimpsed Sara watching him, smiling. Could it get any better than this? Having his brother back? Having Sara back? It was almost too good to be true...

Which meant it probably was. He still had a mission. All the fuzzy feelings in the world didn't erase the fact that he had been saved for a purpose—vanquishing evil in all its forms on countless worlds. That hadn't changed. He'd already bent the rules in taking Sara with him, but he couldn't make a habit out of that.

Could he?

He and his brother separated, with Edward wiping at the corners of his eyes behind his spectacles.

"We'd better get back," Edward said. "Seth'll be madder 'an hell he wasn't the one to find ya."

Michael gawked. "Seth? Seth's here, too?"

Edward laughed and slapped Michael on the back, starting up their walk again. "Oh, man, we got a lotta catchin' up to do."

Inside the camp, Michael saw off-duty soldiers lounging about the open flaps to their worn tents. The men huddled around campfires, laughing, singing, or just sitting in silence. Makeshift instruments made sweet music and Michael felt like he was being welcomed home after a long trip. The men in Edward's squad dispersed, but Edward stayed, a hand on Michael's shoulder to guide him through the camp.

Michael kept an eye on Sara who trailed along behind. She blushed as the men ogled her, and Michael pulled her just a little bit closer.

"C'mere, you gotta see 'im." Edward cupped his hand over his mouth and hollered. "Seth!"

A gangly boy with a stern, mean face and longish dark hair emerged from a tent. The hard set in his jaw looked like it could cut iron, and his gaze was twice as strong. He looked far too angry for a kid his age. Michael gauged he was probably sixteen by now, but even with those years added on, he still looked so familiar. He was still that kid who skipped school to steal smokes with the bigger boys.

No. That was your brother. This is just his double.

It didn't matter, though. His nose stung and he thought he might cry. "Seth."

The boy looked him up and down, cutting eyes at Edward. "No," he said through bared teeth. "No, you're dead. I-I saw it."

Edward took a step forward, reaching out, but Seth batted the hand away.

"No way! No!"

"Come on, Seth," Edward said. "It's him, brother. Look at 'im. It's Mike."

Sara slipped her hand inside Michael's and squeezed. He saw the questioning stare in her blue eyes, and he thought he might know what that look meant. He wasn't their brother. Their brother was dead. It was selfish of him to let this go on any longer, to let these men fighting on the brink of death hold onto the false hope that their Michael Morrison had returned. Sara seemed to be prodding him to tell them the truth, but...

Seth moved closer, inches from Michael's face, surveying his eyes. "It's you?"

Sara's fingers tightened, but Michael ignored her. "It's me, Seth."

Seth's face was like concrete, but he hugged Michael, wiry arms like vices. Michael returned the embrace and Edward joined in. "The Morrison brothers are back," Edward hooted. Others in the camp started to shout, applaud, and whistle. Some came over to congratulate the reunion.

Michael enjoyed the moment, not knowing how long it would last.

6

In Edward's tent, the trio talked while Sara sat quiet at Michael's side. Most of the soldiers had put out their lanterns and gone inside their tents, preparing for a long march in the morning, but the brothers were too excited to sleep.

"I saw it," Seth said, watching Michael with a good helping of suspicion. Or maybe he just didn't want to give in to the hope that his brother was really alive. "You took a shot right to the heart."

Edward studied him too. Michael felt conviction under their eyes. He hated lying to them. It wouldn't matter in a couple days anyway. He'd stay with them, maybe a week. Month, tops, if he were lucky. But, eventually, he would discover his mission, fight whatever battle God had lined up for him, and disappear forever. Then, their brother really would be dead and gone for good.

Why can't we just enjoy the time we have?

Michael wished he would have held onto own his brothers tighter when he had the chance. He cursed himself for the times he'd lied to Edward, the times he'd blown off hanging out with his older brother. Or the times he should have been watching out for Seth, but he'd shirked those responsibilities in favor of doing his own thing.

"What can I say?" He grinned and shrugged. "Yanks are terrible shots."

Edward laughed and Seth joined in after a moment's hesitation.

"It's been a year, though," Seth said, his amusement waning.

"Let it rest, man." Edward chuckled, slapping Seth on the arm. "He's back! Can't you be happy about that?"

Seth ground his teeth in a small smile.

Michael knew Seth's suspicions were not gone. *He shouldn't trust me. After all this time, I'm still lying to my brothers.*

He nearly confessed right then, until Edward pointed a finger in Sara's direction, winking. "Now you gotta tell me where you picked up this fine gal you've got here."

Sara smiled, looking uncomfortable, and tucked her hair behind her ears.

Michael grabbed her hand. "Sara…was one of the nurses who took care of me when I came to. She...she saved me."

Sara met his eyes, her discomfort fading. She beamed at him, glowing. He smiled, too. *I love her. I've got my girl, my brothers—this can work. I can make this work.*

"Aww," Edward said, a bit snarky. "How cute."

Michael felt his face flush and broke eye contact with Sara. He cleared his throat and turned his attention to Edward, getting down to business. "So, tell me. What are you up against? I saw those ships last night."

Edward's face hardened and he nodded. "Yeah, those rolled off the line in Detroit 'bout eight months back. Darndest things. We'd done figgered out how to fight against the tunnelers, so them Yanks took to the skies."

Michael had no clue what a "tunneler" was, but nodded anyway, playing along.

"So they're not aliens?" Sara asked.

Edward guffawed. "Not anymore. We chased those Bugs off our planet. Haven't seen one a'them around here in years. The gadgets they left behind came in real handy. You'd know it, though, that them Yanks in the government just wanted to use it to lord it over the rest of us. This country—now we've had our problems with each other—but we came together when it mattered most. But as soon as the politicians got their hands on that stuff...It wasn't all bad, don't get me wrong. We got running power in a lot of homes, now, and got some cures for diseases we didn't have before. But then they started in on these computing machines. Some kinda 'web' that connected the whole world. It's too fast too soon. It ain't even been three years, and now people are in everybody's business. Nothing's private anymore. Information is policed. Personal opinion can get you arrested."

"They're turning us into them," Seth said, his voice a low growl.

"What?" Sara said.

"*Bugs.*" Seth spat. "We're all linked together in one giant collective. The individual is disappearing. The commune is all that matters now. Believe what everyone else does, or you reap the consequences."

"What do you think the Secession is all *about*?" Edward said. "We unplugged. We ain't gonna be no hive-mind. We didn't fight for our freedom from the Bugs just to surrender it to our own government."

Sara said, "But how long do you think you'll be able to hold your ground, let alone win?"

"Not about winning," Edward said. "It's about making your stand for what you believe in. Winning's just a bonus."

"We're losing," Seth said. "Bad. No doubt about that. General Howard's got his egg heads trying to reverse engineer that crap, but nobody really thinks we'll have our own ships in time."

Sara looked to Michael and said, "Maybe that's why you're here."

Michael's heart hitched. His brothers stared at him.

"What's she talking about?" Edward asked. Seth stiffened beside him.

Sara's eyes went wide and her porcelain skin reddened in the cheek. "Uh, nothing."

"I want to join back up in the war," Michael said in a hurry.

Edward hopped to his feet, and clapped his hands. "Whoo-ee! We'll have them Yanks on the run, now!"

But Seth smoldered where he sat.

Michael studied him. "Got something on your mind, Seth?"

Edward stopped, mid-celebration, and faced his youngest brother. "What's the matter?"

Seth slowly rose, his hands reaching for a shotgun, but his eye never wavering from Michael and Sara. "Something 'bout this ain't right."

Michael tensed, and Sara took slow, firm grip of Michael's arm.

An explosion shook the earth. Loose dirt blew in through the tent flap, showering them. A whine split the air, followed by a second explosion.

"Yanks!" Edward shouted. He grabbed his rifle and rushed out of the tent. Seth was right behind him. "Come on, Mike!" he heard Edward shouting from outside, as the night sky lit up with reds and greens.

Michael jumped to his feet, ready to fight alongside his brothers. A hand touched him. Held him back. He realized it was Sara—he'd momentarily forgotten all about her, focused only on the battle ahead. Shooting bad guys with his brothers at his side.

When he faced her, she looked petrified, but determined. "What do we do?"

"Stay here," he said, trying to pull free.

"I want to go with you." Her voice shook. She flinched as another detonation rocked the ground. "What can I do to help?"

He stared at her, bewildered by her courage. But this wasn't the time for her to tag along. She was weak, and he had to protect her. "There's nothing you *can* do," he told her, slipping out of her grasp.

She looked frightened and confused, but he pushed that look out of his mind. It was time to do what he'd come to do.

Michael darted from the tent, a fresh shower of dirt bathing his face. He spat out soil bits, his eyes squinting against the dazzling light of the explosions. Two night raiders whizzed by overhead, the deafening noise of their engines ringing his ears like a bell. With each flyover, the pronged ships dropped death from above, leaving craters and corpses in their wake. Edward was ten paces ahead, trying to gather his men for a counterattack. Michael saw his brother yelling, but couldn't hear a thing.

Seth, a hothead even on *this* world it seemed, marched off from Edward's huddle and leveled his rifle at the Yankee death ships. The boy fired a shimmering red laser bolt. A tendril of smoke oozed from the bullet hole in the iron plating of the nearest ship. But the ship was unaffected. Michael smiled and shook his head at his brother's defiance.

Edward formed a firing line with the rest of his troops. The men fired, a volley of lit-up ammunition screaming through the night. Most of the rounds missed as the ship veered away from the fire, retaliating with a torrent of shots of its own. The line of men scattered in the midst of more pummeling blasts, but Edward was first to his feet.

"Form up again!" he commanded.

The men scurried side by side, and Michael joined them, taking a discarded rifle off the ground and aiming it at the Yankee ship. "Fire!" Edward hollered and the men obeyed without hesitation.

Even as they concentrated their attack on one ship, Michael turned his eye to the other. It was circling back around, aiming for their rear flank.

"Watch out!" he shouted as the second ship obliterated a swath of trees. Chunks of wooden debris spiraled for them, impaling some men while sending the others running in terror. Michael threw himself on Seth as a hail of shrapnel flew their way. Slivers of wood bounced off Michael's back, creating tiny slices in his already ruined coat and shirt. Once he was sure the devastation had ceased, he took a step back from his brother.

Seth just stared at him, mouth gaping open. "How did you—?"

"Come on!" Edward called his surviving men together. Wobbling and injured, the remaining squad mates formed up and fired again, just as the first flier zoomed overhead, close to the ground. At last, their shots hit their mark, perforating the underside of the passing ship. Smoke billowed from its belly, but the ship carried on, turning around for another nosedive.

"Keep firing! We almost got it!"

The men pulled triggers, sending their laser bolts across the horizon, pelting the mechanical menace. Finally, the ship juked away, trying to dodge the gunfire perhaps, before losing control and spinning sideways to the earth. Edward and his men ran for cover as the ship dug deep rivets in the ground, plowing through the soil.

"Out of the way!" Seth said.

The ship slid closer to them, exploding in a fireball, jettisoning chunks of armor plating in every direction. Michael hurled himself to the ground, narrowly dodging a twisted shard of flaming metal. It stuck in the ground inches from his face, and then all was calm for a blessed moment. Michael rose to his feet and saw that the ship had finally come to a stop.

Plumes of black smoke curled from the fallen flier, filling Michael's vision. His invulnerability spared him from hacking for air as he swatted at the thick fog, calling out for his brothers.

He found Seth, doubled over and coughing. Michael grabbed his arm. "You okay?"

Seth nodded, still struggling for breath. Michael left to find Edward, his Converse kicking up against a dead body. Another. Men who hadn't escaped the path of the crash in time.

"Edward?" He strained to see through the smoke. "Edward!"

"Here," his brother's familiar voice called out from the darkness.

Michael reached Edward. He was on the ground, wobbling on all fours. He helped Edward to his feet as another ball of green light slammed into the earth, denting it. Seth joined them and the three of them shook against the explosion.

"We're not gonna make it," Edward said through bloodied clenched teeth. Michael joined him in looking over the battlefield. Men were left, but they were worse for the wear, disorientated and wounded. "We gotta regroup. We can't take on one of 'em by ourselves."

"Get him inside," Michael told Seth. Then, turning to the field, he shouted to the injured Confederates, "Get inside! Go!"

Edward grasped Michael's sleeve. "What are you doing?"

Michael grinned. "I got this, big brother."

They stared at him until Michael shoved them forward. He turned and raced for the downed ship, then climbed its scorch-marked hull, ascending to the highest point of the metallic mountain. Pain prickled his mind—his warning sense—and Michael ducked instinctively as the second flier zipped above, the backdraft ruffling his hair and jacket. The ship fired and more retreating Confederates were consumed by red and green flame. Michael could hear their screams, even over the din of explosions. He watched, biding his time, as the ship circled back around for another strafing run.

Michael flexed his fingers, waiting for his moment. He held his breath as the ship descended and at the last second he jumped.

7

Sara hid at the far end of the tent, hunkering behind a cot. It was flimsy protection—flammable, at that—but she was too petrified to move. Once more she was in hell, hearing the screams, seeing the flames. She wished Michael were here by her side. He'd protect her. But right now the Confederate army needed him more. That was who he was—a hero. A savior. And not just hers. She didn't know how long it would take her to get used to that. To understand that Michael belonged to the entire multiverse, not just her.

But he does belong to me, she corrected herself. They had fallen in love, she was sure of it. He'd even asked her to marry him. *I refused.* How could she have been so blind? After everyone he'd met in the cosmos, all the daring things he'd done…He was godlike in his power, above the rest of humanity, set apart to be its protector. Yet, in spite of that, he had chosen to love her. Insignificant her with all of her faults and insecurities. How could she turn that kind of love away?

She hated Charlie and all that he'd done to her.

Seth and Edward rushed into the tent and Sara stood, heart beating furious. "Is it over? Where's Michael?"

"He's still out there," Edward panted, covered in soot. "Fighting off the last of them."

Despite knowing Michael couldn't be hurt, worry still gnawed at her stomach. As Seth helped Edward to sit on the edge of the cot, Sara pushed her way to the opening, gazing out at the night.

Her eyes scanned the battlefield, but she saw no sign of Michael. No sign of combat, either. The Confederates were hobbling away, carrying their wounded and dead. One remaining Yankee ship darted back and forth across the clearing, but not firing. Sara squinted against the darkness and glimpsed a shape on top of the ship.

Michael.

He was riding the ship, pulling back plates of steel. Sparks ignited from the tears in the ship's hull, highlighting the outline of his body. She gasped at the sight, cupping a hand over her mouth. Michael tore at the ship with his bare hands, unaffected by the flier's attempt to shake him off. Sara knew Michael would not lose. He was too strong, too determined.

I can trust him with my heart. He's here to take care of me.

She wouldn't run away from that.

8

Michael rent the hull of the ship as its pilot twirled the craft, side over side. He gasped, clutching the plating with his fingertips, gnashing his teeth in exertion.

"Hold…still…" he grunted.

From his vantage point on top of the spaceship, Michael could glimpse into the cockpit, where a human soldier in blue threw frightened looks in his direction. Michael grinned and waved. "Yeah," he called over the noise of rushing wind. "Still here."

The wide-eyed pilot yanked hard on the yoke, taking the flier higher into the sky. Michael slipped and bounced hard on the metal, rolling, sliding down, down, down. Clumsy fingers squeaked against the armor, desperately seeking a grip.

Higher the ship climbed, the air turning frigid and thin. Michael struggled to hold on, but his fingers felt like they had butter on their tips. His efforts proved useless and he simply slipped off, tumbling head over feet through the air in freefall.

Panic overtook him, quickly replaced by the knowledge that he would survive this fall. He had survived all the others. Once the fear of dying was removed, his rage filled the vacancy, surging through his limbs. He shut his eyes against the onslaught of whipping winds and drew upon his hate, his humiliation, and his desire for revenge. He felt buoyed by the power of his anger and opened his eyes to tiny black slits.

The ship, no doubt thinking it had rid itself of its unwanted passenger, had already crested and was now nosediving for the ground for its next attack. Michael bared his teeth, cold power swirling in his gut, and spread his arms out like wings, plummeting downward. His leather jacket billowed behind him, the velocity fraying the tears at the ends, and his long blond hair whipped about, lashing at his face. He worked hard to keep his eyes open against the rush of air. Thinking back to his favorite superhero comics back home, he gripped the flapping edges of his old leather jacket and felt the coat balloon, catching the powerful gale. Grinning with rebellious confidence, Michael zipped through the skies, cutting a path through the violent winds.

Below, he spotted the Yankee spaceship, coming closer and closer to his vision. He tugged on his coat and directed his fall towards the left. Once he had the ship lined up in his sights, he let go of the jacket and catapulted ahead like a bullet.

Timing was everything. Michael watched with predatory patience, as the ship righted itself and began its attack run. As it traveled, Michael took hold of the coat, once more, yanking hard, slowing his descent. Steering, he angled for the ship and landed, tucking his head into a roll. This time, powered by pure fury, he gripped the outer plates of the ship and pulled himself up. Inch by inch, he climbed horizontally, dragging himself to the cockpit. Peering inside, he saw the Yank firing on the camp below, oblivious that his death had finally come for him.

Michael roared, brought both hands up, and then down like a hammer on the cockpit. Glass cracked and the pilot looked up, suddenly terrified. Michael shouted again and pounced on the glass, finally breaking through. The Yankee pilot was screaming something and reaching for a pistol in a thigh holster. He pulled the gun free and fired point blank on Michael, but the bullets deflected off Michael's face and chest harmlessly.

The pilot paled, even as Michael reached down, gripped the man's head by both sides, and yanked with a *pop*. Once Michael let go, the pilot's twisted body slumped to the side and the ship lost control, listing to the left. Michael gripped the edge of the cockpit and rode the twirling ship like a beast. Proximity alarms blared, as he fought against inertia to haul himself inside the open cockpit.

9

Sara watched in stunned amazement as Michael disappeared inside the craft. The aimless ship headed toward the ground for a crash landing. At just the last second, however, the ship stabilized. Decelerated, then landed a moment later.

Michael climbed out of the busted-out cockpit, sweating and out of breath, but grinning. He jumped to the ground and casually walked toward her, his smile widening.

The battle was over.

Sara ran out of the tent, headed for her man from the stars. The man who had come to save her. Before he could say anything, she launched into him, kissing him passionately.

He did not hesitate in returning the kiss, clutching her tight.

They pulled apart, and Sara drank deeply of his eyes.

"Yes," she said, feeling fluttery.

His brow creased. "Yes?"

"My answer. It's yes. I'll marry you."

His frown softened into a smile and he kissed her again.

10

"I'm really proud of you, little brother," Edward said, standing in front of the mirror, adjusting the collar on his officer's uniform.

Following their victory against the Yanks yesterday, the Confederates had rolled into a nearby village and tended to their wounded. Advance scouts had reported that the Yanks were moving on for now, and Edward ordered his troops to take a little R&R. Like most towns in the Confederacy, very little of the Bug-tech was in use, Michael learned.

Nobody was "online" and Edward said electricity was used sparingly as a sign of solidarity for the cause. Michael was still getting used to a late twentieth century town with limited technology, but he'd seen stranger things in his travels. How this world operated was the least of his concerns.

With the war for independence from technology calmed down, it was the perfect time for a wedding. The local parish was very helpful—

especially after Michael retrieved a fistful of cash for the reverend. After that, the whole town was in the mood to help out, putting up streamers, decorating doorways with beautiful flowers. A celebration had come, banishing the war for at least one glorious day.

Michael sat across the room, in a rented brown wool suit, slipping into a pair of stiff and shiny shoes. They were hard and uncomfortable and he spared a moment to look longingly at his Converse sneakers, comfy and worn-in. After adjusting his feet, he stood, shifting his balance, trying to get a feel for his new footgear. Sighing in frustration and disgust, he crowded next to his brother, sharing the mirror in the back room of the small church that had taken them in.

"I look like an idiot."

Edward laughed and slapped him on the back. "Nah, you look fine." He elbowed him in the ribs. "Besides, no one will be looking at *you*. Trust me."

Michael grinned, thinking about Sara, nearly giddy at the thought of seeing her again. In a wedding dress, no less. On their wedding day. And *tonight*... He blushed and tugged at the collar of his formalwear, smiling to himself.

Edward exhaled, as though he'd been carrying a heavy load for a long walk. "Gotta say, Mike, you really did alright for yourself. You don't know how much I worried about you when you were a kid." He chuckled, walking away from the mirror to prop a boot on the arm of the chair Michael had previously occupied, giving his shoes a spit polish.

Michael watched him in the mirror, curious. "Really? You were worried about me?"

Edward laughed. "All the time. It was like you had this dark cloud following you, ever since you were little. Ever since Ma died. You were always so quiet and you had this look in your eye—"

"What look?"

The elder Morrison shrugged, growing quiet. "Just this mean look. Folks were scared of you. And you used to get these awful dreams. Remember those?"

Michael shook his head, forcing himself to remember that this wasn't his brother. That Edward wasn't talking about *him*, but about his double. Still, now that the conversation had started, Michael was more than a little curious about the Michael of this world. "No, I don't guess I do."

Edward rubbed his shoe, grinning. "Lord Almighty, you'd get these nightmares. Hollering at all hours of the night, talking about these monsters. You said they were all grey and nekkid and had no eyes or mouth and just these big fat—"

"Teeth," Michael finished, almost in a trance. At the very mention, he was twelve years old again, dreaming of Chelkan and the devils there.

Edward rose, surprised. "So you do remember?"

Michael's heart trembled. Had he and the Michael of this world experienced the same nightmare? What did that mean? "Just...bits and pieces, I guess."

His brother considered, then shrugged. "Pa was worried mightily about you, but then we joined the Secession and we had bigger things to worry about than bad dreams. Pa got killed shortly after that, and then *you*..."

Edward lingered, his saddened gaze turning to the window. Michael hung his head, unsure what to do.

"Edward, listen, I gotta tell you something."

"But that's all behind us," Edward barked, turning around. He was all smiles now, his arms spread wide. "We're a family again, and ain't nothing gonna tear us apart." He gripped Michael's arms, giving them a firm squeeze, beaming in pride. "Now let's go and get you hitched."

Michael relented with a grin.

11

Sara sat at the vanity in the parlor of the parsonage, as women she did not know busied around her, fluffing her dress and dabbing cake makeup on her face. She studied herself in the mirror, unaccustomed to seeing her hair done up in a bun, and her face beautified by cosmetics.

It was nice, but strange.

"You look lovely, dear," a woman named Miss Pearl, the church organist, cooed. She leaned over to apply blush on Sara's cheeks and nearly suffocated the young bride in her ample bosom. "That boy of yours won't know what to think!"

The other women of the church tittered and fussed as Sara sat in the midst of it all, numb. *I'm really doing this*, she thought. The dress was lovely—if not old-fashioned—and her entourage were more than kind.

And of course there was Michael, who was amazing. She loved him and there was no reason not to marry him.

And yet, she'd only known him for a matter of days. They were still finding out about each other, still learning to trust. *What are we doing getting married already?*

"You okay, dear?" Miss Pearl paused to stare at her, quizzical. "You look a bit peaked."

Sara reddened and tried to hide a nervous smile. "I'm fine. Just—"

Miss Pearl waved her off. "Cold feet." She winked. "It'll pass."

Sara tried to relax, but was unable. Torn between excitement and terror, she was doing her best to quell the rampaging beating of her heart, when the door opened behind her. From her place in front of the mirror, she spied a lean-cut young man in freshly pressed Confederate greys enter. His long, dark hair was slicked back, revealing his sharp, angular face.

She turned in her chair. "Seth?"

He gripped his hat in both hands, wringing the brim, and spoke without facing her directly. "They're...uh...ready."

Miss Pearl propped a chubby hand on her expansive hip. "Well, you tell those men we're *not.*"

Sara was suddenly grateful for Seth's presence and excused herself from the table, eager to be rid of the busybodies. "No, that's okay. I'm ready. I... I think, ha."

Miss Pearl and the others stepped back to behold their masterpiece as Sara stood. The plump organist was already tearing up. "Aren't you a picture. God bless you, dear. God bless you both."

"Thanks."

She stepped up to Seth and he, still stone-faced but flushing just a bit in his high, pronounced cheeks—extended a hooked arm. She gladly took it and the two of them left the parlor. Alone now, she leaned closer to him and whispered, "Thank you."

A sly grin cracked his otherwise stoic appearance. "Figured you needed a little rescuing."

They exited the house and walked across the lawn to the back door of the church. "Can I ask you somethin'?" Seth said, surprising her.

Caught off guard by the sudden question, Sara quickly said, "Of course. Anything."

Seth slowed in his walk, his brow furrowing. "He good to you?"

"Who? *Michael?*"

"Yeah."

"Oh, of course," she laughed, overjoyed. "He's the greatest."

But Seth chewed on his lip, uncertain.

She paused, inches from the church steps. "Why?"

"Nothing." He clenched his jaw and looked to his polished boots. "War does things to a man. It seemed to do worse to Michael. I…"

He seemed increasingly uncomfortable, almost heartsick, prompting Sara to gently rest her free hand against his arm. "Hey, no, your brother—" She hesitated, catching her error. "Michael is wonderful. He takes care of me."

Seth nodded, but still did not look at her. "Good. If he doesn't…" Now he faced her, his eyes full of promise. Of threat. "You tell *me*. Ya hear?"

She gaped at him, shivering inside, and had to giggle to shake loose his ominous tones. "I will," she said through a smirk. "Thanks for looking out for me."

He did not smile, but ascended the steps to the back door and beckoned for her. "Then I guess we've got a date to keep."

12

Miss Pearl played at the organ, bawling, as Sara walked down the aisle, Seth's arm intertwined with hers. Although he was wearing his uniform and had combed back his long hair, Michael still thought he looked like a little punk. He grinned, bemused.

Sara, on the other hand, was magnificent. She nearly glowed in her white dress, radiant. She watched him the entire time, unable to hide a sheepish grin, while Michael waited at the altar, hands clasped in nervous excitement. He'd conquered so much in his journeys—faced enemies that had destroyed planets—but here, in the presence of the girl about to be his wife, Michael felt weak in the knees with fear and joy and expectation. He'd only known her for mere days, but this seemed right. She was the One, he was sure of it. They fit, he understood. She was shy and he was brave. He was loud and she was quiet. She had bested him, cut through his invulnerability and pierced his heart. She was everything to him in that moment, and he'd moved the multiverse to be with her.

Edward stood at Michael's side, grinning like an idiot, the proudest big brother ever. Seth seemed tentatively happy, but there was a seriousness about him throughout the proceedings. Michael knew Seth didn't trust him, and he'd have to deal with that eventually.

But not today.

Seth let go of Sara and she walked to Michael, her head hung low, hiding a blush and an uncontrollable smile. Michael carefully slid his arm around her waist.

Reverend Goodson began, and Michael trembled. He could barely keep up with the preacher's words. The exchanging of vows blurred by as he happily pronounced, "I do" after her. He slipped a wedding ring on her finger, and she his. Michael looked at them—two simple white gold bands.

"I now pronounce you husband and wife. May God bless every one of your days together," the preacher announced. "You may kiss the bride."

Michael gingerly removed the veil and kissed his young wife.

In his mind, there was no multiverse. No redemptive quests for a distant God, no Rip and his blasted plans. No murder or death or fear—just Sara.

Just Sara.

The soldiers in attendance cheered.

Michael and Sara laughed as they ran out of the church and down the steps. A gauntlet of happy and recently wealthy townspeople threw rice at them.

It was perfect. The most perfect day ever.

At the end of the human tunnel, though, Michael glimpsed a strange figure, out of place with the festivities. The man wore a long, tattered coat over a hooded sweatshirt concealing his features. He stood across the street, watching. At first Michael dismissed the figure, then paused. Looked again.

The Hooded Man was gone.

Michael slowed, his smile fading. His stomach quaked. His mission. In all of this he'd all-but forgotten that he was here on God's dime. He had something to accomplish.

Sara clung to him, looking confused. "What is it?"

Something terrible grumbled in his gut. But he restrained it. *Not now,*

God. Not today.

"Nothing," Michael lied. "Come on. Let's go."

13

Michael carried Sara across the threshold of their room above the local saloon as evening fell. She laughed and held tighter to him. Edward had put the couple up for the night, even though Michael tried to tell him that wasn't necessary. He *was* rich after all, but Edward said it was a wedding gift.

"I haven't seen you for a year," his brother had beamed, then turned serious. "Let me do this."

Michael laid Sara on the bed and closed the door. When he turned, he saw her ready for him, propped up on her elbows, looking at him as though she were a lioness and he were a bloody rare steak. His heart picked up, and he his fingers tingled. He'd wanted to make love to her since he'd found her again. Wanted to touch her body, to explore every crest and dip. She was his now. And he was hers.

That night, the cosmos shook.

14

Michael and Sara lay in bed, wrapped only in sheets. Sara had her head on his chest, tracing the lines of the muscles on his abdomen. He stroked her tousled locks and listened to the soft ramble of the bar below. It reminded him of home, of the city. He always did like the sounds of the city after dark.

"What I can't figure out is why it's taken them so long to discover technology," Sara said.

"Think about it. Maybe the guy that invented one thing decided to shoe horses instead. Maybe the person who came up with another invention wasn't even born. Maybe they moved or their parents never met. One decision leads to a ripple effect that could totally change everything. Infinite possibilities in the multiverse, remember?" Michael chuckled, softly. "One time I was on an Earth that shot bubble guns and rode mechanical flying elephants."

Sara laughed, as Michael finished, "You just learn to roll with the punches."

"Does the alternate reality stuff ever drive you crazy?" she asked.

"How do you mean?"

"It's all so weird. Seeing people you know, but you don't know them. Have you ever met *me* before?"

He kissed the top of her head. "No. You're one of a kind."

"Oh? When we first met, you seemed like you'd seen me before."

Michael hesitated. "Well…uh…I mean, yeah. You were on my world."

Sara looked up. "Really? Wow, what was I like? Were we friends?"

"No." Michael said. "We passed a couple times in the hallway at school, but, no. We…never really talked. I had a huge crush on you, though."

Sara leaned back on his chest, snuggling in closer. "That is so funny. Why didn't you ever make a move on me? I'm sure I would have jumped at the chance to be your girlfriend."

"I…" Michael began.

She giggled. "I think I bumped into you once on my world. When I was still in school." She hid her face, drawling, "I may or may not have called you a jerk."

Michael laughed hard, holding her to him, feeling her body move against his.

"It's pretty funny," Sara said. "Can you believe it? Who would have thought that we would be lying here together, like this? Funny how life doesn't turn out at all like you thought it would."

"Yeah. I like the surprises, though."

"Me too."

Sara leaned up and they kissed, long and slow. Michael was ready for more, but Sara pulled away and studied his face. Tears formed in her eyes. "You are so amazing. You've been to all these worlds, done all these things, helped so many people…yet you love *me*. I just don't understand why you chose *me*."

He touched her face. "Because I saw you, Sara. That's all it took."

She gave his lips a quick peck, then nestled against his chest again. "How did you get this job?"

"Will there be no end to your questions?"

She snickered.

Michael said, "I guess it's about penance. I...I killed someone."

Sara didn't react to his confession. Her blind acceptance of him almost made him break down in tears right then.

"How old were you?" she asked.

"I was twelve."

Sara rose up, her eyes alert. "That's...unbelievable."

Michael frowned. "It was Rip's orders. He was the boss. He fed me and my brothers, gave us a place to live. When he gave you a job...you just had to do it. You didn't say no. Which, I guess, is why he was chosen to try to turn me to the Dark after I died..."

Sara laid her head back on him, hugging him close. "What was dying like?"

"Scary. I don't remember a lot of it. I just remember getting shot and waking up in a desert. Rip was there." Michael shuddered. "He gave me the whole bit about how I was chosen to be a warrior for Chaos or whatever. Said that I was special...that it was meant to be. I was supposed to destroy the multiverse."

"Wow. What did you do?"

"I told him no for the first time in my life." Michael paused, thinking about that moment when he'd taken charge of his destiny. "Then I killed him. After that, the Man in the Stetson took me in. Now I guess I kill people for him. It's ironic really. I always believed that God was loving, but I suppose even *he* has to draw the line somewhere. Maybe some people just need killing." He frowned, morose. "Maybe others are just made to be killers."

Sara grew quiet and still. Michael feared he'd said too much. "You've...killed a lot. Haven't you?" she asked.

"Yes."

"But they've all been bad people, right? Like Charlie? Have you ever killed a good person?"

Michael's heart fluttered, and he knew Sara would hear it, laying on his chest.

"Yes. Once."

"Who...Who was it?"

Michael sat up, rubbing at his eyes, feeling sick, and Sara rolled onto her back. "I don't really want to talk about it. It was a mistake. It still...it still follows me around, you know?"

Sara rose up and reached out for him. Kissed his shoulder. "Sorry. I didn't mean to—"

"No, it's okay. We're married now. I want to tell you everything, but…some things I'm just not ready to say yet."

"I understand."

15

Sara was fast asleep. Pale blue moonlight shone through the open window, bathing her perfect body. Michael couldn't sleep, so he sat beside her in bed. Watching her. Studying her. How had his life turned out so great? A week ago, this would have been impossible—just a bittersweet dream that did little to warm him on his lonely nights. Now it was wonderful reality.

Yet, he thought of the Hooded Man. His happiness was dampened by the inevitable. He would have to complete his mission, live up to his bargain with the Man in the Stetson.

But at least Sara will come with me when I leave.

Yeah, that sounded great.

His stomach cramped, coiling in his abdomen. Michael climbed out of bed, clutching his belly, tears building in his eyes from the agony. *He's here.* The pain eased, allowing him mobility again.

Michael dressed. Senses on high alert, he left Sara in bed and moved to the open window. Instinct told him the Hooded Man was close and his suspicions were confirmed with a single glance.

Down below, across the street, the Hooded Man watched him. Staring right into his eyes. Michael thought the man might have been older due to the white hair peeking out from his hood. But he couldn't make out better details in this light. The Hooded Man faded back into an alley, disappearing in shadows.

Michael set his teeth on edge. *No you don't.*

He cast one look at Sara, peacefully sleeping, oblivious to his call. She was an innocent in all of this and he was determined to keep her that way. He needed her that way. Needed something that wasn't tied up in his violent work.

I'll be back, he thought to her, then jumped from the window.

He landed on the dirt street below, kicking up a cloud of dust with his Converse sneakers. The only people still awake were staggering blind drunk out of the saloon, laughing and crowing. Michael ignored them and crossed the pathway to the alley. He slipped inside, finding comfort in the dark's cold embrace.

Michael skidded to a stop, eyes scanning his perimeter. The alley was empty. His stomach cramps were ever-present, a steady beat in his gut, keeping him focused on his task.

"Come out!" he shouted.

A scurry from behind. Michael whirled, fist raised.

Nothing.

His mind exploded with pain a brief moment before something connected with his back, shoving him to the dirt. Michael tumbled forward onto his face. Unscathed but royally hacked, he jumped to his feet.

The Hooded Man stood before him, hands in his pockets. His voice like a low grumble, he said, "Hi."

Michael reared back and threw a punch, but the Hooded Man stepped out of the way, hands still in pockets. Michael roared and charged again, but the Hooded Man held up his hands, in surrender. "Hey, hey, hey. I'm just here to talk."

"I don't like talking," Michael retorted, but he held off from attacking.

"It doesn't have to be this way," the Hooded Man said, low and even, like a snake poised to strike. "I'm here to give you the chance to come back."

Michael snarled. "Come back? Where?"

"Back where you belong. Back to the Rage."

Michael thought of the voice that spoke to him out of the Dark in the In-Between. *Welcome back...*

"I don't know what you're talking about."

"Don't you? Didn't Rip tell you?"

"Rip gave me some crap about destroying the multiverse, yeah. But then I shoved a knife in his heart."

The Hooded Man chuckled. "He deserved that. And worse. I guess I should be thanking you."

"I don't understand—"

"Michael, you can't keep running from It. The Rage has plans for you.

It needs you and you're not getting out that easy. You think you've got it good now, I get it. You're on God's payroll or whatever, and you've got your brothers and that svelte little redhead hanging onto your every word."

Michael tensed. "You stay away from her."

The Hooded Man raised a surrendering hand again. "I'm not here for her. I'm here for you. You've got a beast inside you, kid, and that's the Rage's property. It isn't going to just let one of Its attack dogs running around like a stray. You think you can just take a stroll through the In-Between and not catch Its attention? I've got my orders, just like you've got yours—but I came here, as a courtesy, to tell you to turn back now. Don't make this get ugly."

Michael eyed the man. The hood concealed most of his face, but something about that mouth was familiar. He supposed he could just smash this guy into pudding with his bare hands, but his curiosity won out. "Who are you?"

The man reached up and removed his hood. He was an older man, wrinkled and grey. Michael's parents had died before he'd known them, but Michael had seen a handful of pictures of his father…"D-Dad?" No, that wasn't right. The nose was different, and he was too old.

The Hooded Man laughed. "'Fraid not. Wow, do I really look that bad?"

"Who are you?" Michael asked again.

"I'm you." The man grinned. "Well, you know, a parallel you."

"No…"

"We've got a lot to talk about, and not a lot of time. But I need you to hear me out."

Michael had no words. Just stared numbly. He'd never encountered a copy of himself before, and it was jarring. Like looking into a mirror that had a mind of its own and talked back at you. It was disconcerting to the say the least, and weakened his mental grip on his own identity.

"Forget it. I'm not joining the Rage. No matter what you say to me. Maybe you made that decision, but I'm not you. I'm stronger."

The Hooded Man shook his head, chuckling softly. Patronizing. "Oh, man, I remember when I was your age. Full of hate. Self-righteousness. I felt untouchable, and I swore I would never give in. Never compromise. The ego of youth. But we all sell out, Michael, sooner or later. We lose ground, surrender our ideals, and little by little, we become the thing we never wanted to be: Adults."

Michael took a step back, clenching his fists. "Get out of my way."

"We've been looking for you for years, did you know that? But you've been a tough one to find. You're like a shadow, passing over the multiverse, cutting a bloody swath through 'evildoers'. But now look at you. You've lost your touch. A wife, surrogate brothers. The invincible boy is now just a mortal man. Now you've got something to lose. As long as they're in your life, they'll just be targets. I know, Michael. Better than most."

The Hooded Man nodded his chin towards the bedroom window where Sara slept. His black eyes glistened, growing wet. "I had a Sara of my own. We were married fifteen years. When we were first married, I used to watch her sleep. Do you do that?"

Michael remained silent.

"After a few years you quit doing that kind of thing. Marriage becomes routine. Ordinary. It loses that spark—that fire." The man looked to the ground, his face darkening, his voice hoarse. "It shouldn't be like that, though. You should never forget...If I had it all back..." Now the Hooded Man focused his deep black eyes on Michael's—their perfect reflection. "But the Rage used my love against me. Sara's our kryptonite, kid. It wants me to hurt your Sara, you know? It wants me to kill her, right in front of you. That's what the voices are telling me, but...I can't. Seeing her again has been...harder than expected."

Michael wanted to return to his bride, to defend her. But, as he stared at the older version of himself—so sad and lost—Michael felt only pity. And recognition.

"Please," the Hooded Man said. "Come with me. Once the Rage is done using you, you can come back for her. If you resist, they'll just keep coming for her until you give in. Learn from my mistake, man. If I'd only surrendered earlier, my Sara would still be alive. I could be with her right now."

"What does the Rage want with me?" Michael asked, panicked. "I didn't do anything."

"I told you. You're Its property. It just wants what belongs to It. You can't escape it, you can't deny it. It's your nature, Michael."

"I don't believe that."

"Look, I've seen you in action. I saw how you took down that ship last night. Pretty incredible stuff. Where do you think you got the power to do all of that?"

Michael said, "God. He protects me."

The Hooded Man waved him off, interrupting, "Yeah, yeah. He protects you. We all know about you. You're the one Michael that can't be hurt. The Hand is on you. But God keeps you *safe*. How you pulled apart that ship, though? That was Rage, man. Pure cold, empty Rage. It's inside you, giving you power. Admit it. All those guys you've killed over the years—you enjoyed it. Felt like you were feeding some beast, hiding deep in your belly, right? It's *Rage*, Michael."

Michael clenched his fist, his heart racing. "It...it doesn't matter. I get angry, maybe, but I work for God."

"Do you know how many Michaels I've talked to? On a billion worlds, in a billion realities, existing in an infinite stretch of alternate possibilities—I've met them all. Do you know what I've found? The Rage has called them all. Do you know how many resisted?"

Michael waited.

The Hooded Man leveled him with a withering glare. "*None*. Do you understand what I'm saying here? Every Michael that has ever, will ever exist, has given in. Sure, some held out longer than others, but the Rage has got a taste for the Michael Morrison model. I don't know why. Don't even know if there is a reason. But It's after us. All of us. And sooner or later, we all give in."

Michael felt his fate closing in. "I won't be like them," he said, detecting the quiver in his own voice. "I'll find a way."

"Why? What are you fighting for? Sara? I told you, you can keep her, as long as you do what you're told. Your 'brothers'? They're not even your brothers."

"Are they yours?"

The Hooded Man paused. "No, but I suppose your story starts with him. Their Michael died in battle on the planet Chelkan at the hands of a man—a good man—named Holstead. That Michael was killed the day the Rage called you. You were meant to be his replacement in the game."

"Why not you?"

"We all have our parts to play. I came in too late. I'm not a fighter. I'm just here to explain. I'm here to do Rip's job, after you killed him. The

Maestro has this all planned."

"Maestro?" Michael's stomach swelled with anguish, just at the mention of the name.

"He's worse than anything you know, anything you've encountered. This is all a symphony to him, Michael. You're just an instrument. Play along, get it?"

With each revelation, he felt somehow whole. This sounded right to him, however wrong it really was. But he owed everything to the Man in the Stetson. That was what was right. But what was his mission? The Hooded Man? Hearing him tell these terrible things about his own dark destiny? Why would God bring him to this planet, to face these things?

This is a test, Michael thought. The warm realization pushed out the temptation. "No," he said. "I won't come with you. Tell the Rage he doesn't own me."

Michael stepped past his aged double, feeling stronger somehow. "Don't come looking for me," Michael said. "Or next time we won't just be talking."

The Hooded Man called after him, "You can't run forever, kid. It's *in* you. How can you escape what you are?"

Michael ignored him and headed back into the saloon. For his room. For his wife.

16

Despite the things he'd learned about himself—or rather his parallel selves—from the Hooded Man, Michael slept surprisingly well. He'd made a stand against the Rage...though it settled heavy in his soul knowing that the Rage had found him after all this time. No doubt the Beast in the Void would send another errand boy to convert him. But he'd be better prepared next time. He had Sara now, and he would keep her safe from whoever or whatever was stupid enough to threaten her as a means of controlling him. He had overthrown kingdoms, rerouted the course of worlds—he could protect one girl.

Confident, he considered the case closed. He'd accomplished his mission, he had withstood his test, and soon they'd be leaving. The rift waited for them at the shack out in the woods, but Michael wasn't ready to leave just yet. This was his honeymoon and he'd enjoy it, just a while longer.

Sara woke up none the wiser about Michael's late-night conversation with his double. Around noon, they finally got dressed and stepped out of the saloon, still cuddling and snickering. Michael didn't believe he'd ever smiled so much in his entire life.

Some of the soldiers in Edward's regiment milled about the town, enjoying their semi-vacation, but so far Michael had not spotted either Edward or Seth. He decided he'd catch up with them later, but right now he wanted to spend the day with his girl.

Last night with Sara was...well—

"What are *you* smiling about?"

Michael glanced up quickly and caught her sizing him up, a sly grin on her lips. He felt a little flushed. "What?"

She combed a lock of hair over her ear, smiling demurely, as they passed by the small shoppes along the boardwalk. "I don't know, you just have this big goofy grin on your face all of a sudden."

He paused in their tour and took her by the hand, twirling her like a music box ballerina. "I was just thinking of how perfect everything is."

She laughed in his arms, stealing a small kiss.

Once they parted, she surveyed the stores. "Where to now?"

"I dunno. What do you want to see?"

"Everything!"

He chuckled and gripped her hand, feeling it slip perfectly into his. "You gotta pace yourself."

Sara held on tight and leaned on his arm, laying her head on his shoulder. The two of them strolled down the clapboard sidewalk, passing by villagers. "I guess you're too cool for sightseeing, huh?"

"To tell you the truth, I never stopped long enough to look."

Her hair smelled so wonderful. Her body against his was *right*. Perfect.

"You should," she replied.

Kissing the top of her head, he brightened. "Yeah. Maybe you're right."

She let go of his hand and stood in front of him, a new sense of excitement dawning on her smooth features. "Okay! A game!"

He cocked an eyebrow, amused by her enthusiastic outburst. "What kind of game?"

"Our worlds were so different, but there's got to be *something* we have in common. What was your world like? What did people do for fun?"

"I dunno. What people normally do, I guess. Mess around, get into trouble."

"What about music? What was your favorite band?"

Michael considered. "Ever hear of Metallica?"

Sara pressed her lips into a thin line, her eyebrows rising, until she finally exploded in laughter. "Seriously? That's a real name? What is that?"

"It's heavy metal. It's big. Well, at least it was when I left. Who knows what people are listening to now back on my world." They resumed their walk, and Michael settled into the conversation. "What did you listen to?"

"Did you have Fluber Pixie on your world?"

Now it was Michael's turn for a belly laugh. "*No.*"

Sara pouted. "Shoot. That's a shame. But not surprising. They were underrated on my world too."

"What kind of music is it?"

"Pan flute!"

"Oh, man, really? Pan flute? I don't even know if I know what that is."

"No way. All the best musicians play it."

"What about electric guitar?"

Sara squinted, uncertain. "Yeah…that's around. But, only losers play *it.*"

Michael shook his head. "Your world sounds terrible."

She repaid his snark with a slap to the arm. "Quiet, you."

"Okay, okay, what about movies. Did you have *Boyz n the Hood?*"

Sara frowned. "No. Did you have *Crestfallen Love?*"

"Nope."

She snapped her fingers, gnashing her teeth. "How about books?" Stopping stock still, she took desperate hold of his arms, her eyes saucer-shaped with shock. "Please tell me you have Robert Henry's *Alan Worth: Space Explorer* novels."

He winced. "Sorry. Never heard of it. We had Superman comics, though. He went in space sometimes. Does that count?"

Sara's shoulders slacked and her expression dropped, as though someone had taken a needle to her balloon. "That's sad. I loved reading *Alan Worth.* I used to get into so much trouble reading it in the middle of Coach Seevers' class—"

"Hey!" Michael shouted, smiling wide, startling Sara. "I had Coach Seevers, too!"

She eyed him, suspicious. "You're making fun of me."

"No, I'm not!" He laughed. "He was bald and had a—"

"Bushy mustache?"

"Yes!"

The two shared in a moment of mirth, before Sara said, "Of all the things to have in common."

"I'm telling you," Michael said, wrapping an arm around her as they resumed their afternoon stroll. "The multiverse is a crazy place."

17

The two of them explored the entire village, going in and out of every shoppe. Sara demonstrated the need to handle nearly every knick knack, gabbing excitedly about each discovery.

Michael had simply watched her, unable to remove the smile from his face. The day passed too quickly for him, and finally the lovers retired to the hotel, ready to spend the night together.

Tomorrow we'll leave. He just didn't know how he was going to break it to his brothers. Maybe that's why he hadn't tried so hard to find them today…

Michael closed the door to their room and Sara took a small bag towards the bathroom. "Now wait here," she said, her cheeks reddening, even as she smiled. "I'll be right back."

She gave him one last flirtatious look then disappeared into the bathroom, no doubt slipping into the something she'd bought that day. She'd made a big deal out of making Michael stand outside while she went into the store to buy a special surprise for their second night as a married couple. Michael had protested, but only half-heartedly, excited by any surprise Sara wanted to give him.

While he waited, he leapt onto the bed, the spring coils creaking slightly, and relaxed. Michael decided to have a surprise of his own waiting for his new bride, and stripped out of his clothes before crawling back under the covers. After a moment, the bathroom door opened, and he watched, nearly salivating, anxious to see what she was wearing—but even more anxious to liberate her from its silky clutches.

Sara stepped out in a lavender silk nightie, its frilled hem reaching her mid-thigh. Low cut, the top left little to the imagination, her freckled bosom full and swelled with excitement.

Michael sat up straighter in the bed. "Wow."

Her lips spread into a full smile, but she did not blush this time. "You like it?"

He only nodded as she sauntered over to him, gently rocking her hips side to side. She stood just out of arm's reach, and put her hands on her waist. "What do *you* got?"

Michael snarled, sprang forward, and grabbed her. He pulled her back into the bed in a flurry of kisses and tickles and she kicked and screamed and laughed. Their hysterics melted into soft kisses that burned hotter and hotter. Her fingers dug into his back and he cupped her leg, pulling her closer to him. She moaned in delight, as his lips kissed a path down her neck, to her collarbone, and beyond—

Then there was a knock at the door.

Michael kept kissing, but Sara's body stiffened.

A knock again.

"Ignore it," Michael said, pulling at the straps on her lingerie with his teeth.

"It's Seth," the muffled voice said from the other side of the door. He sounded agitated.

Michael got up and jumped back into his jeans. Sara reddened and disappeared inside the bathroom.

Grumbling, Michael answered the door, without bothering to put on his shirt. "Seth? What's wrong?"

The young man looked haggard, his hatchet-shaped face dark and grim. In his hands he handled two rifles by the barrel. "It's Edward."

"Is he okay?"

"He's missing. He told one of the others he got an urgent message, out past Billy Goat Gruff. It ain't like him to run off without me. Or at least tellin' me. Not after everything we've been through. Somethin's wrong. You got my back on this one?"

Michael hurried to the bed to put on his sneakers. His stomach started rumbling, slowly beginning to tense, just as it had in the presence of the Hooded Man.

Sara came out of the bathroom, fully dressed again, but barefoot. She looked concerned.

"I gotta go," he said in a rush.

Her brow crumpled, forming that knot just above her left eye. "Now?"

"It's Edward. He needs my help."

"Okay." She slumped, leaning against the bathroom doorframe, all her previous playfulness drained from her face. "I'll be...here."

Michael gave her a quick kiss, then slipped on a shirt and his leather jacket. "Let's head out," he told Seth.

"Michael?" Sara asked quietly.

He turned to her, his heart hammering at the thought of what trouble Edward had stumbled into. "Yeah?"

"Is it always going to be like this?"

Hesitating, he asked, "Like what?"

"With you always running off to save the day and me staying behind?"

"It's safer here."

She bit her lip. "Michael, you saved me from one tower. Don't put me in another."

He nodded. "It won't always be like this," he said. "I'll be back."

Sara's lips flickered in a failed attempt to smile. Michael took the rifle that Seth offered him, and left.

Sorry, Sara.

18

Michael stepped through the forest, rifle in hand. He rarely used a gun on his journeys, as they reminded him of the corner card shark he'd executed. It was silly, really—he'd killed scores since then, with his bare hands and with other instruments of destruction. But a gun just felt dirtier somehow. Still, the rifle in his hand seemed natural. Even more natural was the knowledge that he was out here with his brother, at his back, on a quest together. He was still determined to leave tomorrow, just in case the Hooded Man was still keeping tabs on him, but he had to see that his brothers were safe first. He owed them that—or, at least, he hoped someone would do the same for his real brothers back home.

"How far is it?" Michael asked.

He heard Seth's rifle cock. Felt a quarter-sized object pressed to his back. "That's far enough."

Michael held onto his rifle, pivoting slowly to face his brother. "What are you doing?" he asked, uncertain why his warning sense hadn't pinged.

"You're not my brother," Seth said through bared teeth, his eye keenly looking through the iron sights. "My brother died. I know…" The kid took a deep breath, his voice hitching. "'Cause I killed 'im, m'self."

Michael held his ground, unsure of what to say.

Seth gripped his rifle tighter. "Edward doesn't know. He always thought well of Mike. But he didn't know our brother…not like I did. Our brother was cruel. He killed Pa and blamed the Yanks and he…" Seth didn't sob, but Michael heard the emotion in his voice. "He hurt women."

"You're right," Michael said. "I'm not your brother. Your brother is dead."

"It's what he deserved," Seth said with difficulty. "But you don't seem like him."

"I'm not," Michael said. "But Edward. We need to find—"

"Edward is fine. I just told you that to get you out here, alone. Where we could talk. So talk." He juked the gun toward Michael for emphasis.

Michael considered all the lies he could tell, but not a one of them made any sort of sense. Heck, the truth wasn't much saner, but Seth deserved that much. "I'm from another dimension. Sara, too. I'm on a…sort of a mission. I'm trying to help people. Sara and I are just passing through. We don't want any trouble." Thinking of his own brothers, Michael fought down a well of regret and heartache. "You and Edward…you were on my world, too. We were on our own. You were the only family I ever had. I haven't seen you both in years and I just…I missed you. That's all."

Seth grimaced. "This ain't possible. You…you're like an alien? Like a Bug?"

"*No*," Michael quickly corrected. "Not like a Bug. They came from…*up*. I guess you could say I'm an alien, but I came from *over*. The dimension next door."

"Edward hasn't shut up about you," Seth nearly interrupted. "He keeps talking about how things are going to be now. How happy we'll be and how we'll stay a family this time. But you're not sticking around for any of that, are you?"

"I can't," Michael said. "I'm sorry. It was selfish—"

"You're right it was. What am I supposed to tell him when you up 'n leave?"

"I don't know."

At last Seth lowered his rifle, but his hard face still simmered. "Get out. Go back to wherever you came from. You stay any longer, it's just gonna make it harder on him."

"Seth—"

"You're not our brother," Seth said, and stormed off, rifle in hand.

Michael watched him go for a minute, but decided it couldn't end like this. He had to say something, to mend fences. He reached out, his mind already trying to work out a way to communicate what he was feeling when—

A pain split his stomach like an invisible blade. His mission! Danger, on a terrible scale, was at hand! It was the Hooded Man. He was making good on his threat—

"Sara!"

Seth was back at Michael's side in an instant, concern etched on his face. "What's the matter with you?"

"I've gotta get back!"

19

Sara stood by the window of their room, watching life carry on below, feeling a strange, unsettling sense of déjà vu.

She wondered where Michael had gone. What daring venture he was carrying out right now. It was a strange sensation—his job was danger, and she'd never have to worry if he'd come home to her or not. But, oh she longed to be out there with him. To be a part of the adventure, just like in the *Alan Worth: Space Explorer* novels she used to read growing up.

But Michael's words echoed in her mind, stinging. *"There's nothing you can do."*

He was right, of course. She didn't have a fraction of his incredible powers. She wasn't even especially clever. *Just ordinary.* She frowned.

A high-pitched whine cut through her thoughts and she recognized it a second before—

FWOOM!

Red and green fire plummeted from the heavens, engulfing the drug store down the block in flames. It exploded, lighting up the midnight sky. Sara shrieked and sheltered her face. Removing her hands, slowly, she spotted the villagers panic and race for cover, as the sickly-colored lights consumed more of the town. An explosion across the street blew Sara backwards onto the hardwood floor. She scrambled as the saloon quaked. She screamed, expecting the building to collapse beneath her.

Where are you, Michael?

The door to her room burst open. A man stood there, backed by the fearful patrons escaping down the stairs. He had on a long, tattered coat that looked like its edges had been dipped in mud. Under that he wore a dark hooded sweatshirt, the hood pulled over his head and concealing his eyes. But she saw his mouth. Knew him.

"Michael!"

He stepped in and extended a hand. "Quick. Come with me."

His voice sounded strange. Older, and somehow sadder too. She took his hand and looked up, under the hood. "No," she breathed, seeing wrinkles around his black eyes. His blond hair, white. This wasn't right. He was Michael, but…"What happened?"

"No time to explain." He gingerly cupped the small of her back. "We have to hurry."

She hesitated at first, but his familiar eyes…She trusted him.

He guided her down the stairs, through the evacuating customers. With each blast outside, dust shook loose from the rafters, snowing on their heads. They neared the front doors behind a dancer and her admirer. Red laser cut a path through the street in front of the saloon, vaporizing the couple instantly.

Michael pulled her back in an instant, sparing her from the same fate. Once the death ray passed, he pushed her forward. "Hurry!"

Sara entered the streets, saw the bodies caught in the explosions. Men, women…

Oh no. Miss Pearl…

She sobbed, crackling fire eating the village alive. "Why is this happening?" She turned to Michael for an answer.

He removed his hood and surveyed every direction. His face was hard as stone, devoid of the warmth that Michael usually possessed. "It didn't have to be this way," he said, not looking at her.

She wanted to ask him what he meant, but he ushered her down an alley, away from the heat and flames. At last they reached the edge of the village, but Sara couldn't shut out the screams and cries for help.

"Go." He shoved her forward. "Wherever your rift is, head back there. Run, and don't look back."

She clung to him, uncertain. "No, wait. Who are you? Where's Michael?"

"He'll…he'll come around soon. Just go, Sara. Be safe."

Sara took a tentative step back. Her heart felt for this man—just as it did her husband—and she wanted to heal him. He turned to leave, but stopped. Stepped closer to her. Took her chin in his callused hands and drank of her eyes.

"I…" he began.

Sara thought—feared—that he might kiss her.

He flinched and looked away. Shaking his head as if inhaling a whiff of smelling salts, he took a step in retreat, looking composed again. Gently he took her hand. Kissed it. "Good-bye, Sara."

Sara staggered away when another bomb blast rocked the ground.

"*Go!*" he roared.

This time, Sara did not hesitate. She ran for the woods, praying Michael would find her soon.

20

Michael and Seth entered the village. They'd seen the lights some distance off, and Michael knew what he'd find. Knew it wouldn't be pretty.

But what he saw was so much worse.

Seth remained unfazed, his eyes cold and focused. Detached. No doubt he was pushing the terrible sight out of his mind to get the job done. "It's the Yanks," he growled, pointing to the forked flier zipping by, still firing on the people below. "But why? This isn't like them."

Michael knew. It was *him*. The Hooded Man was behind this attack. That's what the quiver in his stomach told him.

And if that were true— *This is all my fault. I refused to join him. This is his retaliation.*

People were dying all around, for no other reason than that they had offered Michael and Sara a place to stay. They had welcomed them, celebrated their wedding. *We were just passing through*, he thought. *This town didn't have anything to do with any of this.* He would make good on his promise to the Hooded Man. He'd find him, and he'd kill him.

"Seth!" Edward shouted, a small band of dirtied troops following behind. They raced forward, rifles in hand. "Where've you two *been*?" he snapped, his voice cracking slightly, and Michael found he had no answer to give him.

Another green explosion. The saloon detonated into a plume of debris.

"*Sara!*" Michael screamed. A thousand tiny snapshots of his short time with Sara blurred behind his eyes. He saw her laughing, crying, the times she looked so deeply into his eyes. The way she smelled, the way she kissed. Her hand in his…

He pushed past the men. "*No!* I have to save her!"

Edward grabbed his arm, pulling him back from the fiery remains. "She's not in there! We just came from there looking for you! She's out, brother. She got away."

His anguish quieted, but now he felt only anxiety. "Where did she go?"

"I don't know," Edward said. "But we got other problems right now."

"Right," Michael said, taking control of his wild emotions. Glowering, he faced the flying ship. Cold rage spread throughout his veins, filling him with power. He closed his eyes, relishing the rush. Emboldened by it. Then his eyes shot open, startled by the depth of his hate.

"You've got a beast inside you, kid, and that's the Rage's property." The Hooded Man's words haunted him, and now Michael knew it to be true. He had a monster buried deep within. Sara soothed it, but now, thinking of all the ways he would punish the Hooded Man for this atrocity, Michael understood that the monster had never left. Maybe it would always be with him.

But I can *control it. Use it to do good. I…I have to.*

"Form a line," Edward commanded. The men fell into rank, aiming their rifles. Michael joined in. He had half a mind to climb a building and leap on the ship during its next pass—that had worked before. But the few buildings left standing were unstable.

"Fire!" Edward shouted, and Michael did.

Super-heated rounds shot out from their line of rifles, scorching the ship. It curled up in the sky, looped, then came back down. Aimed right at them.

The men reloaded and took aim. Dazzling red and green shot out from the ship, punching holes in the dirt road, carving a path towards the soldiers.

"Fire!" Seth shouted.

"No!" Edward corrected. "Move!"

Seth fired anyway, impulsive as ever, even in the face of death, and Michael tackled him to the ground, out of the way of the blast. Edward made it, too, but most of the other men didn't. They ignited in flames, their screams silenced.

"We've gotta run for it!" Edward said. He stood and reached out to Michael and Seth.

"No!" Seth roared, pulling from his grip.

"We've lost this one! We've gotta regroup!"

"I can stop it," Michael said, though he didn't know how yet.

"I'm not losing you." Edward took Michael by the arms, shaking him. "We just gotcha, little brother."

Michael closed his eyes. "I'm not your brother."

When he opened them again, Edward looked as though someone had stabbed him in the heart. "W-What?"

A gun shot rang out and Edward flinched, then slumped forward in Michael's arms.

"Edward?" Michael said, a sob choking him.

Seth pointed down the street. "There!"

Michael looked up. Saw the smoking rifle.

The Hooded Man.

"I'll kill you!" Seth took off after the man, just as the assassin ducked out of sight.

"Seth, wait!" Michael shouted, but it was too late. He carefully laid Edward in the dirt. Edward was still gasping for breath, blood pumping from the wound in his back.

"Mike..." he whispered.

"I'm sorry," Michael wept. "I'm sorry for all of this. This is all my fault."

The light in Edward's eyes darkened and his head lolled to the side. Sobs shook Michael, but he pushed them aside. He'd cry later.

Right now, he had some killing to do.

He glared up at the skies, watched the ship nosediving to strafe again. Michael stood in the middle of the street, spreading his arms wide, rifle in hand.

"Come on!" he screamed. "Do it!"

The vaporizing death rays splashed against him, but Michael still stood. Smoke cleared and he aimed his rifle, the ship bearing down on him, as if to ram. Michael stood steady. Lined up his shot. Glimpsed the pilot in the cockpit. Sneered. "Hey, there."

And fired.

The Yank pilot's head turned to red pulp and the ship dropped instantly, skidding through the dirt, clipping the edges of buildings, bringing this village to its final demise. At last, its descent slowed, as the ship stopped inches from Michael's shoes. This town's nightmare was over.

But now he had a score to settle.

21

Michael kept the gun. He didn't know why. He certainly didn't need it, but it felt right somehow. He'd killed plenty in his time fighting against the Dark, but he wasn't just looking to kill tonight. Killing was clean— didn't require emotion. In fact, it was easier to kill without it. But tonight, he was out to murder. Murder needed hate, and Michael had plenty to spare.

He slipped between the remaining buildings, nearing the edge of town where Seth had chased the Hooded Man. He listened for any sign of combat, but heard nothing. Even the prickling in his mind did little to guide him, only pulsing steady.

"Come out!" Michael shouted into the night.

To his surprise, a trembling voice called back, "You think I wanted to do this?"

Ice cold rage surged through Michael's limbs, honing his focus. He looked for the Hooded Man in the trees. Nothing.

The Hooded Man called out again, raw emotion in his voice. "I didn't want this! You brought this on yourself! You've got to see what's inside you, Michael! If you won't choose to see it, then I'll make you see it! Even if I have to kill all of them, you're going to let it out!"

There! Michael detected the ruffle of the Hooded Man's coat. Roaring, he rose to fire, but halted just as he spotted his brother. Seth struggled in the grip of the Hooded Man, his nose bloodied.

"Seth!"

"Take the shot!" Seth shouted. Michael lined up the sights, his trigger finger itching.

"Please, Michael," said the Hooded Man. "I don't want to do this anymore. You can make me stop. Just give in."

"I'll make you stop," Michael said, baring his teeth.

Seth slammed his head back into the Hooded Man's nose and slipped out of his grip. The Hooded Man stumbled, and Michael didn't hesitate. He fired a laser bolt, right into the Hooded Man's chest.

The killer collapsed backwards on the grass, coughing up blood. Michael moved to his brother.

"Okay?"

Seth nodded, wiping at the crimson on his lip with the back of his hand.

Michael stood over his counterpart. His hood had fallen back and Michael looked upon his mirror image. Michael hated that face. All the misery the man who wore it had created. That man was capable of such wickedness. Tears welled up in Michael's eyes, threatening to undo his anger.

Seth approached, his words shaky. "Mike…it's you. Another one…"

Michael dropped the rifle and climbed on top of the Hooded Man, gripping him by the collar. "Where is she? What did you do with Sara?"

The Hooded Man grinned, not smug, but at rest. "She's…safe. Waiting for you, back at the rift. I-I knew it would come to this. That you'd kill me and leave this place…But it didn't have to be that way. We might have been friends."

Michael didn't know how to respond, but felt his fury melting away.

"You didn't really think I'd hurt her…did you?" the Hooded Man said. "I love her…My Master won't be pleased but…she's our kryptonite, Michael."

The Hooded Man hacked, gurgling against his own blood. Struggling, he spoke, "You can't run from it, kid. I was just the messenger…the Rage has something else in mind to make you submit. It's…worse than you know."

"I'm not giving in," Michael declared, but in his heart he worried. How many Michaels had fallen, all with those same defiant words on their lips?

All of them.

"In that case…when you finally meet the Rage…face to face." the Hooded Man coughed again, his skin turning to marble. "Kick Its a—"

The Hooded Man fell silent. Dead.

22

Michael and Seth buried Edward at dawn. It was an unremarkable grave, off the beaten path. Seth fashioned a wooden cross as a marker and the two stood in silence over the mound of fresh earth, neither one speaking for a long time.

When at last they did speak, it was Seth who said, "You and the girl headin' out?"

Michael nodded, wanting desperately to put his arms around the young man who could have been his brother. But these weren't his brothers. He'd used them. Now Edward was dead and Seth was alone in the world. At sixteen. It wasn't right. Michael had no one to blame but himself.

Michael slipped his hands in his jean pockets. "Yeah. We—"

"Th'sooner, th'better. Wouldn't you say?" Seth hoisted up the shovel, shuffling as though he were readying to leave.

"I'm sorry," Michael feebly offered, but he knew that wouldn't have been enough for his Seth back home, so his words were sure to ring hollow in this dimension as well.

Seth kept his eyes on Edward's grave a moment more, then broke from his stoniness to address Michael. "You're cursed, brother," he said. It sounded less a condemnation than a forlorn resignation.

"I don't believe in curses," Michael said. God was with him—he'd already beaten the odds and withstood the Rage's lure this long. Now that he had Sara, a constant reminder of the good person he could be, Michael was ready to endure for the long haul.

"All right, I gotta take off," Seth said. "The Yanks won't stay quiet for long."

"Take care of yourself," said Michael.

Seth didn't return the sentiment, instead shouldering the shovel and walking away from the grave without so much as a good-bye.

Michael opened his mouth to call out to him, then promptly closed it. He took one last look at Edward's grave, wondering what *his* Edward was doing these days and hoping he and Seth had found some small measure of happiness. With that done, he left the burial site behind.

Up ahead, Sara waited at the edge of the clearing, a light in the darkness.

"You okay?" she asked as he approached. She took his hand in hers.

He felt at home in her touch. "I'll be okay."

Michael and Sara headed back to the shack they'd stumbled upon when they first arrived on this world. The sun shone beautiful and nature sang as wonderfully as it had that day before they'd been taken to Edward's camp. Yet, this time, Michael did not appreciate the beauty. Now it was a dagger in his back.

They came to the piece of paper that was the space-time rift. In a few moments, they'd leave this blasted place in their rearview mirror…but the things he'd faced here, the things he'd learned…Michael couldn't shake them.

His double had killed Edward because Michael hadn't accepted who he was. The Hooded Man's words ran on repeat in Michael's mind. *"You can't run."*

But Michael resolved to do just that. *I'm a hero. I'm not a monster like the Rage wants me to be. I won't be like that.*

The Hooded Man told him that every Michael was just "like that"— they just needed the right push. Maybe Seth was right. Maybe Michael was cursed. Was he really capable of killing his own brother, just as the Hooded Man had done? And all for what? For the Rage? For some stupid destiny?

It scared him to think that he could lose himself like that—that he could fall so far.

Sara brushed the hair out of her face, and stepped to the edge of the paper. When she faced him, she asked, "You ready?"

Seeing her, he remembered what he'd done to another girl named Sara Theresea once upon a time, and understood that maybe he was more like that other Michael than he'd ever care to admit.

There is *a monster inside me…*

The paper waited for him on the grass, and Michael was more than ready to leave. Eager to put one more world between him and the Rage.

You won't catch me.

"Yeah. Let's get out of here."

Sara brushed her fingertips against his. "I love you, Michael."

He wanted to force a smile for her sake, but couldn't. Instead he interlocked their fingers and brought her hand to his lips. "I love you."

She pulled him into a side hug, still respectful of the space he needed, and he put one foot on the rift, instantly pulled in.

You won't catch me…

PART FOUR: MONSTER

1

Twin suns sparkled over the choppy violet waters of Ruggashosh. A lone sailing vessel with sails of pure light stuck out toward the horizon, traversing the waves. The fish-faced Ruggashoshos scurried about the deck in a panic, pronged staffs of crackling green energy in their hands.

The captain, a burly fish no more than a meter tall like most adults of his species, burbled in barely contained hysteria through a ring-shaped filtration device that pumped salt water through his gills. "What will we do, Red-Haired-Scaleless-Fish?" His language was anything but human, but Sara understood enough after three weeks among this strange society to roughly translate his next words. "We're all going to die!"

"He's going to make it. Trust us." She hoped her assurances calmed him.

Sara and her husband had grown to love the Ruggashoshos, their culture, their timid lives. They were a hard-working people of the purple ocean, with large breathtakingly beautiful and complex cities below the surface of the water, she was told, though had never seen herself. They were simple harvesters and miners, burrowing deep into the ocean floor for food and rare minerals.

Until the day their digging awoke something dark and ancient.

In a few short years, the Ruggashoshos' civilization had crumbled. In fear, they fled to the surface, trying to survive on the land. But, even with the water-breathing apparatus, they were dying off. Becoming extinct.

Then a simple piece of paper landed on their world, bringing with it a savior.

Even if not all of the Ruggashoshos believed in such things.

"All is lost," the captain gargled resignedly and clomped across the deck, his crew shuffling to the sides, looking into the murky water below. One of the fish-men shouted and pointed. The others crammed against him, nearly pushing him over the railing into the sea, straining to get a look. Sara rushed too, her heart filling with worry.

Michael had been underwater for a very long time and, though she knew "drowning" was on the long list of things he was immune to, she feared for him all the same. Only a part of her realized that if he ever did die, she'd be stranded on whatever planet or alternate reality they happened to be stationed on at the time.

The boat rocked violently, and the crew jostled with a scream. Some crashed to the deck, one toppled overboard. Sara braced herself on the railing as the captain ordered his men to retrieve the splashing sailor. They hollered orders to one another, organizing the rescue attempt.

Sara stood back and watched, feeling out of place and useless—a feeling she was all-too-familiar with. With each new adventure, Michael had some grand mission to accomplish. Some villain to vanquish, some war to wage. Sara, though, found herself more and more pushed to the sidelines. She wanted to do something, be of some help to Michael in his quest. But she wasn't like him. She was mortal.

But I'm with him for a reason. I've got to believe that. There's got to be something I can do to help.

As she pondered this, the boat tilted to the side once more and a giant explosion ignited behind her. The surf slapped against the deck and a tall, black shape rose out of the water, blocking out the suns. Deckhands screamed and ran for cover. A tremendous shriek filled the air, bringing Sara to her knees. She clenched her teeth, pressing hands to ears to block out the shrill whine, and forced herself to look up, up, up into the dragon face of the sea serpent.

Water rained down from the humongous creature, washing against the deck, carrying sailors over the edge into the sea. Screams of terror and confusion mixed with the monster's cry. Sara was tossed to and fro by the rampaging Ruggashoshos. She stumbled, falling to the floor. A heartbeat later, the slender tentacles dangling from the leviathan's undercarriage writhed and slapped against the boat. Floor, mast, and cabin turned to splinters and shot in every direction, impaling some of the crew. Sara gasped and shielded her face away from the carnage. The captain was barking something, orders or perhaps just telling his men to jump ship and save themselves. Sara couldn't translate in this chaos.

The beast jerked and twisted in the air, fighting against something. Sara heard the distinct sound of "Wahoo!" over the monster's roars.

Michael!

Sara squinted up at the beast's head and saw her husband there, clinging to the thing's protruding snout horn. Michael was barely hanging on, but had a look of utter euphoria on his thin face.

He loved this part.

Tentacles crippled the aft of the boat as the leviathan blindly flailed, trying to dislodge the strange leather-jacketed scaleless-fish on its nose, but Michael kept a firm grip, punching the thing's face repeatedly with his free hand.

Ruggashoshos abandoned ship left and right, but Sara remained standing, watching in awe as her husband fought against a creature a hundred times his size. She wondered what she'd have to do to be remarkable like that.

The captain tugged at her pants-leg and she looked down to see him gesturing to the boat's edge, gargling something vaguely familiar. She thought he was saying *Run*.

A hellish screech assaulted her ears, blurring her vision with pain. Sara stumbled but did not run. She had to stay with Michael, though knew she was no use to him. But it made her feel better to be near him, to let him know that he wasn't in this on his own. And just in case something wonderful happened and *she* could save the day for once.

Michael rode the lurching beast, until the thing jerked its head upward, sending him pinwheeling high into the air.

Sara screamed, watching in dumbstruck horror as the leviathan opened its jaws and Michael fell straight into its mouth.

"No!" she wailed, rushing for the monster's tentacles. To do what? She wanted to climb the tentacles, working her way to the monster's mouth and go down after her husband. But she couldn't.

She didn't have the power.

The captain pulled her back, his small frame little more than a nuisance. Sara fought against tears, reaching out for her husband. "Michael! Michael!"

The beast cawed and snapped, then with a jerk, it coughed and spat bile. Like a falling tower, it collapsed against the boat, halving its frame. Sara and the captain slid across the upended deck and splashed into the water. Sara struggled for breath, swimming back towards the wreckage.

The leviathan lay spasming on a large piece of driftwood, snorted once, then stilled. Sara and the overboard crew held their collective breaths, waiting for the beast to rise up and strike again.

The thing opened its maw, eliciting murmurs and gasps from the Ruggashoshos. But Sara grinned wide.

Michael stood inside, his Converse sneakers standing firm on the thing's tongue, his arms holding up the dead beast's jaw. He was covered in black bile, and his smile beamed all the whiter.

"Your monster's dead," he called out, as though he'd just fixed an appliance. "Try not to wake another one."

Cheers erupted from the bobbing crew. The creature was slain. The Ruggashoshos could return to their underwater domain. Rebuild their world.

Sara caught Michael's attention and the two shared a warm look.

The day was saved, that look said.

Sara knew they'd be leaving this world shortly. Off to fight another battle. Or rather, he would fight. She'd just watch.

Again.

2

After saying their farewells to the Ruggashoshos and gathering in their backpacks what little belongings they had, Sara and Michael returned to the rift and stepped inside.

Once more, Sara experienced the familiar pull, slipping through the In-Between to another world. A bright flash of color momentarily blinded her. It felt like tumbling through a tunnel of rainbow-colored light, terrifying and exhilarating. When she opened her eyes, she was standing on a darkened street, in the rain. A moment later, the adrenaline and fear of the rift jump faded, and Sara all but forgot the time she had spent in the light.

There was always a certain sense of trepidation whenever Sara emerged from the rift. Perhaps it was because her first jump four months ago had landed her in the middle of a warzone. Michael had told her at the time that was just a bad draw. It turned out he was right. Most times, they materialized in the middle of any ordinary day, but Sara was always waiting for some alien or monster to pop up.

A heavy rain drenched them as Sara took stock of their new environment. She and Michael seemed to be on the Main Street of a small town, but there wasn't a soul in sight. In fact, only one store on the strip was even lit—a hardware store—with an old muddy chocolate-colored truck parked out front on the curb. As quaint as the town was, when backlit by crackling lightning it looked fairly ominous.

Coming to a new world was often startling—doubly so given the fact the last world they'd been to had talking fish and was covered almost entirely in purple oceans. But after three weeks on Ruggashosh, they were back on Earth, though a parallel version of it, and Sara had to readjust to a world of streets and cars and *humans*.

Though there were no humans around at the moment.

Michael stood at her side doing what he always did, listening with his senses, detecting if there were a problem nearby. Sara knew her husband well enough to know he'd be itching for another fight soon, still riding high after defeating the leviathan. Michael thrived on hitting things, even more so since they encountered that other Michael—the Hooded Man—some months back.

Michael spoke little of that encounter. It bothered him for reasons Sara could only guess. Since then, he'd thrown himself into his work even more, if such a thing were possible. Always fighting, but not the foes they'd encountered. No, his enemy—his real enemy, the one he *wanted* to be hurting—seemed to be out of Michael's reach. Sara had no idea who that "real enemy" might be. She wasn't even sure Michael was aware of it or how driven he had become since facing his other self.

She worried about him. But he'd open up to her when he was ready. He usually did.

"It's raining," she said with a smirk.

"Brilliant deduction." He led her to the open store with one finger to his temple and concentrating.

"Picking up something?"

"I don't know…Maybe."

"Pretty soon into a jump, isn't it?"

"I'm not in charge of these things, Sara," he said. But something distracted him.

The light in the store ahead went dark and a man emerged, wearing a coat and cap that provided little shelter from the downpour. Hunkered over, he worked at the door—locking it, Sara assumed—then rounded to the parked truck.

"Hey!" Michael called out in the rain. "Think you can help us?"

The man jumped, a peal of thunder chasing Michael's words. As they neared him the man's eyes widened. After spotting them crossing the street his way, his eyes darted over his shoulder, to the side. Sara wondered what he was so jumpy about.

"Hey," Michael said, softer this time, as they approached.

"What are you two doing out so late?" the man asked. He looked to be middle aged, with a craggy, though handsome face. Weathered, like he'd had a life of hard work. "It's not safe."

"Our car broke down," Michael lied effortlessly. "We got caught out in the rain. Think you can give us a lift?"

The man seemed to calm, his features softening. "Sure, sure. Of course. Name's Tom."

He quickly extended a hand and Michael shook it. "I'm Michael. This is Sara. Thanks, we really appreciate it."

Tom kept a lookout, but waved them to his truck. "Come on, we'd better get going. You'll catch your death out here."

He opened the driver's side door and Michael and Sara climbed in, scooting to the other end of the leather bench seat to make room for their host. Tom started up the truck, and pulled away, giving the Morrisons an impromptu tour of the town. Calling it a "town", however, was generous. It was only a few simple neighborhoods, one hanging stop light, a gas station, post office, and school. By the looks of the tractors parked in driveways where cars usually were, and the grain bins dotting the flat fields, they were in a farming community. The single street that split the town in two was deserted thanks to the rain, giving the place a creepy vibe. Sara wasn't one for being creeped-out. Michael could certainly kill anything that jumped out at them from the shadows, but she couldn't deny a certain sense of foreboding, as though eyes were watching her.

"Where is everybody?" Sara asked.

Tom kept both hands on the wheels, his gaze intense and watchful.

"Must be the storm. Rain keeps the folks in." In a hurry, he blurted, "You kids new in town?"

"Yeah," Michael said, still distracted.

Sara wondered if he were getting one of his premonitions. If so, it could only be a headache—a sign of minor danger. If Michael were receiving his mission, he'd be doubled over in agony right now. She appreciated God trying to get her husband's attention, to alert him to the next step in their forever quest, but she didn't know why the Almighty couldn't have been gentler with his "signs." More than once, she just wished God would leave her husband alone. *Hasn't he done enough for you?* But Michael rarely complained about his cross to bear.

Tom took his eyes off the road for a fraction of an instant, flicking them in the couple's direction. "You staying long? Or just passing through?"

"Not sure yet," Michael said, eyeing the night passing on the other side of his window.

"Where would you like me to drop you off?"

Michael scanned the horizon. "Right there. We're staying there."

Sara looked ahead and spotted a cheap motel. It'd feel good to get out of the rain, take a warm shower, and change into dry clothes.

The deluge began to subside as Tom pulled into the parking lot. Michael and Sara got out on their side.

Tom leaned over before they closed the door. His look was serious. "Better stay inside 'til morning," he said, his tone casual, but strange-sounding too. "Might start storming again. Stay inside, get warm. All right?"

Sara nodded. Michael said, "Thanks. Will do."

Tom did not smile as Michael closed the door.

"Well," Michael said as he watched Tom drive off, leaving the two of them behind in the motel parking lot.

"Was it just me or was that weird?"

Michael massaged his temple, his dark eyes watching the night.

"What is it?" she asked.

"Mm…can't tell. It feels like there's something, but…"

"Where's it coming from?"

He looked to her. "Everywhere."

She slipped her hand in his. "Come on. Let's get inside. We'll tackle it in the morning." Sara led him to the motel, aching for a good night's sleep curled up in Michael's arms.

3

Tom drove on, a shard of lightning filling his rear view mirror. His hands tensed around the steering wheel, his mind still on those kids he gave a ride. Where had they come from? What were they doing out on the streets at night? Didn't they know better? No, no, they were new. They'd said that. Just moved here.

But it's not safe.

He should've warned them. He'd tried in his own feeble way, but he should have done more. If anything happened to them on account of him…

The swinging traffic light turned red and Tom pulled his truck to a full stop. He'd lost track of time in the store. He should've been home by now, before the rain started. He just wanted to get home.

The red light stared him down, and Tom considered running it. Not even the cops were out at night. There'd be no one to stop him. He let off the brake, just as a bright flash ballooned in front of his truck. The front tires lifted off the ground then collapsed back on the pavement with groaning metal.

"No," he mumbled. "No, no, no."

Something else exploded behind him, spinning the back end of the truck sideways, knocking his old door loose. Tom toppled out of the truck, scuttling on the pavement, fearing the truck would soon explode. A ring of fire formed around him and the truck, pinning him in place.

"No!" he shouted. "Stop!"

"What did you tell them?" a voice asked as a figure materialized on the other side of the flames. The dark shape's eyes glowed red.

"Nothing!" Tom fell to his knees.

"I don't trust you."

"Stop this! You can't do this—"

"Can't I?" the figure asked, raising a hand, palm out and fingers splayed.

Tom whimpered. "No, please, no…"

170

White-hot light shot out from the hand before Tom shielded his face Intense heat blanketed him.

Then darkness.

4

Come home, little brother...

Michael floats in empty space again, In-Between the worlds. But there is something out there in the Black that growls for him to return. To lose himself in the Void, to become a vessel for the Rage.

Come home...

Suddenly, his feet slowly touch down on broken concrete and the blackness of the Void retreats, revealing a devastated cityscape. Michael knows he's back on Chelkan—the planet of his childhood nightmares that he's never set foot on, but still instinctively remembers. This is the planet where his predecessor met his end.

Rainbow-colored lights undulate from the ruined fortress in the distance, lulling him near. Michael steps toward it, wanting so desperately to be embraced by the lights. To know their mysteries and lose himself to oblivion. He steps over the rubble and strewn bodies, reaching out for the light.

Come home...

The shadows come alive and the strange charcoal beasts with no eyes or nose and only those too-wide mouths of dulled teeth lumber out of their hiding places. The creatures clack their giant spear-shaped limbs against the shattered stone, stampeding for Michael. At first, he hesitates, terrified of the size of their army.

"Don't be afraid," a voice tells him.

Michael peers through the uncountable masses of grey beasts and spots his predecessor. The other Michael with white-blond hair and that spot of black blood painting his stomach. The other Michael crosses his arm and smirks. "They're waitin' for you," he says in a thick Southern drawl. "They need a general. They need you. Isn't it 'bout time you took your place with 'em?"

Michael steps back, away from his mirror image and the legion of beasts that clamor for him. They reach out to him, beseeching him to join them. "No…No, I won't…"

"S'alright," his double says. "Take yer time. We'll be here waitin' when you change your mind. And, believe me…You will."

5

Michael gasped and sat up in the waking world, morning light peeking in through the drawn curtains. Out of breath and shivering with fear, he combed back the loose blond hair that had fallen in his face.

The nightmare again. He'd been having it since his encounter with the Hooded Man, but it'd been a couple weeks since he'd suffered it last. Michael lay back on his pillow, regulating his breathing, savoring the fact that he was here, safe in the motel room and not in the In-Between as in his nightmares or on Chelkan where some dark and unknown destiny awaited. When at last the terrors of his fearful dreams subsided, he sat up, more slowly this time, and looked around the room.

As far as motels go, it wasn't too bad. Of course, they could stay in the most expensive, luxurious hotel, given his divinely unlimited cash flow. But his conscience wouldn't let him. Not with the way his brother worked day and night just to keep food on the table. It seemed a betrayal to Edward somehow.

"Sara?" he called out when he did not immediately see her, his voice a raw croak. He glanced at the nightstand by the bed, where a neatly handwritten note on motel stationery informed him that his wife had gone to gather breakfast for the both of them. A pang of worry nagged at him— not out of any divine warning—just Michael's growing concern for Sara. As they got adjusted to married life in the multiverse, Sara was becoming braver. She'd asked him once before not to lock her in a tower, and he'd tried his best to make good on that request even though he feared for her every time she left his sight. He'd not feared anything for five long years, but Sara had changed everything.

Michael forced himself to relax as he slid to the end of the bed and scrounged for the remote. The bits of images and programs that fluttered as he channel-surfed helped to distract his thoughts from lingering on Sara. She was a big girl. He had to start trusting her more. But, in many ways, she was his heart. The Hooded Man had said it himself—Sara was kryptonite. She made him *human*. If something ever happened to her…

Michael came upon a movie that caught his interest. It was grainy footage, but depicted a costumed superhero type—like right out of a comic book—battling some overseas terrorists. The lead hero stepped into view, dressed in a trimmed-down jumpsuit made of flexible sculpted multi-colored rubber. On his hands, strange mechanical gauntlets. Huge, cumbersome things that hissed with steam and whirred with gears. They covered his forearms and hands, glowing bright red as superheated metal. Exhaust vents kept the things cool, and the glow dimmed to a hot orange.

The hero blasted at gun-toting enemies, giant beams of bright white light igniting from the palms of his gloves, catapulting the terrorists back. It was rather impressive, even by Michael's standards. Then the footage switched to a reporter, commenting on the battle and that's when Michael realized—

He was watching the news.

This was live coverage. This was happening, right across the globe.

Pain raked his mind with cold fingers and Michael dropped the remote, clutching his brow. The reporter held her microphone up to the hero— Light Sphere—asking him questions, but Michael couldn't hear the answers. Just the whine, needling through his awareness. Light Sphere, blond, blue-eyed, All-American, nodded and smiled at the camera.

Michael glowered at the figure, the source of his distress. What did Light Sphere have to do with this little backwater town?

He switched off the TV, hoping it would end the migraine. He wondered what was taking Sara so long.

Michael liked sprinkled donuts.

Sara was useless in a fight but prided herself on being there for her husband after the job was done. It wasn't a glamorous role, but one that she knew she could accomplish and accomplish well. After his daring battle with the Ruggashosh Leviathan, Sara set her mind to walk two blocks down from their motel and score some sprinkled donuts for her man as a reward. It was strange getting accustomed to an "Earth-world" after so long in various alien cultures, and she couldn't quite liken it to coming home, since her home had been just as alien to this type of Earth—Michael's type—as the Ruggashoshos' were to hers. But at least people here spoke the same language and ate similar foods.

Clutching the simple white bag that contained their breakfast pastries, Sara walked back to the motel. It was a humid day, even at this early hour, and her clothes stuck against her body. The town was alive this morning— a stark contrast to the ghost town it had been the night before. People drove to work, honking hellos to each other. Shops were open all down Main Street. Sara stopped by Tom's hardware store to thank him once again for helping them out, but his sign still read CLOSED. She frowned and continued walking.

Overhead a high-pitched squeal grew louder, shortly followed by a boom. Sara squeaked in fright as the ground shook. Everyone on the streets froze and looked up. She joined them and saw a man flying in the sky dressed in black and red with a cape. Another explosion detonated in the air next to the flying man and he stopped. Something on his hands— or *was* it his hands?—glimmered with pink energy and he fired back. Three more costumed people, two men and a woman, flew into sight and dodged his blast. One of them hurled a crackling ball of energy, emitting the same high-pitched sound Sara had heard before. It exploded with a distant boom, nearly hitting the black-and-red costumed man before he flew off. The three figures gave chase, trading more shots in the air as the sounds of their struggle faded over the horizon.

Sara gaped at the scene, trying to process what she'd just seen. She looked to the others around her, hoping for some explanation, but now that the strange sight had passed, the people lowered their eyes and carried on about their lives—completely unbothered as though they'd just seen a near car collision on the road.

Sara picked up her pace and hurried back to Michael. He'd need to know about this.

As she reached the motel she spotted a boy her age, taping a Missing Persons poster to the inside glass of the motel office. He was a bit tall, built lean, and fair-headed—his hair short, curly, and almost stark white. The guy looked lost and desperate, and Sara momentarily forgot about comic book characters. He exited the motel, nearly stumbling into Sara.

"Oh," he said, shaken. He held a small stack of more posters. "Sorry."

"Hi," she said. "You okay?"

The boy looked at her, as though confused as to why she'd addressed him. He eyed her up and down, his brow knit together.

"Are you looking for someone?"

"My dad," he said. Then he awkwardly retrieved the top flier from the stack for Sara.

Sara took the paper. Froze.

It was Tom.

"This is your dad?"

"Yeah, why? You know him?"

"I...I met him last night. He gave us a ride in the rain."

The boy's eyes darkened. "He didn't come home last night."

Sara glanced to the motel. Saw the manager tear the poster off the glass, crumple it up, then shake a disapproving glare at the back of the boy's head. The man walked off and Sara thought him incredibly rude. Redirecting her attention to the boy, she said, "I'm sorry. He seems like a really nice man. Your dad."

"Thanks." He smiled, looking more like a frown. "Nobody in this town wants to help, though. Everybody here is so afraid. They won't say anything. The cops think he just took off or something, but I know the truth."

Sara bit her lip, concentrating. It seemed she had stumbled upon their mission ahead of her husband. It was refreshing. "The truth about what?"

The boy looked over his shoulder. "Ah, it's better not to talk about it out in the open like this." Then he looked at her, his eyes softening. "Maybe we could...go somewhere. Talk about it over dinner?"

Did he just make a move on me?

Sara blushed, combing her hair over her ears. She was flattered, but incredibly uncomfortable. She grinned, her heart fluttering. "I..."

7

Michael paced the motel room, waiting for his wife to return, when an invisible fist slammed into his stomach and folded him over. He dropped to his knees, clutching the bed covers beside him, and gnashed his teeth. His insides were on fire; his guts felt like they were exploding. He clenched his jaw, trying to will the pain away—to think through it. Finally he could stand, his legs numb and tingly. Something was wrong. Like, Big Mission wrong. And where was Sara?

His misery dimmed to an ache now, like a radar, and he followed the leading to the window. Pulled back the blinds. Outside, he saw Sara smiling bashfully, tucking her hair behind her ear. She was blushing and talking to...

Some boy.

Jealousy churned inside Michael and he felt an all-too familiar frigid rage envelope him. Forming a tight fist, he stormed out of the room.

"Hey," he said, approaching the two, trying his best to keep his anger in check. He'd rather just hit the kid. Break his teeth out.

Sara jumped, grinning sheepishly. "Hey!"

The boy regarded Michael in surprise.

"Michael, this is Chris Thompson," said Sara.

Chris held out a hand, gawkily. "Uh, hey, guy."

Michael didn't take it. "What are you doing out here?" he asked Sara.

"We were just talking," she said, tittering nervously. "Chris is looking for his dad."

For a split second, Michael almost said "So?" but relented. God had pulled his mission trigger—this kid was his mission. He had to help. Sara handed Michael a flier.

"Look," she said, her words full of meaning. "It's Tom."

Michael studied the paper, his anger slowly dissolving. *Tom.* "Sorry to hear that," he said and meant it. "What happened?"

"I don't know," Chris replied. "He just didn't come home."

Michael thought back to the previous night—the storm. He had sensed danger *everywhere*. The same sensation he felt when he saw that Light Sphere dude on the TV. What did it mean?

As he mulled it over, he caught Chris' eyes returning to Sara, staring at her. Michael's ears burnt red. The kid was thin with a pouty face, like he moped a lot. He had intense, beady little eyes and gave off waves of co-dependency. With his hunched-over shoulders, he seemed the type of kid who'd talk bad about himself in public in the hopes that those in his company would shower him with praise to boost his ego. Michael hated guys like that.

Or maybe the kid wasn't like that at all. Maybe Michael just didn't like him ogling his woman. Nevertheless, it wasn't his job to pick the assignment. That was up to the Man in the Stetson. Michael was just a grunt, doing what he was told. *Always have been*, he thought sourly. *Maybe I always will be.*

That's why the Rage wants me.

Michael shoved aside the thought. The Rage couldn't have him. He'd keep running across the multiverse with Sara at his side and the Thing in the In-Between would never find him.

For now, he had to focus on the task at hand—finding this kid's dad. It seemed like a cakewalk compared to the last job, and maybe that unsettled him more. Nothing came easy in rift jumping.

When is my life gonna belong to me?

"So…" Chris began. A little hope filled his voice. "You guys brother and sister?"

Michael's gut told him he was here to watch out for this guy, but the obvious look of lust in the teenager's eyes was not going to fly. Michael was determined to set the little loverboy straight right there. "N—"

"Yeah," Sara cut in, beaming anxiously. "Something like that."

Michael glared at her in disbelief.

"I'd better head off to school," Chris said. "You guys are coming, right?"

"No," Michael said, flatly.

"Of course," Sara said at the same time.

"Okay. See you there." Chris gave a little half-wave and was off with a spring in his step.

"What are you doing?" Michael hissed.

"Don't you think you were a little rude?"

"Brother and sister? What was that?"

Sara shrugged, a quizzical expression on her porcelain face, as though the answer were obvious. "He wanted to tell me what was going on in town. I think…I think he kinda likes me."

"Yeah." Michael seethed. "I caught that."

She rolled her eyes. "Anyway, we had to gain his trust and I figured he would trust me more if he knew that we weren't married."

Michael sulked. "Whatever. I still think that was pretty rotten, though."

Sara led the way to their motel room. "There's something else, too," she said. "I think some people have super powers on this world."

"Yeah. I discovered."

"That's gotta mean something, right?"

"I don't know, Sara."

She scratched at her chin, thinking out loud. "Maybe we can get one of them to help us find Chris' dad."

Michael stopped her with a laugh. "Since when did you become the leader, anyway? I thought *I* was the superhero in this family?"

He was only half-serious, but when Sara paused, a real look of hurt and embarrassment crossed her face. He wished he'd not said anything.

"I was just trying to help," she muttered. "You do all the work and I just stand by and watch and occasionally scream. I want you to know that I've got your back. I'm part of the team."

Michael grinned. He stepped in closer, holding her. "Hey," he whispered. "You help tons."

"I do?" Her crystal eyes dazzled back at him.

"Sure. You…" he trailed off, realizing that she didn't really do anything. But that wasn't true. There was one thing she did do that he needed maybe more than a hand in the battlefield. "You love me. That's more than I could ask for."

She turned away, blushing, before giving him a quick hug. Then she held out the white bag. "Plus I get the donuts."

"Sprinkles?"

"Who loves you?" She winked.

"Thanks," he said. He dug into the bag.

"Better eat fast," she chimed, disappearing into their room ahead of him. "We've got to get ready for school."

He froze, half of a glorious sprinkled donut crumbling in his mouth. "Say wha—?"

8

In his time as a rift jumper, Michael Morrison had faced the four-eyed Glegortha of Dranax, fought back the Cult of the Onyx Forever, and thwarted the machinations of a parallel—and cybernetically-enhanced—Adolf Hitler and the mutated goat-men of the Third Reich.

None of those guys had filled him with the same terror as setting foot on the front steps of the local high school.

Sara bounced on her toes to his right, her eyes widening at the brick building, her attention drawn to all the students heading inside. "Wow," she whispered. "This is great."

Michael frowned. "Are you sure this is necessary?"

"Look, Chris is your mission, right? We've got to protect him. Find out what happened to Tom."

"I know, I know." He sighed.

"The best way is to stick with him. Take classes with him. Get to know him."

Michael was about to suggest that Sara have fun with that while he stayed at the motel, but then he thought of Chris eye-groping his wife and considered again. "Fine."

Seeing the school brought back waves of painful memories, suffusing Michael with hot dread. He hadn't seen the inside of a school since...well, not since he murdered...

Now I'm back.

No. It's not the same school. You can do this.

"Let's go!" Sara squealed in delight, taking Michael's hand and racing up the steps.

He trailed behind with the sense that he was being dragged into the very jaws of hell.

9

Michael waited outside the office while Sara signed up for classes. He'd already gotten his schedule and his books, though he'd stuffed the latter in his new locker where he imagined they'd spend the entirety of his short-lived high school career.

While he waited, he glimpsed Sara through the glass, collecting her things and talking excitedly with the office workers. He and Sara had given the school some bogus story about moving into town with their dad. They'd lied and said their records from their previous school were in the mail. They gave the motel as their address and phone number, hoping the secretary wouldn't notice the difference or start asking too many questions. God must have been on his side because the flimsy story had held strong for now.

Kids his own age passed him in the hall, whispering amongst themselves while looking Michael's way. He hated those stares. They reminded him of all the looks he got at his old school. Nothing had ever made him feel so insignificant, so unwanted. Five years of rift jumping—of fighting monsters and saving worlds—gave him purpose and identity. He was above school and all of its ugliness, but now...Now he was right back here in this hellhole. Dealing with cliques and snobs and selfishness and insecurities. It was already starting to have an effect on him as he thought of Sara spending any amount of time with Chris, all in the name of their mission. Chris had that "woe is me" thing going that teenage girls thought was terribly deep and romantic.

Michael knew. He'd worked that angle himself.

Would Sara be drawn into that? After all, she'd gone with Michael when he was in a dark, emotionally vulnerable place.

The whole ordeal made him feel sweaty and twitchy. He was ready to leave this crap-fest. Get back to hitting giant robots and flying laser-armed pterodactyls. Back to the fantastic and away from all of this... ordinary.

Sara stepped into the hall, her arms loaded down with books.

"Here," Michael said, taking them for her. She slipped them into his arms, getting a strange nostalgic look in her eyes.

"Thanks." She blushed.

"Don't mention it."

"So!" she said, waving her schedule exuberantly. "What classes did you get?"

He tucked her books under one arm and used his free hand to retrieve the crumpled schedule from his jeans pocket. Sara compared it to her crisp copy. "Oh, we've only got two classes together. Bummer. Oh! We share lunch! We can sit together!"

"Wonderful," he said, his voice a low growl.

"Come on." She play-slapped him on the chest. "This is gonna be easy. We get to just be normal seventeen-year-olds for a jump. How hard can that be?"

Despite his grumpiness, Michael smiled at his wife's enthusiasm. He hadn't seen her this happy in...Come to think of it, he didn't know if he'd ever seen her this happy. *Isn't she happy with me?*

He wanted to talk to her about it, only mildly aware that that was such a mopey teenage thing to do, when the bell rang.

Sara screeched in glee, leaned over to give him a sisterly kiss on the cheek and grabbed her books from him. She raced down the hall, joining the throng of students. "I'm gonna be late for class! Have a great time!"

Michael slumped towards his first class in five years, convinced that he would *not* have a great time. He entered the din of chatty teenagers settling in, unable to dodge their curious stares or suspicious whispers. The teacher, a slight and mildly attractive young woman, spotted him almost instantly.

"Michael?" she asked, looking back over a clipboard in her hand. "Michael Morrison?"

"Yeah?"

She sized him up. "Where are your books?"

A couple snickers accompanied the question and he glanced down at his empty hands. "In my locker."

More giggles. A murmur rose as the students leaned across aisles, whispering to neighbors.

The teacher stiffened and took a deep breath. Her lips formed a tight line. At last she spoke in a slow, controlled tone, "I don't know what things were like at your old school, but here, I expect you to bring your books to class."

Michael nodded just to get her to shut up, and took a seat in the very back, slouching in his chair. His eye caught two shaggy-haired youths, doing their best to grow in facial hair. One wore a pair of amber-colored Ray Ban sunglasses that would have been antiquated in Michael's own time. The other was the shorter of the duo, his face covered in acne. Both guys gave Michael the thumbs-up, grinning like goofs. Apparently his disregard for his education met their approval. It looked like they were trying to whisper something at him, but he ignored them. Laid his head on the desk.

Went to sleep.

10

"Dude!" Sunglasses shouted, catching up with Michael after class. "New kid, what's up?"

Michael grimaced. "Nothing." He kept walking.

Sunglasses and Pimples hurried along. "Hey, man, what's your name?"

"Michael."

"I'm Dack," Sunglasses said. "This is PJ."

Michael barely nodded, continuing his walk, searching the halls for Sara or Chris.

"PJ and me were gonna have a party at my house tonight. My mom's out of town, seeing her boyfriend for the next couple nights. You wanna head over? It's gonna rock."

"I don't know," Michael said, trying to think of something to say to get these guys off his back. He wasn't here to make friends. "Might be busy."

"Yeah, yeah, that's cool, man. You think about it, all right?"

"Sure."

"Awesome. Later, dude!"

The twosome merged with hallway traffic. Michael tensed as he moved through the sea of students, struggling to stay out of the way and not touch any of them. The place was a madhouse of activity, kids scurrying everywhere, talking, talking, talking. Shouting, screaming, laughing, *talking*! Michael thought of a darkened motel room, alone with his wife, and found a moment of calm.

To think, this would have been his life had he not taken on his mission for the Man in the Stetson. Instead of dueling space pirates with laser-swords, he'd be confined to this cramped building, dealing with homework, young love, and drama.

Give me the space pirates any day.

Up ahead, he saw a flourish of bright orange hair and warmed. Sara. She left her class behind, clutching her books and gabbing with a group of girls. From here, they looked like best of friends and Michael didn't know how she'd managed to blend in so effortlessly in her first class at school.

Sara glanced his way, mid-sentence, and a loving smile stretched across her full lips. She mouthed "I love you" from across the hall. All Michael's complaints vanished.

Sara is better than space pirates.

He was ready to return the sentiment when Chris appeared behind Sara, smiling in greeting. Instantly, the other girls with Sara traded ugly looks aimed at the boy, said their farewells, and hurried away. Michael approached and Chris looked completely deflated that "big brother" had popped up.

"Hey, sis," Michael said to Sara, ignoring the other boy.

Sara frowned at the floor.

Chris coolly remarked, "Hey. Michael, isn't it?" His beady little eyes redirected on Sara. "Hey, Sara, why don't you let me carry your books to class?"

Chris reached out to take them, but Michael butted in, relieving his wife of her burden. "I got it. That's a big brother's job, after all. Wouldn't you say, Sara?"

Sara hid her face in total humiliation. Michael offered his arm and Sara hooked it. They walked for class—this one they shared. With Chris, apparently. He trailed behind them, their third wheel.

Sara whispered to Michael, "Play nice. He's our mission."

"I'm not standing by while he eye-humps you. No way."

"Michael…"

"And it's *my* mission," he added, snapping. "You shouldn't even be here."

She stopped, taking her arm from his. Her blue eyes filled with hurt. Betrayal. "Are you serious, right now?"

Michael glowered. "That's not what I meant—"

"Then what did you mean?"

"I just mean…I don't know. It's probably not safe. You should be back at the motel—"

Sara took her books back and pushed past him. "I don't believe you."

Michael watched her leave, not sure what had happened. Why had he said that? *What a jerk.*

Chris jogged past Michael, joining Sara's side. He offered to take her books once more. Sara looked reluctant, but upon spotting Michael, handed Chris her books. The two walked away.

Michael snarled and punched the nearest locker, denting the metal and sending a small flock of teens scattering in surprise. With his rage released, Michael skulked to class. Sharp nails scratched at his mind and he staggered, in pain. He looked up, expecting Sara to return to his side as she always did, but she was gone. With Chris.

"Dude, you all right?" some kid in black baggy jeans stooped by his side.

"Get away," Michael snarled.

The kid backed up, hands up in offense. "Whatever, dude."

Others in the hall avoided him, giggling at his expense. Michael's vision blurred with tears. Pain swelled in his mind and he looked everywhere, letting the danger sense guide him. At last, the feeling led him to a wall lined with photos. Graduating class photos. His eyes zeroed in as the throbbing beat steadied, guiding him to the photo he needed to see.

There. Some kid that graduated a decade ago. He was baby faced, with a bad haircut, but those eyes were unmistakable. It was Light Sphere. The name under his picture read: Rick Castle.

So Light Sphere had gone to this very school. It had to mean something.

Before Michael had a chance to think on it more, the bell rang and he cursed. He was late for class.

11

Class went by painfully slow. Michael nearly dozed off a time or two, and spent great lengths looking longingly out the window, dividing his attention between thinking about Rick Castle and remembering his own daring superhero adventures. He really wished he was on one right now. He fondly recalled doing battle with the Great Xanawhales Hortex.

Those were good times. He sighed wistfully.

Sara, on the other hand, had somehow become the teacher's pet in a matter of minutes. She took notes and everything, really getting into the role of student. It almost seemed like she enjoyed this. Back at his old school, Michael spent more time in detention than in class. Apart from Coach Seevers, he barely remembered any of his teachers' names, let alone whatever they had taught him.

But Sara was raising her hand, looking to every page the teacher referenced in her text books, and thoughtfully tapping her pencil on the edge of her chin. Michael wanted to apologize to her for what he'd said in the hallway. He was being a jerk. She'd given up her whole life to fight by his side and he'd done little but "keep her in the motel"—his own private possession to hoard. It was selfish, but more than that, it was wrong. Sara was a human being, with her own wants and desires. Not his pet.

Letting go of her, though…She could die. And then what? He'd be alone again. Miserable.

What's wrong with me? How selfish can I get?

He knew what the Hooded Man would say. That Michael was destined to be a monster; that he was already becoming one.

Michael considered writing a note and slipping it to Sara, to tell her how sorry he was, but then he recalled all of his materials were walled up in his locker. He'd just have to talk to her after class and try and smooth things over.

12

Sara stood in the lunch line, her marble-patterned tray in her hands. It looked like it was rectangle pizza on the menu today. She'd been enjoying her first day at school, except after her row with her husband two periods ago, Sara dreaded lunchtime. He'd be here. Would they sit together? Did she want to talk to him after the things he'd said to her?

In a way, she understood where he was coming from. He was the one with the big, fat holy mission. And she understood that. God hadn't chosen her for this gig—that was Michael's calling. But after all that they had been through together, the things they'd seen and done…didn't she deserve better treatment? Wasn't she a part of the team? Sure, maybe just the donut-gathering part but she was capable of so much more if Michael would just trust her. She supposed he was being sweet, in a purely chauvinistic way. Once upon a time she'd needed a leather-clad knight to rescue her from the tower, but that story was over. Now it was time for the damsel to be a part of the adventure, not just an attainable prize.

It infuriated her, but she felt helpless to change Michael's mind. Unless she proved to him that she could do it. That she could solve a case, all on her own.

She spotted Chris sitting alone at the end of a table and decided to join him. He looked lost in thought, no doubt thinking of his missing father. Sara hoped nothing had befallen poor Tom.

"Is this seat taken?" she asked, standing over Chris with her food.

He brightened. Even stood and moved a chair opposite him for her to sit. "Go ahead." He grinned, awkwardly. Sara recognized that look all too well—it stared at her from the mirror every day. "Have a seat."

She did. The boy was quite charming. Sara could tell that Chris was interested in her, but hoped that she could use that to her advantage. To get clues as to Michael's—*their* mission—on this world.

"So, you said something earlier…" she began, leaning across the table in a conspiratorial tone. "About this town."

Chris' smile faded. "Right. That. Nobody wants to talk about it, but there's a monster in this town."

Sara widened her eyes. "Really?" Michael was good at stopping monsters. "What kind?"

He shrugged. "Nobody will say. You hear rumors, you know? Apparently he can shoot fire out of his hands."

"So he's got super powers," Sara said.

He looked at her strangely. "Yeah. Yeah, I guess so."

Excited now, she added, "I saw some of them this morning, flying over the town. They were fighting."

"Yeah, they do that." He grimaced. "They're constantly fighting each other, sometimes destroying whole cities in the process. Of course the heroes will say they're doing it to save people from the bad ones, but when we're all caught in the crossfire, it doesn't seem like they're doing a lot of good. But, what are you gonna say, right? They've got more power in their pinkies than the United States has in its army. They ride roughshod over all of us 'common people'."

"You sound really angry about it."

Chris seemed to catch himself, then softened. "It's something me and my dad always argued about. He wanted to trust the heroes. He believed in them. Said they were great men and women and we should all strive to be like them. But…I don't need heroes."

Sara frowned, seeing his sadness and anger. What had hurt him so? Then she noticed the others kids shooting him dirty looks. He'd been let down, she could see it. She wanted to fix this for him. To make his life better once she left. She would find Tom. She would help them mend their relationship.

Her parents were dead. She'd never get the chance to apologize for the way she'd treated them. The callous things she'd said.

She didn't want Chris to live with that burden.

"What does the monster want?" she asked.

Chris took a drink from his milk carton. "I wish I knew. Maybe if I did…I would know why he got my dad."

"You really think your dad's dead, don't you?"

The boy dug around at his food. "Don't look now. Your brother's here."

Sara swiveled in her seat and saw Michael shoving through the line, disregarding lunch and marching her way like a rampaging bull.

"He really doesn't like me, does he?" Chris asked.

"He's just…"

She didn't know how to finish that sentence. Instead she scooted her chair back and stood, intercepting her husband out of Chris' earshot.

"Don't," she said.

"Don't what? We were supposed to have lunch."

"I think…I think it would be better if you sat somewhere else."

"What?"

"I've got him talking, okay? He clams up whenever you're around. Just let me handle this."

"But—"

"Can't you just trust me? This one time?"

Michael flinched, as though slapped. He quickly recovered, his face like flint. "If he tries anything—"

"He won't. He's not like that. He just needs a friend."

"Fine." Michael marched off, pushing open the double doors to the caf and storming into the hall.

Sara breathed an exasperated sigh and returned to her table.

"What was that all about?" Chris asked.

She shook her head and poked at her lunch with her fork. "Big brothers."

13

Michael tromped across the school lawn, headed towards the parking lot, ready to leave campus. A teacher—a tall, hulking woman—waved after him, flapping her baggy arms. "Hey! Hey, get back here. You can't just walk—"

He ignored her, crossing the street, dodging honking traffic, and joining Main Street pedestrians. He was done with high school. If Sara wanted to take over and be the hero this time out, let her. He could use a break anyway. Head back to the motel with a bucket of spicy wings and watch bad daytime television. What did it matter? He was tired of proving himself to her. Why couldn't she just trust him? He was looking out for her.

She doesn't need me.

The dark thought came unbidden to his mind, and he couldn't shove it aside. Did it threaten him that she was so capable? Did he *want* her to remain the timid young girl he'd first rescued? Deep down he supposed this was all his fault. When he'd convinced her to leave Charlie, he'd given her confidence and encouraged her to take charge of her life. Be her own person.

Isn't that what she's doing? Why are you fighting it so much, man?

Maybe because, if she kept growing—changing—then there wouldn't be room in her life for him anymore.

I can't lose her. I need her.

The Rage was still out there, eyes everywhere in the cosmos, looking to recruit Michael for a career of evil. Without Sara here, loving him, bringing balance to his life…he feared what he would become if she ever left.

He was ready to be away from this world, from high school, and all its conflicted angst-ridden thoughts. If this was what being a normal teenager was like, Michael wanted no part of it. He found it more difficult than laying siege to that fortress in the Middle Ages when some laughing trickster from the future thought it'd be fun to give the opposing army rocket launchers. That had been hard, but still this somehow seemed harder.

And yet Sara had taken to it like a fish to water.

Maybe this is the life for her. But I can't give that kind of life to her. Will she miss it? Will she be sorry she left with me?

Michael turned on Main Street, hands in his pockets, and walked, hoping to clear his head. Whatever his domestic situation was like, he had a mission here—and he was beginning to think that Chris was only a small part of it. His danger sense kicked in around that Light Sphere guy. If Sara wanted to get to know Chris and be his little buddy, then Michael could work the Light Sphere angle.

Already he felt better. He was a hero—he needed to be doing hero-y things.

A tiny prickle pinched the base of his spine. It was just a slight pain, just enough to stop him in place. He stood beside a pizzeria and looked inside the storefront window. The lunchtime crowd was inside, and he thought he was supposed to join them. God was directing him here, dropping bread crumbs. Michael walked inside and the pain immediately subsided.

He dodged the hustle and bustle of the patrons—already recognizing how much friendlier these people seemed than the teenagers at school—and sat on a stool at the front counter. An older man wearing an apron over his dress shirt and slacks called out orders to his staff. He walked over to Michael.

"Welcome to Papa Joey's," he said. "What can I get you to drink?"

"A Coke."

"Coming right up." The man pulled out a dark red plastic glass from behind the counter and went to fill it up.

As Michael waited, the crowd fell into a hush. He looked around, and saw everyone's eyes glued to one of the flat screen TVs mounted on the wall. It was another newscast about Light Sphere. It was hard to hear over the customers' idle chatter, but it seemed that political pundits were discussing Light Sphere's war in the Middle East. Talking about the ramifications of having costumed "Super Powers"—as they were apparently called—waging foreign wars in America's name.

Worse yet, it seemed that Light Sphere had gone AWOL.

"Leave it to the government to complicate things," the older man said. He set Michael's drink on the counter.

"How so?"

"When I was a kid, the Super Powers—the good ones, I mean—they helped people. Plain and simple. They'd just swoop in, right when you needed them, do a good deed and then they were off again. These days, though, the government's gotta regulate everything. America's got her Powers...Russia, Germany, now I hear Iraq's got a few...Sure, they want us to believe that with all the Super Powers fighting our wars, our boys and girls on the frontlines can come home, but...I don't know. Just seems like they're taking something that used to be about being a good neighbor

189

and making it all official."

Michael frowned.

"Ah, what do I know?" He flashed a sad smile before perking up. "You ready to place your order?"

"So, Light Sphere's from around here, right?"

"Oh, yeah." The man beamed with pride. "Yeah, he grew up right here in town. He and his mother used to come by the restaurant all the time. Good kid. Real shy. Not a lot of people noticed him, but he had heart. You could tell once he got his powers. Once you saw how he used them. That's the real measure of a man—how they handle power."

"And what are his powers?"

The man eyed Michael strangely.

"I just moved here," Michael said. "I've heard a lot about Light Sphere."

"Yeah, yeah, he was a local hero for a while."

"His powers?"

"Light. White-hot phosphorous, you know? Yeah, he first discovered it when he shot 'em out of his hands. Poor kid. First time he used 'em, it burnt his hands up. He's got these scars all over them. That's why he wears those gloves now."

"Really…"

The man pointed toward the corner near the front door. "It's all in the comics."

Michael swiveled in his seat to the small rack of sun-faded comics in the front window.

"Those things used to sell like hot cakes when they first came out. But that was nearly ten years ago. People forget, you know? They move on. Especially kids your age." The man shook his head, frowning. "Yeah, Ricky was real good. Helped out around town. He'd take off to the county next door, help there when he was needed too. Now he's on the government payroll and we don't see him around these parts anymore. They've got him too busy fighting over oil to worry about helping cats out of trees, know what I mean? Shame, too…We sure could use his help right now…"

Michael's eyes turned back to the TV. He watched the commentators discuss Light Sphere as stock footage of Light Sphere's battle with foreign powers was broadcast. The headline read that Light Sphere was missing and that the war effort was suffering for it. The pundits wondered where their hero had gone, but Michael thought he already knew.

He's come back home. But why?

"Poor kid," the man said. "Go from being small town farmboy to fighting in a war on foreign soil. Gotta be a shock, huh? I fought in 'Nam. It does strange things to us *normal* kids. Can't imagine what that'd do if you were a Super Power *too*. Leave you all screwed up."

Michael watched Light Sphere's image on the screen closely as "experts" continued their discussion. Something was missing in the superhero's eyes as the old footage showed reporters hounding him with questions:

Hope.

14

After school let out, Sara went back to the motel room and pushed open the door. Michael was lying on the bed, a mess of comic books spread out on the covers. He was reading one marked "Light Sphere." In fact, they all featured Light Sphere.

"Hey," she said softly. "Where were you? We had another class together. I couldn't find you."

"I left." He didn't look up.

She placed her books on the table, but did not sit down. "Michael, we need to talk."

"What?" he asked with barely any interest.

"Chris…asked me out."

Michael threw his comic down and sprang off the bed, face turning red. "I'm killing him. That's it."

She shouted at him, "Why are you so jealous?"

"Are you kidding me? He thinks you're playing hard to get!" He paused, his teeth clenched. "You *are* playing hard to get, aren't you?"

"What's that supposed to mean?"

He turned his back on her, his whole body taut. "Please tell me you told him 'no'."

"I said 'yes'."

Michael whirled on her, the fire of hell in his eyes, but he did not speak.

191

"It doesn't mean anything. You know that. We keep getting interrupted at school. He's about to tell me everything. I just need a little more time."

Michael looked like he wanted to hit her, and a hundred awful memories of Charlie flashed in her mind. But her husband only sat back on the bed, and sagged. "I hate this place."

His eyes watered and he bit at his bottom lip. Was he crying? Sara's heart melted. She sat next to him, hugging him close. "Don't say that. Nothing's changed."

"Everything's changing," he said in a hush. "I don't know what to do, Sara."

"About what?" she asked. She combed his hair with her fingers. "Tell me, sweetie."

Michael faced her, his dark eyes rimmed with red. Her heart broke even more. "Don't leave me. Please, Sara…"

She held his head to her shoulder. "No, no, no. I'm never going to leave you."

"I'm so scared." He sobbed into her shoulder, his dam of emotions shattering. "The Hooded Man told me…"

Sara listened closely. Was he finally telling her what had been bothering him?

She stroked his head. "It's okay, sweetie. You saved me. Let me return the favor now."

"He said you're my kryptonite. That the Rage will try to hurt me—to turn me—by hurting you."

Sara's blood chilled. But she forced herself to be calm for her husband. "You won't turn, Michael. You're stronger than that."

"No," he said, shaking his head. "You don't know the things I've done."

"Like what? Tell me."

Michael stood abruptly. "I'm a monster, Sara. That's why the Rage wants me."

She touched his hand. Kissed his knuckles. "But God wants you, too, right? That's got to mean something. You're a *hero*."

He rubbed at his face, drying his cheeks, his eyes. "I won't let them hurt you. I promise. We'll leave. I went to the In-Between once, I can do it again. I'll go, talk to the Man in the Stetson and tell him we're done. We can stop."

Sara quieted. His hand in hers. "Can I ask you something? And I want you to be honest."

He regarded her with a puzzled look on his face.

"Can you give this up? The rift jumping."

"Of course," he said.

She stood, chuckling a bit, touching his chest. "What then? We'd settle down and get jobs?"

"Yes."

She saw the fear there. The uncertainty. He was trying so hard. "Michael...You can't give this up. It's who you are. And I love you for that."

He shook his head. "But I don't want this for you."

"I've made peace with the fact that my life is always going to be in danger."

"Sara—"

"No, it's not ideal, but I'm okay with that. It's who I am now too."

"Who you are or who I made you?"

"It doesn't matter anymore."

"It does to me."

Putting her hand to his hard face, she smiled back, praying he'd take confidence from her. He'd given her so much, made her a better person. Why couldn't he just let her heal him, as well? "Michael, I've accepted the violence, the running, all of it. But you've got to understand that this is our life. Us. Together. You can't shut me out of it anymore. Train me to fight—"

"I can't," he said. "I don't want you to have to live like that."

"Or are you just afraid of losing me?"

"No. Yes. Of course. I don't know."

He pulled away from her, moving to stand by the window, staring out through the blinds.

After a long moment, Sara said, "I'm going out with Chris."

Michael didn't flinch. Didn't move or say a word.

"You've got to start trusting me, Michael. I love you."

A heavy silence settled between the two. At last, Michael yanked his leather jacket off the back of the chair, slipped into it—his suit of armor. He left the motel, slamming the door behind him.

Sara took a deep breath and sat on the edge of the bed. She was on her own for this one. But she could do it.

She *would* do it.

15

Sara dressed up for her date, but was careful not to be *too* dressed up. She was aware that Chris was attracted to her, and doubly sensitive to the fact that she was walking a very thin line between exploiting the boy's feelings and leading him on.

She thought of Michael. Guilt set in her heart. She was asking too much of him, to act like a normal boy. To pretend to be just another student, worried about grades and parents and all the things she had cared so much about before her family was torn apart. Sara felt warm familiarity with settling in to school work and the more mundane side of life. But she knew that wasn't Michael. He was a hero—just like those she'd seen in the skies this morning—meant to be leaping off buildings to the rescue or fighting down armies of monsters or singlehandedly wrestling a leviathan to the death. He wasn't made for the "normal life."

We're really different. The understanding sank deeper.

It scared her.

Perhaps worst of all, she knew she was expecting too much of Michael to pretend to be her brother. She ached to be near him, too. She wished they were away from this world and free to be man and wife again. Free to be intimate and to talk openly about their lives without all of this code.

Chris arrived at the motel on foot as the sun began its downward crest over the earth. The two of them walked, but talked very little. Around them, shops closed and people headed home for the evening. Sara wasn't sure where they would find a restaurant open. Chris took her hand, balmy and a bit sweaty, and pulled her along to a lone pizzeria still open on the Main Street strip. "Come on!"

They half-ran to the doors and entered. A set of bells over the entrance declared their arrival. The place was empty, chairs upturned on tables, and a middle-aged man in khakis and a dress shirt swept up the place. He had on an apron with "Papa Joey's Pizza" emblazoned on the front. Sara figured him for Joey—first one to arrive, last one to leave. The man looked up, a kindly smile on his face…but it faded once it fell on the couple.

"We're closed," he declared, forcefully.

Chris smiled. "Oh, come on. It's not even dark yet."

"Y-You know the rules. Shops close at sundown, just like…I'm closing up. I'm leaving."

Sara shuffled awkwardly as the manager seemed to get only more riled.

Chris let go of her hand, and stepped forward laughing. "Please, mister. Cut us a break."

"No!" The man gripped his broom with both hands, hurrying for the kitchen entrance. "No, we're closed. I'm about to leave *right now*. I don't want any trouble! Get out! Get out, both of you!"

Sara blushed. "Maybe we should just leave. This isn't really—"

But Chris turned to her, his face reddening. "No. No, we're here already. He's just going to have to deal with it."

Chris followed the man into the back. "Hold on!" he called and disappeared through the door. Sara waited by the front, wringing her hands and wondering where Michael was. The manager was obviously terrified of this elusive monster, and Sara felt exposed standing in front of the glass storefront. She regarded the quiet night outside, tinted in twilight hues, and felt eyes on her.

"Hey," Chris huffed from behind. "I did it. We can stay. Is something wrong?"

"I'm fine. What did you do?"

He grinned. "Gave him an extra forty bucks."

"You didn't have to do that," she said. "Really."

"No, I want you to have a good time. I'm not going to let this town ruin that for you."

She hung her head, unable to keep herself from smiling. He was awfully sweet. Chris took a step back and swept his hand over the empty pizzeria. "So, where do you want to sit?"

She laughed as he made a selection for them. He took down the chairs and held Sara's out for her. She sat, muffling a giggle, and Chris took the chair opposite her.

"Thank you," he said.

"For what?"

"For giving me a chance."

She snickered. "Why wouldn't I?"

"I don't know if you've noticed or not, but a lot of people in town avoid me."

"Ha, yeah, I picked up on that."

"They think...I'm trouble. It's because I'm not afraid. I used to be." His attention drifted to the tabletop, the light in his eyes dulling. "But I'm not anymore."

"Of the monster?"

He nodded. Darkening. "I guess that's why you said you'd go out with me, isn't it? To hear about it?"

Chris looked so vulnerable. Like he was used to rejection. Sara immediately hated herself for using him. He wasn't just a mission...he mattered. "No," she said. "Let's not talk about that right now."

He brightened, as if surprised. His easy grin returned. "What do you want to talk about then?"

"I don't know," Sara said, a warmth spreading through her body. "We've got all night."

16

Michael stood across the street from Papa Joey's. Watched as Sara tittered and tucked her hair behind her ears. Was she laughing? Chris was talking, showing off and kicking back in his chair like he owned the world.

Hate filled Michael's heart, darkening his thoughts. Chris may have meant something to his mission—to God, even—but Michael didn't care about God right now. Didn't care about holy crusades and righting wrongs. He just wanted to kill that kid for trying to steal away all that made Michael's life right. Special. She was his Sara, not this punk kid's.

I won't let you take her away from me.

His hands turned to iron fists and he craved feeling Chris' hot blood splash against them. To murder him, punch his face until there was nothing left but pulpy brain matter.

"You've got a beast inside you, kid..."

Michael loosed his fist. *No. I'm not a monster. I won't be.*

They all give in, though. That's what the Hooded Man had told him. Every Michael Morrison that ever was eventually gave themselves over to the

Rage and became devils.

Sara sat inside the restaurant, laughing and talking and being normal. As much as it pained him to see it, she was having a life. A real life without any fear of the Rage or terrible destinies.

I'm just going to ruin her, Michael thought. *Maybe…maybe she belongs with a guy like Chris. Someone normal who could give her a small town life with all the small town problems.*

The whirlwind of emotions tore at his mind until Michael could stand it no longer. He turned his back on the scene, on his wife, and marched out into the night. There was a monster out there, somewhere, and he was going to find it. And kill it.

17

Michael found Dack and PJ swaying down the deserted sidewalk, arm in arm, singing into the night. They'd obviously been drinking—no doubt at that party they'd invited Michael to earlier—and were continuing the celebration.

"Hey, new kid!" Dack said, his voice like a foghorn in the otherwise silent town.

Michael crossed the street to join them, his eyes cutting a path left and right, watching the shadows. "You shouldn't be out here," Michael said. "I hear it's not safe."

"Then what are *you* doing out?" PJ snickered and sloshed a beer bottle in Michael's direction. "Wanna drink? We got plenty, man."

Michael considered it, a part of him tempted to join in their fun and be "one of the guys" for a night. Sara seemed to be doing so well blending in. "No. Let's just get you home."

Dack's knees buckled and he slipped sideways, chuckling. "Whoa, man…"

Aggravated, Michael helped him up when his mind prickled as though strong hands were squeezing around his head. He snapped a finger to his temple.

"Dude, you cool?" PJ asked. He took over for Michael in getting Dack to a reasonable standing position.

Wincing, Michael scanned the town. The alleyways. The building tops.

A shape passed by, ducking out of sight.

Michael grabbed the boys by their collars and dragged them along. "Come on. We have to go. Now!"

"Dude, let go!" Dack shouted, his voice echoing down the street. "What's your problem? Let go of me!"

"It's not safe," Michael said. "Keep your voice down. We have to—"

A shimmering blast of white energy punched Michael in the chest and knocked him off his feet. Blown backwards, he shattered through a storefront window. Michael picked himself up, tiny fragments of broken glass falling off him like noisy rain. He stared through the window opening and saw a figure approaching on the sidewalk. Colorful suit, All-American maskless face, and bright red-hot iron gauntlets.

Light Sphere.

"Been looking for you," Michael said.

Dack and PJ cursed and staggered away.

Light Sphere raised his hand, palm out and another blast erupted from the constructs on his lower arms. Michael dodged this one, rolling to the side, as the beam cut a trail through the store—a Laundromat, Michael realized. Machines fizzled, sliced in two by the precision beam, and exploded. Michael took the moment's confusion to launch forward through the window and tackle Light Sphere to the ground.

The former hero was no slouch, though, and fell back with the impact, rolling into a ball and hurling Michael off of him. Michael sailed through the air before skidding on the concrete on his face

"You're strong. Stronger than a normal man," Light Sphere acknowledged without the least bit of shock. "You're a Super Power."

"Something like that," Michael spat. He stood to his feet and balled his fists. Cracked his neck.

Light Sphere stepped forward, his body rigid and militaristic. The guy exuded confidence, and Michael was more than willing to knock the freak down a peg.

"And *this* is what you do with your power?" Light Sphere asked.

"You're one to talk. So, going AWOL, huh? What's the matter? Couldn't take orders anymore? Finally snapped, right?"

Light Sphere did not respond. The man's gauntlets glowed and Light Sphere bent his arms at the elbows. The air rippled in front of him, his arms trembling with exertion, as if he were drawing the energy right out of the atmosphere and pulling it to him. An orb of white light formed in his hands, growing—no, charging—and then Light Sphere shoved it forward with a sonic crack. Michael was so spellbound by the dazzling display that he forgot to duck, and the ball of raw kinetic power rammed into his stomach.

Michael catapulted back, his spine smacking horizontal into a light post. The metal bent forward and Michael deflected off it, landing in the bushes of the small Town Square Park. Invincibility didn't protect from vertigo, and Michael was dazed by the impact. He shuffled on the ground, trying to collect his bearings, when another glowing orb pulverized the earth beside him, a fiery conflagration catching him in its shockwave and smashing him through the gazebo.

Wood splintered and Michael was on the grass again, his mouth full of dirt.

Light Sphere stalked toward him, plates in his gloves popping out, hissing steam. Michael realized the gauntlets had to cool before Light Sphere could use his powers again. He took the moment. Michael ape-ran and threw a wild punch that mashed against Light Sphere's chiseled jaw.

Light Sphere grunted, taking the full force of Michael's anger on the chin. He looked startled, and Michael delivered a one-two punch—one to his gut, the other an uppercut. Light Sphere collapsed to the ground. Michael charged in for the final blow, but halted when the Super Power raised a hand, filling the night with a shrill hum. Michael hesitated a half-second before a megablast of energy escaped from the glove, pounding him in the torso.

This time, Michael held his ground. He grit his teeth, roaring, as the blast consumed him, tearing at his shirt, burning strips into his jeans, and fraying the ends of his leather jacket. At last, the energy dissipated, rolling around him and expelling the last of its strength before fading.

Light Sphere gaped. "No one can do that."

"I'm not just no one."

Michael reared back and punched. Light Sphere blocked the shot with a forearm and bashed Michael across the face with hot iron. The impact shook Michael's senses and blurred his vision. *This guy hits hard.* Michael returned the favor, busting Light Sphere's nose, opening up a flood of crimson.

Light Sphere didn't give up. He shoved to his feet and began exchanging punch for punch with Michael. "You're not going to win this," Michael said. "I was sent here to stop you from hurting these people anymore, and I always finish the job."

Light Sphere's brow creased. "Wait—"

But Michael was through waiting. Through discussing. His blood chilled to ice and Michael concentrated only on one thing: the kill.

He pushed forward, swinging his fists like deadly hammers. Light Sphere backed up, trying to dodge the hits. He held his hands out in a defensive posture, the hardness in his face slackening. "Wait!"

"What's wrong, monster? Picked on the wrong guy?"

Light Sphere slipped underneath Michael's extended punch, and curled around, getting Michael in a headlock. Michael twisted, ready to use his leverage to throw Light Sphere off, when the man stammered, "I'm not the monster! I thought you were!"

Michael heard the words, though not sure he heard them correctly through his battle haze. "Say that again?"

18

Sara was enjoying the evening. Chris was awkward and shy, reminding her of herself before Michael had discovered her. He said strange things, as though he hadn't had much interaction with people, which she could certainly relate to. Not once had they mentioned the monster. Sara purposefully steered them away from that conversation, wanting him to feel comfortable. Wanting him to feel like he meant more than just a simple assignment.

Then she heard explosions.

A horrible sound of bending metal echoed through the streets. Sara stood, knocking her chair over. Facing the storefront window, she gasped. "What was that? Was that the monster?"

Chris stood too, easing for the window. "I don't know *what* that was—"

"I've got to get to Michael. He can help."

Sara started for the front door, but thought better of it. Danger lay that direction. She tugged at Chris' arm, heading for the kitchen. "Let's go out the back. Just stay with me. I'll protect you." She crossed the restaurant, looking for the manager. "Hey! Hey, we have to leave! We have to get out of here!" She banged open the kitchen door, prepared to shout once more, but froze.

Joey lay face up on the tile. His eyes were wide open, his mouth gaping like a fish out of water.

He was almost entirely charred black.

Sara screamed, tears distorting her vision. She covered her mouth, holding back the urge to vomit and felt fear grip her heart. The monster had somehow slipped in. She wasn't safe.

"Chris!" she shouted. "Chris, it's here! The monster's here!"

"I know," Chris said, calm.

She spun and saw him approaching. His eyes glowed red. The air around his hands rippled, superheated.

She took a step back. "You…"

"I'm sorry, Sara," he said, no emotion in his voice. "I never wanted you to find out like this."

"Stay away from me." Sara backed through the kitchen, groping behind her, trying to feel for the exit. "Help!" she shrieked.

"Don't," he said. "I don't want to have to kill you too."

"Why? Why did you do this?"

"All my life this stupid town has shoved me around. Looked down their noses at me just because I didn't want to spend my life behind the wheel of a tractor." He held up his hand and flicked his fingers. A single ball of fire emerged and he rolled it along his knuckles, effortlessly. He grinned into the hot blue flame, looking like an addict eyeing a fix. "Then I found out I was special. Now no one messes with me. I'm a god, Sara." Chris frowned and faced her. "But I'm lonely." He squeezed a fist, extinguishing the fireball, then held out his hand to her. "I want you, Sara."

"No!" Sara turned away, running down the hall. She crashed into the exit, nearly tripping over herself. She raced out into the night, wondering where Michael was. Hating herself for not listening to him. For not trusting him.

Chris yelled after her. "Nobody tells me no! I can have whatever I want, do you understand?" Sara felt heat blast her back. She dropped to her knees and covered her head, screeching. A wave of flame surged overhead. "I take whatever I want!"

Sara picked herself up and ran, screaming at the top of her lungs. "Help me!" But the town was empty. There was no one on Main Street. She'd die alone—away from Michael. He'd always taken care of her. But she'd escaped from under his wing, thinking she was ready to fly on her own, and now...

She wept as Chris hollered, "Yell all you want. It won't do you any good. They're all afraid of me now. I let them come out in the day, but the night belongs to me. I say whether they live or die. I own this town!"

Fireballs exploded around Sara like bomb strikes, showering her with asphalt debris.

Chris chased after her and she sobbed openly as she left Main Street and ducked down the neighborhood leading to the high school. Townspeople peeked out their windows, but their frightened expressions told her everything. Chris was the monster they chose to ignore.

They closed their curtains, pulled their blinds, and shut their doors.

Another barrage of fire destroyed the pavement ahead, forcing her to change course.

Michael! Where are you? HELP!

19

"I was called here to stop Chris Thompson," Light Sphere said, releasing his strong grip on Michael. Michael jerked away, his thoughts racing with a thousand possibilities—all of them leading to Sara being on a date with a monster. Panic surged through his chest.

"His father, Tom, called me."

Something like an invisible baseball bat cracked across Michael's forehead. It didn't hurt, but nearly tossed him to the ground, and a voice screeched in his head.

{*Michael! Where are you? HELP!*}

Sara. Somehow, it was Sara's voice, in his mind.

And she was in trouble.

In the distance, Michael spotted a flare of yellowish light, flickering above the buildings. *Fire.*

"We have to hurry!" he shouted. He propelled himself forward, hoping Light Sphere could keep up.

Sara crossed the lawn to the high school and tripped to her knees in the grass. She clambered on all fours, weeping. Chris was on her an instant later, grabbing a handful of her hair, jerking her to a stand.

"Stop fighting!" he cut through her cries. "It doesn't have to be like this. I can be nice, Sara. I can make things nice for you."

Screaming, Sara reached to his face and bit his cheek, sinking her teeth in deep. He cursed and flailed away from her. His eyes flickered with fire even as a river of red pumped from his fresh wound. Sara tasted copper in her mouth, felt his blood down her chin.

She spat it on the ground, defiant.

Snarling like an animal, Chris put his glowing hands out towards her, turning the night bright in a fraction of a second. Sara had just enough presence of mind to throw herself sideways, collapsing to the ground as a rippling current of blue flame pulsed outward, detonating a nearby classroom window. Sara saw the opening and ran for it. Chris still yelled in pain, in misery, in hate. Wild fireballs exploded around her.

Sara leapt for the window, shattering the remaining glass and landing hard on the desks just inside. With a clatter she crashed to the ground, her body aching from the impact. She ran from the classroom and slammed the door shut.

She needed to stay calm. No crying. No calling for help. She had to stay quiet and clearheaded. Had to think. Had to hide.

"Sara!" Chris' voice echoed from the classroom where she'd entered.

He's here!

Sara's shaky hands fumbled along the lockers, her mind struggling to clear. She spotted a janitor's closet across the hall and dashed for it. Thankfully it was unlocked. She ducked inside, closing the door just as Chris blasted into the hall in a shower of flame and wreckage.

"Sara!" She could hear him marching down the hall. She didn't think he saw her hide. She prayed he hadn't. "Don't do this! Don't run away from me! They all run away! Sara, please!"

Sara heard the desperation in Chris' plea. He was lonely—an outcast. Even now, fearing for her life, she pitied him. Wanted to help somehow. Hadn't Michael wanted the same from her? For someone to look past his dark side to see the light underneath?

But Chris wasn't like Michael. Michael was a protector. Chris just wanted to possess.

Chris was like Charlie. Sara ground her teeth, incensed.

Trepidation grew as Chris neared her hiding spot and, once again, Sara squinted against her tears and thought out, *Michael! Please find me! I'm in the school!*

Sara had no reason to believe that Michael could hear her thoughts. But then again, she didn't feel alone. Like someone was there, with her, standing by her side in her terror.

A door opened nearby. Across the hall, perhaps. "Sara?" Chris asked, his voice fading, as though he'd stepped into one of the classrooms. He was searching. Sara heard his footfalls cross the hall and open another door—this one right next to the closet.

"Sara, are you in here?"

His steps became louder, then stopped right in front of her door. The thin crack of light at her feet darkened as he stepped closer. The door knob jiggled.

Michael, hear me! I'm here! HELP!

With a whoosh of air, the closet door swung open.

Chris stood there. Sara screamed.

He grinned, and reached for her. His sweaty hands gripped her blouse, ripping it slightly, as he reeled her in.

"Stop," Sara whimpered. "I just want to go home."

Chris looked confused, fearful, and excited all at once.

"I could do anything I wanted to you," he said. It didn't sound like a threat. More of a thrilling realization.

Sara shook her head. "You're not a bad person."

"I killed my dad, Sara," he said, bluntly, as though understanding the truth for the first time. "He was going to turn me in. I…I couldn't let him. He never understood me. Never wanted me."

She balked. "But you can stop. You don't have to kill anymore."

Chris glared at her, tears building in his eyes. He clenched his teeth. "But I do. That's what the man in my dreams says. That's why he gave me these powers. It doesn't matter what I want. This is who I am now."

Sara relaxed in his grip. Touched his arm, sympathetically. "What are you talking about? What man?"

"You think we just met this morning by accident? I've been dreaming about you for months, Sara. You and your husband. Yeah, I know about him too. This was all supposed to happen. This was my assignment. But I fell for you in my dreams, Sara. I don't want to hurt you."

"Chris—"

Chris' head jerked at a sharp angle and he tumbled sideways to the tile. Michael replaced him in the doorway, snarling in rage, blood on his knuckles. "Are you okay?"

Sara nodded. She flung her arms around him and held her husband tight.

Movement at their side. She looked to the floor where Chris wiped his split lip and stood. Michael placed strong hands on her, easing her behind him.

"You're gonna die," Michael promised, his voice like gravel.

"No!" a new voice said from the other end of the hall, behind Chris. In the gloom, Sara watched a man emerge, clunky iron gauntlets glowing a dull red.

"Stay out of it, Light Sphere. He's mine."

"It's not for you to decide," Light Sphere said. "He's got to be brought before the authorities. There's a way we do things."

Chris looked back and forth to the two men, then balled up his fists. His flesh turned to light. "Screw you both!"

He aimed a hand at each of them and Sara felt the temperature rise in the corridor. Michael pushed her out of the way as a tongue of fire splashed against him, kicking him backward, end over end. Sara shrieked and covered her face from the inferno. She looked down the hall to see Light Sphere meet the bombardment with a wave of white light of his own. The hero managed to deflect Chris' fire with one hand, while bringing up his other gauntlet. The hallway filled with an electronic buzz, and Light Sphere blasted Chris. The boy crumpled momentarily, then brought up his fiery hands and bent the beam, redirecting it, first to a row of lockers to the left where it dented and broke metal, then to the ceiling where it ripped through ceiling tile. Dust and rubble rained down, pelting Sara.

She scurried away, as her husband shot past. Michael charged for one of the broken locker doors and rent it off the hinges. Taking it in both hands he brought it down hard on the back of Chris' head with a terrible dull crack. Chris slammed to the floor and Michael was on him, pounding him in the face.

"Stop it!" Light Sphere yelled. He hurried forward to pull Michael off. But Michael struggled against the hero's restraint, kicking at the wounded boy.

"I'll kill you!" Michael shouted, his voice raspy, terrifying Sara in his wrath and power.

From the floor, Chris laughed through a bloody smile. "Yeah…man…He told me about you…"

Michael paused, his fist cocked back like a hammer, ready to deliver the killing blow, Light Sphere fighting to hold him back. "What are you rambling about?"

Chris coughed up blood, still grinning. "I knew you'd come. He came to me, in my dreams…Gave me power. Promised me more…He's after you, guy. He said the dude in the hood tried to warn you. But you wouldn't come back peacefully…He's got a whole army of people just like me, Mike, to replace you. You'll see…" Chris laughed, his blood gurgling in his throat. "Aw, man, I can't wait til you get yours."

"Who?" Michael screamed. "Who's building an army? Tell me!"

Chris smirked. "The Maestro."

Sara joined Light Sphere and pulled her husband back. "Wait, *wait*." she pleaded. "Don't kill him. We have to help him…we're supposed to help people. You're a *hero*, Michael. Right?"

Michael slowly cooled, the predatory glint in his black eyes diminishing. His face slackened and he, at last, relaxed under her touch, his hands trembling. "Right," he said, as if coming to his senses from an unsettling dream. "I'm…I'm a hero."

But Sara saw the doubt in his eyes, and worried.

21

Michael stood on the darkened lawn outside the school a few hours later, a bruised but standing Light Sphere at his side. Chris Thompson was shackled and being loaded into the back of a black government van. The local PD was out, forming a barricade around the scene with their flashing reds and blues, and all of the townspeople had come out, gathering around in their pajamas to watch their nighttime monster carted away. Some cheered, some hurled curses at the boy. But everyone looked relieved. An impromptu block party had formed, as people laughed, gossiped, and even danced.

Sara was by the van now with Chris in spite of the angry townsfolk. Michael kept his distance. He didn't like her being so close to the killer, but Sara felt she needed to say something to Chris: to forgive him.

"Think there's hope for him?" Michael looked up at Light Sphere.

The Super Power did not face him. "Don't know. The way you told it to me, some cosmic Evil has got its hooks in 'im."

Me, too, Michael thought sourly. *It wants me back...*

"I don't know if there's hope for someone like that," Light Sphere said, morose.

Michael's face hardened. *Is there no hope for me?*

He was convinced that Chris was one of the bad guys, but Sara still held onto hope that the system could reform him. That the Morrisons had been brought into his life to bring him into accountability and to get him help.

Light Sphere said, "My superiors will do all they can for him. They're there to help people like Chris get a hold of their powers and the rush that comes with them. But, whether or not he takes to the training is up to him." The hero shifted his weight, and took a breath. "There's something I should tell you, though."

Michael regarded him, noticing Light Sphere frowning, distressed. "What?"

"We've already done a preliminary test. He's not who you think he is."

"I don't understand."

"Everyone on our planet is born with this certain part of the brain. It houses our powers. For most people, that part of the brain is dark, but, in a Super Power, that part is activated at birth. As we mature, our powers manifest. By now, the government has passed down regulations. The hospitals test every baby born and start cataloging the ones who will become Super Powers. Programs are already in place to watch these children and be there for them when they discover their abilities."

"Okay." Michael shrugged. "So they missed Chris?"

"No. That's what I'm trying to say. That part of Chris' brain? It's dark. Just like ninety-eight percent of the population." Light Sphere caught

Michael's eye. "I'm telling you he's *not* a Super Power."

A chill snaked down Michael's spine. "So what is he? Where did he get his powers if he wasn't born with them?"

Light Sphere set his jaw. "Yeah. That's what I've been wondering. But it doesn't sound good, does it?"

Michael considered it. Chris had said that the *Maestro* gave him power, with more to come. He also said the guy was building an army of firestarters, just like Chris.

To replace me.

"Keep an eye out, will you?" Light Sphere said after a moment's pause. "It sounds like whoever is behind this has got it out for you."

"Yeah," Michael replied, growing quiet. "It's been after me for a while." A burden weighed on Michael's heart. He debated telling Light Sphere. His palms grew sweaty, and at last he relented. "I nearly killed Chris tonight. Almost beat him to death, right there in front of Sara." The Hooded Man's words returned, as they often did these days, *"You've got a beast inside you, kid, and that's the Rage's property. It isn't going to just let one of Its attack dogs running around like a stray."*

Michael remembered looking in the Hooded Man's eyes and saw only evil. *That could still be me.*

"But you didn't kill him," Light Sphere said, facing him. "That's what makes us different. We all have a choice, Michael. Chris made his. You made yours."

"It's so hard," Michael said, almost to himself. "I never used to think about it before, but I wonder if maybe I'm not so far from turning into a monster myself."

"It *is* hard." Light Sphere sighed, crossed his arms, and turned back to watching Chris. "Destroying is so much easier than creating hope."

Michael kept close watch on his wife, lest Chris try something. But the boy seemed subdued, his head low and contrite. Sara said something to him. Even hugged him. Michael tensed, but commanded himself to remain where he stood. Sara was doing something important and he had to accept that.

"I used to be like her," Light Sphere said, smiling at Sara's kind gesture. "When I first started out, all I cared about was helping people."

Michael looked back to the man. "Did that change?"

"Sure. Once Uncle Sam recruited me for the government's Super

Power agency, it all became about fighting America's enemies. It's just fighting now—and all political. Which country has the toughest Super Power. You get caught up in that, after a while. Start to forget about the 'little people' who are looking for their missing kids or who need someone to keep the local bullies in check. Man, you forget…"

Michael had forgotten as well. God had started him on a quest of redemption—of spreading light to a dark multiverse. Michael had accepted that life when he was only twelve. All he'd cared about then was being a better person, to make up for the things he'd done. He wanted to be a hero. But he'd lost sight of that somewhere along the way.

Sara, though, had reminded him there was another path. She was over there, right now, forgiving a man who would have hurt her, or worse. Michael had only become a hammer, pummeling Evil until it stopped, but Sara was doing something truly heroic.

Have I forgotten the real purpose? Did I ever really understand it in the first place?

"Is that why you ran away from the military?" Michael asked.

Light Sphere nodded. "Tom still had my number from back in the old days. He got through to me. Told me what Chris was doing to the town. My town. I've known these people my whole life and I had left them behind. They were hurting. I had to come back. Try to fix it."

"Are you going to be in a lot of trouble when you get back to your bosses?"

"Maybe. Could be looking at a court martial. I did technically desert during wartime. There's a very real possibility I'll be branded a traitor. A coward, at least."

"No," Michael said. "You're a hero."

Light Sphere looked down to him, a mixture of surprise and relief. Once the moment passed, he grinned just a bit. "Thanks. Been a while since I thought of myself as one."

After Chris was safely locked in the van, Sara made her way to Michael. Light Sphere stiffened, facing down the men in black who still waited by the van. Waiting for him. "I better go catch my ride. Take care of yourself."

"You too. Don't go down without a fight."

Light Sphere chuckled, then left without another word. He gave a small wave to Sara as they passed on the lawn. She said something to him that Michael assumed would be short and sweet, then came to join him. The two stood together in silence, watching Light Sphere pass through the cheering crowd, accepting hugs and handshakes. They had their hero back. Once he was through, he stepped into the transport with the federal agents and disappeared into the night.

The crowds continued to celebrate, reveling in their newfound freedom. Despite the jubilee, Michael and Sara remained alone in a quiet spot of lawn. A heavy silence settled over the two. At last, Sara's shoulders shook and she sobbed, clutching her arms and leaning her head against Michael's chest.

She had been strong long enough. Michael put his arms around her as she cried.

"I was so scared." She wept uncontrollably, her words barely intelligible.

"You did great."

"No, I didn't…I messed this all up." She sniffled. She felt so small in his arms. Just as timid as she'd been when he'd met her. He'd loved that then. Loved feeling like he was needed. Like she couldn't get along without him.

But that was wrong.

Rift jumping used to be so simple. Get in, get the job done, get out. But the larger game was coming into sharper focus and Michael knew he was going to have to do something big. A time of decision was coming and the Rage wasn't prepared to take "no" for an answer.

It's going to be war. The Rage is building an army of firestarters against me, and Sara's going to be right in the middle of it.

She wouldn't survive. *What was I thinking bringing her along?*

"You were right." Sara's breath hitched. "I should've stayed out of it. I never should've tried to help. I'll…" she trailed off, looking to the grass. "I'll stay out of it from now on. *You're* the hero."

He watched her, loving her so much. All he wanted was to keep her safe. But…it wasn't a safe life.

He led her back a step. Took her hand. Curled her fingers into a fist. Tightening his expression, he held his hand to her, palm out and flat. With his other hand he guided her slender fist. "When you punch, keep your fist loose until moment before impact. Then, don't follow through with the punch, but give it a snap like a cobra strike. Let out a breath as you punch. Keep your body tight. Compact. Try it."

He wiggled his flat hand before her. She stared at him through tears. "What are you doing?"

Michael did not answer. Just waited. A small grin of understanding flickered on her face, then her forehead screwed up in concentration, the tiny knot forming on her left brow. As Michael had instructed, Sara punched his hand, blowing out a dramatic lungful of air.

He resisted the urge to chuckle at her cuteness. "No, more like a hiss through your teeth. Or say 'hai' really loud. You've got to breathe. Gotta compress yourself. Try it again."

She did. Her hit was a fraction harder. "Is that better?"

Michael nodded.

Sara broke from the somber mood of the impromptu sparring lesson, her eyes searching and passionate. "Thank you. I'll be the best student."

Michael slipped behind her, guiding her body, forging her into the weapon she'd need to be to survive his life. "Spread your feet apart a little. You've got to anchor yourself. Hold your arms like this—with one closer to your side to protect from body shots, then jab with your other."

Sara took her position, her body coiled and ready to strike. Michael stood back, understanding now that everything had changed. War was coming.

But we'll fight it together.

"Now punch."

PART FIVE: FACE THE MUSIC

1

The day was another hot one, but Toby Jeffries had grown accustomed to such blistering heat in his young eight-year-old life. Maintenance workers had already been by to open the fire hydrants, and throngs of shirtless neighborhood boys laughed and danced like exultant tribal worshippers in the spraying water. In the human settlements, most air conditioners didn't work—or were never installed to begin with—leaving the brownstone residents to open their windows, welcoming what scant breeze existed into their broken-down homes. Toby passed underneath those open windows, his hands in his pockets, watching the other kids play in the water. He thought to join them, but he had places to be.

A chorus of bickering spouses and screaming children sounded from most of the brownstones. Toby's parents fought like everyone else, even after their divorce. Toby's dad rarely came to this end of town anymore. When he did, he seemed only interested in quarreling with Toby's mom over old arguments, taking Toby out for a walk, then promptly dropping him back off, promising he'd return again soon. But as Toby's mom was fond of pointing out, his dad was not known for keeping his promises.

His mom, however, was little better. Tanya Jeffries spent most of her weekends out, leaving Toby either alone at their home or with one of her "friends". Toby never knew the names of his mom's friends as they seemed to change quite a bit. When his mom disappeared, Toby would sequester himself in his room while his mom's friends exchanged money and little bags with strangers in the front room. Eventually, Toby's mom would return, a bit dazed and uncertain of how long she'd been gone. Sometimes she'd come back with a new boyfriend, other times she came back with more cuts and bruises and a lot more liquor.

Most times she returned with all three.

Mom's boyfriends moved in sometimes. Toby struggled to stay out of his mom and her friends' way, drawing or playing a couple of video games that had been left behind by one of the many men who had stayed before. But many times, like today, his mother sent him to the corner store to buy junk food for everyone. Compared to the loud swearing, gossiping, and thick smoke he left behind, Toby found the persistent shouts from windows and shrieking children in the hydrant fountain to be a welcome relief. At least no one was talking to him.

Along his trek, he scanned the skies, spotting the giant black motherships blotting out much of the sun's rays. The alien lords had watched over them his entire life. He had grown up under their watch, just like his mom. Toby heard stories from his grandpa that humanity had put up a resistance but proved completely outmatched by their spacefaring neighbors and surrendered ownership of the planet. That was fifty years ago, according to his grandpa. The aliens had been gracious enough to not obliterate the Earth's original inhabitants, instead isolating them into designated cities. Since then, people had lived crammed together in over-populated ghettos while the aliens demolished the rest of the world and rebuilt it to their culture's liking.

Despite living alongside these strangers from outer space, Toby had never seen an alien in person. He'd never been out of his city-zone. Never met anyone else who had either. Not even his mother with all her big-talking men could produce a single adventure beyond the caged perimeter that kept humans from "trashing up" the aliens' Earth.

Toby wondered what the world was like out there beyond the chain link and sentry towers. What wonderful cities the aliens lived in. Clean cities, he imagined. Wealthy ones, too, where people had air conditioning, assuming aliens had need to stay cool. He imagined a paradise where there was no shouting or drug-addled mothers. Where people were happy, well-fed, and safe. Toby imagined he'd never know such places.

He rounded the corner, spotting drug dealers handing out their wares to young and old alike without fear of punishment. The law was something that didn't really exist in the human slums. That was reserved for the alien citizens. Here it was kill or be killed.

Toby passed the dealers, his focus on the small convenience store up ahead, still dreaming of faraway alien cities.

2

Six weeks. Sara Morrison didn't know how much longer she could stand it.

She sat alone in their overpriced apartment that came with no air and no television. Sara hadn't watched a lot of TV on her world, but had become fond of it since leaving that dimension. She'd grown accustomed to seeing a television—or some alternate facsimile—on nearly every world she and Michael had jumped to. It'd become a kind of security blanket for her, she supposed, as most worlds sought visual entertainment of some kind. She'd taken comfort in mindless channel surfing, finding it fascinating to see what constituted for entertainment on the parallel Earths. Some shows remained the same, with maybe one or two actors replaced. Subject matter changed also, from the ridiculously chaste to the outright obscene. Sara learned a lot about the cultural climate of these new worlds by spending an hour watching their TV. Seeing the familiar in a strange world made her feel grounded, connected. But the TV set that cluttered up the corner of their one-room flat hadn't worked in years, the manager told them.

Nor had the air conditioner. Sara sat in a straight-backed wooden chair, in nothing but an undershirt and panties, her bare feet propped up on the open windowsill. She had her red hair pulled back in a ponytail and dabbed at her exposed skin with a wet washcloth, but the effort did little to cool her. Drenched in sweat from the sweltering heat, she watched the skies—more accurately the monolithic sentries that hovered in place.

Six weeks. She sighed. Six weeks they'd been marooned on this planet and Michael hadn't received so much as a headache. God, or whoever was handing out Michael's assignments, was out on a long lunch and had apparently forgotten to leave her husband marching orders. So here they sat. Waiting.

The days were miserably hot and the nights weren't much better. The littered streets below their apartment were akin to a warzone, with squalling tires, shouting and screaming, and gun shots never giving her a moment's peace. Michael's inner warrior was dying to get out, but Sara understood they had to be careful. Michael felt that he could only intervene in another world's affairs when he felt the call of God. To do any more might upset the whole timeline of a world—affect countless generations and not necessarily for the better. Good intentions leading to hell, and all that.

This whole planet was stifling, accentuated by the looming alien ships overhead dominating the skies. Sara was ready to leave.

A shuffle in the hall. A low grumble. A clatter.

Sara put her feet on the coarse and dirtied floor. She quickly crossed the room to the mattress in the corner. By her bedside was the backpack she kept, a small collection of things she'd grown attached to during their marvelous journeys.

Beside the bag lay the blaster rifle she had been given as a gift from a parallel Mars where women were hailed as goddesses of war. She hefted the gun and slapped the power generator fixed to the undercarriage. It vibrated to life, priming the ionic pulse chamber. Sara hustled to the door, pressing her back to the wall, the gun aimed at where an intruder's head might emerge, just like Michael taught her.

Sara's finger stayed touching the trigger guard, needing only a twitch to be ready to fire. She slowed her breathing as Michael had instructed her. Focused. The door slowly creaked open and Sara flexed her grip on the rifle, her heart a steady beat in her ears.

An unruly blond mane popped in, then a hand jerked to the side with animal reflexes and ripped the blaster right out of her hand. Sara let it go with a yelp. She brought a knee up, striking the intruder in the stomach. He pushed her away, but Sara slipped under his hand and came up with a hard right cross, connecting against his jaw. The blaster clattered to the floor and Sara dove for it, coming up and firing the intruder dead center in his stomach. The man folded over, clutching at the smoking mark on his dirtied white T-shirt. Sara stood up, keeping the rifle leveled at his head.

"Don't move," she commanded.

"Not bad." Michael chuckled, then looked up.

Sara smirked. "Did I pass?"

Michael shut the door with a playful guffaw. He charged forward with a mischievous sneer, lifting her off the floor and slamming her to the mattress. Sara giggled all the way down. She wrapped her legs around him, pulling him close as he tenderly kissed her lips. She melted in his arms, feeling desired. *Powerful.* He kissed at her shoulders, moving down her neckline, lifting her shirt to reach her stomach. Sara grinned up at the ceiling. *I passed.*

3

Michael slipped back into his jeans, choosing to leave the shirt off for now. The heat was searing enough without sweaty clothes cloying at his skin.

Sara remained on the mattress, the threadbare sheets tousled around her. She sat up, her hair a matted mess, but her smile unrepressed.

"You're getting better," Michael said, snapping the button on his waistband.

"Oh really?" she laughed. "I'd say I'm pretty outright incredible."

Michael faced her, confused, then chuckled. "No. No, *that* was great. I meant before. At the door. You didn't let my attack surprise you. You kept coming. Adapting to my moves. Kept a level head."

Sara clapped her hands excitedly. "Yay!"

"Don't get cocky. That's—"

"Right, right. First big mistake. Except for you. You seem to pull it off all right."

"Yeah, well." He shrugged, feigning arrogance. "When you're invincible you're cool like that."

"Plus, you make a great punching bag. And I only feel a little bit guilty for hitting you again and again."

Michael crawled back on the mattress and gingerly took her chin. "Really. You're getting the hang of this. I'm proud of you."

She gave him a quick peck on the nose. "I have a good teacher."

Michael got up and moved toward their tiny drink cooler. He pulled out a water bottle and screwed off the top.

"Find anything this morning?" she asked.

"No. I took off as far as the fence, but nothing." He gulped the water, dissatisfied.

"That's twice a day for six weeks, now, and nothing from God. What's going on?" Sara asked.

"I don't know what the deal is," he said.

"I'll go out with you next time." Sara gave up the sheets to find her clothes.

"Okay." It killed him to agree. Were it up to him, she'd stay inside and let him handle the heroics. Sara had accompanied him often on his scouting missions, but even she, with all of her bluster to battle baddies these days, admitted that she was little use when it came to patrol. God never spoke to her, so she was only tagging along, making herself a target to the countless numbers of street scum festering on the streets outside.

But she'd spent her life with Charlie being locked up in a tower, and Michael reminded himself he had no right to treat her the same way.

"I was thinking." She tugged her shirt over her head. "We've been married for a while."

"Ha, ha, yeah?"

"Time gets wonky with all the rift jumping, I get that, but, I don't know. I'd say, if you added it all up, we've been married for about a year. Wouldn't you think?"

Michael shrugged, tossing her the water bottle, which she caught without missing a beat. Her reflexes were getting so much better. "Sure."

"So, maybe we should nail it down."

"What do you mean?"

"A date. We should set a date and say it's our anniversary and celebrate. No God stuff. No holy crusade. Just us, throwing a party for a year of being the coolest couple in the multiverse." She wiggled her eyebrows, chugging on the water.

Michael slid his arm around her. "I like it. We can do that. But later. Not this world."

"Agreed," she groaned. "This place sucks. Let's set it then. Next world we get to, *whenever* that is, that'll be our one year anniversary. Deal?"

She stuck out her hand, all professional, and Michael's heart melted. Five years of punching bad guys, lost, cold inside, and alone. Then one girl enters his life and everything's alive.

This had been the best year of his life.

He shook on it. "Deal."

4

Toby arrived home to a fleet of motorcycles on his front lawn. Beer guzzling leather-clad scuzzos tipped and twirled with their overweight and underdressed women. The front door was wide open, a constant stream of party traffic passing through.

Toby sighed, clutched his paper bag of groceries tighter, and marched for the door.

The boy kept his cool as the bikers hollered his way, asking him what he was doing here, telling him to leave the groceries and get out, calling him "four eyes" on account of his broken glasses. Toby ignored them all, their drunken catcalling easily deflecting off his mental armor. He wondered if the aliens had to deal with crap like this.

He was nearly toppled over as he ascended the front porch. He squeezed around an especially foul-smelling greaser blocking most of the front door.

"Mom," he called. "Got your food."

Women with heaving cleavage and too much makeup cooed over him as he trudged through the hallways. They rustled his unkempt hair, asking if he was old enough for a good time yet. Toby was definitely not interested in any kind of "good time" offered by these women.

"Mom!" he shouted.

"In here!" Her voice sounded from the living room. Toby entered, bombarded by the raucous laughter of the room full of men. In the center of them all, his mom sat on a biker's lap, her arms around him, snickering about something.

Toby dropped the groceries by the couch. "There."

She said something to him, but he didn't hear. His attention was instantly drawn to the two men who sat cross-legged on the living room floor in front of the TV.

Playing his video games.

They laughed and cursed in some digital battle-to-the-death, hammering the buttons on the video game controllers. When one lost, he spat a string of obscenities and hurled the controller to the ground.

"Hey!" Toby shouted, kicking through empty bags of potato chips and beer cans. "Don't do that! You'll break it!"

The offender picked up the controller, ready for Round Two. "Relax, kid."

Toby turned to his mom, who was nibbling at her new boyfriend's earlobe. "Mom! Make him stop! That's my game!" *It's the only thing I've got.* He wanted to cry.

Another defeated holler and the controller landed on the floor with a hard slap. A cracked chip of plastic casing broke free this time. "I've had it with this stupid game!" the man said. Then, with both grimy hands, he reached down, ripped the game system from the wall outlet, and tossed it across the room, where it shattered in the hallway.

"Hey," Toby's mom called out, half-heartedly. "Cut it out, Lee."

Lee shooed off Toby's mom, while his opponent laughed through a stoned haze.

Toby, though, only flared, his hateful stare pinning Lee. Tears streaming down his soft cheeks, he growled, "You broke it!"

Lee lit a cigarette and blew smoke in the kid's face. "Whattya gonna do about it, you baby?"

Hate—cold and strong like iron—laced Toby's bones, his nerves, and chilled his blood. He felt invincible in its power, and stronger than any normal boy. Gritting his teeth, he reached out in base instinct, funneling all of his anger at his mother, his dad, his life, and let it all out.

"I hate you!"

A blast of ice exploded from his hands, flash freezing Lee in that same disgusted snarl. Screams erupted as bikers and trashy women tripped over each other, desperate to get away.

As soon as Toby's outrage had subsided, he relaxed, instantly released. Wide-eyed in shock, he stared at Lee's frozen form. His mom stumbled back, her face a picture of terror. "You're a freak!" Tears streaked her mascara. "Get out! Get out!"

"Lee? I'll kill you!" another biker roared, rushing into the room with a switch blade in place. "Die, you little—"

Toby ducked out of the way and raced for the exit, petrified and confused. He kicked and fought through the throngs of people who didn't belong in his house, finally breaking free. The biker with the knife was hot on his heels, but Toby ran fast, dodging the curses and the threats. He never looked back.

5

Michael left his leather jacket behind in the apartment. He'd not had need to wear it much on this scorching world, but felt somehow defenseless without it. He patrolled down the slum streets that afternoon, Sara at his side. His wife had her blaster slung across her back. Gangs were the natural order and nearly everyone was packing heat. Even the Martian origin of Sara's treasured weapon seemed normal, what with motherships locked in orbit overhead.

Sara kept ready, her bright blue eyes cutting sharp lines across the horizon, scanning alleyways, rooftops. Her senses were honed, ready for action. More than ready, eager. Michael, on the other hand, barely paid attention. He'd let down his guard after six weeks of no action, but Sara was prepared for an ambush at every turn. *She's gonna burn out if she keeps this intense.*

Studying the dark alien shapes looming in the sky, Michael shook his head. "It's gotta be them. We've gotta be here to bring them down. Free the humans or something like that."

"How are we going to get up there, then? We can't get past the armed turrets posted at the fence. Well, *you* can, I guess…" She frowned.

Michael nudged her with his elbow. "Forget it. We're in this together. I'm not going up there unless I can figure out how to get us both up there."

Shrugging, she smiled faintly. "I'm holding you back. Aren't I? Face it, you'd do something crazy and hijack a space ship to get up there and tear down the whole network if I weren't tagging along."

She's right. "We'll find a way, Sara. Just gotta wait for God to open a door."

A rumble of distant motorcycles shook the ground, rattling the nearby windows. Michael paused, feeling a dull throb in his mind. "Oh, wait. Wait."

Sara nodded, reaching around for her blaster, slapping the charger. "You got something?"

The throb turned to an ache, louder. Sharper. He glanced up as a young boy tore around the corner, running straight for them, horrified. Michael was about to point at the boy, then saw the motorcycles rounding into view. The riders were shouting at the child, spitting on him, pointing, revving their engines, bearing down on him.

Familiar pain, still just as startling as the first time he'd felt it, sawed through Michael's stomach like a serrated blade. He grimaced, tears blurring his vision. "There!"

Sara did not hesitate. She aimed her rifle, took a deep breath, then fired. An electric bolt tore the lead biker off his bike, sending his riderless motorcycle smashing into its neighbor.

"Come on!" Sara shouted at the boy. "This way!"

The boy hurried and Michael waved him closer, the pain in his gut nearly driving him to his knees. Once the kid was cleared, Sara fired three more blasts into the biker gang, sending riders and cycles spinning to the ground.

"I'll cover you!" Sara screamed over the rapid hiss of her blaster.

"No!" He passed the shell-shocked boy towards her. "Take him! Get back! I'll cover you."

Sara slapped the charger, recharging her energy clip. "I can do it!"

"*Sara!*"

She bit her lip, fired once more into the mob, then took the boy's hand. "Come on," she said, a bit harsh. "Follow me."

Michael watched her go, feeling bad for snapping at her. She only wanted to help, but she had to learn her limitations. Once she and the boy were clear, Michael's pain quickly subsided, and he faced the bikers. One by one, they picked themselves off the pavement, cut and scraped and madder than before. Knives and guns were drawn as they advanced.

Michael folded his arms, smiling. Without Sara here to protect, he felt unshackled. Like back in the old days.

"Going somewhere?" he asked.

"You're going to die, kid," the one in front with the cut lip grunted, aiming a pistol.

Kid. Michael often forgot that on the outside he looked like a seventeen-year-old kid. *But I feel so much older.* He waved the gunman forward. "Take your best sho—"

BAM!

The bullet punctured Michael's right side, just under his breastbone. He regarded the hole in his shirt, the unmarked skin underneath. *At least it wasn't my jacket.*

Once the bikers realized that he'd not been taken down by a single bullet, they all unloaded on him. Pistols and sawed-off shotguns popped like fireworks, their report echoing everywhere. Michael ran forward, shrugging off the hundreds of impacts, and punched the lead biker hard in the jaw. There was a *pop* as the punch turned the man's head at a wrong angle, cracking his spine. He dropped dead, his fingers still twitching, firing the weapon until it went dry.

The other bikers shouted in horror, backing away, continuing to fire. Michael would not let them escape. With thunderous fists, he smashed the men in their faces, caving in noses. He kicked chests, shattering ribcages. He hurled his attackers against the buildings, busting glass and plaster alike. The sound of staccato gunfire was deafening, but Michael shut it out. Only felt the calm peace wash over him as he dealt death without remorse or mercy.

In that moment he was twelve years old again, people pushing him around, life treating him unfairly, and he only wanted to lash out until all the voices were silenced.

A shrill alarm split through his killing zone and the biker he was preparing to hit vaporized in a puff of black ash. Michael staggered back and looked to the skies. Three small rotating cylinders with hundreds of blinking lights floated overhead. Alien gibberish blared over a loudspeaker on the lead drone, followed by a mechanical voice in English. "HUMANS. END YOUR SQUABBLING OR WE WILL END IT FOR YOU. RIOTING WILL NOT BE TOLERATED."

One of the surviving bikers shouted in defiance and turned his shotgun on the drones. He fired once before they reduced him to cinders. Everyone on the streets yelled and scattered like cockroaches unearthed under a rock. Michael disappeared into the chaos, making his exit while the drones fired indiscriminately into the crowd, vaporizing with abandon, herding the people like cattle.

Michael ducked down an alley, unsure of what to do. Should he stay and take out the drones? Save these people? That would certainly draw the attention of the overlords from their high places. *But you're not here for the aliens. You're here for that kid, for whatever reason.* Michael tensed as a young woman was obliterated into dust right in front of him, mid-scream.

Then, across the street, strangely perched on a street lamp, Michael locked eyes with a man thin as a rail. He was dressed in a cheap and too-small suit, his dress coat sporting long tails. He wore a top hat that cast shadows over a beak-like nose and wild sneer. The stranger tipped the hat to Michael, in greeting, revealing a wild mane of white hair, then flickered like a TV with bad reception, and vanished.

"What the…?"

Above, the cylinder drones finally moved on. The streets settled into weeping for the dead. Michael waited a moment more, watching the three alien monitors fly off, regretting that his time to take the fight to the aliens had passed.

6

Michael entered the apartment building, sidestepping the impoverished people that cluttered the lobby. He watched drug deals being made amidst playing children, and disheveled dead-eyed women exiting rooms with strange men, absently taking the money offered them for services rendered. This world was a hotbed of disease and tainted with the worst of humanity. Why did his mission have to be this boy? It was the aliens who needed overthrowing. That was the only way these people had any hope of rising above this hellhole and starting a new life for themselves. *Can't God see that?*

Michael ascended the trash-ridden steps and down the hall towards his and Sara's apartment. He slipped his key in the lock and turned the knob to enter. Immediately he sensed Sara by the door, her blaster aimed at his head.

"It's me," he said.

Sara lowered the rifle and locked the door behind him. "You look terrible." She gaped down at the tattered remains of Michael's shirt.

He stripped it off, throwing it into the trash bin in the kitchenette. "Where is he?"

Sara nodded towards the corner and the bespectacled boy poked out from his hiding place behind the deceased television set.

"Any trouble getting here?" Michael asked in a hurry.

She shook her head, setting her gun on the small stained kitchen table. "You?"

"Drones showed up." He dug around in their belongings for a new shirt. "Started blasting the place."

There's more, Michael thought to say. There was the thin man in the coattails. Sara needed to know about that, but he didn't want to talk about it yet. Not until he knew what was so important about this one little boy. Michael approached the kid, trying to soften the adrenaline edge. "Hey, kid. What's your name?"

The boy looked to Sara first, as if silently asking for permission to speak. Sara nodded, and Michael saw that they had already developed a trust. *Good. We'll need that.* "Toby."

"What did those guys want with you?"

Sara stepped beside Michael, her face stony. "It's okay," she said to Toby. "You can trust him."

Toby concentrated on a spot behind Michael as Sara gently pushed her husband back a step. "Better move," she said.

Michael watched as the kid raised a hand. A prickly stream of ice jettisoned like a rocket from the boy's palm, turning the trash bin with Michael's shirt into a jagged lump of ice.

"Whoa!" Michael ran a hand through his hair.

He faced Sara and she nodded.

"I'm a freak," the boy said, slumping to sit in Sara's wooden chair.

Michael pulled his wife toward the kitchen. "What's this all about?"

Sara shook her head. "I don't know. He doesn't either. It just happened for the first time today. He was mad at those biker guys and it just…came out."

Aliens were one thing, but now there were Super Powers on this world too? That didn't make sense. They'd been here for six weeks and had seen some pretty crazy things—but nothing like this. Super ice-blasting powers didn't belong on this world.

Who is this kid?

"He's our mission, right?"

Michael watched the boy. Toby wiped at a few stray tears from his eyes, looking to the floor. "Yeah. I believe he is."

"This doesn't feel right."

"Sara, listen, there's something else I've gotta tell you. Back there after the fight, I saw someone. A thin man. One minute he was there, then he wasn't."

"Teleporting?" They'd encountered teleportation a time or two in the last year.

"I don't know. But he was watching me. Like he knew me."

Sara heaved a great sigh. "Your friend in the Stetson really picked an awesome time to be out for lunch."

7

As dusk fell, Michael kept watch from the miniature balcony. For what, Sara didn't really know. But he was determined that they were smack in the middle of their mission on this world and he was in full "game on" mode. He was wearing his bullet-riddled leather jacket despite the heat, which showed he meant business.

While he watched and waited for something to happen, Sara and Toby huddled in the cramped living space. Sara sat on their sleeping mat, her Martian rifle draped across her legs. She had out her dirtied rag and wiped the blaster down, caring for it as an old friend. Toby sat opposite her. He was near catatonic when they'd brought him in, but he'd certainly loosened up since.

"You're putting me on!" Toby laughed in disbelief, and Sara joined him, surprised and amused by his sudden outburst. "I don't believe you're from another world."

"It's true." Sara chuckled. "My husband and I travel across alternate dimensions, helping out whenever we can."

Toby's eyes widened more. "And you're here to help *me?*"

Sara craned her head. Got a good look at Michael, stiff as a statue, examining every avenue of attack. She faced Toby again. "Looks like."

He blushed. "Is it because of…what I can do?"

"We don't know yet. Michael sort of hears from God. It helps him figure out what he's supposed to do next."

"Who's God?" Toby's brows cinched up.

"You don't know who God is?"

Toby shook his head.

Sara huffed, under her breath. "Maybe you're better off."

"What?"

Sara waved him off. "Nothing. Don't worry. You'll be safe with us."

"I feel safe," Toby said. "I never felt safe back at home. Mom never…never did a very good job of protecting me."

Sara's heart broke for him. The kid was abandoned. He was as good as an orphan now. *Just like me and Michael.* Further hurt set in, though, when she realized that Toby would be left behind, again, when she and Michael jumped out of here.

Or would he? Michael changed the rules when he brought her along. Maybe…

{*Sara.*}

She heard Michael speak her name in her mind. Ever since their encounter on Chris' world, they had begun to develop some type of telepathic bond. Neither of them had any clue how such a thing was possible, or why it was happening. It wasn't always on, either. It was like they had each found a door to the other person's mind—but they still had to knock to get in. They hadn't yet tested the limits of their new ability and were hesitant to rely upon it until they knew more about it. But it sure came in handy in a fight sometimes.

Or when they were being watched and had to keep a low profile.

Sara glanced up. Michael stared her down, his face twisted in discomfort. {*I feel it. They're getting—*}

FWOOSH!

A pillar of fire fell from above and incinerated the balcony. Sara yanked Toby to his feet and shoved him behind her. In one automatic move, she gripped her Martian blaster, slapped the undercarriage.

She watched the raging inferno, waiting for Michael to emerge as he always did. She searched for him with her mind.

{*Michael?*}

Sounds outside the door. The door burst open. Sara's instincts took over. As she and Michael had rehearsed a thousand times, she pressed her back to the wall and aimed the blaster. A purple-skinned alien poked his head in, and she pulled the trigger.

A static bolt of rippling blue caught the alien's head, pinwheeling him to the floor. He was immediately replaced by another intruder—this one a young Asian woman with long blue bangs combed to one side. Sara fired again, but the woman dodged the blast and punched Sara hard in the stomach. Sara staggered back and dropped the gun. She took a deep breath and came up with an uppercut, knocking the attacker off balance. Grabbing the woman's hair, Sara brought head down into knee, and the intruder was out cold.

Two more men—one human, one vaguely triceratops in nature—took her place. They charged Sara, one securing her from behind. Sara kicked at the human, pushing off his groin and connecting a knee to his lip.

He grunted and spewed blood from his mouth.

Sara smashed the back of her head into her dino captor's snout. He released her and she slipped to the floor, reaching for her gun with one hand and waving Toby towards her with the other. "Hurry!"

Whoever these guys were, they weren't bikers. She needed to get out of here. To regroup. Think. Find Michael.

With the boy holding on, Sara fought against the flames and pushed to the edge of the fiery maw where the balcony and her husband had once been. "Michael!" She searched the rising heat and smoke, but couldn't see him in the flaming rubble on the streets below.

A hand clamped around her ankle and she shrieked. It was Michael, hanging on to the ruined wall of the apartment. His clothes were charcoal and smoking, but he was unharmed. Sara let go of Toby and knelt down, pulling on her husband. Together they worked until he was back in the room with them.

"Are you okay?" he asked, looking to the four intruders moaning and bloodied on the floor. "Wow. Did you do that?"

Sara looked back, feeling an intense sense of pride filling her. "Yes. Yes, I did."

"Who are they?" Toby asked, his voice tense and shrill.

A second wave of figures—a bizarre mix of mostly humans with a smattering of aliens that couldn't *all* be native to this world, who were all clothed in the same long black coats—filled the doorway. "I don't know, but there's more!" Sara shouted.

She fired into their numbers, her back pressed to the opening and three-story drop. The attackers ducked out of the doorframe, dodging her bolts, then hurled fireballs into the room.

"Firestarters!" Michael hollered.

The room caught fire where the burning orbs touched down. One fire-bomb struck her gun, turning it white-hot. Sara dropped it into the conflagration that threatened to claim them all.

No, not all. Michael will survive. He'll always survive. Always be stronger than me.

"We have to get out!" Michael said.

"Here!" Toby shouted, scurrying to the blown-out wall of the apartment. He squinted and lifted his hands. A blast of ice shot out and formed a misshapen bridge to the ground. "It's like a slide!" He hopped on the lumpy ice hill and half-slid, half-bounced through the flaming mouth to safety.

Sara reached for her blaster, but Michael pushed her down the slide next. Touching foot on the ground below, Sara looked up as Michael slid down to join them. Seconds later, the apartment exploded in a devastating fireball.

{*No!*} she screamed inside, thinking of all the things she'd collected over their adventures. All the pieces of their life together that meant so much to her.

Michael gripped her arm and hurried her forward. {*Sara, forget it! We have to move!*}

The three of them ran down the street full of panicked people. More black-clad firestarters poured out of alleyways, doorways, from rooftops.

{*They're everywhere!*} Sara thought to him as her heart thundered in her chest, and she nearly lost hope. She and Michael had been through a lot, but this felt like the end.

❽

The Rage found me.

Michael hurried his wife and the boy down an alley, his soul trembling with fear. The Hooded Man had told him it'd come to this: *"You've got a beast inside you, kid, and that's the Rage's property. It isn't going to just let one of Its attack dogs running around like a stray."*

Chris Thompson had confirmed it: *"He's after you, guy. He said the dude in the hood tried to warn you. But you wouldn't come back peacefully…He's got a whole army of people just like me, Mike, to replace you. You'll see. Aw, man, I can't wait til you get yours."*

Now it had finally come down to this moment. His end had caught up to him. *How can I win against this?*

The Rage wasn't something he could hit. It was something he didn't understand. Some formless beast waiting in the Void in the In-Between.

How could he combat something like that? He'd done his best to train Sara, make her ready for this day. She'd held her own, but they were up against so much more than he could have prepared her for.

"Up here!" He hurried to a fire escape, running on pure adrenaline. He had no plan, no idea what he would do or how many they were up against. He just knew he had to get them away.

Sara helped Toby go first, then followed behind. Michael nearly shoved them to the rooftop. They reached the top and Michael dropped low, peering over the corner. The army of firestarters rushed like a flood through the alley below. In moments they had passed. Their carnage had attracted the attention of the drones. Five of them zipped and zoomed across the street, examining the burning pyre that had been Michael and Sara's home for six weeks.

Michael laid flat on his back on the roof, breathing life back into his lungs. Toby huddled, quiet and unmoving, as if waiting for the firestarters to come back. Sara crawled by Michael's side, her voice barely above a whisper. "What do we do?"

He shook his head. "I don't know."

9

Hours passed, and the three of them hadn't moved from the rooftop. Michael had taken to pacing in silent concentration. Sara hated it when he paced. She wished he would calm down. Talk to her. Figure this out together. She knocked on the door to his mind, but he wasn't answering.

Toby kept to himself a small distance away. Sara feared for the boy and wanted to comfort him, but now wasn't the time. The Rage had sent its attack dogs after them, her only means of defending herself was gone, and her husband—the only one who had the power to do anything about all of this—had clammed up.

"There can't be that many, can there?" Sara asked Michael at last, unable to stand his brooding quiet any longer.

"There was at least thirty after us back at the apartment." He gestured wildly to the smoking ruins across the street, agitated. The alien drones had extinguished the immediate inferno, but ignored the debris. The aliens couldn't care less about rebuilding for the humans. "But thirty is enough.

I can't protect you both from that many."

"You don't have to protect me."

"Sara, stop." Michael sighed. "We don't have time for this."

She folded her arms. "Time for *what?*"

"What are you trying to prove anyway?"

She snapped around, walking away. "Forget it."

"Hey," he called out, hotly, and took her arm. "You're really going to do this *now?*"

"I'm sick of trying to prove myself to you! I'm not just some dumb kid anymore, okay?"

"Don't you think I know that?"

"No! Stop trying to take care of me like you're my babysitter. We're partners. When are you going to get that?"

"When are you going to get that I love you?" he roared back at her. "You are all I have, Sara. You are the most important thing to me. What am I supposed to do? Just stop caring about you?" He cooled and shook his head, looking to the night sky. Sara saw regret on his face. Regret that he'd yelled at her, perhaps?

Or regret that he'd even met her? Brought her along?

Her heart sank.

"Are...are they after *me?*" Toby finally asked, his voice sounding small amidst the shouting.

Michael and Sara paused their bickering and looked to him.

"No," Sara said without hesitation.

"We don't know," Michael said after a moment.

Sara calmed and walked over to the boy. "We can't know for sure."

"Yes. We can," said Michael.

Sara stared at her husband. "No."

"I'm going out there, Sara—"

"No."

"Stay here."

Michael moved for the fire escape, but Sara gripped his arm in a heartbeat. "Don't do this."

"I'm the only one who *can*, Sara. They can't kill me."

"There are worse things than death." Sara looked deep into Michael's eyes, fear slowly pushing aside her pride. "This is the Rage we're talking about. Don't...don't underestimate it. I don't want to lose you, either."

"You won't," he said and leaned in to kiss her. She resisted at first, but allowed a small peck on the lips.

Michael pulled from Sara's grip and descended the fire escape. Sara watched him leave, angry. Angry at Michael, at God, at herself. She didn't know. But her fists shook and her jaw clenched so tight her teeth hurt. Wherever the Man in the Stetson was hiding, Sara hoped he was the kind of guy who pulled through for his friends when they needed him most.

10

Michael walked down the ghetto streets, ignoring the hungry and defeated faces that surrounded him. He'd grown up like a lot of these people. Hand to mouth, fighting for every last scrap of food. It was a living death, what they were experiencing, and he felt guilty knowing that if he and Sara survived this mission he'd jump right out of here for greener pastures. Meanwhile, these people—Toby—stayed behind. Michael thought back to his brothers, Edward and Seth, and all that they had been through growing up. It'd been a hard life. A bad life. Still, he craved to be with his brothers again so much sometimes that he felt like cursing God if it'd get him out of this "forever quest" deal and let him get back to them. Back home.

Sara was his home now, though. If he could just keep her in one piece.

Sara wasn't a big fan of God. Michael understood that. He wasn't much of a fan himself some days. But even through the long periods of silence, Michael could look back on the things the Man in the Stetson had given him and he couldn't hate him. The Man had salvaged Michael's body when Big Joe's men had gunned him down. He'd given Michael new life, a purpose. Protected him all these years, on all these wild battles.

Above all, he had given Michael Sara. That was the greatest blessing of all. He loved her more than words could say, more than his actions could show. She was inside him, all the time, permeating every thought, every reaction. They were connected in ways he had yet to understand, only to know that they were one.

What am I doing to her?

With each passing world, Sara was growing harder, losing the soft innocence she'd had when they first met. *I'm changing her.* He didn't want that. He didn't want her to be like him.

Though the thought of war with the Rage scared him, he was secretly glad that it had finally started. He'd grown tired of looking over his shoulder, fearing this moment. Now that it was here, he could face it. Hit it. Kill it. At least, he hoped he could, but Sara was right. The Rage wasn't a monster he could attack. It was some ethereal thing operating in the hearts of men.

God, I could really use some direction down here.

On top of firestarters, now Michael had Toby to worry about. First he had to figure out what he was saving Toby from. After that, then what? Drop the kid off on a random doorstep? Condemn him to the same hard life Michael had needed a miracle to survive? *I can't do that.* And the alternative? Take someone else with him on the inter-dimensional road? Bring some little kid into this war with the Rage? That's all he needed. Someone else to teach how to kill and survive. Someone else's innocence torn away because of his selfishness.

I should have left Sara on her world. As much as it kills me to think it, it was wrong to bring her with me. Life would have been hard for her, but not like this. She's going to die and Toby will too, if I take him with us.

Michael just wanted all of this madness to end.

A prickling at the base of his neck silenced his doubts and Michael spun around, narrowly dodging a ball of churning flame. He braced himself, fists tightening, and watched as a laughing figure with glowing red eyes emerged from the darkness between two houses.

"Hiya there, guy."

Michael's dark eyes narrowed. "Chris Thompson."

Chris wore the black turtleneck and long leather coat as the other firestarters. His hair had grown out, the white curls tight and frizzy. His face was harder than before, indicating that years had perhaps passed on his world, but he still bore the mouth-shaped scar on his cheek where Sara had bitten him.

"I thought you'd still be in custody," Michael quipped. He watched the shadows, waiting for more firestarters.

"Nah, I quit their school." Chris shrugged playfully. "What could they really teach me there, anyway? To control my power? Why control it? It was a gift. Gifts are supposed to be used."

Michael braced himself for a fight, mentally daring Chris to get within punching distance. *I'll cave in that smug face of yours, don't you worry.* "What about Light Sphere? I'm sure he had some things to say about that."

"Oh, he did." Chris laughed. "But he's not saying much of anything now."

"I'm going to kill you." Michael glowered. "You know that, right?"

"So, what do you think about our little gang?" Chris said. "Did you think I was lying when I told you what the Maestro had planned?"

"I've fought worse."

Chris nodded, circling Michael, his eyes dancing with mischief. "Maybe. But it's just the warm-up act. See, there's this little legend. About an army of grey-skinned monsters. One that would make *our* little group of firestarters look like a preschool class. Turns out they're stuck on this planet, though, called…" Chris tapped his lip in thought. "Chekla, Chelkis—"

Michael barely contained a gasp. "Chelkan."

Chris' face lit up. "Heard of it, have you?" He sneered. "Or maybe saw it in a dream? I have, too. We all have. The monsters, see, they were *looking* for something. What, I have no idea. No one's told us yet, officially, but you hear things."

"What things?"

Chris ignored him, leering. "But the way I hear it, the monsters are stranded now, after their last general died. You were supposed to be his replacement and start up the search again, but, well…we see how that's turned out."

The terrible boom-boom-boom rumbled his stomach and Michael swooned, as though he were slipping back into those vivid dreams.

Chris winced. "Oooh, you feel that? Yeah, it's like everything's making sense, now, isn't it?"

"Do you ever shut up?"

Chris came to a dead stop, his grin waning. "Look, you thought you were hot stuff, but you're old news. Everything the Rage had planned for the multiverse is halted because you won't pick up your birthright and lead the monster army. So now you got people like me. We're the new breed of soldier. But, see, there can only be one of us. The Maestro only has to find one general to lead the lost army on Chelkan. And all it takes to get the promotion is to get rid of *you*."

"Ha," Michael chuckled through a dark grimace. "You'll all die trying."

Chris held up a finger. "Ah, but that's where I have an advantage. I know you better than the others. I know your one weakness."

Michael bared his teeth, cold rage oozing its way through him.

"And how *is* Sara?" Chris smiled. "Still fine as ever?"

"Say her name again. I'll rip your tongue out of your mouth."

Chris leaned forward. "Sa—"

Michael was on him in an instant, his vice-like hands wrapped around Chris' throat. Chris looked legitimately surprised, as if he really thought he could get away with taunting Michael. He gagged and placed his hands on Michael's arms, firing them up. But Michael pushed through the blaze, maintaining the stranglehold. "I should have done this the moment I met you."

Somewhere behind him, Michael heard a snap—like fingers—and felt an incredible wave of pain wrap around his body. He immediately released Chris and dropped to his knees, screaming louder than he'd thought possible. It was like his stomach cramps multiplied by a thousand—unlike anything he had ever experienced before. Michael felt the veins in his head pop and blood ran down over his eyes. "God!" he shrieked, falling on all fours and throwing up vomit and blood.

"He's busy," said a new voice. "Just you and me, Michael."

The pain vanished and Michael rolled over on his back, clutching his stomach, bleeding from the pores in his skin. He coughed up the remnants of the blood in his mouth, and spotted Chris massaging his throat.

"You said you weren't going to let him hurt me," Chris said.

Michael angled himself to get a good look at this new figure. It was the same thin man in the top hat and coattails. Like some cheap stage magician, but an unmistakable power in his eyes challenged Michael to voice that comparison out loud.

"Who are you?" Michael croaked.

"I've been called many things by many worlds," the man said, flatly. "But the name is not important. My symphony speaks for itself."

Michael coughed. "The Maestro."

"The Rage has been looking everywhere for you."

"You found me." Michael spat again. He sat up, preparing to stand. "Good job."

"Oh, I'd say so. Time to go home now. You've been a very bad dog."

Michael laughed, knowing the Maestro would probably see through the bluff. Michael wasn't so convinced he could do anything about this, after all. "I'll pass on leading your monster army. Thanks for the offer, though."

"That offer is no longer on the table," the man said, with no humor in his voice. "You are obsolete. Now we'll just settle for locking you up in the worst hell imaginable for the rest of eternity. And you *will* heel, boy. If not— Well…I've brought friends."

A snap of the fingers and an army of firestarters flickered into existence.

Sara and Toby were with them.

Sara struggled in the arms of her captor, while Toby did not move. Just hung his head.

"No…" Michael shut his eyes, tearing up without shame. They'd used Sara against him, just like he knew they always would.

The Maestro waved a hand to the others, looking bored as though he had an important meeting and Michael was a simple nuisance holding him up. "You're outnumbered. Even with all that power, you can't stop us all and you can't save your friends."

Michael shared a look with Sara. He focused and thought to her, {*Babe, can you hear me?*}

Sara stopped squirming. {*What's the plan? I can get free—*}

{*Don't. Stop. This isn't the way.*}

Sara's eyes narrowed, filling with tears. {*Don't do something stupid.*}

{*I'm not. But I'm tired of fighting. We thought we could run away forever, but…we've gotta go back home eventually.*}

"What's it going to be, Michael?"

Michael lowered his head. {*Sara, I'm sorry.*}

{*No! Don't do this! We can fight them! I trusted you! I left everything for you!*}

{*I love you, babe.*}

Sara went limp in her captor's arms, weeping. {*…I love you, Michael. I love you so much.*}

Michael raised his head, faced the Maestro straight on. "Nobody has to get hurt. I'm ready. I won't fight."

Sara roared and twisted. But her abductor was fast and prepared, easily putting her back into submission. The Maestro sighed in relief. "Splendid. Let's get this going, then."

He snapped his fingers and, before Michael had a chance to look back to Sara—to say good-bye to the love of his life—the ground beneath him buckled and broke away and Michael fell into the abyss, lost to the In-Between...where the Rage would be waiting.

Welcome home.

11

Sara screamed, kicked and brawled and bit. But it was no use. She collapsed, crying hysterically.

The Maestro regarded her blankly. Then he moved past her to stand before Toby.

"Stay away from him!" Sara shouted, her throat burning.

Toby faced the man, his brown eyes brimming with tears.

"Hello, Toby," the Maestro said with more care than he'd used before. "Ready to come along?"

Toby balked. "What?"

"Those powers of yours are very special, Toby. But they come with a price. My Master will want to use you too. We have beautiful music to make."

"No." Toby whimpered.

"Oh, my Master will want to get a look at you. You're unique. When he gave out his powers, they manifested as fire. Blinding, rage-fueled fire, like in my friend Chris, here."

Sara was startled to hear the name. Even more startled to see Chris Thompson stepping into view, grinning maliciously. "Chris?"

"Hey, Sara. Good to see you again."

The Maestro continued. "But not you, Toby. You took that power, and your rage was so powerful that you turned it to *ice*." Nearly gasping in amazement, the devil said, "Do you understand how unique that is? You must have some real hate inside you, little boy. There's a whole army on Chelkan that could be yours to command."

"Hey," Chris said, nearly stumbling forward in his haste. "That wasn't part of the deal. I handed you Michael. *I* get the army."

The Maestro ignored Chris, stroking Toby's chubby chin. "Would you like me to kill him for you, my lord?"

"Toby! Don't listen to him!" Sara screamed.

"I can teach you. No one will ever pick on you again."

"Chris!" Sara pleaded. "If you ever cared about me, don't let him do this. Stop him!"

Chris hesitated, eyeing the Maestro. "We got Michael like you wanted. You said we'd let them go. Hurting Sara is not an option."

The Maestro regarded Chris with a baleful look. Chris' head suddenly jerked to the side unnaturally, breaking his neck. His lifeless body dropped to the dirt in a heap, without fanfare. Sara hung her head, gnashing her teeth. "I hate you!" she screamed.

Turning back to Toby, the Maestro frowned. "I'm sorry for my impulsiveness, my lord. Please forgive me."

"Leave him alone! He's just a little boy!" Sara seethed.

"Not when I'm through with him."

"God!" Sara shouted to the heavens. "Where are you? Help us!"

The Maestro left Toby behind and strolled to Sara, eyeing her curiously. "And you. You, you, you."

Sara faced him, baring her teeth through tears. "Come closer. I'll give you a kiss."

"I'm sure you'd like to. My Master had plans for you too."

"I'll bet he did. You wanna know where he can shove his plans?"

The Maestro smiled for the first time since this horrible nightmare. It chilled Sara to her depths. "Michael's rubbed off on you, I see. Good. You'll need that edge for what's in store. We've invested a lot of time in you, Sara. Myself most of all."

Sara's blood ran cold and her bravado faded. "What do you mean?"

"Your lover was never going to win this. Even if he'd fought off my firestarters, we always had a back-up plan that he would have never seen coming. Pity it won't come to fruition now. That was one of my finest concertos. Your parents' death. Charlie. Misery is like a song, Sara, and your suffering was the most beautiful music of all. I hope you enjoyed my work."

Sara was so bombarded with thoughts and emotions and questions. So many things she wanted to ask, to know. But, she thought of Michael being pulled into hell, not as a hero, but as a prisoner.

She spat in the Maestro's face.

He wiped the spittle away. "Everyone's a critic."

"Sara..." Toby said.

She looked to him. Saw him, so small and innocent. *We would have been good parents to you. We would have taken care of you.*

"What, Toby?"

"I'm ready to go now," he said, frowning. "Are you?"

She laughed through her cries. "Yeah. Yeah, I'd like that."

His eyes crinkled into a smile. "Go left."

Sara frowned in confusion before Toby threw his head back and shouted. A shockwave of power blasted forth, flash-freezing the man who held him, and the two nearest him. Sara took her moment and leaned over, using her leverage to knock the already distracted firestarter to the ground. She kicked loose of him and ran for Toby, scooping the boy in her arms.

"Hold on!" she shouted, running down the street.

Fire rained down around them, but she dodged to the best of her ability, as Toby countered the attacks with his own power.

We might make it out of this yet.

12

For untold millennia, Michael resided in hell, his body reduced to bloodied leathery strips, rebuilt, then torn down again. All around him he could hear the inhuman wails of the damned and the clanking of great steel hooks and chains. Consumed by fire, by pain, by evil, he tossed and turned in the dark, screaming until he had no voice to shout. No thought, no conscious, just unending death. Forever and ever.

Then he saw only white.

Michael stood in the presence of some Great Light, and was overwhelmed by the feeling that he was safe. For a moment, he forgot Sara, forgot his past and the fighting and the rift jumping—all of it. Here, in this White Place, his body healed. His clothes returned. Even the leather jacket that he'd come to think of as his second skin fit snug. The hell that held him a second ago seemed like three lifetimes away, distant memories removed of pain. They sat like someone else's experiences in his mind and he had no idea why. He felt complete, and for the first time, at perfect peace.

"Michael," a Voice addressed him, though he heard no words. Rather, he *felt* them. Felt their intent, the compassion behind them, and understood them in his heart.

Michael shielded his eyes as a new brightness approached him. Squinting, he could barely make out the semi-familiar shape of that stranger he met so long ago in the desert. He had only known him as the Man in the Stetson, the soft-spoken wizard in the funny coat and cowboy hat, but here he sat in all his splendor, and Michael realized he had never really known the Man at all. "You..." he breathed.

This was heaven, and before him stood its King. *How could I have thought of Him as anything less?* The last time he'd spoken to the Man, by that quiet church in the country, Michael was cocksure and arrogant, certain of everything. Demanding answers, as though he were owed them. But in the White Place, the Truth stood revealed to him, and he *knew* now his place in Creation, he grasped God's sovereignty and love and wisdom. Here, Michael finally understood perfect trust and oneness with God in a way he never could've back in the crude, material world. Michael thought back to this past year, his doubts, his accusations against God, his fears, and he felt ashamed for all of it.

"I'm sorry." He wept, dropping to his knees, pressing his face into his hands.

The Light spoke to him. Not in words, but in intent. In love. Michael felt the words in his heart, internally translating them to Michael-speak.

"How long was I there? In hell?" Michael asked, feeling old yet brand new.

"There is no time in these places. Only existence. You were there. Now you are here. I brought you out. This is a place of the spirit, but you are here in flesh, as well. You don't belong here."

"Then...why am I here?"

"I am sending you back to Creation."

Michael sobbed. "No...please, don't. I don't want to. I don't want to leave."

"You are not ready for this place, Michael." The Light emoted patience. Mercy. "There is more to do. But you need to understand. There are things I must tell you. Things I couldn't explain while you were in the multiverse."

Michael rose. "Like what?"

"You are not your own."

"The Rage…" Michael looked to the ground.

"It has many names. For you, it's the Rage, for that's how you knew it. For others, it's Greed, Lust, Envy. All facets of the same Beast. Evil in its purest form. It corrupted my fallen angels, it tainted Creation, fragmenting it."

Michael stood, thirsty to hear more. "Fragmenting it."

"In the beginning I formed one world. One creation. I introduced choice into the world, and with choice came the possibility of disobedience. It was Adam's disobedience in the garden that brought sin, rebellion, and death into the order. Every choice—every possibility— leads to a new world. Infinite possibilities."

"The multiverse."

"The multiverse comprises the whole of Creation, but is, in itself, mirrors of the original."

Suddenly, the White was gone and Michael was standing in empty black, but not the Black of the In-Between where the Rage waited for him. In this black, a lone mirror stood before him. Michael felt compelled to move his right arm up and down, and watched as his reflection moved its left in likewise manner.

"What is real? What is reflection?"

I'm real, Michael thought, but suddenly wasn't so sure. *Am I just a reflection?*

In a flash, more mirrors appeared. Everywhere Michael looked, he met himself. Some looked identical, like a boy his own age, skin like marble, lean body wrapped in leather. Behind this grim figure stood the ruined world of Chelkan, a horde of grey beasts laying siege to everything. There were other Michaels, too, but some were warped, barely human at all. Alien.

"The multiverse is like a funhouse mirror," the Light said, now in words. Startled, Michael turned to his side and saw the Man in the Stetson there, his hands in his pockets, an easygoing smile on his face, and everlasting mercy in his cobalt blue eyes. The Man nodded to the mirror. "It casts many different reflections of a single truth."

Michael considered this revelation as, once more, the Man began to speak, almost conversationally, "The Beast exists in between the layers of the multiverse, corrupting everything it touches. It wants to shatter the mirrors."

Michael faced him. "That's bad? Wouldn't we be down to the one world again? The True One?"

The Man in the Stetson raised his hand in a simple wave, and more mirrors blurred by. Within them, Michael glimpsed the untold worlds of the multiverse. He saw Myriad Prime—his first jump—as well as so many others. Some he recognized, but still more were alien to him. He felt dwarfed by the impossible size of it all, and even more dwarfed by the awesome might of the One who created and sustained it with no effort whatsoever. "The multiverse is a product of choice—a natural order that serves as Chaos' prison. For every one who rebels against me, there is a possibility that they will return to my protection. The Rage would see that choice revoked. No multiverse, no choice. No order. Only Chaos."

Michael struggled to recall his life before this place and it felt like reaching back through untold eons. "When Rip first found me in the desert, he told me that the Rage was offering freedom. Free from your will, free to make my own choices."

The Man smirked, as if amused. "The Rage would have you believe that by choosing It you are choosing freedom, but you've seen yourself that you only enter into bondage. I've come to bring freedom to Creation—to every facet of it."

Michael frowned and stared back through the portals, seeing so much turmoil and war. "But how do I stop it?"

"You are not *meant* to stop it, Michael," the Man told him patiently. "Only to protect the balance. Choice must exist—including the choice to rebel. There will always be those who reject me. There will always be those who choose to go their own way. But as long as the choice remains to follow me, then Creation will hold and the Beast will have lost." Pausing thoughtfully, he said, "I want my creation to love me, but I won't force you. It is in the choosing that I am pleased. Knowing that you had the opportunity to reject me, but that you loved me still…"

The Man grew silent and Michael watched him, finally understanding the pain that all of his doubts and disbelief had caused.

"I get it now," Michael said, soft. "I really get it. I choose you."

Taking a firm, fatherly hold of Michael's shoulder, the Man said through a proud smile, "Then the Rage has no hold over you anymore."

Michael warmed, but could not return the smile. He hung his head, turning to watch the mirrors. He had to believe there was goodness out there in the worlds, but all he saw—all he'd ever seen—was the pain. The death. "You said you were sending me back... I have to fight more?"

The Man took a deep breath, his hand still on Michael's shoulder, and gave it a reassuring squeeze. "Michael, I didn't choose you to destroy the Rage. My order will remain as it has since I first formed it, no matter what the 'Maestro' has planned. The Rage will always lose in the end, though there are terrible and dark days ahead for my Creation. But those times must come to pass, as difficult as it will be for you to understand. Chaos cannot stand—it will always destroy itself."

The mirrors faded until only one remained. Through it, Michael saw a most familiar sight: himself, twelve years old, nearly swallowed in Rip's leather jacket, trundling through the Desert of Choosing. Lost, terrified, and homesick.

"You came to me in that desert, wanting a change," the Man said, a fondness in his voice. "Wanting redemption."

The image changed, and now Michael relived his career as a rift jumper on fast forward. Memories assailed him in flickering images: There he was at twelve on Myriad Prime, captured and beaten by those horsehead creatures. He'd used his own shackles to strangle his equine master, finally ending the monster's legacy of terror. Next he was thirteen, sleeping under a bridge in a glittering futuristic city, shivering in his coat, seeking shelter from a deluge. He was fourteen, now, at the forefront of an army of black-clad medieval knights with laser-lances, charging a horde of lycanthropic creatures. Still only a boy, but wearing the armor of a man, using steel and laser to hack and slash at the werewolves, their blood splattering his own feral face. Now he was fifteen, leaping about, dodging blasterfire from a gang of cyborgs. He laughed as he leapt and dashed, then slipped through their defenses and literally disarmed them, sparks spewing from their wounds. He saw those who sought to train him—dozens of alien martial warriors, teaching him to kill more efficiently. He saw battle after battle, more and more slaughter, and he gaped, having never before realized the extent of the death he had spread.

Taking a deep breath, the Man in the Stetson continued, "Along the way you forgot that. You thought that you could use your anger to fight my battles, but you were deceived."

Michael's eyes watered with emotion as he watched himself—

245

seventeen, now. Only a year ago. Seventeen and gaunt and terrifying. The shadows pulled apart and he stood revealed, his eyes devoid of compassion as he beheld poor Tony Carlson. Michael watched in revulsion how easily the boy in the mirror dispatched of the gangster, snapping his neck without a second thought.

"You were becoming what the Rage had in store for you all along," the Man said, somber.

"I didn't know," Michael said, trembling with regret.

"But not all was lost," the Man chimed in, hopeful, and Michael forced himself to watch the mirror. In it, he saw the junkie from Frazetta's office. *Candice*, he thought was her name. She stabbed him and he wanted to kill her, furious that she'd gotten the drop on him.

He watched, moved by his own choice when, after a lifetime of destruction, he let her go. Michael grinned.

"This." The Man in the Stetson pointed at the girl. "This is why I called you. I chose you to live your life as my son, mending the broken lives that the Rage has destroyed in its defiance against me. That was always meant to be your mission. This has never been about fighting Evil, but merely loving in spite of it."

Sara's face suddenly filled the mirror, breathing relief into Michael's soul. He felt tears fill his eyes at the sight of her, smiling back at him.

"That's what Sara was meant to teach you. How to find joy and peace in the midst of a corrupt Creation. She was able to bring you back to me, but only part of the way. You still have to make the choice—once and for all. Who will you serve?"

Realization dawned on Michael, the implications of that statement almost too enormous to grasp.

Now the images in the mirror began to change, and Michael no longer saw the war. Only those he'd helped. The lives he'd touched. People he'd forgotten, laughs he'd shared with them, quiet conversations. He never made a habit out of forming friendships in his transitory occupation, but there had been those who'd helped him along the way. Soldiers who'd fought by his side, civilians who'd found their courage. Among them he saw the Johnny Frawl from Sara's world, and Light Sphere, too. Lastly, he saw Toby and sensed an incredible responsibility.

"There are battles to be fought, yes. Chaos is searching for the key that will unlock Its prison, and defeating It will come with great personal cost.

But the real victory is here. These people are what is important, son. They always have been. Love them. Protect them. *Teach* him, Michael. Lead your family."

Michael faced the Man.

The Man in the Stetson looked upon him with joy. "You who were set apart by Chaos for evil, will show them that there is another way. That the choice is always with you." He grinned wider, his eyes crinkling. "*You* are the promise of the multiverse fulfilled."

He nodded, shaking in anticipation. "I'm ready. I'm...finally ready."

The final mirror faded and perfect light shone from the Man's features, suffusing Michael in white. Already he felt his awareness dimming and knew that he was phasing back into the multiverse.

"Go back, now," the Light spoke. "Stand firm. And above all else, love."

13

Sara's lungs burned with exertion. Her arms stung, threatening to give in to fatigue and let her rider drop. Toby had his legs wrapped around her, firing ice blasts behind them while the firestarter army pursued.

"Now we're kicking butt!" he said, hooting in triumph.

"I...I can't..." she panted, slowing down, her legs faint.

"Don't stop now!" Toby's body burned with fever. Sara had never considered what prolonged use of his powers could do to him, but she didn't want to risk it. With Michael gone, Toby was all she had left.

She ducked down a neighborhood, cutting a path through crowded backyards to the loud objections of the homeowners. "Out of the way!" Sara shouted, dropping Toby to his feet so they could scramble over fences.

The neighbors' cursing and shouting turned to screams when the firestarters caught up.

A tremendous rumble stopped Sara in her tracks. She held her breath, wondering what terrible thing was going to happen next. The sky three feet above her flickered with lightning. There was a dazzling flash of rainbow-colored light and she shielded her eyes, wondering if she'd died and not even known it.

When she realized she was still alive, she opened her eyes and saw him. "Michael...?"

He was on his hands and knees, much the same position as when he left. His clothes smoked, but he looked okay. He was *okay*.

He stood, patting the smoke off his leather jacket. He looked at her with his dark eyes, and smiled. "Hi."

Sara forgot all about firestarters or Toby at her side or the Rage or any danger they might have been in. She ran forward and crashed into his arms, weeping, kissing him as hard and as passionately as she ever had. Nearly devouring him, she held on tight to her husband, finding salvation in his breath, his hands, his chest.

They broke from their kiss and Sara pulled him close. "I thought you were gone."

"I'm back," he breathed, looking shell-shocked.

Sara stepped back. "But the Rage—"

Michael opened his mouth to perhaps explain when he suddenly screamed. Sara tried to hold him up as he roared in pain and dropped to the ground on all fours.

"No!" she shouted. "I just got you back! NO!"

"I don't know how you returned, dog," the Maestro said, stepping out among the firestarters. He applauded lightly, mocking. "But you're just going right back."

14

Michael bit back the pain, but he knew he couldn't last. Sara stood by him, her hands moving over him, trying to help him stand, to fight. The sense of peace, of completeness, he had experienced in the White Place not a minute before was fading into the recesses of his mind. Being pulled away by the Rage.

No. I can't forget.

The Maestro approached, backed by his pyrokinetic jackals. "When are you going to understand that you are property, Michael? My Master owns you. You can't run from him."

"Not...anymore," he grunted, fighting through the pain to glare at the Maestro. "I've made my choice."

Michael snapped his eyes shut, feeling a tremendous weight leave him, like something had dislodged inside of him and was rushing for the surface. He felt cold tears on his cheeks, slithering down his angular face. When he opened his eyes again, everything looked clearer. Absently he wiped at the thick tears and pulled back his fingers to see them covered in a sticky black goo. When the strange tears escaped his body, the pain disappeared too. He stared down at the dark puddle that had formed on the ground, feeling…he couldn't explain how he felt, other than to say it was wonderful.

"Michael?"

He stood, carefully at first, making sure he had his balance, then was surprised to discover how strong he felt. How clear-headed he was. The anger that usually sat like a load on his back was gone. The hate he'd carried since he was a boy had evaporated, a distant dream now.

"Sara…" He looked to her. Saw her staring at him, a mix of fear and uncertainty. "What is it?"

"You…" She frowned, the small knot forming on her brow. "Your eyes…they're blue, not black. Your hair. It's darker."

Michael touched at his bangs, pulled them down to get a look. The washed-out blond had been replaced by new chestnut color. New life. His mind rushed with excitement, understanding as he'd only known in the presence of the Light flooding through. "I chose God," he said, dawning. "I chose love. The Rage doesn't have any power over me. Not anymore."

"The Rage." Sara looked to the grass, to the tiny pool of black that Michael had cried on the lawn. Michael looked to it, as well.

That was inside me. All these years, that was holding me prisoner. I'm free. I'm really free.

The Maestro advanced, one eyebrow raised in surprise, his mouth slightly agape. He flicked his fingers, ready to conduct his orchestra, but Michael stood tall, feeling no effect at all. Instead, and much to his surprise, the small pool of black goop twisted and jerked—alive—and rose.

Sara and Toby ran behind Michael, seeking refuge, as the thing lashed out with wild tentacles, growing, snapping and gnashing at the firestarters nearest it. They cried out, but were cut down or snatched up in the spindly arms and beat against the ground into a pulp. The thing that had lain hidden inside of Michael for his entire life thrashed and grew, pulsing with malevolent force.

From the gelatinous blob, arms and inverted knees emerged with a sickening *snap* of tearing elastic: a Behemoth birthed of the Rage and Michael himself. The monster took a vaguely humanoid form with muscular arms, and three-fingered hands and three legs. At the top, a terrible head emerged, its facial features slowly coalescing. The thing screeched, shrieked, and danced in violent mirth.

Michael felt tears of pity sting his eyes, finally seeing his soul laid bare. He did not fear or hate the Behemoth, but embraced it for what it was— the part of him that was dying. His old life, his old decisions, his old desires. All along, *he* had been the villain plaguing his steps, sabotaging his happiness. The rage that had ruined him from the beginning was finally dying, setting him free to find a new life with new things.

"No!" the Maestro cried out, working a strange pattern in the air with his hands. Rage like that, Michael recognized all too well, could not be tamed. Muted for a time, perhaps, but it was always there, ready to cut loose.

The Black Behemoth's face solidified, forming eyes, nose and chomping teeth, and Michael knew that face.

"What is it?" Sara gasped.

Michael stared in dumbfound amazement and relief. "Me."

The thing pulverized the firestarters, though they tried to fight back, lighting up the black sky with their fireballs like the Fourth of July back home. But their attacks only angered the Behemoth and it wrecked half of their numbers with a single strike, utterly destroying them.

Lights overhead bathed Michael and his family in bright white. The alien drones had arrived—five of them now. "ATTENTION, HUMANS. VIOLENCE OF THIS SCALE WILL NOT BE TOLERATED. LEAVE OR SUFFER PENALTY."

The firestarter gang fought and died in the dervish of violence that was the Behemoth—now two stories tall. It curled its fat fingers around their bodies, squishing them and discarding their ruined corpses to the horizons. Other firestarters dodged the Behemoth's reach, throwing shimmering fireballs at it, to no ill effect. At last, the drones opened fire.

Michael grabbed Sara and Toby. "Run!"

They did, as the drones' blasts vaporized what was left of the army, first, before turning their attention to the creature. Michael helped Toby and Sara over a neighbor's wooden fence, but paused long enough to see five laser beams firing on the Black Behemoth. It squealed and smacked one drone, sending it hurtling through space before detonating into a house. The drones zipped as the beast lashed out with its oily muscular arms, until it paused. Turned its head, as if looking for something.

And glared right at Michael.

It blew steam out of its flaring nostrils and swatted a drone against another, both exploding. The Behemoth pounded the earth with thundering fists, snapped and snarled, then galloped straight for Michael, roaring. Michael's mind had a fraction of an instant to warn him to run, but his body didn't respond fast enough. Instead he stared dumbly as the Black Behemoth—wearing a twisted version of Michael's own face—lumbered for him and shouldered him through the fence. His feet kicked over his head as Michael catapulted through the wooden barrier, shards jutting into the ground beside him. Dazed, Michael pushed himself on all fours, but the beast dashed again, a gallop now that shook the ground and vibrated a nearby lean-to to rubble. Fists and feet trampled Michael, rolling him on the dirt and gravel.

He tucked in his arms and legs, compressing himself into a ball, and followed along the roll. Once the monster passed, Michael tumbled to his sneakers, standing tall. The beast slid along the grass, digging deep ruts into lawns and loose rocks, wheeling itself about. Its eyes narrowed to slits, its teeth gnashing. It let loose a half-bark, half-roar and stampeded for Michael once more.

This time, Michael was ready. He bent at his knees gathering his strength, and pushed hard, cartwheeling through the air, narrowly avoiding the rampaging creature. It pulverized what was left of the wooden fence, scrambling in broken boards, screaming in mighty anger.

Michael landed deftly on the ground, facing down the monster.

Looking at it there, struggling to free itself that it might kill him, Michael felt no anger. Felt no desire for vengeance, no compulsion to kill. The Behemoth was simply some mindless animal operating on instinct. It had been locked inside Michael his whole life, fighting to force Michael to do its will. But it was loosed now. Michael was loosed, too. He felt weightless, the burden of his hate removed from his shoulders. That joy was followed by an acceptance of all the terrible things he'd done, yet he knew he wasn't that person anymore. He was severed from the monster within, able to live his own life. Make his own choices without the Behemoth screaming in his ear.

The dread monster finally broke free of the tangled boards and stood. Grew. It flexed, its muscles popping, expanding, mutating. Michael inched back, waiting to face his demon. He wondered where Sara and Toby had gone. If they were safe. Michael quickly scanned the area, but saw no sign of the Maestro. Had he died in the attack? Or did his kind ever die?

Clacking its teeth, the Black Behemoth craned its head to study him. Michael clenched his fists, ready for more

The drones returned. This time an even dozen, circling like angry flies. Once again they shouted their automated commands, demanding surrender. Michael ignored them.

So did the monster.

With a backhand the size of a Buick, the Behemoth smacked away a persistent drone, shattering it to sizzling pieces.

"It's you and me," Michael shouted.

The creature beat at its own head, its chest, snapping like a rabid dog. Michael readied for another charge, but the Behemoth instead leapt straight up into the night sky. Michael stumbled backwards, his eyes probing the dark beyond. A tiny dot grew larger as the Behemoth plummeted straight down.

Michael hurled himself to the side, rolling on the lawn, as the Behemoth crashed into the earth. Dirt and debris filled the air. Michael shook the loose dirt from his hair and tried to gain his bearings in the black haze. The beast clambered out of its fresh-made crater, mashing giant fists into the ground. Michael leapt out of the way of the first wild swing, but a second caught his side and sent him spinning through the second story of a nearby building.

Glass and brick shattered as Michael's body punched a hole through one end and out the other. He landed head-first on the street, covered in brick dust and the raggedy leftovers of Rip's old leather jacket. He had just enough time to glance up when the building he'd momentarily occupied exploded in a hail of brick, wood, and glass. The Behemoth had simply jumped *through* it, devastating the structure in a single stroke. It galloped toward him.

But Michael had had enough.

He curled his fingers into a steel fist and swung wide. His tiny punch connected with the giant, startling it out of its rage-fueled stupor.

"Yeah." Michael glowered through clenched teeth. "I hit back."

The thing made to grab him, and Michael leapt onto its wrist, scaling its sinewy obsidian arm. He climbed on the monster's face and punched again, painting the street with black gunk. He punched again, creating large potholes in the creature's visage that immediately refilled with oil.

The squealing monster whirled and wobbled like a drunk as it reared back, trying to dislodge Michael. But Michael dug his fingers deep into the creature's dark viscous hide and held on. Bright lights suffused the warring duo as the drones caught up to the scrap.

"ATTENTION, HUMANS. VIOLENCE OF THIS SCALE—"

"Will not be tolerated!" Michael finished, grunting against the inertia of the rampaging beast. "I know, I know!"

The drones opened fire, but the devil sludge danced between their rays. Laser beams skipped by the two combatants, devastating broken-down cars, fences, and homes—slicing through the neighborhood. Out-of-use telephone poles were halved, collapsing onto roofs and streets. Those who had been hiding in their hovels scrambled for safety.

"Stop! You'll hurt the people!" Michael knew it was useless to shout at the drones. They were just machines, operating on a pre-programmed command.

The monster lashed out to one of the robots, but it zagged underneath the monster's reach. Then a flying dagger of solid ice pierced the drone. It fizzled and dropped hard to the ground. Michael jerked his head and spotted—

"Toby!"

The kid shot more ice blasts at the drones. Sara was there, too, in the mob, trying to herd people away from the battle.

They're heroes. Even in this chaos, Michael felt an immense amount of pride.

Once all the people were out of the way, Sara raced closer to the twirling devil. "Michael! Get clear!"

A drone's laser heated up the air inches from Michael's face. "I'm a little busy!"

Sara cupped her hands around her mouth, shouting, "They want something to shoot! Give it to them!"

A drone turned to target Toby as a new threat. One pinpoint of white-hot light cut right for him. Sara rushed over and knocked the kid to the ground. Rising up, she looked back to her husband. "Do it!"

Michael pressed his sneakers to the Behemoth's face and pushed. He sprang backwards, tucking into a curl, and landed with a skid on his feet. The Behemoth shook its head and pounded the concrete like a spoiled child throwing a tantrum. Large chunks of broken concrete burst from the ground, forming an asphalt mountain range. Michael easily dodged it, running over to Toby and Sara. He grabbed them by the hands and ducked down an alley between two houses.

The monster roared and the trio halted, throwing one last look behind them. The buzzing drones directed the full force of their attack on the Behemoth. They beat at it with lasers, but the creature continued to retaliate against the tiny robots, destroying many.

But not all.

"We have to go!" Sara shrieked.

Michael held his ground. "No. I have to see this."

Sara tugged at his arm, but Michael felt serenity as he watched his demon die, once and for all.

The drones concentrated their efforts, beating back the creature until, finally, the phosphorous beams super-heated the Behemoth and it bulged, stretched, then exploded in a shower of ash.

Quiet immediately settled over the street.

The drones retracted back into the air to rejoin the motherships.

Michael stared into the night, watching the ships' lights twinkling like stars. He had no idea how long he stood there, grinning like an idiot. He felt the familiar touch of Sara's hand on his cheek as she gently turned him to face her. Her blue eyes glimmered with tears that caught the alien starlight.

"You did it, sweetie," she whispered. "You're free."

15

As day broke, Michael stood beside a back alley Dumpster, the tattered remains of Rip's leather jacket in his hands. Sara kept a respectable distance, giving him time to reflect. He'd always thought it was stupid to hang onto this coat, but it had been a tether to his past. For so long, it had been his only constant on his journeys—like a child's security blanket, he now realized. *Time to let it go*, he told himself. Michael held it up, smelling it, the scent of a thousand worlds ground into the fabric. Throwing it away would mark the end of an era, and seemed to only reinforce that he had no idea how long God would have him on this gig, rift jumping all over the multiverse. Holding onto the jacket made him feel like an end was in sight, but it seemed the mission would outlast the coat.

He wasn't the same person that he'd been when he'd first slipped this jacket on. That person was dead and gone, and he had a new future to look forward to.

Saying good-bye to an old friend, he patted the worn leather, alien dust pluming, then tossed it into the bin.

Gotta keep moving. Work to do.

Sara slid next to him, intertwining her fingers with his. "Hey."

He grinned at her, wondering if he'd ever get used to walking around without a jacket. Maybe he'd have to buy a new one. "Hey."

"So, did we do it? Is the Rage finally dead?"

"Ha. I wish. But, no. God already told me that It can never die. It'll always exist. But a part of It died last night. The part inside me. I think that's victory enough."

She reached out to touch his chestnut-colored locks and winked. "Gonna take me a while to get used to *this*." She lay her head on his shoulder, giving him a side hug. "So, what now?"

"Keep moving on," he said. "I think the real work's just starting."

"The Maestro's still out there. He'll want revenge."

Michael shrugged, allowing a playful grin to surface. "Ah, let him. I'm not afraid. He doesn't have any control over me anymore. Besides, I've got a good partner to watch my back."

Sara squeezed his hand, her smile widening. "'Til the end."

He groaned, then laughed. "Oh, don't say that. That sounds so *ominous*."

She laughed, too, and kissed him, deeply. When they parted, Sara looked off to the side where a small eight-year-old boy waited for them, pushing the frames of his broken glasses on his button nose.

Sara frowned. "What about *him*?"

16

Michael and Sara walked Toby back to his house that morning. It seemed the party that Toby had described had long since disbanded. Not a biker in sight, the place looked cleared out. Michael and Sara waited on the sidewalk at the entrance to the chain gate out front. Toby hesitated by their side, eyeing his house.

"Will I ever see you again?" he asked, quiet.

"No," Michael said, knowing the truth wouldn't make this easier. But he owed Toby an honest answer. He wanted to take Toby with them. The boy had a well of untapped power. A power given him by the Maestro, himself. Surely that had to come with a price. It could be Toby who ended up on Chelkan, taking up the mantle of general of a massive demonic army. Toby needed guidance. Support.

Two things Michael was fairly certain Toby would never get at home.

But he was reluctant to bring in another rift jumper. Sara had sacrificed so much. Besides, he couldn't just steal an eight-year-old boy from his mother, no matter how justified he might have felt.

"This is where you should be." Sara laid a reassuring hand on Toby's shoulder. Michael felt a pang of regret, knowing Sara would never be able to go home again. Neither would he, for that matter. Could he submit Toby to that same life?

"Go on." Michael grinned to hide his doubts. "We'll cover you."

Toby shared one last look with them, then began the short trek to his front porch.

Michael felt Sara slip her hand in his. "Are we doing the right thing?" she whispered to him as they watched Toby. "Is he really safe with his mom?"

Michael didn't have an answer for that. Instead, he prayed that God would show him the way.

Now on the porch, Toby reached out for the doorknob. Before he could touch it, the door swung open and his mother was there, aiming a shotgun.

Right at her son's face.

Her eyes were red and puffy and long, dirty streaks betrayed recently shed tears. "Get out," she said, her jaw clenched so tight her words were garbled.

"M-Mom?"

Michael pulled from Sara's grip and stepped forward.

"Get away from here!" she screamed, spittle dotting the top of the shotgun. "Don't ever come back!"

Toby hung his head and started to weep. Michael stood behind the boy, defiant. "He needs you. He's your son."

"You ain't no kid of mine!"

Sara pushed past Michael, putting herself between the gun and Toby. "You *stupid* cow!"

"You got two seconds to get off my porch before I start shootin'. Take that freak with you."

Sara took Toby's hand and led him away. "Come on, Toby. You don't need her anymore."

Michael continued to stare down the woman. The shotgun wobbled in her trembling hands and he saw fear in her eyes. He chose his words carefully. "I'll take care of him. Don't worry." He wondered if she'd sober up in a few days and realize she had lost her little boy forever.

His sentiment seemed to momentarily penetrate the blockade around her heart and the woman nodded, new tears building. Michael turned and left.

He had his answer.

Michael caught up with Sara and Toby down the street. The boy was sitting on the curb, his arms crossed on his knees, his face buried in them. He was crying. Sara sat next to him, hugging him with one arm, speaking gentle words that Michael could not hear.

Sara met her husband's eyes when he approached. She was weeping, too, but he thought her pain was out of anger rather than grief. He suspected she'd unleash a swearing tirade on the boy's mother as soon as Toby was out of earshot.

Michael stood before the boy, blocking out the sun. "Toby."

The kid lifted his head, looking miserable. "Something's wrong with me...isn't there? That's why I have powers, right? The bad guys want to use me."

Michael felt instantly back in the desert nearly six years ago, reminded of when he was a scared boy. Back then he'd met a man out in that wilderness—a wolf who would have used him for evil. But Michael had met another man, as well. This one in a Stetson. A teacher. A Father. They'd had a strange relationship over the years, but Michael felt as though he was finally beginning to work that out.

Maybe this is what growing up is like.

Was that it? Had he become a man at long last?

Michael had made his choice in that terrible wasteland, a choice he hadn't truly understood until last night. Now that choice was Toby's.

Michael poked a finger at the boy's chest, bold and certain. "They don't get to choose for you. You choose who you're going to be. Who you're going to serve: the Light or the Dark."

A ghost of a hopeful smile tickled at the corners of the boy's mouth.

"I could teach you," Michael said. "I can help you find your way. You were good out there last night, but not good enough. Yet. I could train you. You could come with us, but you'll never see your home again."

The boy nodded, and looked at his feet. Sara pulled the boy close, loving him when his mother had not. Toby would need that. But he would also need to be taught harder lessons, too. About sacrifice, hard work, and doing the right thing. He was going to need a father.

Am I ready for that?

Truth was, it didn't matter if he was ready. Toby needed a father right now. Michael couldn't be the child anymore—he had to grow up and pass on what he'd learn to the next generation.

"I'm serious, Toby. I miss my home every day. Sara does too. It's not an easy life if you come with us. It's not an easy life if you stay. This is a decision you've got to make for yourself."

Toby wiped his tears and shrugged out of Sara's embrace. The boy stood, looking into Michael's eyes, without fear. "I don't want to stay here anymore. I never liked it here. I want to go with you."

Michael wanted to hug the kid, but restrained himself. Instead he extended a hand, as brothers. As equals. Toby shook it.

Sara jumped to her feet, and joined Michael's side, beaming. "Then let's get out of here."

A half-hour later, the three of them returned to the rift and stepped into the radiant fountain of rainbow-colored light. Then the simple sheet of paper lifted off the dirt and drifted away into the great unknown.

Their journey ends here.

Michael and Sara's final story.

Read on for an exciting preview of:

VOLUME 2: SARA'S SONG

The New Multiverse Novel by Greg Mitchell

Coming Soon from

Back at the Krinvox village, Michael sat by one of the small fire pits that dotted the camp, staring into the flame, his hood pulled over his head—partially for warmth, but mostly for privacy. Around him, the Krinvox danced in celebration. They had the Glor trussed up like wild game and some of the men were gutting it, disseminating all of the giant's parts to be used—not just for the cure to their plague, but for meat, clothing, tools. None of the ogre would be wasted and Michael supposed he was grateful for that, but to think of all that *was* lost… An entire species, wiped from existence. And for what? A few drops of blood that the beast was willing to offer in return for a little peace and quiet.

The electro-barriers around the perimeter of the village hummed, one of the few technological advances that the otherwise primitive tribe possessed. The force-field was there for protection against predators, but Michael wondered if maybe the real monsters were already inside the camp.

Ak-Huel approached, surrounded by a dozen screaming, laughing, rambunctious children. They clung to their papa, as did most of the tribe tonight. He was a hero, the only of their soldiers to return following the Glor hunt. Ak-Huel gave Michael's back a hard pat. "Happy! Glor dead! We saved!"

Michael nodded and forced a small smile. "Yeah, Ak-Huel. Your people will be okay."

Ak-Huel's kids tumbled around him like newborn pups, until the alien scooped up three of them in his elongated arms. He nuzzled their necks as they laughed, his expression softening. His one eye glistened with tears and he managed a small, meaningful nod. "Thank you, Mych-El. Thank you."

Once again Michael offered a half-hearted smile in response as the man of the hour and his joyful brood rejoined the festivities. Though Ak-Huel's fallen compatriots were mourned by family and friends, the general mood of the settlement was one of relief, a peaceful comfort resonating from the villagers who could now rest easy without fearing the plague. Looking deeper into the celebration, Michael saw Toby playing chase with the other kids and showing off some of his ice powers by creating snowballs for the children to pelt each other. Laughs were shared all around and the boy he'd adopted appeared happier than Michael had seen him in a while.

Michael hadn't told Toby about the Glor's true nature. The kid had a hard enough time adjusting to a life of rift jumping; he didn't need unnecessary guilt to compound all those confused feelings. He was only eight, for crying out loud.

Eight…

What have I done by bringing him into this?

Up ahead, Sara excused herself from her own warrior's welcome to approach Michael by the fire. She moved her lithe form like a cat. When he'd first met her, Sara had been a mousy girl, afraid of her own shadow. Now she was a fierce and powerful woman, confident and in full command of her body. She was undeniably gorgeous, but Michael was unsure about some aspects of her transformation. Confidence, he'd always wanted her to have. But she was prideful now. Arrogant.

Sara's broad smile glowed with excitement and accomplishment in the company of the villagers, but she visibly diffused as she neared him.

"Can I sit?" she asked, somber.

He nodded and she crouched beside him, hands draped over her knees. She stared into the fire as Michael studied her face, hoping to see remorse there. Instead, he saw nothing.

Nothing at all.

"You're upset about the Glor, aren't you?" she asked after a moment, tossing a small pebble into the fire.

Michael looked back to the crackling flames. "Yeah."

"I thought it was a threat. I thought I was rescuing you."

"I know."

"Had I known what you told me about it being a good guy, you know I wouldn't have hurt it."

Michael wasn't so sure. "I know."

She angled her blue eyes on him and he forced himself to hold her gaze. Her eyes used to sparkle. Like the clear blue waters of Dronaj in the Ufghar Galaxy. But now the shine had dulled. The waters were muddied. "Michael, we did what we had to do. We saved these people. That's what we do."

Was she trying to convince him or herself? He didn't offer a response either way. Just frowned and looked away.

Sara chuckled darkly. "Hit first and ask questions later, remember? That's how we've survived this long. *You* taught me that."

Michael stood, dusting off his jeans. "I know. That's the problem."

"Michael," Sara called after him, standing.

He stuffed his hands in his jeans pockets, lifted his eyes, and faced her more directly. She looked like she wanted to say something, to ask something, perhaps. Her face was marred by a concerned frown, that little knot forming on her brow just above her left eye. He wanted to say something, too, but wasn't sure what. Something *needed* to be said—maybe a thousand things. Apologies, confessions…the truth.

But the truth scared him, and he wasn't ready to face it just yet.

A tremor rumbled beneath his feet and Michael held out his hands to maintain his balance. Shrieks of surprise and worry erupted from the camp. Michael scanned their surroundings as Sara stepped to his side, searching as well.

"Are we being attacked?" she asked, drawing her chukrahas blades. "Do you think it's the Empire?"

Michael bit his lip. "Not sure."

Sara eyed him, alert. "Any headaches? Does your stomach hurt?"

"I told you, I don't get those anymore."

"But we need some kind of sign! How else are we supposed to know what we're supposed to do?"

"Faith," he said, saddened because he already knew from past experience that she would not accept that answer.

Sara's jaw tensed and she was careful not to look at him. "We need to rally the soldiers. Form a perimeter around the women and children."

"Sara." Michael gently took her arm, ignoring her instructions. She regarded him coolly, her eyes like slits. "Faith is all I have. This is who I am, now."

She nodded automatically, but her cold eyes did not thaw for him any longer. "I'll go find Toby."

The quake continued and the Krinvox ran haphazardly about, gathering children, spouses, weapons, items from their huts—anything they could get their hands on. Ak-Huel raced to Michael, a child in one arm, his spear in the other. His alien face was lit with terror. "Mych-El!"

The slender blue tribal warrior fumbled for his English, but Michael waved his hand, easing him. "I don't know what's happening."

One of the other Krinvox pointed a finger to the nighttime horizon, exclaiming something in her strange tongue. Michael looked to the skies and the camp followed suit, growing quiet.

Sara whispered, "What *is* that?"

Michael's heart thundered in his chest, his fingers growing numb. Across the prairie landscape, headed their way, was *black*. That was the first thought that entered Michael's mind. Examining it closer, trying not to hear the screams around him, he surmised that it was a cyclone made of solid black, flickering with purple lightning. The column of empty space churned violently, ripping apart the earth around it, sucking chunks of grass, of dirt, of rock, into its void.

No, Michael realized. Not just earth. *Sky*. It was eating sky. Snuffing out stars by the hundreds, devouring everything. Devouring reality itself.

Michael stared in dumb disbelief, watching the pillar of black as it erased the world, right before his eyes.

Headed his way.

The wind picked up, tugging at his hoodie, his long hair. Sara tucked a blade in her belt then tugged on his arm. He suddenly realized she was yelling at him. "Run! We have to run!"

Michael came to his senses, trying to tear his eyes away from the terrible empty void that sought to consume them. *It's the Rage*, he immediately knew, for he'd encountered the terrible consciousness in the dark spaces between the worlds. Was the Rage freed from Its prison to destroy reality as It saw fit?

But how? Why?

How would he ever stop it?

"*Come on!*" Sara shrieked in his ear, yanking on his arm.

He shook his head clear and turned back to the camp. The winds proved deadly, leveling the small hovels, then just as quickly sucking them into the sky— hurtling towards the vacuum. The Krinvox screeched, clawing at anything they believed might anchor them, but one by one were yanked from loved ones' arms. They tumbled through the air, end over end, landing in the black space and disappearing forever. Wiped from existence.

Michael spotted Toby, lost in the crowd, frightened. The boy searched the faces of the tribe, his chocolate-colored eyes widening behind his glasses until they spilled over with tears when at last he glimpsed Michael. The boy raced for his caretaker and Michael hefted him up in his arms.

"What's happening?" Toby roared over the high winds, clutching Michael in a death-grip.

The cyclone was almost upon them now, swallowing earth and sky, flesh and blood, its hunger never satisfied.

"We have to get to the rift!" Sara yelled, her long red hair thrashing wildly, slapping her face. "If we don't, we'll die!"

Michael knew she was right. He handed Toby to her. "Go! I'll be behind you!"

Sara balked at him. "Where are you going?"

"We have to take them with us!"

"Who?"

"The Krinvox! They'll die here!"

"*Are you crazy?* How do you even know if that'll work? What if they can't breathe on the next world?"

"I have to try!"

Sara briefly considered, then nodded. She hurried to him and kissed him. "Come back to me."

He warmed inside. "I will. Promise. Now *go!*"

Sara fumbled and dropped the chukrahas still in her hand before tucking Toby close to her breast and racing through the camp, away from the ebon tornado, headed for where their rift first touched down. Michael surveyed the camp, saw bodies pinwheeling through the air, meeting their oblivion in the encroaching void.

"Follow me!" he shouted to the first Krinvox he saw—one of the men, shielding a female. "Come on! This way!"

The Krinvox couple nodded, then reached for him, but were both pulled off their feet and lost to the spreading darkness.

Michael gritted his teeth, and stepped away from the buffeting winds. He felt light on his feet, felt the draw to the Void, and could hear, once more, the voice of the beast In-Between.

The Rage.

{*You'll never outrun me, Michael…*}

For years, Michael had done just that, trying to escape the Rage, to break his own dark destiny. He struggled against his own wicked impulses, the urge within him to do terrible things. At last, he'd surrendered to the Being in the White Place. The Rage's hold on him was finally broken now.

It seemed, however, that the Rage was a sore loser.

Is it doing all of this just to get me? The entire planet—maybe even this entire galaxy—was being erased. *Is it my fault?*

"Mych-El!"

Michael turned at the sound of his name. Ak-Huel had one arm hooked to a post in the deactivated perimeter fence. In his other hand, one of his babies. Ak-Huel's gangly grip held tight to the little pup's arm, but the mewling babe was dangling in mid-air, drawn to the Void.

Michael shot forward, moving closer to the cyclone, his clothes whipping about, threatening to drag him into the black oblivion. Ak-Huel cried hysterically, something Michael had never seen the warrior do. The sight broke something inside of him.

"Where are your other kids?" Michael screamed.

Ak-Huel only wept, clutching onto his child. His last one, Michael feared.

Michael reached for Ak-Huel and pulled on the lanky figure, dragging him away from the abyss. "We have to get to my rift!" Michael said. "We have to get you out of here!"

"Daught-er! Save my daught-er!"

Michael extended his arm, trying to grab the child, but couldn't connect to her tiny frame. "I can't reach! Pull!"

Ak-Huel tugged against the vacuum, but Michael felt his own feet beginning to lift off the ground, as though the planet's gravity was slowly being turned off.

"Can't!" Ak-Huel spoke. "I—"

The child slipped out of her father's grasp, crying as she fell into the Void.

Ak-Huel screamed a throaty rattle, tears spilling from his eye. Michael cried, too, shouting after the child, watching in horror as she simply plopped into the blackness, gone.

Michael yanked on his alien friend, but now Ak-Huel fought against him. "Let go! My daught-er!"

"You'll die!"

Ak-Huel pulled free from Michael's grasp and leapt forward, snatched out of the air and ripped through the black cyclone.

Michael stared at his empty hands, blinking back tears, then looked around. The Krinvox were gone. Only loose debris remained where homes once stood. A lone patch of Earth and sky surrounded Michael, and, at the edge of it, Sara, waving him forward.

Guilt churned his gut, and he felt like vomiting. *Everything's gone.*

Determination set in. Anger. Michael didn't know how this had happened or why. But he would find out and he would stop it from ever happening again, even if he had to punch his way through hell and damnation to do it.

Gritting his teeth, he took off for Sara, fleeing the whine of the cyclone barreling towards him. With every step he took, the ground he left behind was pulverized and consumed in the abyss. Stars blotted out overhead, and endless darkness dogged him. Sara came closer into view, but he couldn't see Toby. The boy must have already stepped onto the sheet of paper at his wife's feet that served as their vehicle to travel the multiverse. At least he prayed Toby was safely through. If he lost the boy or Sara in all of this—

A terrible scream shook the space behind him, a banshee's wail that sent a shiver into to his soul. He reached Sara and instinctively faced the whirlwind once more. The scream persisted, and there, suspended in the air by the purple lightning but unaffected by the pull of the cyclone, was a lean shadowed figure, its fingers splayed, reaching out for him. By the frame and by the cry, he judged it to be a woman. Gaunt and clad all in black, the short-haired woman leveled her hands at him and screamed, a shrill, frightening sound.

Sara hollered, "*No!*" then grabbed Michael by the shoulders and threw him into the rift.

Michael was blinded by white, then his vision returned. New information from this latest world assaulted his mind: *Daylight. Hot. Desert. Mountain. Cliff!*

Michael's Converse sneakers slid in loose gravel, undoing him. At once, his ankle buckled and he lost his balance, tumbling down a steep embankment. With each roll, he slapped up more dust, and his fingers desperately sought purchase. He dug them deep into the loose topsoil, finally slowing his descent. Suddenly exhausted and disorientated, he momentarily lay his head in the dirt, catching his breath.

After a moment's pause, a tiny cry carried over the still, empty air and Michael's head jerked upright. "Toby?"

Only a terrified shriek answered him. Michael scrambled to his feet and turned about. For the first time, he realized how high off the ground they were, as a breathtaking and empty desert stretched out to the horizon. High winds pushed against him, and Michael stumbled about, shouting "Toby! Toby, where—"

He saw the tops of little digits clutching the edge of the sheer cliff. Michael hurried and slid to his knees, peering over. Toby dangled helplessly over a wide chasm, the color gone from his face. Tears were frozen in his wide, petrified eyes, his cracked lips trembling. "I-I fell," he sobbed.

Michael lay flat on his stomach, grappling for the child. "Hang on, man. I got you."

As soon as Michael's arms were extended, Toby latched onto them, frantically pulling himself up. Michael took firm hold and brought the kid to safety, even as vertigo distorted his vision. In no time, both of them were sitting, turned away from the ravine. Toby continued to shake, his teeth chattering, and violently hugged Michael. The boy buried his face in Michael's shoulder, and Michael gave the kid a dusty pat. "It's okay. We're okay."

A dazzling burst of rainbow-colored light exploded from the piece of paper that served as their doorway to other worlds. Sara emerged from the quickly fading light, dazed-looking and pale. Michael eased Toby off of him and stood fast. "Sara, watch your step."

She managed to maintain her balance, but her eyes were distant. Glassy. She looked like she'd been crying.

Michael nodded to Toby. "Wait here."

The boy returned the gesture, finally laying on his back and heaving a great sigh of relief over his ordeal. Michael climbed up the slope and held out his hand for Sara to use as a guide. She took it, but did not face him.

"What is it?" he asked her, searching her for injury.

"Did you see her?" Sara asked, her body trembling. "Hanging in the sky?"

Finally her eyes locked on his, relaying stark terror. Michael nodded. "Yeah. I don't know who she is or why she did this, but we'll find her. We'll figure this out. We'll make her pay. For Ak-Huel, his family, *all* of them."

"No." Sara slowly shook her head. "That's not... I don't mean that..."

Michael frowned. "What?"

Sara fixed him with a wide-eyed gaze, a mad glint in her eye.

"The witch," Sara said, shaking. "It was *me*."

www.ingramcontent.com/pod-product-compliance
Lightning Source LLC
Chambersburg PA
CBHW032209190626
46810CB00019B/2362